Praise for Th[e Veil]

"[*The Veil*] was full of action, a steady [...] slight romance element, and an interest[...] world building. Any and every urban f[...] read this."

"*The Veil* was truly a fantastic read and most certainly one of my top reads for 2015 thus far. If you're a fan of Chicagoland Vampires, you will fall in love with *The Veil* . . . and Claire and Liam." —Literary Escapism

"The world building was fabulous; the characters were likable; the plot and tension provided a great 'what's going to happen next?' feeling that kept me engaged. . . . I loved it and basically devoured it in only a few sittings." —Paranormal Haven

"A great start to a new paranormal series from an author I love! If you don't have this on your to-read list, make sure you get it there ASAP! I think it's going to be an amazing ride!" —Fiction Fare

"Action-packed and fast-paced, with enough sexual tension to keep a girl hoping. And with a cast of characters that I couldn't have picked better myself. This book was exactly what I needed to restore my faith in the paranormal. Yes! There can be a new series that catches my interest and gets me giddy again!" —Under the Covers Book Blog

"Neill is truly a master storyteller!" —*RT Book Reviews*

"A fast-paced read that you won't want to put down once you pick it up." —A Book Obsession

"A fabulous beginning . . . filled with nonstop action and drama." —Fang-tastic Books

"This was absolutely enthralling, entertaining, and completely original. . . . This truly was a wonderful start to what promises to be a standout series." —My Guilty Obsession

OTHER NOVELS BY CHLOE NEILL

THE CHICAGOLAND VAMPIRES NOVELS

Some Girls Bite

Friday Night Bites

Twice Bitten

Hard Bitten

Drink Deep

Biting Cold

House Rules

Biting Bad

Wild Things

Blood Games

Dark Debt

Midnight Marked

Blade Bound

"High Stakes" novella in *Kicking It*

Howling for You (A Chicagoland Vampires Novella)

Lucky Break (A Chicagoland Vampires Novella)

Phantom Kiss (A Chicagoland Vampires Novella)

THE DEVIL'S ISLE NOVELS

The Veil

The Sight

THE DARK ELITE NOVELS

Firespell

Hexbound

Charmfall

THE HUNT

A DEVIL'S ISLE NOVEL

CHLOE NEILL

BERKLEY
NEW YORK

BERKLEY
An imprint of Penguin Random House LLC
375 Hudson Street, New York, New York 10014

Library of Congress Cataloging-in-Publication Data

Names: Neill, Chloe, author.
Title: The hunt: a Devil's Isle novel/Chloe Neill.
Description: First edition. | New York: Berkley, 2017. | Series: Devil's Isle; 3
Identifiers: LCCN 2017018327 (print) | LCCN 2017024969 (ebook) |
ISBN 9780698184558 (ebook) | ISBN 9780451473363 (softcover)
Subjects: LCSH: Magic—Fiction. | Good and evil—Fiction. | New Orleans (La.)—Fiction. |
Paranormal fiction. | BISAC: FICTION/Fantasy/Urban Life. | FICTION/Fantasy/Paranormal. |
FICTION/Romance/Paranormal. | GSAFD: Fantasy fiction. | Occult fiction.
Classification: LCC PS3614.E4432 (ebook) | LCC PS3614.E4432 H86 2017 (print) |
DDC 813/.6—dc23
LC record available at https://lccn.loc.gov/2017018327

First Edition: September 2017

Printed in the United States of America
1 3 5 7 9 10 8 6 4 2

Cover illustration by Blake Morrow
Cover design by Adam Auerbach

I was born for a storm, and a calm does not suit me.

—*Andrew Jackson*

THE HUNT

CHAPTER ONE

Early January
New Orleans

It had once been a lovely kitchen, with pale wood and granite, a pretty view of a courtyard garden, and an enormous refrigerator still dotted with photographs of what looked like a big, happy family. Father, mother, daughter, sons, and an enormous black dog, big enough for the kids to ride on.

But they were long gone now, cleared out like nearly everyone else in New Orleans when Paranormals flooded into our world, leaving most of our city and much of the South in ruins.

I was searching through what they'd left behind, looking for a diamond in the rough.

"There is a house in New Orleans . . ."

I winced at the throaty croak that echoed from the other end of the kitchen. "Like a frog being strangled," I muttered.

"They call the Rising Sun!"

I leaned around the cabinet door. "Moses!"

Inside the pantry, something thudded, rolled. "What? I'm working here."

"The singing."

A head, small and pale, with glossy black horns and irritable green eyes, peered around the pantry door. "What about it?"

"It's not great."

He snorted, doubt written across his face. "Says you."

"Yeah, says me."

Moses walked out of the pantry, three feet of Paranormal attitude. And, for the five weeks we'd been sneaking around New Orleans, my best friend.

"Someone might hear you," I reminded him.

He grumbled a curse, walked through the shadowed kitchen in my direction. He held up a bloated silver can, its seams bursting from age, heat, and rot. By the size, I guessed it was tuna fish. Very gnarly tuna fish.

"Jackpot," Moses said.

"You aren't going to eat that," I said. "It's spoiled."

"Don't be persnickety." He sniffed at the metal, closed his eyes in obvious pleasure. "More flavor this way." He held it out. "You want a sniff?"

My stomach flipped in revolt. "I do not. It would probably kill me."

He waved off the concern. "I've done this tons of times. Maybe I just have a stronger constitution than you, Claire."

"Hmm," I said noncommittally. Better to avoid going too far down that rabbit hole.

Moses was supposed to be locked up in Devil's Isle, the prison for Paras and anyone else touched by magic. Some Paras had wanted our world for their own; others, like Moses, had been forced to fight via magical conscription. Unfortunately, the Paranormal Combatant Command, the federal agency in charge of Paras, didn't much care about that detail.

I was a Sensitive, a human affected by magic that had seeped in from the Beyond. That magic gave me telekinesis, but at a cost: Too much magic would destroy my mind and body. Keeping that balance was a trick I was trying to master.

I'd kept my power secret until a cult called Reveillon—people who believed magic in any form, including the city's remaining Paranormals, should be eradicated—had attacked Devil's Isle. I'd had to use my magic to bring down Reveillon's founder. The PCC now considered me its enemy—and didn't get the irony.

There were signs the PCC might eventually come to its senses, acknowledge that magic wasn't all bad and not all Paranormals had been our enemies on purpose. It had even authorized temporary leave for a select few Paranormals who'd fought in the Battle of Devil's Isle.

Sensitives like me hadn't gotten the same consideration. We weren't Paras, and we weren't humans. We were different. Paras couldn't become wraiths—the pale, skeletal monsters into which Sensitives transformed if we failed to control our magic, to balance all that heady power. If we weren't careful, the magic would corrupt us, turn us into twisted creatures obsessed with absorbing more and more power.

So despite my efforts in the battle, there'd be no pass for me. I was too unpredictable, too dangerous, too untrustworthy.

Moses, having already snuck out of Devil's Isle and having skipped out again during the battle, didn't need a pass. He was already on the lam.

We'd tried playing the game, helping Containment, the PCC unit in charge of Devil's Isle, track down Reveillon and fighting on their side. And except for the few token passes, nothing had changed.

So we'd been sneaking around New Orleans, working to avoid Containment. And since they were treating us like criminals, we figured we'd might as well act like criminals. We'd decided our job was to challenge the PCC and its refusal to acknowledge the truth about magic, about Paranormals, about Sensitives.

Along with the other members of our crew, which we called Delta, we'd been covering Reveillon's antimagic billboards with our own messages, using contacts outside the war Zone to rally the rest of the world to our side and gathering supplies for the Devil's Isle clinic.

The facility—and the wraiths secured there—weren't on Containment's priority list. Reveillon's attacks had put a big crimp in the PCC's supply chain, so even if the clinic had been on that list, consumables were getting harder to come by. We were in this house to gather up what we could for delivery to Lizzie, who ran the clinic.

Moses walked toward the kitchen island with his slightly sideways gait, then slung a mesh bag of equally swollen cans onto the granite countertop and added his newest find to it. "You find anything?"

It took me a moment to reorient. I closed the cabinet, held up a carton of sea salt and a tin of tea bags. "Salt's half full, and the tea bags still smell mostly like tea." No small feat, given they'd been stewing in heat and humidity. "Still," I said, "you'd think there'd be more here."

"It's a nice house," he said, glancing around the room. "It would have been one of the first ones sacked after the war—or during the battle."

"Yeah," I said.

Reveillon had ransacked Devil's Isle—and every neighborhood the members had blown through along the way. They'd been like a hurricane scouring their way across New Orleans. Not the first storm the Big Easy had faced down. But over time, hell and high water took their toll.

Reveillon's members had hurt the city and those who lived here—

and some, including Liam Quinn, didn't live here anymore. The bounty hunter I'd fallen for had been hit by magic, and he'd left New Orleans to fight his resulting demons.

I hadn't heard from him since.

I knew Liam was with his grandmother Eleanor in what Malachi called the "southern reach," the bayous and marshes of southern Louisiana, where small communities of Paras worked to stay out of Containment's crosshairs—and out of Devil's Isle.

Malachi, another of my Paranormal friends, had told us that much when he'd returned from reuniting Liam and Eleanor.

But that was all I knew about Liam's location or the effects of the magical hit he'd taken. It was a point of pride that I hadn't asked Malachi for any more details, for updates as one week after another passed. I'd tried to force thoughts of Liam to the back of my mind, giving him the time and space he apparently needed. In the meantime, I'd focused on Delta, on our new work for New Orleans, on controlling my magic. Because even though I knew why he'd gone, it still hurt to be left behind.

I put my hands on my hips and sighed as I looked at our meager harvest. "Oh, well. You add it to the bottled water, the aspirin, the radio. That's something."

"It's something," he said. "You know they don't take things for granted."

They hadn't. If anything, they'd been too grateful, and that didn't make me feel any better about Containment or our situation.

"Oh, found one more thing," Moses said, pulling something from the bib of his denim overalls. He'd found the overalls during a previous scavenger hunt. They were way too big for him—the pants rolled up at the bottom—but he loved that front pocket.

He moved toward me, offered his hand. In his small, meaty palm sat a silver robot with a square body perched on blocky feet. Probably three inches long, with a canister-shaped head topped by a tiny antenna. A metal windup key emerged from its back.

"It was wedged behind a drawer," Moses said.

"It's old," I said, taking it gingerly and looking—as my father had taught me—for a manufacturer's mark or date, but I didn't find anything. "Probably from the fifties or sixties." That was much older than the fancy cabinets and countertops in there. "Must have missed it when they renovated the house. Let's fire it up." Carefully, I cranked the key, listened to the gears catch and lock, then set the toy on the countertop.

The gears buzzed like hornets as it moved forward, its feet rotating in sequence, the little antenna bobbing. We watched silently as it marched to the end of the countertop. Moses caught it before it reached the end, turned it around, and sent it back in my direction.

"Huh," he said, monitoring its progress with surprising affection in his eyes. "I like that."

"Yeah," I said, "so do I."

We wound it again and let the toy repeat its parade across the granite.

"Shame they missed it when they left," he said.

"What did they miss?"

We both turned sharply, found a man behind us.

Malachi was tall, over six feet, with the broad shoulders of a soldier. He looked like an angel: tousled blond curls that reached his shoulders, a square jaw, luminous ivory wings that folded and magically disappeared while we watched, and eyes of shimmering gold. That gold was a signature of some Paranormals—and it was the color I'd seen in Liam's eyes after he'd been hit and before he'd run.

Malachi had been a general in the Consularis army—the caste of Paras who'd ruled the Beyond before the war, the same Paras who'd been magically conscripted to fight us by their enemies, the Court of Dawn.

We hadn't heard the usual *thush* of wings that signaled Malachi had alighted—and apparently walked right through the front door. He wore jeans, boots, and a faded Loyola T-shirt.

Malachi smiled at Moses, then let his gaze linger on me. My heart met that look, delivered by a man beautiful enough to be carved in marble and preserved for eternity, with an answering thump. It was an instinctive response, triggered by the sheer power of his gaze.

Paras had very different conceptions of romance and attraction. We were just friends—even if we'd become better friends over the last few weeks—but that didn't make his power any less potent.

"They missed our new toy," I said, answering his question. I wound it again and set it to work.

"Ah," he said, then picked it up to study it. "An automaton."

"Or humans' sixty-year-old idea of one. How'd you find us?"

"We followed the sound of mating cats," Malachi said, sliding a sly smile to Moses.

Moses lifted his middle finger. "I got your mating cats right here."

I guess the gesture translated. Good to know. "We?" I asked.

"Someone wanted to talk." He glanced back as footsteps echoed on the hardwood floors at the other end of the shotgun house.

A man stepped into the doorway, his figure only a shadow in the harsh sunlight behind him.

For a moment, I was lost in memory, back at Royal Mercantile, my store in the French Quarter. Or it had been, before I'd been forced to abandon it. In my mind, I was in an antique bed on a rough-hewn floor, a slip of a breeze coming through the windows and a man sleeping next to me. Dark hair. Blue eyes. Body lean and honed like a weapon.

The man I'd fought beside.

The man who'd left.

Then he took a step forward. Memory faded, putting another man in the doorway. Similar to the one who'd left, but not the same.

"Gavin," Moses said.

This wasn't Liam, but his brother. But it was still surprising that he was standing here with Malachi. I hadn't seen him since the battle.

"Claire. Mos."

"What are you doing here?" I asked.

Gavin didn't waste any time. "Jack Broussard is dead."

Broussard was a Containment agent, and a generally despicable human.

"No loss there," Moses said.

"Maybe not," Gavin replied. "But they're saying Liam killed him."

CHAPTER TWO

"Liam's not in New Orleans," Malachi said simply. "He couldn't have done it."

"There's supposedly physical evidence he did," Gavin said. "And Liam and Broussard had a bad history. That seems to be enough."

Liam was a bounty hunter, or had been, and Broussard had been his handler before their relationship had soured. Because Liam understood Paranormals weren't all our enemies, Broussard believed Liam was a traitor to humankind. That was the kind of attitude Delta was fighting against.

"Tell us what happened," Moses said, crossing his arms.

"Broussard didn't show up for a shift at the Cabildo," Gavin said. Containment headquartered in the historic building on Jackson Square. "Containment sent someone to take a look, and they found him in his house. It was bloody. His throat had been slit." He paused, seemed to collect himself. "The knife was one of Liam's—a hunting knife I gave him. Had an engraved blade. And 'For Gracie' was scrawled on the wall—in Broussard's blood."

The silence was heavy, mixed with eddies of horror and fury.

Gracie was Gavin and Liam's late sister, a young woman killed by wraiths. Her death had haunted them, and that was one of the obstacles that had stood between me and Liam.

Moses narrowed his eyes. "Someone's setting your brother up."

"That's how it reads to me."

"Bastards," Moses spat. "Scum-sucking bastards for using your sister like that."

"Yeah," Gavin said, running a hand through his hair. "I can't argue with that."

"Why set Liam up?" I asked. "Containment doesn't have anything against him—or didn't. Do they know he has magic?"

"Not that I'm aware of," Gavin said.

"Maybe Containment didn't arrange the frame-up," Malachi said. "Maybe the killer did. He or she could have a vendetta against Liam, or may not care who's blamed, as long as it's directed away from him or her."

"Yeah," Gavin said with a heavy sigh. He looked tired, I realized, his skin a little paler than usual, his eyes shadowed with fatigue. "I lean toward that. Containment's issued a bounty for him."

"Gunnar wouldn't do that." Gunnar Landreau was second-in-command at Containment, and one of my best friends.

"He wouldn't have a choice," Gavin said. "An agent's been murdered, and the evidence points to Liam. Gunnar's hands are tied. Containment's already been looking for him. Now that the bounty's issued, the search is going to get more intense. Containment is also looking for Eleanor."

"For leverage," I said, sickness settling in my belly.

"Probably," Gavin said. "I hear they've been through her place in Devil's Isle, tore up what wasn't already torn up after the battle. I haven't been to Liam's, but I imagine it didn't fare any better."

"How do you know all this?" Moses asked. "You talk to Gunnar?"

He shook his head. "I just got back into town, had a drink with a source at the Cabildo. That's where I got the details."

"You're here to warn us," I said. "Because now they'll want us for another reason—to find Liam."

Gavin nodded. "Containment's been looking for you, but they haven't been looking very hard. They know you helped in the battle; Gunnar knows you helped. But with this, they'll double their efforts to take you in."

Moses snorted. "They can try."

"We'll be careful," I said. "What are you going to do about Liam?"

"We're going to warn him," Gavin said. "Me and Malachi. That's the other thing we wanted to tell you. We'll be gone for at least a couple of days, more likely three."

"You know where Liam is?" Moses asked. "I mean, specifically?"

The bayous and marshes of southern Louisiana covered thousands of square miles. They were also isolated and difficult to get through.

"We know where they were," Malachi said. "Erida checks in when she can." Erida was a goddess of war and one of Malachi's people. She'd accompanied Eleanor into the bayous. But to make it harder for Containment to find them, Erida, Eleanor, and the other Paras moved frequently. "I received a message three days ago. By the time we get to that location, she'll have moved again."

"It's a place to start," Gavin said with a nod. "That's all we need."

"They could follow you back to him," I said. "That might be their plan—to send you running to him, to Eleanor. And if they find him, they might find the others."

I didn't know how many Paras lived in the bayou, but I knew their existence needed to remain a secret. Given the smile on Gavin's face, he wasn't very concerned about that.

"They might think we'll lead them to Liam and the others. But I've walked through PCC recon camps without being spotted. If I don't want to be seen, I won't be seen. And I'm fairly confident Malachi has the same skills."

"I do," Malachi confirmed. "It's not without risk. But we can't not warn them of what might be coming. Of the storm they may be facing. And we can't wait until Erida checks in again."

I had a sudden image of Liam on his knees in front of the cypress house, hands linked behind his head, gun at his back. Whether from fear or premonition, a cold sweat snaked up my spine. Because Liam Quinn was still mine.

"I'm going with you."

"No," Gavin said automatically. "It's too dangerous."

I gave him my best stare. "You want me to remind you what we faced down five weeks ago? What I faced down?"

"I don't mean physical danger; I know you can hold your own, not that I'm eager to throw you into a fight." He moved toward me. "Like I said, Containment wants you even more now. Parading you around isn't the best idea."

"I wouldn't be parading," I said flatly. "And they'll expect me to be in New Orleans. Near the store, near my friends. They won't be looking out there."

"Claire might help Liam," Malachi said. "Could be good for him."

"And he'll string me up if anything happens to her," Gavin said, flashing him a look. "You want to take that punishment for me?"

"If Liam wanted to keep an eye on me," I said, "he could have stayed in New Orleans."

Gavin opened his mouth, closed it again. "I can't really argue with that."

Moses snorted. "That's a damn lie. You'd argue with a signpost just for the fun of it."

"That's the Irish in me," Gavin admitted.

"That's the mule in you," Moses corrected. "Anyway, I think it's a good idea." He narrowed his eyes at me. "Gets her off my back for a little while."

I just rolled my eyes. I'd missed one day of visiting him since the battle—during a gnarly tropical storm—and he'd hounded me for a week.

Gavin tapped his fingers on the countertop as he considered. *Tap-tap-tap. Tap-tap-tap.* "Give us a minute?" he said, glancing up at Moses and Malachi.

Not one to take orders from Gavin, Malachi looked at me. When I nodded, he gestured to Moses, and they walked into the next room, leaving us alone.

"I don't want you to get hurt," Gavin said, then held up a hand when I started to argue. "I don't mean by Containment."

He softened his tone. "He hasn't been gone very long, not really. And if he's trying to come to terms with his magic, he may not be ready for company." He paused, and my stomach clenched at what I knew was coming next. "He may not be ready for you."

That was the other side of the coin. The possibility that time had changed his mind, or his heart, had been gnawing at me. And the teeth grew sharper each day that passed without a message.

But it was a risk I had to take. I'd given him time and space to cope. Now it was time to act. To flip the coin.

Gavin must have seen the hurt in my eyes. "Liam wouldn't feel good about running away. About bailing on you, on New Orleans, on me, on the life he was finally beginning to build here. But that doesn't mean he's ready to come back."

I nodded. "I know."

"And you still want to go?"

I turned to lean back against the counter, crossed my arms. "I don't like that he left. I know why he did it, but I don't like it. And I don't feel good about being left behind, probably any more than you do."

Gavin didn't answer with words, but there was no mistaking the quick flinch. Liam had hurt both of us. He might have had his reasons, but the pain was still there, the wounds still fresh.

"But he's in danger," I continued. "Eleanor's in danger. I'm not going to sit on my ass in New Orleans while you guys do the hard work." I looked over at him. "If it was me out there, he'd look for me. Even if he thought my feelings had changed."

He looked like he wanted to argue, but realized there wasn't anything to argue about.

"And Containment?"

"You suddenly a coward?" I asked with a grin.

He puffed out his chest. "I'm not afraid of Containment. Or anything else. But still." He made a vague gesture in the direction of my hair. "Your hair . . . It's noticeable."

Rolling my eyes, I pulled my long red hair into a bun and unsnapped the Saints cap I'd fastened to the back of my jeans. Then I stuffed my hair into it, adjusted the fit.

"Boom," I said, and flicked the cap's bill. "Instant disguise. I won't get caught."

"You willing to stake your life on that?"

I lifted my brows. "I've been staking my life on it since I learned I had magic. And since the battle. You think I've spent that time underground?"

"Not according to what Malachi's told me." He glanced over at me. "I saw the billboard on Magazine. 'Free the Consularis. Seek the truth.' And a pretty little triangle in the bottom corner. The Greek symbol for delta."

"It's amazing what you can do with seven-year-old house paint."

"It was one of Reveillon's?"

"It was. Now it's one of ours."

Gavin shook his head, but there was pride in his eyes. "He ever tell you you're stubborn?"

"Connolly," I said, grinning and reminding him of my last name. "I'm also Irish. And you know I can handle myself."

To prove my point, I raised a hand, gathered up the tendrils of power that lingered in the air, and used them to lift the robot off the counter and into my hand. When it was in my grip, I scratched a bit of grime from its body.

"You're getting better," Gavin said. "Smoother."

I had gotten better, both at controlling it and expelling the left-over magic to keep it from wrecking me.

"I've been practicing." Robot still safe in my palm, I looked up at him. "We go, we talk to them, we come back. An easy two days," I said, repeating his promise. "Three at the most."

"Rude, using my words against me."

"Handy, giving me words to use."

Gavin leaned on the countertop, muttered something in the Cajun French he and Liam used when their emotions ran high. But my arrow had found its mark. "Fine. We meet at Moses's place at dawn." His expression changed. "In the meantime, Malachi said you have a place to stay. A place that's safe."

"He's right." The fewer the people who knew about the former Apollo gas station my father had rehabbed, the building where I now lived, the safer it would remain. It had to stay safe because it was the last bastion of a trove of magical objects my father had saved from destruction. So I wouldn't give Gavin any more details.

Gavin nodded. "I figure you, like Liam, had reasons for the choices you made."

I narrowed my gaze. "Now who's using words against whom?"

Gavin left. "We'll talk," Malachi said, and then he was gone, too.

"Was he telling you or me?" I asked Moses.

"Could be either," Moses said. "But I'm pretty sure he meant you."

Moses and I packed up the things we'd found, then closed up the house again. We walked in silence through the alley that bisected the block.

"Did you know Broussard well?" I asked as we moved through shadows made by the high afternoon sun. It wasn't exactly discreet to walk through the city in broad daylight, but there were so few people in the neighborhood—and the sound of anyone was so easily heard in the silence of the city—that we usually risked it.

"Not well," he said, pausing to kick at a shining spot of metal in the gravel. "Knew enough to stay away from him. Saw the world as good or bad. You were either on his side or on the wrong side." Apparently not impressed by whatever he'd found on the ground, he started walking again.

"Yeah. Liam said something similar. You know anyone who'd want him dead? Maybe any Paras in Devil's Isle?"

Moses snorted. "Who didn't want him dead? But hated him enough to take him out? No." He stopped and leaned down, pulled a random bit of wire from a patch of scraggly grass, regarded it with a nod, stuffed it into his bag. Moses had never met an electronic component he didn't like; he'd had a store of discarded radios, computers, televisions, and every other available gadget in Devil's Isle before it had been destroyed.

As a woman estranged from her store, I could sympathize.

"Humans," he said when we were moving again, "think they're the only things we think about. Seven years we've been in Devil's

Isle. We've got lives and worries, probably the same kind of crap humans worry about."

Malachi had warned me once not to make assumptions about Paras. He'd been right then, just as Moses was right now.

"So who does that leave? Did he have enemies?"

"You mean other than Liam? They want to frame him for this, they couldn't have picked a better fall guy."

"Yeah. No love lost there." I glanced at him. "Maybe you could poll your Para friends? Find out what they know?"

"How would I do that? They're in Devil's Isle, and I'm out here in the wasteland." But he took a big huff of fresh air and held it in for a moment, as if savoring the sensation.

"I know you and Solomon communicate," I said. Solomon was the Paranormal kingpin of Devil's Isle. He was also Moses's cousin.

"That would be illegal. And risky."

I stopped, gave him a dry look. It took a minute, but eventually he withered a little, hunched his shoulders.

"I'll find out what I can."

"Good man. And I guess I'm going into the bayou."

"It's a good decision."

I looked back at him. "I thought you were opposed to it."

"The danger, yeah." He lifted a shoulder. "But not the idea. It's Liam, and you're Claire. I may not be people, but I got a sense of how they work."

"He may not want to see me."

Moscs rollcd his cycs.

"He left," I pointed out.

"You know why he left." His voice was low, quiet, and a little bit sad. "He'll want to see you. He'll *need* to see you."

I hoped so. Because I didn't really have a backup plan.

"Look," he said, "let's just put it out there. He left, and even if he has his reasons, it's real damn hard not to take that personally. But you haven't been whining and moping. You got your shit together, and you hung out with me." He pointed a stubby finger at me. "Now you go find that boy, and you call his ass out."

I thought of Gavin's warning. "What if he won't talk to me?" The words spilled out and with them the fear.

"Well, fuck that," Moses said, and started walking again. "He'll talk to you, if only because he's gotta face this Broussard situation. He may have his issues, but he's not a coward." He looked at me speculatively, onyx horns glinting in the sunlight. "I figure he gets a good look at you, he probably remembers how good he had it."

That made me feel better. "And what are you going to do while I'm gone?"

"Try and get my damn comp up and running. Managed to find a working power supply, but I still can't get the OS to boot."

We reached the end of the alley, prepared to turn right down the sidewalk, and stopped short. Across the street, a man in fatigues sat inside a Containment-branded jeep. Another man walked toward him, opened the front passenger door, and climbed inside. RECOVERY was printed in large letters on the side.

Moses and I were the types they wanted to recover: Paras and Sensitives who weren't in Devil's Isle, where we belonged.

"Shit," Moses said, stepping back into the shadows. "We wait here or run?"

There was no way to tell if they were here for us—if they'd followed us across the neighborhood—or if there were others on the hit list today. "Wait," I said. And watch. Figure out what they did, and which way we'd need to run.

The sounds came first, high-pitched and spitting with anger.

"A wraith?" Moses said.

But as two agents dragged the man out, I realized we weren't that lucky.

The man they'd found wasn't a wraith or a Sensitive. He was a Para, short and slender, with elfish features, pointed ears. His name was Pike. He was a friend of Liam's who'd helped protect Eleanor when she'd lived in Devil's Isle.

"I didn't know he made it out," Moses said, voice tight with concern.

"Me, either." I hadn't seen Pike during the battle or in the brief time after that I'd been in the Quarter, and I hadn't been back inside Devil's Isle since. If he'd been on the streets the entire time, I hadn't seen him there, either.

I didn't know Pike well. If Liam trusted him, Pike was smart enough to be careful. But Containment had ways of finding people. I glanced up and around, looking for the magic monitor, found it hanging on a light pole across the street. The light blinked green. The power was on in this sector of the city, and Pike had done something magical, which tripped the alarm.

I started forward, but Moses's fingers tightened on my arm. I tried to shake him loose, but he held firm. He may have been small, but he had plenty of strength.

"Let go," I said. "I have to help him."

"You can't just run out there. We're outnumbered."

"I can use magic." I could clear a path for Pike, get the agents out of his way, and put him somewhere safe—as long as I could do it quickly. I could usc only so much magic without having to managc its side effects.

"Okay," Moses whispered, "let's assume you get out there and kick some ass with your magic, and they *don't* take you into Devil's Isle. Gavin already told you they've moved you up the most wanted list. You do this, you definitely can't risk going into the bayou."

And wasn't that a shitty choice? I felt angry, guilty, helpless. "We can't just let them take him."

"He'll go back inside," Moses said. His voice was quiet. "There are worse places for him to be."

"Even if freedom's the other option?"

"There's a time and place," he said. "And out here on the street, in broad daylight in front of operational magic monitors ain't either of those."

Pike hadn't stopped struggling, so the agents forced a jacket on him—a special restraint usually used to control wraiths—and moved him into the back of the vehicle.

A moment later, they climbed inside and were gone. When the neighborhood was quiet again, the birds began to chirp.

"We'll talk to Lizzie," Moses said. "Make sure she's got an eye on him."

Right now that didn't feel like much consolation.

It had been a gas station—a corner business with atomic-era architecture and a couple of garage bays. It was now a bunker and a secret archive of banned magical objects. And my home sweet home.

Inside, there were long wooden tables and shelves along the walls, each holding priceless and completely illegal weapons, books, masks, and other items. My father had hidden them here to keep them away from Containment bonfires.

For now, I was outside and above the magic. I lay on a blanket on the roof, where the low walls gave me cover from Containment patrols.

Tomorrow would be the first night I'd spent out of New Orleans in years. My father had refused to evacuate, even when the city was bombarded. We'd lived together in a house until he died, and then I moved into Royal Mercantile. After the Battle of Devil's Isle, I'd walked to the gas station and spent the first of many nights here. It had become my home, my new piece of New Orleans.

Tonight I watched the sun sink in the west, sending streaks of brilliant orange and purple across the sky. The sight was beautiful enough that I could nearly pretend the world was whole again. But nearly wasn't enough. Nothing—and no one—in the Zone was whole anymore.

The gas station sat on what had been a busy road. But in the weeks I'd been here, I'd seen fewer than a dozen people nearby. An older couple lived up the street in a double camelback. A man lived two blocks up in the kingdom he'd made of a former Piggly Wiggly. Everyone else had been moving: passersby, nomads, Containment officers.

"I understand I missed some excitement."

I jumped at the sound of Malachi's voice, sat up to find him standing behind me, his body a dark silhouette against the brilliant sky. "You have got to stop doing that."

His wings retracted, changing his shape from Paranormal to human. "You have got to listen harder."

I shouldn't have been surprised; Malachi had a habit of visiting me at night. Darkness reduced the chance he'd be seen, and I think he enjoyed the company and the quiet. I hadn't let him inside the building—too many secrets there—but I'd given him the address. I knew I could trust him to keep the location secret, and I didn't have to worry about his evading Containment if they somehow found out about it.

"Containment agents found Pike," I said. "They took him in."

He walked toward me, sat down on the edge of the blanket. His body was big and warm, and he smelled faintly like woodsmoke. "Moses told me."

I stared hard at the horizon, guilt punching through my chest. "I should have helped him."

"There's a time and a place."

"That's what Moses said."

"He was right. We have to pick our battles. They aren't all winnable."

I glanced at him. His face was inscrutable, his golden eyes shimmering in the fading light as he scanned the horizon, as if keeping watch for marauders. "Is that a lesson you learned here, or in the Beyond?"

"Here," he said thoughtfully. "In the Beyond, we were in power and took much for granted." He glanced at me. "I've told you it was an orderly society. Rigidly so. If it hadn't been so rigid—if we'd been able to evolve, to change—perhaps we'd have been able to prevent the war."

"Maybe," I said. "Or maybe the Court would have been dissatisfied with everything you offered to do. Sometimes the ones who cry loudest for war don't really want change. They just want the fight and the power."

He nodded. "Humans and Paras are very similar in that respect."

I sat up, crossed my legs. "You didn't object to Gavin's request—to leaving New Orleans and traveling into the wilderness. Is that a winnable battle?"

"I don't know. But I've been in that particular wilderness before. There's a lot to recommend it."

"I don't like snakes."

Malachi smiled, ran a hand through his tousled curls. "Then the bayou may not be the best place for you."

"What is?" I asked. I didn't really fit in anywhere right now. "What's the real story about Broussard?"

"I don't know anything beyond what Gavin said. But whatever it is, Liam seems to be the key."

"The key to what?"

"I don't know. Something important enough to kill a Containment agent for. Or something important enough to frame Liam for. Or both."

I looked up at the stars that had begun to pierce the settling darkness. "Life is never simple."

"Death is simpler." He smiled a little. "But too simple for most."

"At least everybody gets a turn."

He lay back, looked up at the stars. "That's one thing we certainly all have in common."

CHAPTER THREE

I sat on the floor. It was just dawn, and sunlight would have filtered through the windows if they hadn't been painted over to shield the magical goods inside from prying eyes. I still wore pajamas—a V-neck T-shirt and shorts. I hadn't yet begun to pack for the trip.

I'd committed to going. And I was going. But in the meantime, I was having seriously cold feet.

I knew why Liam had left. Understood well the fear and doubts he'd have had about gaining magic. I'd had doubts, too, and I hadn't had a sister who'd been killed by wraiths, by magic gone bad. Having gained magic, he would have to deal with those complicated feelings.

And it was probably worse for him, because he didn't clearly fit on the human-Sensitive-Paranormal scale. Unlike me, he and Eleanor hadn't just absorbed magic; they'd gotten it through strikes by magical weapons.

But five weeks still felt like a long time. A long time with no messages, no checking in, no making sure that I was all right. Maybe it was selfish of me, maybe not. But the silence hurt. Maybe, like Gavin had warned me, Liam's feelings had changed.

If they had, what was I going to say to him? How was I going to face that down?

I shook my head. At least I'd find out one way or the other, I reminded myself, and ignored the hollowness in my chest. I wouldn't have to wait, and I wouldn't have to wonder. Plus, I'd get out of New Orleans for a little while. I'd spend time with Malachi and Gavin, who were usually entertaining, and I'd see parts of Louisiana I hadn't seen before. If we found them, I'd see Eleanor again.

We hadn't even left yet, and I was lining up the consolation prizes.

"Way to be brave, Connolly." I muttered it to myself, but climbed to my feet, then took the small back staircase to the basement.

I walked to the far wall, grabbed one of the hanging backpacks that was already half full of emergency supplies my father had decided we'd needed, and began adding to it.

Today, I was going into the bayou. I'd see Liam. And the shape of my future would become clear.

The sky was gray with clouds and humidity, and even the breeze was heavy and wet and carried the scents of earth and water. The scents of New Orleans.

The temperature would continue to climb and the humidity probably wouldn't diminish, but we'd also be facing bugs of every variety, and God only knew what other crawling and flying horrors rural Louisiana would have to offer, so I opted for long cargo pants and a short-sleeved shirt, and folded a thin waterproof jacket into my pack in case of deluge.

In Louisiana, there was always a chance of deluge.

My travel mates stood together in the alley behind Moses's house—one human and two Paranormals. Moses, in a shirt of screaming red that made him look more like an impish devil than made me comfortable, Gavin in lived-in jeans and a technical shirt, and Malachi in a V-neck and jeans. Gavin had the strap of an army surplus pack in one hand, a double-barreled shotgun in the other.

He looked at me, smiled. There was so much Quinn in that smile. "Looks like we're all here. Would y'all like the good news first or the bad news?"

"I'd prefer there not be any bad news," I said, adjusting my pack. "Is that an option?"

"No," Gavin said. "I talked to Gunnar this morning. He doesn't think Liam's guilty, but the theory's got legs within Containment. There are folks who think Liam had too much leeway dealing with Paras and got special treatment because of his family."

Eleanor was an Arsenault, an old and wealthy Creole family connected to very powerful people outside the Zone—the people we'd been contacting in our efforts to bring to light the truth about magic.

"They sound like allies of Broussard," I said.

"Yeah. They have no trouble believing this is Liam's doing. And they've increased the amount of the bounty."

"It's only been a day," I said, concern for Liam tightening my gut. "They never increase that quickly." I'd done a little bounty hunting with Liam; it had been good cover for keeping an eye on Containment. Increases in bounties were rare, and happened only when time had passed without a lead on the particular prey.

"And what's the good news?" Malachi asked.

"It's not raining. Yet."

We just looked at him.

Shameless, Gavin lifted a shoulder. "As leader of this particular mission, I figured you needed the stick and the carrot. Except I didn't have any carrots. So I went with the weather."

Moses shook his head, lips pursed. "You this good on all your missions?"

"There's a reason I usually work alone," Gavin said, shouldering the pack.

"Where, exactly, are we going?" I asked. There was no one else around, but I dropped my voice anyway. This wasn't the time to attract attention.

"Houma," Malachi said. "Vicinity of Erida's last location."

Houma was about an hour's drive from New Orleans.

"There," he continued, "we'll meet some friends, see if we can get a sense of where she went."

"Friends?" I asked.

"Paranormals with passes."

I lifted my eyebrows. "I was actually beginning to think that was a myth. Since Moses didn't get one, I mean. Or you."

"I won't request freedom I already own," Malachi said. "And Containment isn't in a position to give us passes from Devil's Isle, since we're already out."

I couldn't really argue with that.

Gavin gestured to the beat-up jeep at the curb. "The wheels will take us to Houma. Then we'll leave the vehicle, travel on foot."

"If we get to the Gulf, we've gone too far?" I asked.

"Something like that." Gavin looked me over, took in the pants, shirt, shoes, and gave a nod of approval. "What's in the bag?"

"Water, poncho, knife, atomic bug spray." I might not have been out of New Orleans in a while, but I'd been in it long enough. I had a pretty good idea how to survive in the wet and the heat.

"Good," Gavin said with a smile.

"I'll meet you at Houma," Malachi said.

"Wait," I said, sliding him a narrowed glance. "What do you mean you'll 'meet' us? You aren't going with us?"

He smiled. "I mean I don't need a ride." He unfolded his wings, and twelve feet of ivory stretched out behind him, feathers gleaming in the sun.

"You're going to fly the whole way?"

"Boy, will his arms be tired!" Moses said, waving a fake cigar.

Gavin's eyes narrowed at me. "I hear you let him have a joke book."

"He found it in an abandoned house, which made it fair game. I couldn't exactly stop him from taking it."

He shook his head. "Let's hit the road. Every mile toward Houma is another mile away from jokes that start with 'Two Paranormals walked into a bar.'"

"I need a minute," Moses said to me, then moved a few feet away.

"I believe you're being beckoned," Malachi said.

"Evidently," I said, and joined Moses. "You rang?"

"I want you to remember something," he said, pointing a stubby finger up at me. "You've worked hard for the last few weeks, done some good around here. Whatever happens, no one can take that away from you."

I lifted my brows, surprised at the emotion in his eyes. "You under the impression I'm gonna have a breakdown in the bayou?"

"I'm just saying, whatever he says or does"—he paused, seemed to look for the right words—"there's more to the world than dames."

I looked at him for a minute, appreciating the thought but confused by the message. And then I figured it out. "You didn't just take the joke books. You took the detective novels, too, didn't you?"

"They're good," he said with an embarrassed shrug that I found almost absurdly endearing. "I like this Sam Spade character. Straight shooter. Anyway." He cleared his throat. "You be careful out there."

"I'll be fine," I told him. "But I don't like leaving you here alone."

"You think I can't take care of myself?" He pointed a thumb at his chest, which was puffed out a little. "I'm the one who's been taking care of you—not the other way around." But there was something soft and sweet in his eyes.

"You're right. You'll tell Lizzie why I'm gone?"

"That you're taking a relaxing spa weekend? Sure thing."

"Hilarious, as always." I hugged him. "Be careful."

"No need to get emotional," he said, but his arms were steel bands around me. "You're only gonna be gone a few days."

Assuming we found him and managed to make it back alive.

"We'll be fine," I said, trying to assure both of us.

"Damn right you will. Now get in that jeep, start your hunt, and claim your bounty."

The clouds had burned off by the time we reached the edge of New Orleans, and the sun beat down on Highway 90 like a drum, sending up shimmering waves of heat. It was much too early to be this warm, but magic hadn't just affected electricity; it had made our weather less predictable.

We stayed on the highway as long as we could, then veered off to Old Spanish Trail when Gavin caught sight of a Containment convoy—jeeps and trucks heading into New Orleans with goods and sundries to be distributed to stores around the city.

Royal Mercantile would probably be getting some of the freight. Bottled water, soap, maybe a few sticks of butter packed in dry ice for the trip. But that was Tadji's responsibility now. She was my beautiful and brilliant best friend, the woman I'd given the choice to run the store or let it sit until I came home again.

She'd decided to enter the exciting world of postwar retail and was doing a damn fine job of it, based on what I'd seen the couple of times I'd managed to sneak into the Quarter. She'd apparently gathered up every volunteer left in the neighborhood to fix glass broken in the battle, to reorganize overturned furniture and scattered stock. From what I could tell, business was booming. Tadji might have been trained as a linguist, but she was really, really good at merchandising. Even in the mostly deserted Quarter, people had milled around, looking at the goods and making purchases.

I wondered if the convoy had skipped this road to keep from destroying the vehicles and the cargo. I had to grab the jeep's handle as we bounced over pitted asphalt.

"Are you hitting the potholes on purpose?"

"Man's gotta have a hobby," Gavin said.

The narrow highway ran between railroad tracks on one side and the remains of stores, small houses, and mobile homes on the other. Rural parts of the state hadn't been hit by Para attacks as hard as the urban areas, but there were even fewer services out here, and a lot of people hadn't stayed after the war. Plenty of solitude, if that's what you preferred, but the living was hard.

We passed a store on stilts, a bait shop with "fresh" painted in rough black letters along one exterior wall. The windows were boarded up, and a rusting car sat on blocks in front. Once again, my mind tripped back to my store, to the Quarter.

I pulled out my water bottle, took a drink, trying to focus on something else.

"Tadji's handling Royal Mercantile," Gavin said.

I guess his mind had taken the same turn.

"Yeah," I said, screwing the lid back on the bottle.

"Have you talked to her?"

I shook my head. "I check in on the store every once in a while. But I don't want to put her in danger. The less she knows about me, the better." As far as I was concerned, plausible deniability was my friend's best option. "Have you talked to her?"

He shook his head. "I haven't been around." The vehicle shuddered, and he slammed a hand on the dashboard, which seemed to settle the issue. "I left after the battle."

My eyebrows lifted. Yesterday, he said he'd just gotten back into town, but I didn't know he'd been gone the entire time. I'd assumed he'd been here but was doing his own thing—or he'd been avoiding me. That he'd been out of town made me feel a little better, and more curious.

"Where were you?"

"Reconnaissance contract," Gavin said.

"For Containment?"

"For Containment. They were surprised by Reveillon. They don't want to be surprised again."

"Do they think there are more Reveillon members out there?"

Gavin made a sarcastic sound. "Nobody doubts there are more Reveillon members out there. Or at least sympathizers. Plenty of people hate magic, blame magic for what the Zone's become. Containment's looking for organizing, collective action. Any sign that people are clustering again, planning violence, posing a threat."

"Find anything?"

"Lot of talk, no action to speak of." He gave me a sideways glance. "Did you think I was in New Orleans and just avoiding you?"

He'd nailed it, which made my cheeks burn. "Kind of, yeah."

He shook his head, looked back at the road. "We're family, Claire. Granted, kind of a weird, dysfunctional family, but family all the same."

"Yay," I said, and spun an imaginary noisemaker. But family was family. And it wasn't so bad to have this one.

Before we hit Houma, the rain started up, the kind of heavy and steady downpour that set in for the day.

Twenty minutes later, Gavin pulled the car off the highway and onto a long gravel drive.

At the end of it, stately as a queen, sat a plantation house. White, with two stories, both lined with porches, fluted columns, and floor-to-ceiling windows. The front yard featured a boxwood hedge in a pretty pattern, and the drive was marked by enormous oak trees whose branches bent in graceful arcs toward the ground, with Spanish moss draped like scarves across the boughs.

There weren't many plantation houses left in Louisiana. There'd once been dozens along the Mississippi River outside New Orleans. The Civil War had knocked down some of them. Time and history had knocked down others. The war with Paras had done a number on the rest, especially after Paras targeted the petroleum facilities that shared the prime real estate along the river.

This house had survived, and it looked like it had been well cared for. It wasn't the only thing that had gotten attention. Row after row of skinny green stalks filled the fields around the structure. It was sugarcane, acres and acres of it stretching across the delta to the horizon. A dozen Paras—or so I guessed, given the rainbow hues of their skin tones—were pulling weeds among the stalks.

Gavin moved slowly down the drive and came to a stop in the shade of an oak tree. A wooden sign swinging in the rain read VACHERIE PLANTATION.

"What are we doing here?" I asked, after we'd climbed out of the car.

"One, leaving the car, so grab your pack."

I did as he suggested, shouldering it on. "And two?"

He met my gaze over the hood of the car. "Malachi's friends work here. The Paranormals with passes."

"Correct," Malachi said.

This time I'd caught the soft flutter of wings.

"Back up," I said. "Paranormals who have passes out of Devil's Isle are working in sugarcane fields?"

Malachi looked at me, his golden eyes keen. "What did you think they'd be doing outside Devil's Isle?"

"I'd assumed they were out there"—I made a vague gesture—"enjoying freedom." Not pulling weeds at a plantation house.

"They are entitled to employment," Malachi said. "And feeding the Zone is a big industry."

"I'm not arguing they don't have the right to work. But, I mean—working in sugarcane fields? Does that make anyone else uncomfortable?"

"You mean the overtones of indentured servitude?" Gavin asked.

"Yeah, let's start there." And jump right into slavery. "How is this freedom?"

"Because they're paid," Malachi said, and there was tension in his voice now. "Because they can be productive after seven years of feeling like victims. Because they can sleep outside Devil's Isle for the first time in years. And because it was the only option given."

So passes weren't really the magnanimous gesture that Containment made them out to be.

"I'm sorry," I said. "That's pretty conniving on Containment's part. And it's not really comfortable, given, well, U.S. history."

Malachi nodded. "Paras have their own history and uncomfortable parallels. The landowners are allies, and the Paras want their wages and their freedom. They know this is their best route to that—at least for now."

At least, he meant, until Containment proved it wasn't willing to go further. Containment had acted in good faith by giving the passes, so the Paras would act in good faith, too. For now.

"Come on," Malachi said.

Gavin and I followed him toward the house, then around it to several barns and outbuildings. The grass was short, the areas between buildings dotted with enormous copper kettles probably used for preparing cane syrup.

"They sleep in the main house," Malachi said. "While they're getting ready for the harvest, they'll repair the barn and the house, work on the subsidiary crops. When the cane's ready, they'll trim it, cut it, process it."

The detail made me smile. "You a farmer now?"

He looked down at me, a curl falling over one eye. "I take an interest in my friends' interests."

"Does that mean we're friends?"

"Close enough."

"Is it safe for you to be here?" I asked him.

"The humans here know me as a friend of the Paras." He smiled a little. "They believe I'm connected with a charitable organization, and I haven't bothered to correct them."

"Is it safe for Claire to be here?" Gavin lifted his gaze to the magic monitors that dotted the grounds.

"The monitors are inoperable," Malachi said. "Although Containment isn't aware of it."

A whistle split the air, high-pitched enough to break all wineglasses in a five-mile radius. I put my hands over my ears a little too late.

"Damn," Gavin said, wincing. "Please destroy that whistle immediately."

"Not a whistle," Malachi said. "A skill."

A man emerged from behind one of the outbuildings, his skin pale, his hair long and white and straight. He was on the short side, his body lean and compact beneath bright orange scrubs. The color,

I guessed, was for visibility, should he or any of the other Paras attempt to escape.

"And the line between freedom and imprisonment gets thinner still," I murmured.

"Uncomfortable," Gavin quietly agreed.

"Djosa," Malachi said. "This is Gavin and Claire, human and Sensitive."

We nodded to one another.

"What brings you here, General?" Djosa asked, his voice deep, his diction precise.

Malachi had been a general in the Consularis military.

"We're looking for Erida and two travelers with her," he said. "Neither of them Sensitives. Both changed by power from others. One without sight. One with golden eyes."

His brows lifted. "You don't know where your subordinate is hiding?"

"We know where she *was*. We do not know where she *is*."

Djosa gave us a suspicious look. "I imagine that's for her security and yours."

"It is," Malachi agreed. "But circumstances require that we find her."

"Because?"

"Because the humans are being hunted," Malachi replied. "And we bring a warning."

"Or you lead soldiers right to them."

"We're being careful," Malachi said, impatience growing in his voice. "We acknowledge the risk, but there's no helping it. They must be told."

"We don't know anything about where they are or might be." He looked back at the fields. "And we need to get back to work."

"Do you like the work?" I asked him.

"Would you?"

"Probably not," I admitted.

He seemed to appreciate the honest answer. "This isn't forever," he said determinedly. "It's for now, and it's freedom. Maybe not the freedom we want forever, but the freedom we can get now."

He held up his hands, his skin marbled with dirt and stained green from weeds. "Do you know how long it's been since I've had earth beneath my fingers? Since I've felt her heart beating? Felt her stirring beneath me?"

Given the lust in his voice, he might as well have been talking about a woman. That created some uncomfortable mental imagery.

"Too long," Djosa answered, saving me from filling the silence. "This is a chance for us. It may not be the best chance, but it's the one we've been given. And when you've been in our skin for seven years, you take freedom as it comes."

Good enough for me. It was his life, not mine, and we all had to find our path.

Screaming pulled our attention away from Djosa. A woman who looked to be human—slender, with tan skin, straight dark hair, and dark eyes full of concern—ran out of the barn.

"Djosa!" she screamed, waving him toward her. "Help!"

Djosa didn't waste any time, but took off at a sprint toward her. We let Malachi take the lead, then followed him.

The barn was enormous, a tall wooden rectangle with a sharply pitched tin roof. The double doors stood open. We were about to follow Djosa inside when three men emerged from the door and jumped into our path.

They had tan skin, hooded eyes, hair dark as ravens, and a cascade of dark feathers that appeared to run from the crest of their heads to the bottom of their feet. "Appeared to," because they were wearing the same bright orange scrubs as Djosa.

The trio split apart and moved around us, the shifting light illuminating purple and black tones in their gleaming feathers.

The feathers along their spines lifted like the hackles of an angry dog, and the men made low, snipping noises as they circled, raising hands that revealed gleaming talons nestled among finer feathers.

They prepared for attack, so I did, too. I reached out a hand, felt for the magic in the air, just in case I needed it.

"These are the Tengu," Malachi said, spreading his hands out as if to shield me and Gavin from an attack—or to keep us from drawing first. "They don't know us. Give them a moment to settle."

They didn't seem interested in settling. Ominous magic colored the air, staining it black. I could feel the magic circling around us now, spinning like a hurricane and bending the cane around us, as we stood in the eye of the storm. The Tengu screamed, the sound sharp as fingernails on a blackboard.

"I don't think they're settling," Gavin murmured, blading his body for a counterattack.

"Kahsut."

The simple word, spoken by Malachi, apparently in a language from the Beyond, echoed around us. It was more than a word; it was a bone-deep order, full of power.

I wasn't sure if the Tengu recognized the word or understood the demand, but they stopped moving and lowered their arms. Then each of them knelt in front of Malachi and gave another whistling cry.

"Are they your . . . subjects?" Gavin quietly asked, clearly groping for the right word.

"Not precisely," Malachi said, then repeated the word. The Tengu rose and shifted away from us, giving us room to walk.

Subjects or not, he got results.

The path now cleared, we walked into the barn. A dirt floor, with hay in piles and rusting implements leaning against the walls. A piece of bright green farm machinery was parked near the opposite end, streaked by shafts of sunlight.

In the middle of the space, a woman lay on the floor, her skin and hair the same pale shades as Djosa's, her legs folded like she'd simply fallen in place. Even from a dozen feet away, it was clear to see her skin was sallow, her body shaking with chills, or fever, or both. There were red dots on her arms, and her breath wheezed in and out.

Djosa knelt at her left side and took her hand in his.

"Anh," Malachi said to the woman who'd yelled for us and who now stood behind Djosa, looking worriedly at the woman on the floor. "What's happened?"

"She was ill," Anh said. I hadn't realized how petite she was—barely over five feet, and delicately boned. "But she refused to stop working. She'd had chills, collapsed suddenly. Now she's burning up, and her breathing is shallow. Her heart is beating so fast."

I could have imagined it was just a difference in biology, except for everyone's obvious concern. "What's her name?" I asked.

"Cinda," Djosa said, without looking up. "Her name is Cinda."

One of the Tengu moved closer, began chattering at Malachi in what I assumed was the same language Malachi had used to calm them.

"They believe she was exposed to something out here," Malachi translated, then paused while the Tengu spoke again. "Something she wasn't exposed to in Devil's Isle."

Another pause, and Malachi's brows lifted as he listened. "Containment warned them this might happen, gave them immunity boosters before they left Devil's Isle . . . to strengthen them against the enemies here."

"The enemies?" I asked as more people came into the barn, humans and Paras who smelled of earth and sweat, who'd probably left their work to investigate.

"Wildlife," Gavin said. "Animals and bugs, humans from outside Devil's Isle. New vectors."

"Freedom made her ill," I quietly said.

"Yeah." There was regret in Gavin's voice.

"We need to get her to a hospital," Malachi said. "I assume the closest one's in New Orleans?"

Djosa shook his head. "They won't treat her. They'll send her back to Devil's Isle. Our passes last one week," he explained. "We sleep here, in the big house, because they don't want to transport us back and forth every day. That's too much trouble if the power goes out. And if Containment decides she's hurt," he continued, anger rising in his words, "they won't let her out again."

Anger burned in my chest, but it was useless against the tide of Containment's power.

"We can't just leave her like this," Anh said. "That can't be the only option."

"Are you sure she'd trade her freedom for her life?" Malachi asked Djosa, his voice calm and composed even in the midst of panic.

"Yes," Djosa said, his gaze clear. "She would. But this is just an illness. She'll get rest, and she'll be fine. She'd want to take the chance."

"Then we treat her," Malachi said, and looked at Anh. "Prepare a bed inside the house, away from the others. Only she will sleep there. You have ice?"

Anh nodded.

"Get ice, a fan if you have a generator. You need to get her temperature down. She'll need liquids, salt. Go," he said. Anh dashed off.

I wished I'd brought the salt I'd found yesterday; it hadn't even occurred to me that it might be useful.

"I cannot heal her," Malachi said, crouching beside Djosa. "But I can perhaps soothe her. That may help."

"Do it," Djosa said, wiping his brow. The barn was in the shade, but there was no breeze in it, and the air was stifling.

"Maybe we should move people back," I said, since we had no other way to help. Gavin nodded, turned to the crowd.

"All right, everyone," he said, "let's give them some room to help her."

The Paras and humans, united by hard work and concern for their colleague, shuffled around and backed up as Malachi pushed the damp hair from Cinda's face. He closed his eyes, his lashes crescents against his golden skin, and placed his hands, palm down, above her heart.

She whimpered, and he smiled down at her with warm and confident kindness. Exactly the kind of expression you'd expect to see on an angel. If you hadn't seen them fight in the war.

"There's no need to be afraid," Malachi said. "Consularis are strong. Djosa is strong, and you've inherited your strength from him."

So Djosa was Cinda's father, I guessed.

"Illness is part of life," Malachi said, "just as pain is part of healing. It is a natural reaction. I cannot interrupt that process, but I can make you more comfortable while your body heals."

Malachi didn't touch Cinda, but moved his hands above her body, back and forth, as if manipulating air—or maybe energy.

I'd felt Malachi's magic before, when we'd snuck Moses out of Devil's Isle and when he'd begun to train me to better use my magic. We'd managed a few more lessons in the last few weeks, and I'd sensed it then, too.

Here in this hot and dusty barn, as his magic unfurled around us,

I realized that those had been mere glimpses of the breadth of it. Like looking into a greenhouse and seeing shapes and petals through a filter of fogged glass.

This was like standing in a field of brilliant crimson poppies.

Malachi was a master of control, and he often seemed distant because of it. But his magic was wild the way wolves were, untamed like the staggering peak of a snowy and rugged mountain. And it was strong—the strongest magic I'd ever felt from a Paranormal. It was like the torrent of a raging river. This was real magic, not the pale frost that I could access.

After a few minutes of steady movement, Cinda appeared to relax, and her breathing calmed again. Malachi slowly lifted his hands, then stepped away as Anh rushed back in.

"We're ready," she said.

At Malachi's nod, Djosa picked Cinda up, limp in his arms, and carried her out of the barn.

We waited for a moment in the humming silence, while the other workers went back to their tasks.

Malachi led me and Gavin outside, then pointed toward a stand of trees about a hundred yards away. "The trail begins there, and it's blazed. Follow it to the woods."

"You want us to leave?" I asked.

"I want to be sure she's comfortable, and she doesn't need an audience for that. We also don't want to wear out our welcome, as we've yet to get information about Liam and the others.

"Get started," he continued. "The trail forks a quarter mile into the woods. Go left when you reach the fork. You'll find a creek about twenty yards down. The water's potable, and there's shade. You can fill your bottles and wait there. I'll meet you when I'm done."

"All right," Gavin said, glanced at me, and I nodded.

"Be careful," Malachi said, then turned and strode toward the house.

"Are you okay?" Gavin asked when we were alone. "Your pupils are still dilated."

My cheeks warmed. "He's got powerful magic."

"I bet," Gavin murmured. "Let's get moving."

CHAPTER FOUR

The trail was hard dirt that skimmed between a sugarcane field on one side and a treelined creek bed on the other. The woods were in front of us, a dark wall battling back oppressive sunshine. The temperature dropped ten degrees the second we stepped into shade, but the trees and foliage quickly formed a canopy over the path, closing in the humidity.

"It's like trying to breathe through a wet blanket," I said, wiping my brow.

"Yeah," Gavin said, pausing to inspect a tree along the trail—and the small symbols carved into it.

"Para trailblazing?" I asked.

"Yeah. I don't know the meaning, but at least we know we've hit the trail."

We walked until trees surrounded us on all sides and we could no longer see the fields open behind us.

"Creek's nearby," Gavin said as the sound of moving water grew louder.

A few seconds later, the trail spit us out to a short bluff over the narrow creek, which flowed invitingly between tree-covered banks. "Steps" had been worn into the sharp drop to the water, held in place by roots that popped up through the dirt.

"And here we are," he said. We took off our backpacks, pulled out our bottles, and headed down the bank. Gavin went first, sliding a little in the slick mud, and turned back to offer me a hand when he hit the bottom.

"You want help?"

"Not going to say no to that offer," I said, taking his strong fingers and easing my way toward the water. I ran-skipped the final few feet, then grabbed a tree limb to keep from pitching into the creek.

"Momentum's a bitch," Gavin said with a grin, uncapping his bottle.

"Yeah." But the view was nearly worth it. The water wasn't deep—only a foot or so—but it was crystal clear, moving quickly over a rocky bottom. A tree limb dipped nearly to the surface on the opposite bank, and Spanish moss hung like lace above the ribbon of water as it flowed past.

Except for the gurgle of water over rock, the world was completely silent. If anything else moved in the woods, the sound was muffled by the stream. That was a reason to take a minute to relax—and a reminder that we needed to be aware.

"It's beautiful here."

"Yeah," Gavin said, taking a drink from the bottle he'd already filled. "There's a reason I don't spend much time in the city. Out here, it's easy to pretend the war never happened. That everything's peaceful again and you're alone in paradise."

I looked at him. "You like going solo."

"I'm used to it," he said, but didn't elaborate. A tender spot, I guessed.

I dipped my bottle into the stream until it was full again, took a long drink. The water was sweet and cold, probably untouched by humans since the war.

That was one of the few benefits of the battles that had racked

Louisiana. Most humans and industry were long gone, and nature had reclaimed the land in their absence. A few years ago, pesticides probably would have made the creek water undrinkable. The world had, in some ways, healed itself.

I screwed on the bottle cap again, then splashed water on my face and dried it with the bottom of my T-shirt.

Back on the bluff, which was easier to get up than climb down, I looked it over for enemies—snakes, spiders, ants—and took a seat.

"I'm going to take a moment," Gavin said, gesturing into the woods. "A private moment."

"I don't need the details," I said, holding up a hand. "Do what you need to do. I'll be right here."

"Stay put," he said with a warning glance. "We don't know who or what's roaming around these woods looking for Liam or you."

"Not a problem," I said, patting the log. "Me and Mr. Tree will hang out right here."

With a nod, he wandered back down the trail.

He'd been gone less than a minute when I heard his footsteps behind me. "Found the little boys' room already?" I asked.

It took me a moment to realize they weren't Gavin's footsteps.

And that was a moment too late.

The hand that clapped over my mouth was thick and callused and smelled of dirt and gasoline.

"Keep ya mouth shut, and you'll be fine." His voice was over my head and to my right. He was tall, and the spread of heat radiating at my back indicated he was wide as well. His other hand was clamped on my shoulder.

"You got her?" The second man stepped out from behind a tree. Average height, average weight, average looks, dark hair, pale skin.

He wore a T-shirt, jeans, and boots. No uniform, which meant he wasn't a Containment agent. Or he wasn't on duty as one, anyway.

"I got her," the man behind me said.

My heart was pounding so fiercely it might have broken through my chest. But panic wouldn't help me, so I made myself stay calm and hoped they might let their guard down.

"Let me go," I said, when he moved his hand away from my mouth. But he kept his meaty hold on my shoulder.

"Oh, we can't do that." The second man's voice had a rough edge, as if he'd dragged each word over a serrated blade. "You appear to be Claire Connolly, and I know plenty of Containment agents who'd like to question you. And what's more, my research says you know one Liam Quinn. He's right at the top of my list, and I understand he's been seen in these parts."

"We aren't gonna hurt you," the man behind me said. "Just take you into New Orleans."

Not a trip I wanted to take today, and certainly not with these two. But before I could object, Gavin stepped onto the trail, his eyes wide, an apple halfway to his mouth. If he was alarmed to see me in my current position, he hid it well.

"Well, hello there," he said, crunching into the apple, as he looked from man to man and then to me. "I am not sure what I've come across here, but I don't want any trouble."

"True enough, friend," the second man said. "This is Containment business, so just be on your way."

"Containment business?" Gavin looked excited. "That's actually really great. I don't suppose you gentlemen have any matches to trade? Mine got soaked, and I've been looking for someone on the trail for two hours."

"Your name?" the second one asked.

"You can call me Lafitte," Gavin said, naming the most famous pirate in the history of New Orleans. "I'm not aiming to make friends." He held up his hands. "You don't have what I need, I'll be on my way."

The man behind me let me go, giving me a look at his face. He was older, easily a hard-earned sixty, with long, frizzy gray hair and a mustache of the same color that fell well below his chin. He wore jeans and a T-shirt with a leather vest covered in patches.

He reached into his pocket, pulled out an old Altoids tin. And from that, he extracted three thick matches.

"Thank God," Gavin said, relief clear on his face. "I've got MREs, an extra knife, some wire and rope I found up the way. Any of that interest you?"

"All of it," the younger man said, "if you want the matches."

Gavin's gaze narrowed, jaw working as he considered. "Price isn't worth it for me. Two MREs, wire, and rope."

"You aren't exactly in a bargaining spot."

Gavin's brows lifted. "I'm not?"

"You don't seem to know who we are."

"I can't say that I do."

"Hunters," said the older man. "And lots of people want to talk to her."

Gavin looked at me doubtfully. "About what? She doesn't look like much of a threat."

"She did something that pissed off Containment," the older man said. "The details ain't no business of mine."

"I guess I can't argue with that." Gavin took another bite of the apple. "Bounties make for good work? I haven't gone that route yet, prefer staying outside New Orleans—which is Gomorrah if you ask me—but I'm always looking for viable employment."

"It's viable," the younger one said, "if you're skilled."

"Sure," Gavin said, eagerness in his nod. "Of course."

"Biggest bounty is for Liam Quinn," the older one said, excitement coloring his words. "Biggest bounty Containment's issued in three years."

There was a hard knot in my stomach. Gavin's eyes shifted quickly to mine, a warning in his gaze that told me to keep my mouth shut.

"Jimmy," the younger one said, "zip it."

Jimmy pursed his lips. "Sorry, Crowley."

Crowley was the older one. He nodded, looked at Gavin again. "We've got business now. If you want the trade, let's get on with it."

"Sure thing." Gavin took a final bite of the apple and tossed the rest into the woods. Then he wiped his hand on his pants, pulled his backpack off his shoulder, and set it on the ground. "Shit," he said, wincing as he yanked at the zipper. "Damn thing's stuck again."

"Let's go," Crowley said, after Gavin had wrestled with it for another solid minute.

Gavin looked up, held out the bag. "You want to give it a go?"

Crowley stepped forward, and Gavin took his chance. He used the bag like a baseball bat, slamming it toward Crowley. But Crowley dodged at the last moment, so the bag only smacked his shoulder.

"Son of a bitch!" Crowley yelled. He took a knife from the leather holster on his belt and sliced down, aiming for Gavin's chest. Gavin, who still held the bag in one hand, spun it again, this time knocking the knife away so it disappeared into the foliage. Crowley growled and charged, pushing them both to the ground.

His hand still around my arm, Jimmy yanked me back down the trail toward Vacherie. I tried to pull away, but he outweighed me by more than a hundred pounds and didn't mind dragging me.

"We have to make a damn living, too," he muttered, his uneven fingernails digging into the skin on my arm.

"Everybody does," I said neutrally, my gaze darting around the narrow trail, looking for something I could use.

Since he wasn't sure why Containment wanted to talk to me, I didn't think it was a good idea to call up magic and clarify that for him. So unless Gavin got to me first, I'd have to deal with Jimmy on my own.

And when I saw what I needed, I made my move.

"Ow!" I cried. I leaned down, touched my ankle gingerly, then hopped a bit for good measure. "I stepped on something wrong. I think I might have sprained it, maybe?" I let my voice do a simpering little whine.

"Freaking women in the woods," Jimmy muttered. He dragged me over to a chopped-off cypress stump and pushed me down onto it. "What the hell's wrong with you?"

When he leaned over to look at my foot, I brought my knee up hard against his chin.

Kneecap slammed into jaw and sent pain ricocheting up my leg. Jimmy howled and stumbled backward, his momentum stopped by a tree on the other side of the trail.

"Son of a bitch!" he said, his words muffled by the hand he'd slapped over his mouth.

While I scrambled to my feet and snagged a thick branch that lay beside the stump, he pulled his fingers away, and his eyes went hot with anger at the sight of the blood on them.

He roared and jumped up again. I waited until he was close, then dodged to the side, lifted the branch, and brought it down across his back. He stumbled forward, hit the cypress stump, then rolled over it to the ground. He was up in a second, clothes striped with mud and moss and plenty of piss and vinegar in his glare.

I raised the branch again, but he was on me before I could swing. He grabbed it and tried to pull it away, but I put my weight into it, and his mud-slicked fingers lost their purchase. He cursed and I stumbled and hit the ground. The branch skittered off.

Jimmy wiped blood from his face. "You couldn't just go quietly?" He stalked forward, and I scrambled backward, trying to give myself enough space to get to my feet. "You get into trouble with Containment, that's your fault. Man has a right to make a living out here, damn it."

Since Liam and Gavin were hunters, too, I didn't object to the principle. But I objected to being anyone's prisoner. "I don't have anything to say to Containment."

"That's not what Containment says."

I finally managed to get to my feet, sweat snaking down my back from the heat, the humidity, and the fight. My heart was still pounding, my adrenaline high. "I guess that makes us enemies. Why don't we both just walk away?"

"I don't think so." Jimmy reached out and swiped at me, but I managed to avoid him. Problem was, the path was narrow, bounded by swampy woods on both sides. Jumping into that mess wasn't going to help me get away from him. "Why don't you be a good little girl and come with me?"

"Because I'm not a good little girl." I kneed him in the balls. And when he hit the ground, moaning and scrunched up with pain, I grabbed the branch from the ground and knocked him in the back of the head.

"Freaking women in the woods," I said, chest heaving. Then I tossed the branch away.

There was clapping behind me. I looked back, found Gavin leaning against a tree and applauding me congenially.

"Thanks for the help," I muttered, wiping my hands on my pants.

"Didn't need my help," he said. "You can handle yourself on your own."

"Thanks," I said dryly. "You get your guy?"

"He's out."

I cocked my head toward the man on the trail. "I guess we'll need to do something with him."

"You wanna kill him?" he asked.

Once upon a time, that question would have horrified me a lot more than it did now.

Still. "No, I don't want to kill him. I'd really like to get out of this trip without anybody dying," I said. The fight did confirm this trip had been a good idea, though; Liam and Eleanor needed warning. And they needed it fast.

"Lafitte?" I asked.

"Beau Q. Lafitte," Gavin drawled. "One of the identities I use on ops."

"And nobody guessed 'Lafitte' was borrowed from 'Jean Lafitte'?"

"It's Louisiana," he said with a grin. "Anyone who recognizes it wants to hear the backstory."

"Which is?"

"He's Beau's grandfather, a dozen generations back. And in between, you've got your wenches, privateers, the illegitimate son of a U.S. senator."

"That's a lot of fake backstory."

"I spend a lot of time alone," Gavin said. "I made a chart."

This time, I heard the flutter, saw the silhouette of wings against the sky as Malachi maneuvered through the trees and touched down on the trail with impressive grace.

He looked at Jimmy. "Bounty hunter?"

"Yep," I said, then gestured down the trail. "There's another one that way."

"They're going to wake up soon," Gavin said.

"They won't trail us to the others." Malachi's statement was as much warning as promise.

Gavin smiled. "I've got an idea about that. You know Montagne Désespérée?"

Malachi didn't smile, but there was definitely amusement in his eyes. "I do."

"What's that mean? 'Desperate Mountain'?" I translated.

"'Hopeless Mountain,'" Gavin corrected. "Right off Bayou Black. And it's not a place you want to be stranded. Which is unfortunate for them."

Montagne Désespérée couldn't have even impersonated a mountain, except by the standards of flat southern Louisiana. It was a hump of land about twenty yards across, like a man's balding dome topped with scrubby vegetation and ringed by cypress knees and dark water. And it would be the temporary home of Jimmy and Crowley, whom Malachi and Gavin had hefted down the trail.

"This isn't an accidental hill," Malachi said, looking it over.

"No," Gavin said. "Built by Native Americans five or six thousand years ago. It used to be higher. But again, the water's rising."

"How do we get over there?" I asked, glancing dubiously at the swamp that lapped at our feet, water bugs skimming like ice-skaters across its surface.

"In a skiff," Gavin said. "I just have to remember where to find it." He picked up a stick and began poking into the leaves, fronds, and moss that littered the ground and probably held more than a few spiders and snakes.

I stayed well back from the search. And sure enough, after a couple of minutes, Gavin hit something wooden and hollow, then used the branch to push debris off a gnarly-looking boat upside down in the dirt, well hidden from passersby. But not, apparently, from people in the know.

"How did you know that would be there?" I asked.

"Because it's not my first time on Hopeless Mountain," Gavin grumbled, and I knew I'd need to weasel the entire story out of him later.

"Let's flip her," he said, and we took positions along the boat, pushed it up and over, and found the oars wedged beneath the seats. We carried it to the water and set the nose firmly in the muck at the edge so it wouldn't float away. Gavin watched for a minute, hands on his hips, waiting to be sure the bottom didn't leak and fill with water.

"Who left you here?" Malachi asked.

"That's a story that doesn't need telling. Suffice it to say I woke up on the mountain one morning with a helluva headache and no skiff."

"You swam for it?"

"After I gathered up the nerve. Place is teeming with gators. But I made it out again. Point is, if you're on the correct side of the bayou," Gavin said, "the skiff's here for the borrowing. If not, you take your chances with the water.

"Boat's fine," he pronounced, then glanced over at the hunters, now on the ground and still unconscious. Then he looked at me. "Three in the boat at a time. You want to help or watch?"

"Land is fine by me."

We moved Crowley first. Gavin and Malachi paddled the short distance to the hill while I watched Jimmy. Then they unloaded Crowley, made the return trip, and repeated the process.

"What do you think?" Gavin asked me, arms crossed as he looked over their work. He and Malachi had placed the two men beside each other against a tree, arms slung over each other's shoulders like buddies sleeping off a bender.

"I think they're going to be pissed when they wake up." I slapped a bug on my elbow, hoping for at least a couple of reasons that I wasn't going to be in the vicinity when that happened. "How long will they be here?"

"Probably less than twenty-four hours," Gavin said. "If they don't want to wade back to shore, shrimpers will find them."

"I'm surprised there are shimpers this far out," I said.

He shrugged. "Life was already hard in this area, so the war wasn't much of a change. Anyway, these two *couillons* will only have to wait out the mosquitoes." Right on cue, he slapped a bug on his neck.

Malachi and I helped Gavin turn the boat upside down and cover it again. Then Gavin picked up his backpack, slung it over one shoulder. "Let's get moving. Just in case they had friends."

Malachi's conversation with the Paras had kept him out of the bounty hunters' sight. Since he'd come back with a snack, we could forgive his missing the fight.

"Sweet rice cakes," he said, offering a waxed paper package containing two small round snacks in pretty pastel colors. "It's one of Anh's family recipes."

Gavin grabbed one and took a bite. "Nice."

I took the other one, nibbled on the edge. It was sweet and soft, and textured on the inside like a honeycomb.

"I believe her parents were from Vietnam," Malachi said. "They were here before the war and stayed when it was over."

"They give you any information?" Gavin asked, stuffing the rest of the cake into his mouth and licking sugar from his fingers.

"Djosa says he saw Erida," Malachi said. "But not Liam or Eleanor, and they don't know where Erida was going."

"Is he telling the truth?" Gavin asked.

Malachi nodded. "He might evade, but I don't think he'd lie about the details. But he did have one suggestion—that we visit the Bayou Black Marina and speak with a woman named Cherie."

"I Icy," Gavin said, brightening up, "I know her. She's actually a friend of mine."

When we both looked at him, he hunched his shoulders. "What? I have friends."

Malachi's brows lifted. "Seriously?"

Gavin looked at Malachi, then me.

"He's been working on sarcasm," I explained. "I think he's getting pretty good at it."

"You let Moses have a joke book, and you're teaching Malachi about sarcasm. Of all the things you could illuminate about the human experience, you opted for those?"

"Man's gotta have a hobby," I said with a grin. "Didn't you say that once?"

Gavin grumbled and led the way down the trail again.

It was the ugliest building I'd ever seen, and it sat like a sentinel at the edge of Bayou Black.

Maybe less a building than a three-year-old's imitation of a building—flotsam and jetsam assembled into a rough cube perched on top of wooden piles to keep it out of the water.

But letting the water take it might have been a small mercy. The walls were shards of other buildings—red shiplap and weathered cypress and aluminum siding—and the windows were oddly sized and mismatched, probably salvaged from the same buildings. It was ringed by a rickety dock that connected land and sea and hosted a single skinny gas pump.

"That is . . . interesting," Malachi finally said from our spot on the shoreline.

"It's ugly as sin," Gavin said. "And the proprietor's a pain in the ass. But she knows her stuff."

"And there will be shade," I said, wishing we'd decided to hunt down the Arsenault clan on a cloudy day.

"Let's go," Gavin said, and we strode across the bouncing dock to the door.

The inside didn't look any better than the exterior. Mismatched tables and mismatched chairs atop a sheet of linoleum that curled around the edges. There was a bar on the far end made of an old shop counter with a glass front, the case now filled with faded buoys and tangles of fishing nets.

Only one chair was occupied—by a man whose tan skin had the texture of sandpaper. He was roughly bear shaped, wore a T-shirt, jeans, and rubber boots, and worked on a bowl of food with grim determination. He looked up when we entered, apparently found nothing worth commenting on, and returned to his lunch.

There may not have been much to look at, but there was plenty to feel. An air conditioner roared in a small window on the other end of the room, and the bar was at least twenty degrees cooler than the air outside. The striking difference made my head spin, and I didn't mind a bit.

"Close the goddamn door." The voice came from behind the bar. The woman—tall, broad-shouldered, and dark-skinned—stepped around it. Her hair was short and dark, her eyes narrowed with irritation. "You think electricity comes in with the tide?"

"I think if you've got AC in here," Gavin said, walking to the bar as Malachi closed the door, "electricity isn't a problem."

"It's always a damn problem." She looked him over. "What's not a problem is that sweet, sweet face. You are a beautiful example of a man."

Gavin's eyes narrowed. "It's good to see you, too, Cherie. Can we steal a few minutes of your time?"

She looked over at us, took in me and Malachi. "Six ears is three times the price."

"I can pay," Gavin assured her. He pulled bills from his pocket and put the wad on the counter. She slipped the packet into a pocket of snug, worn jeans in a practiced move that said this was clearly not her first bribe.

"Your friends?" she asked, looking us over.

"Call them Tom and Jerry."

She looked dubious, but gestured at a table. "Take a seat," she said. She opened a cooler behind the bar, and condensation rose into the air like steam. She pulled out an unlabeled bottle of what I guessed was homebrew, popped the top, walked back to our table.

I guess the payment didn't include beverages.

Cherie pulled out a chair and practically fell into it. The movement shook the entire structure, and I had to swallow the urge to grip the edges of the table for support. At least if the building crumbled beneath us, we would hit the water.

"Helluva morning," she said, and took a long pull from the bottle. "PCC patrol rolled through here a few hours ago."

My heart tripped at the possibility they'd already narrowed down Liam's location—and made it farther and faster than us.

"PCC patrol?" Gavin asked. "Looking for someone?"

"Don't know. They drove past on the levee road, didn't stop." Gaze narrowed, she looked at Gavin. "You here because of Containment?"

Gavin slid a questioning gaze to the loner at the table.

"Don't worry about him," she said. "That's Lon. Shrimper. Lives in his trawler half mile up the water. He doesn't hold with Containment."

"In that case, I'm here because of my brother."

She chewed on that for a good fifteen seconds. "Word is, your *frère*'s wanted for the murder of a Containment agent."

"Incorrect," Gavin said. "He wasn't in New Orleans when it happened."

"Heard that, too."

"That's why we're here. We need to find him. You know where he is?"

She shook her head, twirled her bottle on the table. "I haven't seen him, don't know anyone who has. Could be I could speculate. For the right price."

Gavin's patience was obviously wearing thin. "I already paid you."

"For the time," she said, and took a drink. "Not for the answers."

For a long moment, she and Gavin just looked at each other, poker players gauging each other's hands. "What do you want?"

"Booze. We can't get shit but skunky beer up here." Still, she took another pull on the bottle. "Skunky beer's better than nothing, but it don't help business much."

She didn't seem to get the irony of "better than nothing," given that she was demanding more from us. But there was no point in complaining. Not when we needed information, and not when I could do something about it.

"Done," I said. Getting goods into Containment was my particular skill, after all. And even if I wasn't at the helm of Royal Mercantile, I still had contacts.

Gavin kicked me under the table, but I ignored it.

Cherie narrowed her eyes at me. "You answered fast. Maybe I didn't ask for enough."

"You didn't let me finish." I leaned forward. "Done—if you give us the right information."

She watched me for a moment, calculating. "What kind of booze?"

"Depends on what they're bringing in that week. But if it's on the truck, I can get it."

She wet her lips thirstily. "I might know where you can find a friend of his. Word is, there's a woman living in a cabin near Dulac, only been there a few days. Word is, she doesn't see in this world, but she sees in others."

That was Eleanor, almost certainly. But I kept my expression neutral and didn't let her see the victory in my eyes.

"That's an unusual condition," Gavin said carefully.

"It is," she agreed. "The kind of thing that would interest Containment. Or maybe already has."

"The PCC patrol?" Gavin asked.

"Don't know, but that certainly seems possible." Our time apparently up—or because she didn't like the Containment talk—Cherie rose and pushed back her chair with a squeak of metal. "Word about bounties spreads fast around here. Take a break if you need it, but don't stay too long." She grabbed her bottle by the neck and headed back to the bar.

"Thank you, Cherie."

She held up the bottle as she walked away, her back to us. "Get me some decent brew, we'll call it even."

"We're going to end up owing a lot of people on this trip," Gavin muttered when we'd stepped outside again. "Let's get out of here. Being out in the open is making me twitchy."

"Also," Malachi said, "you may need new friends."

CHAPTER FIVE

We made good time toward Dulac, but even still, it was slow going. The farther south we moved, the thicker the mosquitoes and the deeper the humidity. We found more water, but I was sweating it out as quickly as I was taking it in.

We walked for two hours, until woods gave way to grasslands and fields, land with a road and a few houses on stilts became occasional slips of earth between bayou or marsh. And that water was rising. From the middle of one road, we could see the remains of three aboveground tombs slipping into the advancing water.

"It was a full cemetery," Gavin said. "But land in southern Louisiana is sinking. The Mississippi's controlled to keep it from flooding, but flooding is what deposits the silt that puts land in the bayou. Without the silt, the Gulf gets closer; the water gets higher. The tombs are slipping into the bayou, like most everything else around here."

"And there's no one to pull them out again," I quietly said.

Gavin nodded.

The thought of my loved ones' remains sliding alone into the water was disturbing and incredibly sad—and it made me eager to find high ground.

"What's the plan for tonight?" I asked.

"Depends on Dulac," Gavin said, breaking a granola bar in half and offering a piece to me. I took it. "And whether we find anyone there."

"They won't be in the city proper," Malachi said. "It would be too easy to track them—as we've done. There's a cabin in the area we've used before. But if they aren't there, we may still be looking when night falls." He looked at me. "Either way, we'll find a place to sleep."

"Away from the water," I said as a chunk of mortar from one of the tombs splashed into the bayou. "High and dry."

"No argument," Gavin said.

We crossed the road and moved into a drier area of knee-high grass that had probably grown unfettered since the war began.

"Let's take a break," Gavin said, pointing at a hand-operated water pump in the shade of a weathered barn with old gas and oil signs nailed to its sides.

We stepped into the shade, took off our packs.

"I'm going to check out the barn," Gavin said. "See if there's any sign of them, or anything worth grabbing."

We hadn't passed any evidence of people in a few miles; even the stilt houses had looked empty. So there likely wasn't much to find. On the upside, odds were also low that we'd be taking someone else's property.

Gavin disappeared around the corner . . . and then his body flew backward toward us, bowed in the middle like he'd taken a kick to the gut. He hit the ground with an audible *"Ooof."*

And before we could move toward him, Erida stepped out of the barn's shadow, a satisfied smile on her face.

I moved to Gavin, went to my knees beside him, patted his cheeks. "Hey, you all right?"

"No," he said, eyes still closed, wincing as he rubbed a hand over his abdomen. "She still standing there?"

"Yep."

"She look at all bothered by my jab?"

Erida was tall, with dark curly hair that spilled over an army-green tank top, buff leggings, and knee-high boots. Her skin was tan, her features lush, and her eyes narrowed. This wasn't the first time she and Gavin had come to blows—and it wasn't the first time she'd won.

"No," I said quietly. "But I'm sure she's suffering on the inside."

In truth, she looked perfectly unruffled.

But while Erida didn't look flustered by Gavin, she looked pretty unthrilled to see me. I'd seen that look on her face before, a kind of flat disdain, the first time I'd met her in the New Orleans church we'd used as a meeting site before the battle.

"Ow," Gavin said, pushing himself to his feet. "Was that really necessary?"

"I owed you from the last time," she said, putting a hand on her hip. Her voice was faintly accented, and plenty arrogant. Not surprising for a goddess of war.

Swearing under his breath and gripping his ribs with one hand, Gavin walked back to her. "Let's call a truce for now."

She just lifted her gaze to Malachi, the question in her eyes.

"Peace is faster," he said with a nod. "We're looking for Eleanor and Liam."

"What's happened?"

"It's involved," Gavin said.

Erida's thick, dark brows lifted. Then she shifted her gaze to the woods. "He's at a fishing cabin up the road. Checking traps. He'll be back soon."

Liam was nearby.

We'd met Djosa, Anh, Cinda, the Tengu, then Cherie. We'd moved from Houma to Vacherie, from Bayou Black to Dulac. One person at a time, one place at a time, we'd been getting closer to him. And now we were nearly there.

For weeks, I'd wondered what it would feel like to stand right here, to be on the verge of seeing him again. Every muscle in my body seemed to tense in anticipation, in hope, in fear. So many emotions, all of them pummeling me.

"Eleanor?" Gavin asked. "She all right?"

"She is. She's at the main house." Erida looked surprised by the question, but then her face went all business. "You weren't followed?" she asked her boss.

"No." Malachi's response was flat.

"Very well, then," she said, and turned on her heel. "Follow me."

The field where the barn sat gave way to another border of trees. And that border gave way to the bayou.

Cypress trees, dark water, and Spanish moss covered the land on both sides of the path Erida led us down. The sounds of wind blowing through grass gave way to the croaks of bullfrogs and insects, to the whoops of enormous birds, and when we reached a patch of open water, the swoop of a pelican.

The house sat near the shore, wooden and unpainted, the planks probably made of cypress—wood that would last in the heat and humidity. It was a small, two-story box with a peaked roof and deep front porch, and it stood on ten-foot stilts that kept the water out of the living room.

Eleanor Arsenault sat on one of two white wooden rocking chairs that flanked the front door. She was a lovely woman. Slender, with medium skin, cropped gray hair, and a regal face. She wore a simple dress and white sneakers, and a delicate knitted wrap around her shoulders even in the heat and humidity. There was more color in her cheeks than I remembered; maybe being out here had healed her in some important way.

"I've brought guests," Erida said as we approached the house.

"Well, I believe that's Claire," Eleanor said with a smile, leaning forward, eyes bright. The magical attack had taken her sight but left her with the ability to see magic, the unique shades and tints that colored power from the Beyond.

"And Malachi," she added, her eyes going bright with pleasure. She didn't need to see Gavin to be glad of his arrival. "And my grandson. You've come a long way."

Gavin climbed the steps, took her hand, and pressed a kiss to her cheek. "You look well, Eleanor."

"I feel well, although I'm surprised to see you." She glanced in my direction. "Claire, your color is beautiful. Deep and rich—more than the last time I saw you." Her voice softened. "It's been a while, hasn't it?"

"It has. It's good to see you again, Eleanor. I'm glad you're safe."

"I am." But her smile faded. "I have to wonder what brings you here—and away from New Orleans."

"Let's talk inside," Malachi said to Erida. "Give them a few moments."

When they crossed the creaking porch planks and disappeared into the house, Gavin gave Eleanor the details, told her about the murder, the accusations, the bounty.

Her hand, small and elegant, flew to her chest. "But Liam hasn't even been there. Someone is blaming him for something he didn't do . . . on purpose."

"That would be my guess," Gavin said.

"They're looking for him," she went on, "and if they're looking for him, they're probably looking for me." Eleanor didn't bother with tears; she just narrowed her gaze, screwed her features into what I guessed was DNA-deep Creole stubbornness. "I don't hold with false accusations. I assume you're here to warn us?"

"We are," Gavin said. "Erida said he's checking traps?"

She nodded. "He's at the cabin."

"How far?" Gavin asked.

"Not far at all," Eleanor said, and the words sent another flurry of nerves through my belly.

She looked toward Gavin. "There's firewood in the shed behind the house. Would you be a dear and grab a few cords for later? The smoke helps with the mosquitoes."

His expression said he knew he was being dismissed, but he didn't argue. "Sure thing," he said, flicking a glance my way.

If she was dismissing Gavin, I assumed she had words for me. I wasn't sure how I felt about that.

"Come," Eleanor said, patting the arm of the second rocking chair. "Have a seat."

I did so, the chair creaking beneath me, and let my gaze shift to the bayou in front of us, the sway of moss in the light breeze.

"How are you, Claire?"

"I'm managing. How are you?"

She closed her eyes, lifted her face to the sunlight that filtered through the trees. "I'm good. It's peaceful here. Not easy living, but peaceful."

Silence fell, broken only by the sounds of birds and insects. I looked over the water, watched the sun begin to dip into the bayou, watched the light go golden. An egret flew past, long and white and elegant as a dancer, and unfolded its legs to drop onto a cypress stump.

"He missed you."

The words were a lance, and they found their mark.

"I'm not sure if he's able to tell you that yet, but don't doubt that he missed you. I'm sure you know he had reasons to leave—good ones. But it never feels good to be left behind." Eleanor looked toward me. "Or, I think, to come looking for the one who left you."

"Not easy," I agreed. "Kind of terrifying." I paused, gathering my words like carefully picked flowers. "I've missed him. Worried about him. And sometimes I've been angry at him.

"Malachi and Gavin didn't want me to come," I said after a moment. "I'm still not sure if my coming was a good idea or not, if I'm interrupting him or breaking some unspoken request for space and time. But I needed to come. It's time to face the music, for both of us."

Eleanor smiled as she rocked. "I had a sense you'd be good for him. I'm glad to know I was right."

I appreciated the sentiment, but that she thought I was good for him didn't mean he felt the same way.

"His magic?" I asked, but she shook her head.

"That's for him to tell."

"It has a color?" I wasn't entirely sure what that would tell me—the color of his magic. But it was one characteristic that she would know, and that I thought she might confess.

"It doesn't have *a* color," she said after a moment. "It has *all* the colors."

I didn't know what she meant, so I waited in silence for her to elaborate. And when she didn't, I realized she wasn't going to say anything else. I'd have to wait—just as I'd been waiting—to see what magic had done to him.

"I won't tell you what to do," Eleanor said. "You have your own feelings, your own reasons, and you're entitled to them. I'm sure the last month hasn't been easy for you. It hasn't been easy for him, either. Even though he believes he did the right thing, he also knows it was the wrong thing for both of you.

"What have you been doing for the last few weeks?" she asked, and it took me a moment to catch up with the conversation shift.

"Spending time with Moses. Trying to do what we can for Paranormals. And to change Containment's mind."

She smiled cannily. "Good. It's good to have a companion in Moses. And it's good to give those in power a little pinch every once in a while. It reminds them who they work for."

She reached out, patted my hand. "Thank you for listening to me, Claire. Liam and Gavin are my boys, and I love them more than good sense should allow. And I want them to be happy. I imagine you could use a little of that, too."

"There's happiness out there," I said, thinking of bloated cans and tiny robots. "Sometimes it's easier to find than others."

Gavin rounded the corner, arms full of wedges of wood, sweat on his brow. I hopped up and opened the door so he could carry the load inside, where a stone fireplace with a deep hearth dominated a small sitting room. A single hallway led to the rest of the house, probably to the kitchen, bedroom, and bathroom.

"Damn," Gavin said, when he'd added the wood to the pile on the hearth and wiped his hands on his pants. "Hard to believe a fire's necessary when it's this hot out."

"Anything that keeps the bugs away," I said.

"I guess."

Erida and Malachi came in with Eleanor. "Time to get Liam?" Malachi asked.

"Yeah," Gavin said, using the hem of his shirt to wipe his forehead. "Let me get a drink."

"Cold water in the fridge," Erida said. He nodded and headed in that direction.

"What will we find?" Gavin asked over his shoulder.

"He's angry," Eleanor said. "Getting used to his new reality."

"Picked a helluva way to do it," Gavin muttered. He came back with a Mason jar of water and continued, "Middle of the bayou, PCC roaming around. But that's my *frère*. God forbid he should do anything the easy way." He drank the entire container of water, then looked at Erida. "Cabin's down the road, you said?"

She nodded. "Walk until the road ends, then take the trail to the right. Maybe half a mile down from there."

Gavin nodded. "Claire and I will go." He looked at me. "Unless you prefer to stay here."

He was giving me an out, and I knew it. Giving me an opportunity to pretend I was just along for the ride—or giving himself an opportunity to prepare Liam for the fact that I was here.

For a moment, I considered it. I considered playing the coward, sitting in the rocking chair and letting the world spin around me, letting fate fall where it would. But I didn't like the idea of being cowardly. Not when I'd come this far.

And selfish or not, I didn't want to give Liam the chance to adjust, to prepare, to school his face if regret was going to show there. I wanted to know his heart. So I'd see him, and he could see me. And we'd both see.

"I'm going," I said. I saw the approval in his eyes.

We walked outside, and Eleanor gave me a fierce nod.

"I'd say we're all on your side," Gavin murmured with a laugh as we walked back to the road.

While I appreciated the sentiment, I needed only one person on my side right now. And the time had come to face that particular fire.

"Not a road," Gavin said as he and I squelched toward the trail. "Just muck between trees."

Since my shoes were covered in it, I couldn't argue.

We picked our way through and across the muck, then down the narrow trail that led to even lower ground. By that point we were sloshing between cypress knees.

The bayou was beautiful—the water, the trees, the haunting stillness. There was something undeniably wild and vital here. But that also made it seem undeniably ominous. I was convinced that every tendril of Spanish moss brushing my shoulder was a cottonmouth with an attitude. Two snapping turtles eyed us warily from a log that poked up through the murky water, and I heard splashing in the distance that I was pretty certain was an alligator on the hunt.

"If a gator is man-eating," I wondered, pushing away a tangle of moss, "does it eat woman as well?" I was making jokes because I was nervous, because my body was jittering like a live wire. And not just because of the wild things in the woods.

"A timely question," Gavin said. "If one charges at me, I'll push you in front."

"That's very thoughtful."

We reached the end of the trail, where dirt gave way to clumps of grass and scrubby palms that nearly hid the cabin a few yards away. It was a smaller version of the main house, with unpainted planks, a roof of tin, and a small porch in front.

"I'll see if he's inside," Gavin said.

"I'll wait," I said. But only because the cabin was tiny and looked empty to boot. Not because my heart was beating so hard I could hear it in my ears.

I could see a strip of glassy water through the trees, so I headed toward it, passed a pile of ancient and rotting buoys and traps, reached a short, weathered dock.

And there he was.

Liam Quinn stood at the end of the dock in jeans and dark green rubber boots, his short-sleeved shirt soaked through with sweat.

He looked completely different, and exactly the same. The same leanly muscled body, the same black hair, the same strong, square chin, and the wide mouth that tended to curl up at one corner when he was pleased. Broad shoulders, long legs, strong hands. But his cheekbones, already honed, seemed sharper, and every muscle was more distinct, as if the generous sculptor who'd created him had come back to refine his work.

Muscles bunched, moved as he added bait to a mesh crawfish trap, then dropped it into the water. He pulled up a second trap from the bayou, emptied the wriggling contents into a bucket on his left, baited it with leftovers from a bucket on his right, and dropped it back into the water. Another trap, and then another, and another. They'd feast on crawfish tonight.

Liam looked natural here, completely at home surrounded by woods and water. I wondered if he'd learned this skill—smoothed the rough edges of the movements—at his family's cabin near Bayou Teche. There was something so practiced in the movement, so hypnotic in the dance of it, that I forgot myself. I just watched him, *admired* him, while pent-up emotions rushed back to the surface.

A crack as loud as a gunshot split the air—and jolted me out of my reverie.

His head shot up, like a wolf scenting danger, eyes widening as he stared at the tree limb—more than a foot in diameter and nearly ten feet long—falling toward him from a tree that stretched above the bayou.

Instinct had him throwing up his arms, but that wouldn't save him. And I wouldn't let him be hurt on my watch.

Moving just as quickly, I grabbed a fistful of magic, wrapped the invisible filaments around the branch, and brought it to a jerking stop eighteen inches above his head.

Still staring, he dropped his arms, and his gaze. And for the first time in weeks, we looked at each other.

The world went quiet, its revolution slowing, as his eyes locked onto mine like a weapon on a target. The vivid blue was still ribboned through his eyes, but they were shot through now with streaks of gold, a residual effect of the magic that had struck him.

Liam Quinn had always been beautiful. Now there was something devastating about him.

I half concentrated on the magic, spent the rest of it to search his face, his feelings. I saw utter surprise, as if I was the last person he'd expected to find standing on the dock behind him.

Something else lurked there, too. Something darker that I didn't understand.

"Claire."

The word was full of emotion, but he didn't take even a single step toward me. Instead, his body was rigid, like he was holding himself back.

I didn't trust myself to pick apart why that might have been. And I didn't say anything, afraid that voicing his name would give away too much about my own feelings and the fact that seeing him here, today, only solidified them.

Foliage crackled, and Gavin stepped onto the dock. He glanced at me, at Liam, and at the branch hovering above Liam's head.

"You threatening to kill him, or stopping that thing from doing it?"

"Stopping it," Liam quietly said.

Gavin nodded. "Then there's no point in overdoing it." He touched the hand I still held outstretched, the hand that still gripped the tangled reins of magic.

I flicked my fingers and sent the branch soaring into the water, where it landed with a splash, bobbed once, then twice, and moved on downstream.

Liam looked as surprised by the quick release as he had by my being there in the first place. Good. I liked the idea that I'd awed him.

"I guess we found you," Gavin said.

That statement broke the spell, had Liam pulling back into himself. The surprise on his face disappeared, and his other expressions shuttered.

"I guess you did." His tone was as flat as his gaze. "Why are you here?"

"Because you've become suddenly popular," Gavin said, glancing around. "Let's get out of the heat, sit down. We need to talk."

We waited while Liam finished rebaiting the traps and grabbed the bucket of crawfish. Then we walked back to the cabin.

I wouldn't have thought my heart could beat faster than it had when I'd looked into his eyes for the first time. But now it raced with a different kind of nerves and challenged the hollowness that made my chest ache.

We'd seen each other, and there'd been no hug, no embrace, not even a look of excitement or gratitude or relief. There'd been nothing. That flatness sent a chill down my spine and a frisson of worry through my belly. Had his feelings changed? Had that been the obvious and simple reason I hadn't heard from him?

Maybe this had been a mistake.

"Go on in," Liam said, flicking a glance my way as he dealt with the crawfish at a small table on the porch.

"You all right?" Gavin whispered as we walked through the screen door. The question added embarrassment to my churning emotions.

"I'm not sure."

Like the main house, the fishing cabin had walls and a floor made from planks of wood, with what looked like old newspapers stuffed into the gaps. There was a wooden bench topped by a pelt of dark, shiny fur and a kitchenette with a gas camping stove and a sink. A small wooden table sat in the opposite corner, its top a slice of cypress with wavy edges. Two wooden chairs were tucked beneath. Through the open doorway, we could see the foot of a small brass bed covered by a handmade quilt.

"This is like Grandfather's place," Gavin said when Liam came in behind us.

"Yeah." Liam gestured to the chairs. When we took seats, he walked to the sink, turned on a water spigot that probably was hooked up to a rainwater cistern. He washed his hands and dried them on a tea towel. Then he opened a plastic cooler on the small counter, pulled out three bottles of water, passed two of them to us.

He didn't make eye contact when he handed me the bottle, was careful to avoid touching me. Gavin must have noticed it, too, because his brows lifted in surprise.

Liam walked to the fur-covered bench and sat down. His body seemed bigger in this small room, as if his strength strained against the walls.

"What's the problem?" he asked. He glanced at me, seemed to satisfy himself that I was in one piece, then looked at Gavin. "Eleanor?"

"She's fine. With Erida at the main house. It's about Broussard."

Liam's brows lifted. He hadn't been expecting to hear that. "What about him?"

"We've come too far to beat around the bush," Gavin said, "so I'll get to the point. He's dead, and you're the prime suspect."

For a moment, Liam just stared at him. "What?"

"Broussard was murdered, killed in his house. They think you did it, because 'For Gracie' was scrawled on the wall above the body."

There was no hiding the emotion in Liam's gaze now, no suppressing the rage that boiled there. "Someone is using our sister's death to frame me for murdering a Containment agent." His voice was low, dangerous. A panther, angry and pacing.

"That's part one," Gavin said. "Your knife was used to slit his throat."

Brow furrowed, Liam felt for the small utility knife holstered on his belt. "What knife?"

"Well, not that one, obviously. The blade mounted to the antler handle. The one I gave you—what was it, two years ago? Three? The one I found in Mobile."

The confusion in Liam's eyes faded to what I thought was speculation. "I haven't seen that knife in months. I don't even own it anymore."

"You gave away my knife?"

"You gave the knife to me. It was mine to keep or give away."

Gavin rolled his eyes, made a frustrated sound. "Who'd you give it to?"

"Not to anyone who'd kill Broussard."

"All evidence to the contrary," Gavin sniped. "I want a name."

"I'm not giving you one."

"Stubborn bastard," Gavin murmured. "Who has the knife?"

Liam shook his head, which sent Gavin on a tear of Cajun French.

"This isn't helping," I said sharply, cutting through the cursing.

They both looked at me, then dragged hands across their jaws. I wondered if the move had been buried in their DNA.

"I don't know who has it," Liam said. "That's the truth. I could find out. But that needs to be . . . careful."

There was humming silence for a moment. "All right," Gavin said. "Sleep on it. Then you owe me names. There's a bounty on your head, and I'm not giving you up that easy."

Liam finished off his water, began to strip the label from the bottle. He did that when he was agitated. "Is someone eager to get me back to New Orleans, or just to pass the blame?"

"Hard to say." Gavin finished his water as well and recapped the bottle. "Could be either. Both."

"If Containment wants to close the book on the murder," Liam continued, "they say Broussard's dead, Liam Quinn did it, so no need to look further?"

"That's my guess, and Gunnar's. There are people in Containment who believe it. You've got a few enemies. Maybe not as many as Broussard, but enough to make trouble."

Liam pushed the wadded label into his pocket and began to flip the bottle idly in his hand. After a moment, he looked up. "Who'd Broussard piss off?"

"We don't know," Gavin said. "We don't know of any specific enemies, or at least not any new ones. Plenty of people didn't like him. We don't know anyone who hated him enough to kill him."

"Who'd I piss off?" Liam wondered. "I mean, why me particularly?"

"Maybe someone," Gavin said. "Maybe no one. Could be as simple as opportunity: someone knows you had a beef with Broussard, thinks you're a convenient target."

"Only if they don't think too closely about the fact that I didn't have the opportunity to kill him."

"Your innocence doesn't seem to matter," Gavin said.

"Have you talked to Gunnar?" Liam looked at me. It was the first question he'd asked me directly.

"Not since the battle."

"He hasn't come by Royal Mercantile?"

"Couldn't say. Tadji's running the store now. I haven't been there since the battle."

Whatever he was feeling, his face gave nothing away. "I see."

"Containment's offered passes for some of the Paras," Gavin said. "But they haven't changed their position regarding Sensitives. Claire used magic during the battle. Ergo . . ."

"Ergo," Liam quietly agreed. He shifted his gaze away, his expression still unreadable. And again, I wavered between feeling hurt, worrying about him, and being flat-out confused.

"Speaking of, you need to be careful out here. We talked to Cherie; she said a PCC patrol had been by the marina. And we met two hunters on the way in. They wanted to execute the bounty on you, take Claire in for the field goal."

Liam looked at me. "You're all right?"

"I'm fine. It was a minor incident, all things considered."

Emotion flared gold in his eyes. "An attack on you isn't minor. I don't want you getting hurt on my account." He said nothing else. He didn't reach out, didn't try to comfort or soothe. But if his feelings for me had disappeared, or faded away, why the emotion?

When Gavin cleared his throat, Liam shifted his gaze toward him. "I assume you didn't let them follow you here?"

Gavin gave him a look of brotherly irritation. "It's not my first day on the job. We left them at Montagne Désespérée."

For the first time, a corner of Liam's mouth lifted. Even after many nights and miles apart, and regardless of his feelings, that wicked smile had a powerful effect. "Not a bad idea."

Gavin grunted. "Easy for you to say." He looked at me, pointed at Liam. "He's the bastard who left me there."

I risked a glance at Liam. "And why did you do that?"

"He needed a time-out." He watched me for a moment, and I met his gaze beat for heavy beat. "Your magic is better."

"I've been practicing. How is yours?"

To his credit, he didn't look away. "Fine."

"The magic was enough to make you leave," I said, "but not enough for you to talk about?"

"It's not that simple." Liam rose, obviously restless, and put the bottle in a bucket. Then he came back and looked down at us, his gaze settling on me again. "You're here to warn me?"

If the question was a test, I didn't know the right answer. It was Gavin who spoke.

"Yes," he said. "They've also mentioned looking for Eleanor. If they're willing to plant evidence and send out hunters, they're willing to do worse. We want to be sure you're both safe."

Liam acknowledged that with a nod. "Then thank you for warning me."

Gavin nodded, and Liam headed for the door. "It's getting dark. Let's get back to the house."

CHAPTER SIX

By the time we made it, darkness had fallen.

"You'll stay here tonight," Eleanor said. "We'll have a fire."

Since I was bone-deep tired—physically and emotionally—that sounded good to me.

The Quinn boys prepared the bonfire, logs and branches in a brick fire pit, and arranged camp chairs around it.

Eleanor and I took neighboring chairs, watching forks of flame lift and crackle. Beyond the fire's reach, the world was dark, but the bayou was loud with frogs, insects, and the calls of animals.

Liam came out and took a seat on Eleanor's other side, the chair angled just enough for his gaze to fall on me.

And fall it did. Intense and searching. But he still hadn't given voice to anything he was feeling, whatever that might have been.

"Dinner," Malachi said, and I shifted my gaze from the fire to the enamel mug he offered. The metal was hot, and the steam that wafted up smelled of meat and onion and the bright green flavor I recognized as filé.

He sat down beside me, his broad shoulders and muscular body almost comically large in the slender chair.

"Nothing for you?" I asked. He'd brought only the one cup.

He shook his head and crossed his arms, watching Liam warily beneath half-closed lids. I'd assumed Malachi and Liam had discussed Liam's magic, but maybe I'd been wrong. Maybe Gavin and I weren't the only ones who hadn't seen it, who didn't know what kind of power he was carrying. Or how it had affected him.

"I'm fine," he said.

"Spoon," Gavin said behind him, pulling two from his pocket, offering one to me. "I'm not entirely sure what variety of gumbo this is."

"Probably crawfish," I said. "Or didn't you recognize the traps?"

"I don't trap," Gavin said, fanning a mouthful of still-steaming gumbo. "Hot," he confirmed, and swallowed with a wince.

I pulled out a spoonful, but let it cool before I took a stingy bite. It was thick enough to stand the spoon straight up, dark as coffee, and absolutely delicious.

"Not a bad way to spend an evening," Gavin said, casting a glance at Liam. He leaned forward as if studying the fire, hands clasped in front of him.

"The fire is good," I said. "The bayou is . . . intimidating."

Gavin smiled. "Didn't spend much time out of the city, did you?"

"I camped at City Park once for a field trip. But otherwise, no." Even the gas station, which was supposed to be an emergency bunker, was loaded with tech, including the air conditioner, dehumidifier, and solar generator that had kept my father's collection safe.

A steady beat began to fill the air, and it took me a moment to realize what I was hearing.

"Is that—is that the Go-Go's?" Eighties pop didn't find its way into the Zone very often.

"It is," Erida said, pulling a chair to the fire. Like Malachi, she didn't carry a bowl. But she did have a beer, which raised my opinion of her. Or at least made her seem a little more human. "Our esteemed general has a great love of eighties music."

I looked at Malachi, tried to imagine him—tall and broad-shouldered, a young god's cap of wavy curls—dancing to Bananarama or Michael Jackson, or wailing away on an air guitar to Journey. The image didn't work.

"Please provide details," I said.

Malachi smiled. "It's . . . hopeful." He lifted a shoulder and seemed faintly embarrassed by the entire discussion. "And very different from the music of the Beyond."

He'd said the Beyond was orderly and regimented. "So what did you have?" I smiled at him. "Baroque classical music? Maybe lyres? Golden harps?"

"Consularis Paranormals do not care for instruments," Erida said.

"Don't do instruments?" Gavin asked, pulling a shrimp from its tail with his teeth and tossing the tail into the darkness over his shoulder.

"Instruments are unnecessary when the voice is prepared," Malachi said, his gaze on Erida. "That's the tradition in our society."

"So, like a cappella?" I asked.

"Yes," Erida said. "Although with complexities not recognized in the human form."

"Dozens of voices in careful and precise layers," Malachi said. "Well-ordered, as are most things in the Beyond. Intricately constructed, each song prepared and performed for a very particular circumstance."

No wonder he liked eighties music. It wasn't "intricately constructed," and it was certainly more emotional and spontaneous than the music he was describing.

"Give us a taste," Gavin said.

"Please," Eleanor added. "I'd really enjoy it."

Malachi looked at Erida, who nodded.

I couldn't have said when the song began, only that it slowly surrounded us. No words, just the gentle rise and fall of their voices, which danced together, then swirled apart into higher and lower notes, then dipped back together again. The melody was complex, even with only two voices performing the parts, and it lifted goose bumps along my arms.

By the time they stopped, my head was swimming. Residual magic, I guessed.

"Damn," Gavin said, running a hand over his head. "Powerful stuff."

"What was it about?" I asked.

"It's a tale of battle and bravery," Erida said. "And the honor of loss."

"There's nothing honorable in loss," Liam said.

"In your world, that may be true," Erida said. "Our world was different."

Their world sounded cold and constrained. That didn't justify the Court's attempt to bring their revolution to our door, but I could understand how they'd have felt straitjacketed.

"We've now told you about one of our rituals," Malachi said, glancing at me. "Tell us one of yours."

"One of ours? You've lived among humans for years."

"I've lived *near* humans for years," he said, "but outside their communities, and in a place mostly denuded by war."

I hadn't thought of it that way, of how much he'd have missed by living in the Zone instead of outside it. Not to mention the fact that nearly all humans would have considered him an enemy if they'd known what he truly was.

"Okay," I said, and let my mind wander to the place where I kept my memories of life before the war. "Kids had slumber parties, where you'd go sleep at someone else's house for fun."

Malachi blinked. "Why would it be fun to sleep in someone else's home?"

"Because there would be food," Gavin said. He'd finished his gumbo and stretched out, ankles crossed, and hands linked across his flat abdomen. "And music. Booze, if you were old enough." He grinned. "Girls, if the parents were out of town."

"So it was a mating ritual?" Malachi asked.

"No," Gavin said with a laugh. "The kids at slumber parties weren't usually old enough for that. And if they were, there wasn't much slumbering."

"We had football games," I said. "A game involving a ball and a march down a field. You'd have liked it," I said to Malachi. "It's regimented and orderly, like two armies facing each other across a battle line. That's how a lot of people in Louisiana spent their weekends."

"Marching down a field or facing off across a battle line?"

I knew he was teasing me. "Watching football on television. And drinking beer."

"That doesn't sound very rigorous," Erida said. I didn't think she was teasing.

"Don't tell the members of my fantasy league that," Gavin said. At Erida's raised brow, he shook his head. "Never mind."

"So humans," Malachi began, "for entertainment, slept in a stranger's house and watched strangers engage in battle?"

"It's a little more complex than that," Gavin said, and lifted his gaze to his silent brother. "And what about you, Liam? What rituals do you remember that you'd like to enlighten our friends about?"

"Do plumbing and electricity count?"

"They do," Eleanor said with a smile. "Very much so. I love a good ceiling fan in the summertime."

I glanced at Liam, expecting to see at least a half-smile on his face, but his body had gone rigid. I looked up, watched silent warning flash across Erida's and Malachi's faces, and followed the direction of their gazes.

Deep in the trees, where cypress knees emerged from shadowed water, hovered a pale green light. It was the color of spring leaves, and it floated like a cloud a few feet above the ground. But there was no bulb or fork of flame. Just a fog that grew nearer, transforming dark and silhouetted branches into threatening claws.

"Feu follet," Gavin whispered. "Will-o'-the-wisp."

The hair lifted on the back of my neck. But Liam and Malachi rose. Erida and Gavin moved closer to Eleanor.

Instinct told me to snatch a torch from the fire, run back to the house, and lock myself inside. But I wasn't going to run—and certainly not in front of this crowd—so I slowly stood, locked my knees tight, and moved behind Liam and Malachi.

Without taking his gaze off the light, Gavin reached out, took Eleanor's hand, whispered something to her. She nodded, glanced casually in the direction of the light . . . and smiled.

"Friends," she said quietly, taking another sip from her teacup, as smoothly as a woman at high tea. I trusted her instinct and relaxed a little, but kept my gaze on the light.

It drew closer, the single cloud separating into a dozen smaller pinpoints.

Malachi chuckled. "Not will-o'-the-wisps," he said.

"No," Erida agreed. "Just run-of-the-mill Peskies."

Peskies were tiny Paras with dragonfly wings, curvy bodies, and not a scrap of clothing. They were about twice the size of hummingbirds and four times as nasty.

They didn't like being called "run-of-the-mill." They let out shrieks sharp as an ice pick and began to dive-bomb us. One buzzed around my face, her wings moving so quickly they were a haze behind her. Then she gave me an ugly stare and flipped me off.

The gesture *definitely* translated.

"Right back at you, honey," I said, and got a double eagle in response.

"Don't antagonize the Peskies," Liam said, his gaze still on the trees.

"She flipped me off first," I grumbled, and swatted her away when she tried to blitz me again. That triggered a stream of foreign cursing. But I didn't need to understand the words to get the gist.

They stepped out of the woods in sequence, led by a tall man with a barrel chest and thin legs in jeans, a T-shirt, and rubber boots. He carried a bucket in one hand, a shotgun in the other. Although a gun in the hand of a stranger should have made me wary, the three kids—all with their father's skinny legs—appeared behind him, all smiles.

All four of them had tan skin, high cheekbones, and dark hair that came to sharp widow's peaks.

"Good evening," said the man in front. "Looks like a good fire."

"Roy," Liam said, walking to him and offering a hand, which Roy pumped heartily. *"Comment ça va?"*

"Comme ci, comme ça." He shrugged. *"C'est la vie."*

"Looks like you've got a Peskie infestation," Liam said.

Roy grinned. "Found 'em in one of my muskrat traps. Released 'em, for all the good it did. They been following me 'round since."

"They like you," Malachi said. "They're grateful for the rescue. And they're enjoying the crawfish."

"Who doesn't?" Roy said. "You speak their language?"

"Enough of it."

"Roy Gravois," Liam said, "Malachi, a general in the Consularis army. My brother, Gavin Quinn. Claire Connolly. And you know Erida and Eleanor."

Roy nodded at us in turn, his gaze stopping when he got to me. "Nice to put a face to a name."

I nodded, and couldn't help but wonder which of them had mentioned me. "Nice to meet you."

"Roy lives up bayou," Liam said. "Takes the crawfish before they get down to me."

"Problem is, you don't bait your traps worth a damn." Roy looked back, held out a hand to those who'd come with him. "My family: Adelaide, Claude, and Iris." He pointed to each of the kids in turn.

"All members of the United Houma Nation," Liam said.

"Born and bred," Roy agreed with a nod.

"Roy," Eleanor said, "would you like some gumbo? We made too much."

Roy smiled at Eleanor. "I'm good. Just came by to return these tools." He offered Liam the bucket. "Appreciate the loan."

Liam took them. "You fix the generator?"

"Did. I tell you what I was doin' with it?"

Liam shook his head.

"Took the windshield wiper motor outta the old Plymouth on the Fortner place. Hooked it up to a pole, then plugged it into the generator, made my own little spit. Roasted the rest of the wild boar last night."

"Cajun ingenuity," Liam said with a grin. "The boar good?"

"Mais ya," Roy said, kissing the tips of his fingers.

The conversation carried on like that for a few more minutes—food, trapping, life in the bayou.

Like on the dock, he seemed comfortable here. Maybe that was something positive that had come out of whatever had happened to him during the battle; he'd been able to come home, at least in some way.

I wondered if it also meant he should stay here. Live here. Which made my heart ache painfully.

"Listen," Liam said, "while you're here, you should know—there's possibly trouble on the horizon."

"What kinda trouble?"

When Liam glanced at the kids warily, Roy nodded.

"It's all right if they hear. If there's trouble, I want them prepared. They can handle it."

Liam nodded. "Containment agent in New Orleans was killed a couple days ago. I'm the prime suspect."

Roy's brows lifted. "Interesting you killed a man in the city while you were out on the water with me."

"Isn't it, though?"

"They issue a bounty?"

"They did."

The initial curiosity in Roy's face faded, and his gaze narrowed. "They wrong accidentally, or on purpose?"

"We have the same question. Given I wasn't even in the parish at the time, we think it's on purpose. But we aren't sure why he was killed, and we aren't sure why they settled on me, other than because Broussard and I didn't much get along."

Roy made a snorting sound. "If we killed everyone we didn't get along with, the world would be a much smaller place."

Liam smiled.

"Have you seen anyone looking around?" Gavin asked, rising from his spot at Eleanor's side and stepping forward.

"Haven't seen an agent or hunter this far south in years. Present company excluded." Roy grinned. "They know better than to come into the southern reach without a guide. End up lost and stranded on a good day, gator meat on a bad."

"Be on the lookout," Liam advised.

"For storms, for gators, for hunters, and for agents," Roy said. "We'll stay careful." He looked down at Claude. "Right?"

When Claude nodded, Roy ruffled his hair, pulled him close. "Should get home, get the little ones to bed and check on Cosette and the baby." He looked back at Liam. "What you gonna do about those charges?"

"Not sure yet."

Roy nodded thoughtfully. "You need a character witness, you call me. You need someone to talk about your expertise on the water, you'll have to call somebody else."

With another jaunty wink, Roy and his family disappeared into the trees again, Peskies lighting their way.

We took turns adding branches to the fire, stoking it to keep the flames dancing in the humidity and occasionally slapping at the mosquitoes that hadn't been deterred by the rising smoke.

I grew more comfortable as the night went on. Not that I was getting used to the bayou, but I was getting used to the sounds—the frogs, rustles, splashes that signaled things moving in the dark. And I was getting used to Liam sitting near me, to the gravity of his body only a few feet from mine.

Somewhere around midnight, Gavin stretched, yawned. "We should call it a night. We've got an early day tomorrow."

"I'll sleep at the cabin," Liam said, rising

Gavin nodded. "I'll join you."

"Claire can sleep in the house with us," Eleanor said.

I looked at Malachi. "And where will you go?"

"I prefer to be outside."

Yes, we'd spent more time together in the last few weeks, and I'd gotten to know more of his thoughts and moods. But he was still a mystery to me in so many ways. "Where will you sleep outside?"

"Wherever seems best," Malachi said. "I'll see you all in the morning." And he walked into the darkness, disappearing beyond the edge of firelight.

"Let's get you settled," Erida said, rising. I did the same, and followed her into the house without another backward glance. Liam hadn't made a move to talk to me, at least not yet. And while I was pretty sure we'd need to have some kind of talk, I wasn't emotionally or physically equipped to do it tonight.

The steps creaked beneath us, and the porch and floorboards did the same. Erida pulled a rolled-up green sleeping bag from a high shelf, then pointed to a small, empty room off the kitchen. "You can sleep in there. There's a cot in the back room. It's folded up, but you can get it, bring it in if you don't want to sleep on the floor."

She said it like a dare, as if she expected me to refuse and demand a feather bed and silk sheets.

"Either way is fine," I said.

"You may not think that after you see the cot. But the spiders are probably gone."

I tried not to think about the possibility of dozens of legs crawling on me in my sleep. "The floor is fine. I've slept on worse." I held out a hand, and she offered me the sleeping bag.

"I knew your father."

That jerked me out of my arachnoid nightmare. I looked over at her. "What?"

"There were many of us in New Orleans. Hidden there, at least until we fled. We were, at first, convinced humans would come to understand the difference between Court and Consularis, and release from prison those who hadn't chosen to fight. They did not."

The words were spoken like a judgment, a declaration of guilt. There'd be no acquittal for humans from Erida.

"How did you know him?" I asked.

"He helped us. When he became aware of his power, like other humans in his position—he became more sympathetic. He was a good man. He—"

She stopped herself, went silent and still for a solid fifteen seconds. So still she might have been a statue of some ancient human goddess. And since she seemed to be grappling for words, I waited her out.

"He was kind," she said at last. "He was good and he was kind. He helped those of us stuck in New Orleans when he could, gave us supplies. He gave us trust and friendship."

But when she said "friendship," there was something beyond friendship in her eyes. Longing, if I had to put money on it.

I'd seen my father with women, a date or two here and there with the divorced mother of a middle school friend, the woman who baked croissants at the European bakery on Magazine. But I hadn't seen him with Erida. Hadn't seen Erida before the moment she'd walked into Delta's church.

"Friendship," I quietly said.

She looked at me, met my gaze, and didn't say a word. Much like Malachi, she held her cards close to the chest.

"Did you see his magic?" I asked.

She gave me a questioning look.

"I didn't know he was a Sensitive," I said. "I didn't know anything about his magic, about what he'd done to help until . . ." Until Broussard had spilled the beans. And now Broussard and my father were both dead. "He loved me, but he didn't tell me as much as he should have."

"He was a bringer of light," she said quietly.

I nodded. "That's what I heard."

"He didn't know about you, either?"

I shook my head.

"I see," she said, but her voice said she didn't really see but maybe was trying to reconcile the man she'd known with the one I'd just described.

She wasn't the only one.

"I also knew your mother." Her gaze stayed on mine, but her expression had gone very cool.

I tried to maintain control of my own expression, to keep the fear that flooded my veins from overwhelming me, from showing on my face.

My father had told me my mother had died when I was a child, many years before the war, before Paranormals had even entered our world. I didn't remember her; it should have been impossible for Erida to know her.

But the war had expanded what was possible. Stretched and contorted it. I'd seen a woman with red hair, a woman who looked like me, trying to force open the Veil at Talisheek. The same woman whose photograph had rested in a trunk in the gas station's basement.

I had good friends, but I didn't have a family, and I longed for that connection, for something that had been gone a long time from my life. But I was afraid of what I might learn. Because if there was some connection between me and that woman, it meant my father had lied to me my entire life.

And it meant the woman who'd tried to open the Veil, who'd nearly destroyed us, was my mother. So the questions I might have asked—*Is she alive? Is she our enemy?*—stayed strangled and unspoken.

I wasn't ready to accept either possibility, so I shook my head. "My mother died a long time ago."

Erida watched me carefully for a moment. "I see," she finally said. "Then perhaps I was mistaken."

The ice turned to heat that burned in my chest, tightened my throat. I nodded at her. "Sure."

"Well," she said after a long silence, "you'll have an early morning. You should get some sleep."

And then she was gone, leaving me with more questions than answers.

CHAPTER SEVEN

Chicory coffee was scenting the small house when I woke. Gavin offered me a spatterware cup that matched the one in his hand, while I blinked myself awake in the sleeping bag.

I sat up groggily and took the mug, the enamel still hot. The first sip was so sweet it made my teeth ache.

"Eleanor apparently didn't get quite enough sugar in Devil's Isle," Gavin said with a grin. The shoulders of his T-shirt were dark with moisture from his still-damp hair.

"And apparently she's making up for lost time." I gestured to his shirt. "You take a swim this morning?"

"Me and the gators," he said with a wink. "Water's great if you want a turn."

It took less than a second of consideration to decline the offer. "There isn't enough money in the world to get me to take a bath with a gator."

He grinned. "You step into the bayou, you might find just that, cher. Get that coffee in you and get dressed. There's omelet in the kitchen, with crawfish pulled out of the traps this morning. We're leaving in twenty."

I didn't have an appetite, but I gave myself time for a few heartening sips of coffee. Then I poured water into a basin in the small bathroom and cleaned up as well as I could. I'd slept in my clothes in case we needed to make a quick getaway, so I changed what I needed to, brushed my teeth, and twined my hair into a braid that would keep it out of my face for the journey home. Then I shoved everything else back into my bag and zipped it up.

I went outside, dropped the bag on the porch, and headed for the dock again. This time, it was empty, so I walked a few feet out over the water.

A low fog covered the bayou, thick as a cloud. It was speared by sunlight, which reflected off the fog and cast an eerie light across everything. Everything was still, like I'd walked into a photograph of a bayou frozen in time.

An arrow of white split the stillness—an egret flying from one bank to the other. It disappeared among the trees, and bullfrogs began to croak in the vacuum of sound.

It was beautiful here. Desolate and empty in some ways, teeming with life in others. This was a world that had existed before humans and had managed to survive them.

Today, we would walk away from the bayou, and from the people who lived there. I wasn't ready to face the loss that would mean again—either walking away from Liam or watching him let me walk away. But I had to prepare myself, emotionally and physically. And I had to be ready for the journey and whatever we might face. With hunters on the prowl, there was a good chance I'd need magic before we got back to New Orleans. I had to be ready for that, too.

Sensitives absorbed magic daily, which would rot us from the inside out. Once a Sensitive became a wraith, there was no way back. Simply using magic didn't help, as Sensitives' bodies just tried to absorb more, to fill the vacuum that using the magic created. The only way to get rid of it was to consciously let it go, send it back into the universe.

It had been a few days since I'd done that, and that was dangerous. It felt like a living thing within me, something that wriggled and burned and ached to turn me inside out. Something that wanted more.

So I had to take steps.

As I walked back to the bank, I saw a short stool on the porch. Like the table in the cabin, the top had been cut from a slice of cypress. I grabbed it, found a quiet spot with a view of water and cypress, and took a seat.

I hadn't brought the box I usually used to store the excess magic. I hadn't wanted the weight of it in my backpack, and I hadn't wanted it to accidentally open along the way and spill the magic back into the world, where it would keep creating the same problem. I needed an alternate holder. I found one in the cleanly cut cypress stump a few feet away. Probably the same tree sacrificed for the table and stool.

"Apologies in advance," I said, then closed my eyes, let my mind drop down to the spot where I imagined the magic sank and gathered and filled. Its shimmering filaments hummed with power, as if anticipating more. The magic always wanted more. That I knew that now—that we were so connected I could sense its desires—was disconcerting. But it's where I was. Removing it was the only control I had, so that was what I would do.

I gathered up as many of the threads as I could metaphorically hold and pulled them up and away from their hidden center. I struggled against them for a moment, against their tentacular grip on my body, but demanded that they move, and they did. Movement, after all, was my particular gift. And curse.

I directed them away from my body, let them pour into the wood until I felt lighter, until the pulse of power was softer, a hum instead of a drumbeat.

Then I blew out a breath and opened one eye to take a squinting look at the stump.

I hadn't blown it up. I hadn't set it on fire, and it wasn't glowing with otherworldly radiation. It just sat there, as stumps tended to do, and went about its stump business.

"Success," I muttered, giving myself a mental high five. Then I stood up, stretched muscles that felt loose and relaxed, and glanced at the slow-moving water.

Like a lithe and nimble god, Liam rose from the bayou, body wet and slick and naked down to his now-damp cargo pants. Water dripped from his torso, sleeking down the curves of his hips.

It took a moment for me to grasp that he was real, and not some mirage conjured by my traitorous imagination. Eyes closed, he ran his hands through his hair, tightening every lean cord of muscle.

And then his eyes opened, and his gaze met mine . . . and we stared at each other until the air seemed to sizzle with electricity, with heat.

This time, he didn't seem surprised to see me.

"Sorry," I said, turning on my heel before the image of his body seared further into my brain. "I was just taking a look before we left. At the bayou," I added quickly.

"It's fine," Liam said, but the tightness in his voice said exactly the opposite. He pulled down a towel hanging from a nearby branch, slung it around his neck. "I'm glad you're here."

I turned around slowly, looking for a sign of what he might be feeling. Was he glad I was here because he'd wanted to see me? Or because he appreciated the warning?

But once again, his face gave nothing away. And that left me asking, once again, what he was trying to hide. Or hide from.

"Are you all right?" I asked him.

"I'm fine."

But there was a tightness in his voice, something behind the words, something he clearly wasn't ready to talk about. A conflict I didn't understand.

"Really?" I asked. "You don't seem okay."

Gold flashed in his eyes. "What do I seem, Claire?"

"I don't know. You tell me. Or show me," I murmured, and took a step closer. For the first time I was near enough to feel the magic that spun around him.

Instinctively, I lifted a hand to touch the threads of it, to let them brush through my fingers—and Liam took a step back, putting space between us.

"You don't want to do that."

Before I could ask what he meant, Gavin stepped into the clearing.

"Sorry to interrupt, but we need to get going. We're getting a later start than I'd intended."

My chest went tight, stuffed with words that needed to be said before there were miles and miles between us again. Before I lost him again.

Liam shook his head, kept his eyes on me but spoke to Gavin. "I'm going with you."

"Oh, no, you aren't, brother mine." Gavin took a step closer, a fight brewing in his eyes. "I didn't haul my ass down here into the bayou so you could turn yourself over to Containment. I came down here to keep you out of trouble. You and Eleanor both."

"I'm the one accused of murder," Liam said, sliding his gaze to his brother. "You think I'm going to stay here, cower here, while someone frames me? Convicts me in absentia?"

"You seemed okay with coming down here after the battle."

"That was different," Liam said, each word carefully bitten off. "There were reasons—" He shook his head. "I can't get into that right now. If someone's willing to frame me, they're willing to do worse. If I don't go back, if I don't challenge this, who else will stop it?"

"We will," Gavin said. "That's why we're here, after all. You go back, you endanger everyone."

"I stay here, I endanger everyone. Including Eleanor, Erida, Roy and his family. Plenty of hunters aren't concerned about who they hurt to get their quarry. If I'm here, they might use him—or the kids—to find me. If I'm gone, he can be honest, tell them where I've gone, maybe even get a little money out of it."

"And they'll tail you back to New Orleans," Gavin said. "Where Containment is waiting to haul you in. If something happens to you because I made the call to come down here, I won't be able to live with that."

Liam took a step toward Gavin. I'd seen them come to blows before, and I wasn't sure if we were headed there now. "Someone murdered Broussard in my name. I can't live with *that*."

Gavin didn't answer. The sounds of the bayou crept into the waiting silence.

"I go with you," Liam said, "and you're there to help me, or I go back by myself. Which do you prefer?"

Gavin cursed, then turned and stalked back to the house, fury in every step. I followed him, and Liam followed me, close enough that I could feel the punch of heat from his body.

Malachi and Erida waited on the porch.

Liam gave his hair a scrub with the towel, then tossed it over a railing, took a T-shirt from a waiting duffel bag, and pulled it over his head.

"Going somewhere?" Malachi asked.

"With you," he said.

Malachi looked at Gavin, who glared back. "Stubborn ass is going back whether we like it or not. He might as well go with us."

I guess that decided that. And I decided I'd probably better not think too hard about what it meant for me. I was going to have to either wait Liam out or decide he wasn't worth it. And I wasn't ready to make that decision.

Erida shifted slightly, drawing our attention to her. "I can stay with Eleanor, but I think we'd need to move again. Perhaps make it look like the house has been deserted for a while."

"I think that's a good idea," Gavin said. "At least until this Broussard situation is done."

Erida nodded.

"And now that you've made a plan, do I get to speak in my own defense?"

We looked back. Eleanor had stepped onto the porch. Gavin moved forward to help her, but Erida held out a hand, shook her head.

Eleanor moved slowly to the rocking chair, using her hands as guides, then sat carefully down. "I'm content to stay out here," she said. "The bayou is growing on me. But Liam should go back to New Orleans. His home is there, not here. This is his birthplace. And I'm not saying he shouldn't come visit every once in a while." She shifted her gaze, settled it near Liam. "I've loved spending this time with you. But it's time for you to go home. As if you haven't been planning that all along."

Her gaze slid toward me, and I felt my body jerk, but refused to give in to the temptation to play with those words, to let them roll around in my mind, so full of possibility. He'd been planning to come back? When? How?

And, most important, why?

"Plans go awry," Liam said, and that snipped off the growing stem of hope. "I don't want to leave you alone."

Eleanor smiled like a cat who's done a fine job of pinning the canary. "My boy, I lived on this earth for decades before you were a glint in your father's Irish eyes. You have business to attend to. It's time you attend to it."

She rocked once, wood creaking against wood. "Now, be on your way, and get that business done."

And like the bayou's Creole queen, Eleanor looked over the trees and water and waited for her bidding to be done.

Liam having no counterargument to his formidable grandmother—and who could?—we helped Erida prepare some of Eleanor's belongings, including the book in which she'd cataloged the colors of the magic she'd seen over the years. Malachi found Roy, who steered a boat up to the dock. It was big and pale green, a former trawler with the net spars removed.

We helped Eleanor into the boat, and then they were gone, ready to move even farther downriver, farther toward the flat saltwater marshes and the Gulf of Mexico.

When the sound of the motor had drifted away, Gavin put a hand on Liam's shoulder. "To everything there is a season."

The hand dropped away when Liam growled.

"You may not have had enough coffee," Gavin muttered. "But it's too late now. Let's hit the road."

We walked in single file: Gavin, me, Liam, and when he wasn't doing above-the-ground scouting, Malachi. I could feel the weight of Liam's gaze on my back, like his stare was a tangible thing. His silence was nearly as oppressive as the heat and humidity, but we were focused on making progress.

It didn't help that I didn't know what to say to him and he wasn't ready to say anything to me. Every sticky mile made me more irritated about that.

"Anybody need a break?" Gavin asked. The trail veered away from the levee to our left, which held back the Mississippi, and toward the railroad tracks on our right.

Gavin walked to a short line of trees, pulled off an orange, sniffed. "Ripe," he said. He plucked a few more, began passing them out. Even Malachi took one, and we climbed up the levee to eat them. The path up was steep, but the top was rounded. Below us, the river frothed brown as it rushed south.

"I always thought it looked like café au lait," Gavin said, throwing off his pack and taking a seat.

"Which is how you ended up a hundred yards downriver one fateful Saturday afternoon."

Gavin grinned at Liam. "Got me out of Sunday school, which was fine by me."

I put down my backpack, sat on it, and began peeling my orange. Only then did I realize we hadn't passed an orange tree on the way to Dulac. We were taking a different route back.

"We bypassed the marina," I said.

Gavin chewed, nodded. "Didn't want to push our luck."

"You don't trust Cherie?" I asked.

Liam made a sound of doubt and began to peel the orange rind in a single long spiral, just like he'd peeled the label from his bottle the day before.

"Cherie's out for herself," Gavin said. "And no one else. I can't fault her for it in this day and age. But you have to stay wary."

"She's probably already sent people our way," Liam said.

"She might have," Gavin said. "But we needed information. That's the risk we took."

If she was going to tell Containment about us, I wasn't going to hurry in getting booze sent her way.

"So where are we going?" Liam asked. "This isn't a straight path to New Orleans."

"Jeep's at Houma," Gavin said. "Vacherie Plantation."

Malachi nodded. "I want to check on Cinda."

"Who's Cinda?" Liam asked.

"One of mine," Malachi said, biting into a segment of fruit. "She was ill when we passed through the first time. I'd like to see how she's doing."

"And maybe Anh has some more of those rice cakes."

Malachi gave Gavin a dour look.

"But obviously check on Cinda first," Gavin amended. "Because the care of our Paranormal friends is more important than my stomach." He glanced speculatively at Liam. "That work for your agenda, *frère*?"

"Fine by me."

"You given any thought to where you'll be staying in the city? Can't get you back into your town house in Devil's Isle."

"I'll borrow a house." He would sleep in an abandoned home, he meant. "That's safest for everyone. And I want to see Broussard's house—the scene."

"Wait until we talk to Gunnar," Gavin said. "Maybe he can make arrangements for me, and I can get you in."

"I can't make any promises." The orange denuded, Liam pulled off a segment and took a bite, then gazed over the water.

"You won't do us or Eleanor any good if you get caught," Malachi said.

Liam looked at him. "I'm a pretty good judge of what I should and shouldn't be doing."

Malachi slid his gaze to me. "I'm not sure that's accurate."

Gavin snorted, then covered it with a fairly unconvincing cough.

"I want your opinion, I'll ask for it."

"Not opinion," Malachi said. "Fact."

Liam's gaze went hot. "You have something you want to say to me?"

"No." Malachi's expression was utterly bland. "Should I?"

Liam tossed away the rest of his orange and stood up, gold blazing in his eyes.

"Ladies," Gavin said, "this isn't helping. Malachi, please quit antagonizing him. You're too old to be acting like idiots. Well, I presume." He looked at Malachi. "I'm not actually sure how old you are."

"I think we need to discuss some things," Liam said, his eyes still narrowed on Malachi's. "Feel free to take a walk."

"I'm available for a conversation," Malachi said.

I rolled my eyes, then rose and pulled on my backpack. "Let's walk," I told Gavin. "We've got miles to go before we get to Vacherie."

"The voice of reason," Gavin said, following me down the levee. I glanced back once, saw Malachi and Liam—light and dark—facing each other like warriors preparing for battle.

"He's not helping anything," I said.

"He's not trying to help. He's trying to be a pain in Liam's ass, and it's working."

"And what good does he think that's going to do?"

Gavin looked at me. "You cannot be that naive. He's trying to get Liam to pull out the stick that's wedged thoroughly up his ass and talk to you. He's obviously still in love with you, Claire."

I snorted. "Whatever. He's barely had two words to say to me."

"Stick, ass," Gavin reminded me with a smile. "He's as stubborn as they come, and I'd know, seeing as how we've got the same genetics. My guess is the magic's eating at him. Maybe also guilt about

Gracie, anger at being stuck out here while you're in New Orleans alone. If you can't see that on his face, you aren't looking. Or maybe that's the problem—you aren't looking. He stares at you like you're the first water he's seen in months. I know you've at least seen those looks he's been giving Malachi."

"There's nothing between me and Malachi. We're just friends, and Malachi's antagonizing him."

"Yeah, but you can't antagonize someone who doesn't give a shit. Trust me—he cares. He'll just have to work his way around to figuring that out, or telling you about it."

And how long was I supposed to wait?

It was twenty minutes before Malachi and Liam caught up to us again, and after noon by the time we reached Vacherie. We'd grabbed a few oranges for the road, but were still hungry.

"Rice cakes," Gavin said again. "Just to confirm, that's item number two on the agenda. Checking on Cinda being item number one."

"You're so magnanimous," Liam said. The first words he'd spoken in miles.

"Diplomacy is my particular art," Gavin said. Which nobody really believed.

We reached the edge of the woods and saw the house perched like a crown amid the fields. And from somewhere on the plantation, the sound of wailing and weeping carried toward us on the breeze.

"No," Malachi said, pushing in front of us, his body bowed and tense. "No, no, no." He ran forward and his wings unfolded with a sharp *snap*, then propelled him into the air.

Cinda was my first thought. She'd taken a turn for the worse.

I ran down the trail and toward the plantation, ignoring Gavin's calls behind me. I flew out of the knee-high sugarcane and emerged in front of the barn to stand beside Malachi.

I saw the Tengu first, standing in a semicircle, hands linked, feathers lifted. Paranormals followed, crying and keening, then two men with a linen-covered board on their shoulders, a body laid carefully upon it.

He wore white, and his hands were crossed over his chest, his hair falling white around the shoulders of the men who carried him. It wasn't Cinda; it was Djosa.

"No," Malachi said again, an exhalation and a cry. Then he stepped in line with the rest of the mourners as they walked.

"Oh, shit," Gavin murmured as he and Liam joined me.

More Paranormals joined the procession, and we watched silently as Djosa was borne from the barn to a grass path between cane fields.

I glanced at Gavin, unsure of the etiquette.

"It's all right to follow," he said. "But let's keep our distance."

The Tengu began to sing, a keening cry of sadness and loss as the group moved through the fields beneath the glaring sun. The Paras carrying Djosa must have been parched, but none seemed to complain. Given what little I knew about the Consularis, I guessed they saw the task as a privilege, a way to honor their fallen friend.

The sown fields gave way to tangled and gnarly woods, where nature was winning its battle against the forces of human agriculture. Humidity closed in around us again, and even the smells changed, became damper and greener.

We wound through the woods to a small clearing where I could just make out broken stones that littered the ground. This was a cemetery, a very old one that had probably been used by the plantation since its inception. There were no elaborate aboveground tombs here, and barely any markers. Just a small plot of land where the deceased could be laid to rest beneath live oaks and moss.

But they weren't going to put Djosa in the ground. They'd built a small platform of two-by-fours and plywood, and carefully placed the board that held his body atop it. The Tengu moved closer, picked at his hair and clothes to resettle them. To arrange them.

A Para I hadn't seen before stepped forward, began to speak to the crowd in their particular language. And it was a crowd, I belatedly realized, that didn't include Cinda. I wondered if she'd been too ill to attend her father's funeral.

Gavin pulled off his cap. I did the same thing, so my braid fell across my shoulders.

Drawn by the movement, the Tengu looked in our direction, caught sight of us.

They went crazy again—feathers raised like an animal's hackles, voices that had been singing now screaming. With fear or fury, I wasn't sure, but they didn't want us there. Didn't want us watching. The other Paras turned, shot nasty looks in our direction, made it clear they didn't welcome either the interruption or our presence.

Without argument, we left them alone with their grief.

CHAPTER EIGHT

We were sweating by the time we took seats beside the jeep and beneath the oak tree in front of the main house. We waited nearly an hour for Malachi to walk around the hill. In the meantime, I stayed quiet, while Gavin and Liam talked through Containment's personnel roll, trying to pick out the person who might have had some vendetta against Liam.

"It was an illness," Malachi confirmed when he joined us. "Djosa had been feeling weak, tired. Felt worse before we arrived yesterday, but didn't want to seem weak in front of me." He looked away, shook his head as he gazed at the plantation house.

I wasn't sure how to comfort him, so I went for the obvious thing, which still felt pointless. "We're sorry for your loss."

Malachi nodded. But there was something hard in his eyes—something that said he wouldn't be forgetting about Djosa's death anytime soon.

Southerners—whether in New Orleans or out of it—loved to talk about lessons. What you learned even from bad experiences. What they were supposed to teach you. How they were part of a bigger plan. But I was having trouble seeing how this man's death could have been part of anyone's plan.

Gavin pushed himself up from the ground, wiped his hands on his jeans. "He shouldn't have gotten sick at all."

"No," Malachi agreed. "He shouldn't have."

"At the risk of sounding incredibly callous," Gavin said, "we should get moving. Presuming it's contagious, you don't need any further exposure. We don't want you getting sick, and we don't want to take anything home with us, spread it further."

"I'll go my own way," Malachi said, then glanced at me. "Would you like a ride into New Orleans?" He extended his wings, the ivory feathers reflecting back the sunlight that dappled through the tree limbs.

Although the thought of getting a bird's-eye view of New Orleans was interesting, the thought of flying all the way back in the arms of a rogue Paranormal was not.

"Rain check," I said.

"We'll see you there," Gavin said. "We should probably meet tonight, discuss the plan of attack, so to speak." He slid his brother a glance. "Since this is no longer just a warning mission, but an investigatory one."

Liam nodded. "We need to find out what we can about Broussard's death. The why, the how, the when. That will lead us to the culprit."

"I'll speak with Moses," Malachi said, and gave Liam the address. "We'll meet there, unless it's not safe." He nodded at me.

"I know the system," I assured him. A string of Mardi Gras beads—yellow, with enormous plastic monkeys holding enormous plastic bananas—hanging on the front door meant the coast was clear. If the beads were gone, it wasn't safe, and we were supposed to keep on walking.

"Then it's a date," Malachi said, and took to the sky.

I held a hand over my eyes, watched his body rise, wings smooth and powerful against the thick air, until he became a thin sliver of white against the brilliant sky and then disappeared.

When I looked back again, Gavin was clapping Liam on the back, then walking toward the jeep, singing as he strolled, *"Do you know what it means to miss New Orleans . . ."*

At least he was better at it than Moses.

Liam wasn't any more communicative in the jeep than he had been during the walk.

"If we play I Spy or the alphabet game," Gavin said, catching his gaze in the rearview, "will you contribute to the discussion?"

"Doubtful."

"Grouchy ass," Gavin muttered.

He went back to singing and tapping his fingers on the steering wheel—until he suddenly went quiet.

"Forget the words?" I murmured, my eyes closed as I tried to take a catnap in the passenger seat.

"No," he said, and there was no humor in his voice. "Look. Roadblock."

My eyes flashed open, and I blinked in the brilliant sunlight, caught a glimpse of four vehicles, two on each side of the divided highway. On the side heading into New Orleans, the vehicles were parked nose to nose, just enough space between them to allow one car to pass at a time.

Gavin swung the jeep onto a gravel road, sending a spray of dirt and gravel into the air.

"I'm sure they won't notice that and think it's suspicious," Liam muttered.

"Defensive maneuvers," Gavin said.

"Why is there a roadblock around New Orleans?" I asked. Had something happened in the two days we'd been gone? "Was there another attack on Devil's Isle?"

"Doubtful," Gavin said. "Someone would have gotten word to Malachi."

"Is this because of Broussard?" Liam asked.

"It couldn't possibly be," Gavin said, tapping the top of the gear-shift. "Shutting down access to New Orleans to find a suspect in one murder? Not to diminish what happened to Broussard, but that's not procedure. That's overkill."

"The entire thing is overkill," Liam said. "The murder, the literal writing on the wall, the frame job. Maybe this is bigger than Broussard."

"Maybe," Gavin said, but he didn't seem convinced. He glanced back, looked at his brother. "What's the plan?"

"I can swim in," Liam said.

"Swim in?" I asked, meeting his gaze in the rearview mirror. "You're going to swim into New Orleans?"

"Just to the river," Liam said. "Containment doesn't patrol the canals. You stay low along the wall, and you can move in and out of the city pretty easily."

"You want to meet down the road?" Gavin asked.

Liam shook his head. "I'll take the ferry when I get to the river. Meet you at Moses's place."

"That's a long trip," I said.

Liam's gaze on me was intense. "It's safer for all of us if we split up."

"And speaking of safety," Gavin said, looking at me, "the road-block wouldn't be for you, but that doesn't mean they won't take you in if they can. Can you swim?"

"I can swim, but I'm not strong enough to go through miles of canals." And that didn't take into account the gators, snakes, rats, and nutria, among other things. "So no."

"Then you pretend to be someone else," Gavin said, turning in his seat to glance at me. "Grab that cap, please."

"I'll do you one better," I said, and rummaged through the backpack at my feet to find the wig I'd thrown in. It was cut into a short, dark bob, not unlike Darby's. She was a former employee of PCC Research and a member of Delta.

I pulled off the cap, twisted up my braid, then leaned over and stuffed the wig on. It took a little adjusting in the mirror to get it straight and to tuck up the stray ends, but I didn't look like an obvious redhead anymore. I pulled the cap down over it, then turned to Gavin, lifted an eyebrow.

"Not bad." His appraising look turned to an appreciative one. "Not bad at all." He wiggled his eyebrows suggestively.

"Focus," Liam said, elbowing the back of Gavin's seat.

"A man can focus on multiple things at once."

"Focus." This time I said it. I checked the car's side mirrors again, since I was expecting a Containment vehicle to come storming down the gravel road any minute.

"Be careful," Gavin said.

Liam nodded. "I know how to stay below the radar."

"Then let's do this," Gavin said, starting the car again.

Liam climbed out, shut the door, and glanced through my open window. "Be careful," he said, and gave me a long look before walking away.

"Is he brave, or stupid?" I asked.

"Both, obviously." Gavin's face changed, became serious, as he pulled the car around to head back to the highway.

"I'm with Containment," Gavin reminded me, "or close enough. Hunter on my way into the city for a meeting. And you are?"

"Your girlfriend, along for the ride. Name's . . . Mignon."

"Excellent choice," he said. "I've always wanted to date a Mignon."

I sat back, crossed my arms, and tried to ignore the butterflies in my belly. I'd been purposely avoiding not just Containment but nearly everyone and everything from my previous life that Containment could have used to get to me. Now we were running toward the trouble, and there was no turning back.

Gavin waved out the window as we came to a stop. Two agents in dark fatigues, guns strapped to their waists, approached us.

"Sir," said the one on Gavin's side. "Ma'am." He was big and beefy, with pale skin, shorn hair, a square jaw, and a puggish nose.

"Agent," Gavin said. "I'm no sir, and she's no ma'am." He yanked away an ID clipped to his visor, offered it to the agent. "I'm Special Ops."

The agent looked at the badge, then up at Gavin again. "Reason for visiting New Orleans?"

"I live there, as my badge says." He checked his watch. "And in particular, I've got a meeting with Gunnar Landreau in half an hour."

"And your business outside New Orleans?" the agent asked.

"Not at liberty to disclose to anyone without sigma clearance. Containment can confirm."

The agent lifted his eyes to me. "And you?"

"Field trip," I said, sounding as bored as possible. "Although this ain't exactly what I had in mind."

The agent gave the badge another careful study, then looked at me and did the same. "Step out of the car, please."

"Sure," Gavin said. "But can I ask why?"

"You're on the list."

Shit, I thought.

"What list is that?"

"You may have information about persons of interest."

"I'm sure I do, having sigma status. But as I noted, I'm not authorized to give out that information."

"We're looking for Liam Quinn. Your brother."

Gavin's jaw went tight in a pretty good imitation of someone very, very angry at Liam.

"Merde," he muttered, really pushing the Cajun accent. "The hell has he done this time?"

"Killed a Containment agent, name of Broussard."

Gavin visibly jerked, then pulled his sunglasses off very, very slowly. "Say what?"

"Killed Broussard in his own home. Bounty's been issued. He's a wanted man, and Containment wants him inside sooner rather than later."

"I guess so—you've got a roadblock. But I ain't seen that *couillon* in weeks. We had what you might call a bit of a falling-out after the battle."

He gestured to the roadblock. "Containment thinks he's outside NOLA?"

That was a good strategy lesson: Containment knocks down your door, take the opportunity to get what information you can.

"Don't know. Just following orders."

"Of course you are." He swore, shook his head. "He thinks I'm going to save his ass again, he is very mistaken. *Tête dur.*" Gavin wet his lips, looked at the agent conspiratorially. "How much is the bounty?"

The agent threw out a number that would have kept Royal Mercantile in the green for months. Containment was serious about getting Liam.

Gavin whistled. "I didn't ask this question, but just so I'm sure—family members get the bounty, should they come across him?"

"I believe so." He stepped away for a moment, had a conversation with the other agent, spoke into his communicator. Gavin, who looked completely cool from the neck up, squeezed my hand.

The agents came back.

Let us go, I murmured. *Just let us go.*

"Sir, please step out of the car," the agent said again. "We need to take a look inside."

Gavin nodded. "Of course, Agent. I'm being an asshole, and you're just doing your job. I'm coming out," he said, then opened the door, climbed outside. "But if I'm late for my meeting," he added with a grin, "could you write me a note?"

I exited under the watch of the other agent.

"Hands on the hood, please." We were both steered to face opposite sides of the hood, and we put our palms on the car. After baking in the sun, the hood was hot enough to fry an egg. But at least it kept my hands from visibly shaking.

Gavin winked at me, which helped a little. But I knew some of that was bravado he didn't feel. If someone was willing to frame Liam and put Containment on his trail, it wasn't hard to believe they'd bring in his brother, too.

They opened the doors, began sorting through the Jeep's contents. Gavin's backpack, my backpack. I did a quick mental inventory of what I'd thrown in there and if there was anything damaging.

"Well," said one of the agents.

I froze, swallowed down a hard ball of fear, and glanced around the vehicle.

The agent, whose cheeks were flushed pink, held up by two fingers the raunchiest bit of black lingerie I'd ever seen. Cheap black lace with bows and cords, and strategic cutouts that seemed to defeat the point of wearing lingerie in the first place.

I glared at Gavin.

He managed to scrounge up a blush, coughed delicately. "So, I may not have cleaned out that bag very well after its last use."

Since I was playing a role, I figured I might as well go for the gold. "You asshole!" I lunged at him across the hood of the car, managed to get in a couple of slaps on his arms before the agent dragged me out of range, pulled back my arms. "What the hell is that? Why the hell is there lingerie—*lingerie*—in your bag?"

He held up his hands, all innocent. "Mignon, baby, it's nothing. I swear."

"You *asshole*! Was it Lucinda's? You promised me you wouldn't see her again! You *promised*!"

He looked at the agent who held my arms. "Could you please give us a minute here?"

"Ma'am," the agent said, "you going to control yourself?"

I curled my lip at Gavin. "You mean like how he controls himself? Can't keep his fly zipped. Can't keep his damn hands to himself."

"Ma'am."

"Yes," I said. "Yes, *fine*. I can control myself."

He let me go, and I adjusted my shirt, then brushed a hand over the wig to smooth it.

When I turned back to Gavin, glaring at him over the hood, the agent stepped carefully away and joined the other agent at the back of the jeep.

"You're violent," Gavin murmured.

"You're a pervert."

"It's not *my* underwear."

"Yeah, that was my point. Do I want to know why you have it?"

"You do not," he said matter-of-factly. "Lucinda?"

"Mean girl from sixth grade. Hated her." I couldn't let it go. "Were you hoping you'd find a little company on this trip?"

"I mean, I'm not saying I can't appreciate a good time when I find it, but no. I really did forget it was in there."

Probably best not to dig too deeply into the rest of it.

Five awkward minutes later, the agent came back and avoided all eye contact with me.

"You're free to go," he said. "We appreciate your cooperation, and we're sorry for the, um, domestic issues."

"Not your fault he's an asshole," I said, giving Gavin one last leer.

The agent nodded awkwardly, looked back at Gavin. "If you see your brother, call Containment. He needs to be stopped before he hurts someone else."

"I couldn't agree more," Gavin said, and we climbed into the car again. "We appreciate your service."

We pulled away, both of us still checking the mirrors, waiting to be followed. But the cars stayed parked where they were.

"That was easy," I said.

"Too easy," Gavin said, his gaze still flicking between the road and the rearview mirror. "And . . . there it is."

I checked the side mirror. About a quarter mile behind us, a silver sedan pulled onto the highway.

"Who is it?"

"A Containment tail would be my guess. They probably assume I'm lying about Liam—or they hope I am—and figure I'll either lead them directly to him or I'll take them to a drop-off spot, and they can lie in wait."

"You don't actually have one of those, do you? A drop-off spot?"

He smiled. "Not one, no. More like"—he paused, lips moving silently—"eleven, at last count. Twelve? No. Eleven."

"Why?"

"It's a big city. You never know where you're going to wake up."

I snorted. "That sounds like a personal problem."

Gavin grinned. "Personal, but never a problem. A tail, though, would be a problem. And confirms that Containment is very serious about finding Liam. What the hell did he do to get so much interest?"

"Wrong place, wrong time?"

"I don't know. I really don't."

We watched the sedan draw closer.

"How, exactly, do they plan to tail you? It's pretty obvious they're back there."

"Multiple cars," he said. "They'll do a handoff a mile or two up the road. Watch," he said. And sure enough, the sedan drew closer, then pulled into the other lane and passed us, as if totally oblivious to our car.

"This car will pull off the road ahead. Another car will pull in behind me, follow me until they hopscotch again, and so on. It's a good trick."

"And you've got a plan to deal with it?"

"Of course I've got a plan. Which, unfortunately, is going to mean ditching this jeep. Which is a bummer, because I really like it. Found it in the Garden District behind an old bookstore. Full bottle of Jack Daniel's." He smiled, patted the dash lovingly. "She's been good since the beginning. Alas. I'll leave the keys in it for the next person who might need it. And maybe I'll come across a Range Rover." He glanced at me. "You buckled up?"

"I am," I said, and pulled the seat belt to check the tension, just in case.

"Then sit back and enjoy the ride."

With a grin on his face, he gunned it.

Between the two of them, I'd figured Gavin for the risk-taker, Liam for the planner. If Gavin's driving was any sign, I'd been exactly right.

Gavin knew how to handle a tail. He played oblivious, weaving through Carrollton—up and down side streets, occasionally stopping to chat up some random person he spotted on the street and forcing the cars tailing him to stop and hide. I kept the wig in place while we drove. There was no point in riling them up with the thought of more quarry.

After half an hour of cruising through the city, and no loss of interest by the agents watching us, Gavin waited until the next handoff, then took a chance and pulled the jeep into an alley, driving through it until he found an empty garage. He backed in and turned off the engine while I jumped out and closed the garage door.

The trick worked. They drove right past us. We waited and listened for them to circle back, and when the coast was clear, we pulled out and headed toward Mid-City.

I'd already given Gavin my drop-off location, an alley a few blocks from the gas station that wasn't close enough to clue him in to my secret lair. I wanted a shower and food before I headed to Moses's place for round two.

"I don't suppose you'll let me drop you off right in front, so I'll know where you are, can keep an eye on you?"

"I will not." I climbed out of the car, grabbed my backpack. "Thanks for the ride. If you tail me, I'll be pissed."

"You're entitled to your privacy," Gavin said. He paused for a moment, seemed to debate saying what he said next. "Look, Claire. You and Liam are none of my business."

"But you're going to power through it?"

"I think you should consider something."

One arm atop the jeep, I sighed, looked back in. "What?"

"You're cocooning."

"I'm—what?"

"Cocooning." He stuck his thumbs beneath his arms and pretended to flap wings. "Like a butterfly."

I just kept looking at him.

"Jesus, you're both being purposefully obtuse. You're hunkering down in this secret lair of yours so you won't hurt anybody. Gunnar or Tadji or the store."

"I don't have a secret lair." But I totally did. And even if I did, wasn't that the right thing to do?

"Don't you think Liam was doing exactly the same thing?"

"Maybe," I said. "But he's back now. Whose side are you on?"

"He's my older brother, and you're my friend. So I'm on my side, naturally. I'll see you at Moses's."

I closed the door. "If I don't show up in a couple of hours, you can come back here and start your search."

"Fair enough," he said. "And Liam?"

I shouldered the backpack on. "That wasn't a question."

"I've gotten him back to New Orleans. The rest is up to you. So get to it."

CHAPTER NINE

In a war zone, a long shower was a miracle. That was especially true after a day of moving bayou residents, wandering trails, witnessing a Paranormal funeral, and getting stopped by a Containment roadblock.

I was tired, my legs ached, and I was starving. I wouldn't have minded spending the night in the station, futzing with one of the projects I'd started to keep myself busy. The backup dehumidifier that didn't want to turn over, or the few Paranormal artifacts that needed repair. But that wasn't in the cards. Containment was on the hunt, and we were on the clock.

I capped off my shower by eating a can of peaches with a fork. It had been sunny when I'd arrived at the gas station, was pouring by the time I left. I pulled up my Windbreaker hood and started my second hike of the day.

By the time I arrived at Moses's house, dusk had nearly fallen. An enormous white Range Rover was parked outside, and since I didn't know anyone who drove one, I figured Gavin had made quick work of finding a new car.

There were still plenty of vehicles in the city, but not many luxury cars or SUVs that hadn't been stripped or trashed, or turned into rusting hulks after seven years of sitting. And yet, he'd somehow managed to find one in a matter of hours—presumably one that ran. I hoped that kind of luck was contagious.

The beads were on the door, so I took the steps to Moses's Creole cottage, but paused for a moment on the porch to prepare myself for round two with Liam. Whatever that might involve.

I found Gavin and Malachi in the small front room of the house. It had what rental sites would have called "Authentic New Orleans Charm." Brick walls, old hardwood floors, floor-to-ceiling windows.

Along with narrow rooms, old plumbing, and the constant risk of flood.

Before his place in the Quarter had been torched, Moses had amassed a huge collection of electronics. He was making a pretty good dent in filling up this room around his workstation—a padded stool and metal desk. There was a couch for visitors, but unless he'd gotten into a decorating mood while we'd been gone, the race car bed in the back room was the only other piece of furniture in the house.

Because he was small of stature, it fit Moses perfectly.

"You bring me anything?" he asked from his stool, swiveling to look me over.

"Did I bring you anything?" I asked, closing the door.

Moses gestured to Gavin and Malachi. "These two take a field trip, leave me to guard the entire city, don't even bring me a souvenir."

Knowing an opportunity when I had one, I unzipped my backpack, pulled out two of the oranges we'd nabbed near the levee. "I guess they aren't as nice as I am."

"I knew you'd come through," he said, hopping down from the stool, taking the oranges and putting them proudly on one corner of the desk.

Gavin leaned toward me. "You didn't get those for him."

"No comment."

"Now that we're all assembled," Moses said, "shall we get to business?"

"We're actually still missing one," Gavin said, just as we heard a perfectly timed knock at the door. He opened it and let Liam inside.

Liam had cleaned up and changed into a snug DEFEND NEW ORLEANS T-shirt that highlighted every nook and cranny of strong muscle and taut skin.

He gave Malachi and Gavin quick looks. Gave me a longer one as a lock of dark hair fell over his face. He brushed it back, then looked at Moses, who'd hopped onto his stool again and was giving Liam a wary gaze. "Well, well. Look what the damn cat drug in."

"Mos," Liam said with a nod.

Moses lifted his brows. "That's all you got to say?"

"It's good to see you," Liam said. "It's just been a long day."

"Long five weeks, more like," Moses muttered, sending me a look I dutifully ignored. "Where the hell you been?"

"Where it's wet," Liam said.

"Eleanor?"

"She's good."

They stared at each other for a moment, and smiled, and that was that. Weeks evaporating like fog over the bayou.

"Well," Moses said, "I'm glad to see your ugly face again. How was the trip home?"

"Malachi lost a friend," Gavin said.

"A friend?" Moses asked, and Malachi told him about our visit to Vacherie and the death of the Paranormal.

"Damn," Moses said. "Can't stay in Devil's Isle, can't leave it, either."

"Roadblock on the way back into the city," Gavin said. "Nearly got pinched. They wanted Liam, wouldn't give us details. We also met a couple of bounty hunters on the way down there. They said Containment had a bounty for Liam, wanted to talk to Claire."

"Talk, my ass," Moses said. "They want to haul you away." He pointed a finger at me. "I didn't go to all this trouble for you to get rounded right up."

I couldn't help grinning. "What trouble, exactly, did you go to? And be specific."

He just snorted, glanced at Liam. "Looks like they didn't waste any time coming after you, either."

"Evidently not."

"And since that's why we're all here," I said, "you find out anything about Broussard while we were gone?"

"Lizzie doesn't know a damn thing," Moses said. "Plenty of people have plenty of things to say about him, none of it friendly, but none of it specific. Usual complaints, far as I can tell."

"He was an asshole," Liam said. "Pretentious. Narrow-minded. But that's not unusual among humans, much less agents. I will give credit, say he usually thought he was doing the right thing. He and I just disagreed about what was right."

Including, I thought, *whether I'd been harboring magic-wielding fugitives.*

"But that's not our only source of information. While you've been frolicking through the meadows, I've also been working on this gorgeous girl." Moses waved a hand at the electronics on the desk.

It was shaped vaguely like an elephant, but I was pretty sure that was just a coincidence. Large gray body on a platform with four feet, power cords serving as the trunk and tail. A couple of monitors were squeezed in beside cases full of dangling wires and what I thought were speakers and fans.

"Does it work?" Liam asked.

"Does now that I found a power supply a couple houses down. In the damn garage, if you can believe that. People hid all their good shit before they left."

"How dare they?" I asked with mock outrage. Moses ignored the question and the tone.

"Since we're all here and this machine is up and running, I think it's time to see what we can do with it."

"What are you going to try?" I asked, moving closer.

"Try? I'm not going to *try* anything. I'm going to *do*. In particular, I'm going to worm my way into Containment-Net and see what we can see about Mr. Broussard."

"Should I mention that's illegal?" I asked. It wasn't the first time he'd hacked his way in; he'd done it the very night we'd met in order to erase evidence that I'd used magic. In other words, he'd saved my ass.

"Of course you shouldn't." He typed furiously, one screen replacing another as he worked through Containment's systems. "Figured we'd check Broussard's files, take a look at what he's been working on."

"In case what he was working on got him killed," I concluded.

"That's it," Moses muttered as he typed. "Added some new security, think I can't make my way through it? Assholes. Gunnar's the only good one in that entire group. Not counting you two," he said, glancing back at the Quinn boys.

"Technically," Gavin said, "I'm an independent contractor and Liam's"—he glanced speculatively at his brother—"in his post–independent contractor stage."

Liam grunted his agreement.

"All right," Moses said. "Recent docs." He clicked on a folder with Broussard's name on it, revealing another set of folders.

"Put his docs in reverse chronological order," Liam suggested. "Let's see what he was viewing before he died."

"On that." Moses moved from folder to folder, pounded keys, then repeated the process. "Here we go," he said after a moment, when the screen filled with bright green text.

If that text was supposed to mean something, I didn't get it. It was a mishmash of letters and numbers and symbols, like someone had simply rolled a hand across a keyboard.

"Is it encrypted?" Gavin asked, moving forward with a frown and peering at the screen.

"Don't think so," Moses said as he continued to type. He did something that made the text shrink, then rotate, then expand, then shrink again. "Huh," he said. "Not encrypted. Just not the entire file. It's a stub."

"A stub?" I asked.

"What's left of a file after someone tries to delete it." He looked back at us. "Deleting a file doesn't really destroy it, at least not completely, and sometimes not at all. There's almost always at least something left—the stub."

He swiveled back to the screen. "This looks like someone tried to do a pretty thorough delete, dumped a lot of the bytes, but not all of them. This is what's left." He typed, then hit the ENTER key with gusto.

One of the tower's panels flew off, followed by a fountain of orange sparks and flame. The panel hit the brick wall and bounced to the floor, and the machine began to whistle.

"Shit!" Moses said, swatting at it with his hand.

The brothers moved faster than I did. While Gavin grabbed a towel from a nearby stack and covered the flames to block access to oxygen, Liam yanked the power cord—overstuffed with plugs—from the wall.

Without power, the screens went dark, and the hum of electronics went suddenly silent. Gavin futzed with the towel and the case until he was satisfied the fire was out.

The room smelled like burning plastic, and a haze of smoke gathered near the ceiling.

"Huh," Moses said after a moment, brushing smoke away from his face and leaning around to get a look at the case.

"Do try not to burn the house down," Gavin said. "Tends to make Containment pay attention."

"You think that bus you've parked outside won't?" Liam asked.

"It's New Orleans," Gavin said matter-of-factly. "Anything goes in the Big Easy."

Moses hopped off the stool, gave the case a thump with his fist. When nothing happened, he peered inside it, began fiddling with parts.

He yelped in pain, and we all jumped forward to help. But he pulled his hand out, perfectly fine, and wiggled his fingers. "Humans," he said affectionately, and shook his head. "So gullible.

"This is the problem," he said, then extracted a black box—probably four by four by three inches—with a very melted corner. "Power supply. Hoped it would last a little longer. If you wanna get back into the file, I need another one." He looked at me and Liam speculatively, which put me instantly on my guard. "I need a favor."

"What?" I asked.

"This," he said. He tossed the box at Liam. "House down the road's got a pretty good stockpile of parts, and I think I saw another one of these in there. It's a Boomer 3600. Number will be written on the side."

"Which house?"

He gestured vaguely to the left. "The one with the shutters."

"Mos," I said with remarkable patience, "it's New Orleans. They all have shutters." When he opened his mouth, I held up a finger. "And don't say the one with the balcony."

He grinned. "Got me there. It's the butter one."

"The butter one," Liam repeated.

"I think he means yellow."

I asked Moses, with brows lifted.

"That's it, Sherlock. Two houses down, in the garage."

"Be more specific," I said.

"There's a house, with a garage, and there's a pile of damn computer parts in said garage. It's just like that box Liam is currently holding, and it will be inside a case that looks like mine." He gestured over his shoulder with his thumb at the stack of ten or fifteen empty computer cases, which didn't help narrow things much.

"You'll know it when you see it." He turned back to the pile of tools beside his keyboard, pulled out a screwdriver, tossed it at me. *"Go,"* he said emphatically.

The order given and screwdriver in hand, we headed for the door.

It was pretty obvious he was setting us up, putting us together so we'd have to talk to each other. I didn't disagree that the conversation needed to be had, but it had been a long day, and I didn't feel much like being manipulated. If Liam wanted to talk, he could damn well open his mouth.

After checking that the coast was clear, we walked down the block. It was quiet out compared to the bayou. Maybe the city's wildlife was also waiting to hear what we'd have to say to each other.

But we didn't say anything. We just walked, and I worked really hard to pretend being out here with Liam was no big deal. To pretend I couldn't sense him beside me, strong and cruelly handsome.

"This one," I said, coming to a stop. Even in the dark, the color was clearly buttery. There wasn't an attached garage, so we walked down the driveway—two strips of gravel nearly covered now by grass—to a courtyard behind. The entrance to the garage was on the other side of the courtyard, a narrow box just big enough for one car. It had a pull-down door with a row of glass panels across the top and painted white handles along the bottom.

We each took a handle, lifted, then turned on the skinny flashlights we'd borrowed from a stash in Moses's living room.

"Damn," I said, staring at the volume of junk stuffed inside the narrow space. There were boxes, crates, electronics, and bundles piled to the ceiling.

"Stockpiler? Or hoarder?" Liam asked.

"Who knows?" I said, glancing around. "Doesn't look like it's been disturbed much, except for that." I pointed the flashlight at the narrow path that wound through the piles. "Probably Moses's trail."

Liam nodded, and I stepped into the path, followed it around a pile of busted bikes and television sets.

"I bet he picked this house because of this garage," Liam said, shifting things behind me.

"Probably. Electronics without corrosion are hard to come by."

The trail spiraled into the center of the garage, where the junk shifted to electronics. Cases, wires, connectors, screens. There were a lot of cases that looked like Moses's, so I started to pick through those.

He must have heard me moving around. "You got something?"

"Maybe." I shone the light into the cases, one after the other, until I saw a dusty box similar to the one Moses had had, with 3600 in red letters across the side.

"Found it," I said, and set about unscrewing it from the case. After a moment of work, it popped free into my hand. I didn't see any corrosion, but it was hard to tell with just a flashlight.

Prize won. I put away the screwdriver and began to weave my way back to the garage door. I stopped when I came to an old metal sign. SNOBALL was written across the rectangular piece of metal in pink three-dimensional block letters, each topped with a mound of snow. Flavors—strawberry, rainbow, praline—had been punched across the bottom.

Snoballs were the New Orleans version of shaved ice, a summertime tradition that hadn't survived the war. I hadn't seen a sign like this before, and I loved the memory it triggered.

My first instinct was to grab it for the shop, either to hang in the store or sell to someone looking for tangible reminders of the city's history.

But I didn't have a store to hang it in.

"Are you okay?"

"Just feeling nostalgic." I held up the power supply. "Got what we needed."

Liam nodded. We walked back to the garage door, and both reached for the same handle. Our fingers brushed, and the shock of hunger that arced through me left me nearly breathless.

Proximity shouldn't have made me suddenly ravenous, weak with want and need. I shouldn't have wanted to grab fistfuls of his hair, meld my mouth with his. I shouldn't have wanted to fall into his arms, to feel safe—and understood. But I did.

And I wasn't the only one affected; Liam's groan was a low, deep rumble. Then he stepped away, putting space between us, and ran a hand through his hair.

"What's going on?" I even sounded breathless. "Tell me what happened to you—what happened at the battle."

He shook his head. "You wouldn't understand."

I didn't think he meant to hurt me. But that didn't matter much.

"What wouldn't I understand, Liam? Magic? What it's like to run from it?"

"This is different."

"How?"

Liam shook his head, the war he was waging clear on his face.

"I don't know who you are right now," I said. "And I don't know what you want from me."

"I want nothing. And everything." He took a step closer, heat pumping from his body, muscles clenched like a man preparing for battle. "I haven't stopped wanting you. But it's inside me like an organism, a living thing full of fuel and anger. You think I'm going to bring that to your door?"

"I don't need protecting."

"Don't you?" He grabbed my hand, pressed it against his chest. His heart pounded like a war drum. "Feel that, Claire. That's because you're here. Because I see you, and I want to claim you like a goddamn wolf."

I stared at him while heat pulsed between our joined hands, and goose bumps rose along my arms. And it was long seconds before I had the composure to pull my hand away. I fisted my fingers against my chest, like that would cool the burn and diminish the power of his touch.

"Tell me about your magic."

My question had been a whisper, but it still seemed to echo through the garage.

I watched him shut down, shutter his expressions. But there was something he couldn't hide, a flash of something in his eyes. Not just anger, and not just stubbornness. There was *fear.* I recognized a man facing down his demons, because I'd faced down demons of my own. I was still facing them down.

"If you won't tell me what you're going through, I can't help you. And I can't fight your monsters on my own."

When he stayed silent, although it made my chest ache to do it, I walked out and left him behind.

The air had already been heavy with humidity, with heat. Now it was heavy with things left unspoken, things that weighed on both of us.

When we reentered Moses's house, everyone turned to look at us. To gauge what had happened—and what might happen next.

"Power supply," I said, walking to Moses and handing him the box. "You need anything else, you can find it yourself."

His gaze narrowed, but he turned it on Liam. "I'm so glad the trip was productive."

"Install the damn thing," Liam said.

Moses muttered something under his breath, then hopped off the stool and began to tinker with parts in the case. Plastic, now charred and black, went flying, as he made room for the new piece. He hooked it up, plugged in the system, and looked back at the screen.

But there was only silence. No whirring motors, no bright letters.

"Hmm," Moses said.

"Maybe it was corroded," Gavin said.

"Might have a trick," Moses muttered, then reared back and whopped the case with the side of his fist.

The entire tower shuddered, let out a belch of grinding plastic, and then whirred to life.

"And away we go," he said, and we all moved closer to watch the screen. Liam slipped in beside me, putting his body between me and Malachi.

That was fine. He could do whatever he wanted.

And so could I.

It took Moses a few minutes to get back into Containment-Net, and Gavin cast wary glances at the tower the entire time, waiting for another round of sparks. But the system held together, and Moses made it back to the stub of the file Broussard had reviewed.

"Here we go," he muttered. "File was called . . . Icarus."

"Isn't that a myth?" Gavin asked. "The guy who flew too close to the sun and his wings melted?"

"Yeah," I said, "that's the myth."

"That mean anything to anybody in this context?" Gavin asked. "Regarding Containment or New Orleans or Paranormals?"

When we shook our heads, Gavin looked at Malachi. "The theory is that a lot of our myths come from the Beyond. That we anticipated your existence, or were visited before."

"I know the theory," Malachi said. "And I know the myth. But there's no comparable story in the Beyond. We don't need wings made of wax."

"Fair enough," Gavin said, and glanced at Moses.

"I don't know anything from my corner of the world, either," Moses said, turned back to the screen, pressed a couple more keys. "Presuming Containment's telling the truth about when he died—and who knows if it is—Broussard opened this file less than an hour before he kicked."

"Coincidence?" Gavin asked.

"Maybe," Liam said quietly. "But it's the only lead we've got."

"Did Broussard create the file?" I asked.

It apparently took a moment for him to check. "He did not. The stub doesn't show who created it, only that it wasn't Broussard. It's some kind of binary security feature. 'Yes' if the creator looked at it, 'No' if a stranger to the file's looking at it." Moses traced a finger across the screen, following a line of letters. "I can tell you he sent this file to someone. Can't tell who, but based on the metadata, he looked at it, transmitted it. And that's the last task he performed."

"Can we see the stub again?" Liam asked. "Or what was left of it?"

"You got it," Moses said, then clicked keys emphatically. There was a music to his typing, like he was building songs with the percussion of stubby fingers on keys. "Here we go," he said, and swiveled back so we could see the screen.

"No flames," Gavin said, stepping forward. "That's a good start."

"Har-dee-har-har," Moses said as he frowned at the screen.

"I can't make heads or tails out of it," Gavin said.

The numbers and letters didn't mean anything to me. But the longer I stared at it, the more I thought I could make out a shape.

"It looks like part of a model," I said.

"A model of what?" Gavin asked.

"A molecule, maybe?" I frowned at it, trying to remember something of Mrs. Beauchamp's chemistry class. "We had to make one for our eighth grade science fair with painted foam balls and straws."

When they all gave me blank looks, I waved it off, then pointed at two clusters of letters. "Here and here," I said, "like these are foam balls, and see how they're kind of linked together by these things?" I pointed at the lines, now crooked, that I thought were supposed to connect them. "But instead of balls and straws, there are numbers and letters."

"A molecule," Gavin said. "So this is something scientific." He glanced around the room. "I don't think any of us are scientifically inclined, other than Balls-and-Straws over here, but anybody got any ideas?"

"None," Liam said.

"Science in the Beyond is differently constructed and imagined," Malachi said. "But even so, this doesn't look familiar. We need to talk to Darby."

This would be right up her scientifically minded alley.

"I think I can clean it up," Moses said, fingers busy at the keys again. "Let me do that, and I'll get you a hard copy. She can work her scientific magic on it."

Malachi nodded. "All right."

"It's also probably time to go see Gunnar," Gavin said. "Tell him what we know, and find out what he knows." He glanced at me. "I assume you want to go?"

"Of course. It would be good to see him." The thought of it made me simultaneously excited and nervous. I was pretty sure we had the kind of friendship that could make it through an absence, but this was the first time we'd been apart for so long.

"I'm going to dig around here a little more," Moses said. "Maybe I can find something else."

"Like what?" I asked.

"Identity of the person who created the file, when, maybe a note about related docs. I'll see what else he worked on, in case this is a blind. Lots of information to look through. Whoever among your ilk invented metadata gets a thumbs-up from me."

"We'll be sure to tell him or her," Gavin said, then gestured to the door. "Saddle up."

CHAPTER TEN

Once upon a time, St. Charles Avenue had been an ode to architecture, a boulevard marked by one mansion after another, and the lead-in to a neighborhood of gentility and Southern wealth.

The Landreaus had owned one of those houses, the so-called Palm Tree House, which was as yellow as the cottage near Moses's, had long porches, fancy columns, and dozens of palm trees. The family had refused to give up on or abandon New Orleans. Instead, they'd repaired the damage war had done to the house and lived there still—Gunnar, his parents, and his siblings. It was a testament to their love of New Orleans—and their absolute stubbornness.

It also occurred to me that every one of my friends was stubborn. Probably in part because it was the stubborn people who'd stayed.

Gavin parked on the otherwise empty street, and we took the cobblestone sidewalk to the front door. The house was dark but for the front room, which glowed with light.

He gave the brass door knocker a questioning look, then rapped it lightly.

Seconds later, the door was yanked open. And the man standing there—tall and handsome, with dark, rakish hair that fell over his forehead and teasing, intelligent brown eyes—opened his arms.

I ran past Gavin and into Gunnar's arms.

"It's been too long," Gunnar said. He was tall enough to rest his head atop mine, and his arms were banded around me like I might fly away if he didn't hold tight enough.

"Yeah, it has." I reached up to knuckle away the only tear I'd let fall. "It's good to see you."

He brushed back my hair, pressed a kiss to my forehead. "It's good to see you, too." He looked up, offered nods to Gavin and Malachi, then glared at Liam.

"Well. Look who's here." If anything, Gunnar's embrace tightened. "Let me guess—you pissed off everyone outside New Orleans, too, so you've come home again?"

"Landreau," Gavin said, cutting off the argument. "We need to talk. Can we come in?"

"Just telling it like it is," Gunnar said. He looked down at me, concern in his eyes. "But do come in. I actually have something for you," he said, then released me to push open the door.

She sat on the couch, one leg tucked under the other, a binder in her lap. Her dark hair was curled now into tight ringlets that brushed her shoulders.

"What's going—," Tadji began, then looked up. Her brown eyes went wide with surprise. Then she made a half-scream sound before jumping up, dumping the binder on the floor, and running toward me, the flowy tank she'd paired with leggings and boots shimmering in the air like wings as she moved.

She yanked me into the house, then wrapped me in a fierce hug that almost broke the few ribs Gunnar hadn't managed to crack. She squealed as we swayed back and forth—at least until she let me go and slapped me on the arm. Hard.

"Ow!" I exclaimed, rubbing it. "What was that for?"

"For showing yourself," she said, her eyes brimming with tears. "You're not supposed to be running around the Garden District."

But she pulled me into a hug again. "And I have missed the crap out of you."

Then she pulled back again, slapped my other arm. "Why are you here?"

"Stop the cycle of violence," Gunnar said, extending a hand between us. "Claire, Tadji's glad to see you and concerned about seeing you." He smiled at her. "That cover it?"

"It does." But her eyes were narrow. "For now."

"Good," he said. "There's water in the refrigerator, and the bar's open," he said, as the others filed inside. But no one moved for booze. Not when there was work to be done first.

He closed the door, then turned back to me, ran his hands up and down my arms. "And how are you?" he asked quietly.

"It's been a long couple of days."

Gunnar's gaze found Liam. "I take it that's how long he's been in the universe again."

I nodded, really glad to be back among my allies. "Pretty much."

"He say anything about what happened? Why he left? Maybe groveling for mercy for leaving you behind?"

"Not yet."

Gunnar nodded, looked at Liam. "Never fear, Claire-belle. If the way he looks at you is any indication, it's on its way."

"Where are your parents?" I asked, thinking the house seemed unusually quiet. "Your brother and sister?"

"They left after the battle," he said. "Couldn't stay in the Zone any longer." He glanced back at the room, the fancy Southern décor, like he might be imagining them there, cooking or talking or laughing.

"I'm sorry," I said, and squeezed his hand.

He nodded. "I'm managing. I assume you want to talk about Broussard?" he asked as we moved to stand with the others.

"Among other things," Gavin said. "Let's sit down."

Gunnar didn't look thrilled about taking orders in his own home. But when Gavin took a seat on a yellow gingham sofa, Gunnar went to the windows and began lowering the shades.

"All right," he said, when he'd secured our privacy. "Let's talk."

We joined Gavin on the couches in the living room. Or everyone but Liam did. He stood by the window, apart from the rest of us.

Gavin did the talking, telling Gunnar the parts of the story he hadn't yet heard—from our trip to the bayou, to the bounty hunters, to the roadblock.

Gunnar didn't speak until he looked at me. "You walked into the bayou?"

"Yes."

"With gators and snakes?"

"Yep."

"Should I be pissed you hiked around southern Louisiana even though the Containment heat's been turned up? Or should I be proud you walked among gators and snakes?"

"Technically," Gavin said, before I could answer, "we drove for part of it."

Gunnar slid his gaze to Gavin. "This was your idea?"

"All due respect, since she was a trouper, Claire's really not the focus of this particular story," Gavin said. "We're more concerned about Broussard and this very obvious frame job. And Icarus."

"What's Icarus?"

Gunnar's expression was blank, and he looked genuinely confused. Which was probably what Gavin had been testing.

"The last file Broussard reviewed before he was killed. Assuming Containment's telling the truth about his time of death."

"I'm not going to ask how you know what files Broussard was looking at. But I don't know what Icarus is, and I don't have any more details about the murder than I did the last time we talked." Gunnar looked at Liam. "I'm not involved in the investigation."

"You're second-in-command of Devil's Isle," I said. "How are you not involved?"

"Because you've been shut out," Malachi guessed, and Gunnar nodded.

"He was killed outside Devil's Isle, so his murder is technically outside our jurisdiction. Any normal day, that wouldn't matter. But it seems to matter now, and to people at a higher pay grade than mine. Investigators have been assigned. I don't have access to files, reports, or anything else. I'm shut out completely."

"This the Commandant's doing?" Gavin asked.

"Above his pay grade, too. I don't know who's pulling the strings, but it's someone in the PCC, someone who ranks high enough to shut out the Commandant." He looked at Liam. "Being that I'm the curious sort, I talked to one of those investigators, asked what he believes set you off—why you attacked Broussard when Gracie has been gone for nearly a year. He didn't have a satisfactory answer; he's just assuming you did it."

"That's a shitty investigation," Gavin said.

"It is. I realize Containment isn't perfect. But it's usually minimally competent. That's not what this is."

"It's bigger," I said.

"Yeah. Let's go back to Icarus. What is it?"

"We don't know," Gavin said. "Found a stub of a file that someone tried very diligently to erase."

"And someone else, probably a Para with electronic skills, managed to dig out?" Gunnar asked.

"No comment," Gavin said with a thin smile.

"And did this individual get anything of substance in that stub?"

"It looks like something scientific," Gavin said, glancing at me. "But we don't have enough information to figure out how or what it is."

"You going to talk to Darby?"

"That's the plan."

Gunnar nodded. "That he looked at the file last could be just coincidence."

"Could be," Gavin said. "But it's the lead we've got, so we're following it through."

"Who else knew Liam and Broussard didn't like each other?" I asked. "Does that narrow it down?"

"It doesn't," Gunnar said, and looked over at Liam. "I assume you don't disagree?"

"No," Liam said. "He didn't like me or trust me, and he wasn't shy about sharing that with others."

Gunnar furrowed his brow and nodded. "I can look into this Icarus deal quietly. Assuming it's not personal nonsense he happened to store on our network, it could be a PCC project. If it is, it's not one I'm privy to."

"Is that unusual?" Liam asked.

"Not necessarily. We oversee operations in Devil's Isle, Containment operations in the New Orleans quadrant. That's a small slice of the PCC's pie. But Broussard was one of our people. I'd know about anything he was working on."

"And what was he working on?" Liam asked.

"Nothing unusual," Gunnar said, meeting his gaze. "We're more than a month past the battle and still processing the intel on Reveillon, working through the individuals we arrested. He's been in on that. But Reveillon's old news, according to Gavin's report."

Gavin nodded. "Sporadic discussion in the Zone. No action I could find."

"Like I said, I'll look into it. And I'll let you know what I find."

"There's more," I said, and looked at Malachi. "There are Paranormals at Vacherie. One's sick, and one was sick but passed away. Both were friends of Malachi's."

"Man, I'm sorry," Gunnar said.

Malachi nodded.

"What kind of illness?"

I described what we'd seen. "Does that ring any bells for you? Sound familiar? It's unusual, and we want to make sure it's not spreading."

"I'm not aware of anything," Gunnar said. "Lizzie would know better than me, since she's at the clinic, but she'd have reported something unusual, and she didn't. She did tell me she appreciated your package."

That was something, anyway. "The Paras are being treated at the farm, because they think if they come into the clinic, they won't be able to leave again."

"That's a possibility," Gunnar agreed after a moment. "Based on the phrasing of the regulation."

I nodded. "If you've got any extra medics, maybe you could send someone out to look at them?"

"I'll see what I can do."

"Appreciate it," Malachi said, and Gunnar gave him a nod.

"Go back for a minute," Liam said. "What package did you give Lizzie?" He'd introduced me to her; she'd been his friend first.

"Goods for the clinic," Gavin said. "Delta's been busy in the last few weeks."

"Gunnar arranged the logistics," I explained. "Moses and I scavenge. Lizzie gets whatever we can find for the clinic, and we don't get nabbed for dropping it off."

"How do you do that?" Liam asked.

"Delivery entrance," Gunnar said.

"Devil's Isle doesn't have a delivery entrance."

"It does now," Gunnar said with a smile. "The battle did some damage to the walls. We took the opportunity to do some upgrades."

"They're going to build a gym," Malachi said. "For the residents."

"A gym?" Gavin asked.

"Recreation facility," Gunnar said, "for the kids who've been born in Devil's Isle."

"Innocent kids," I said, and he nodded.

"Yeah. Kids who need an outlet."

"How'd you get the taxpayers to foot the bill for that?" Liam asked.

Gunnar's smile widened. "They didn't. It will be built thanks to a very large donation from the Arsenault Foundation."

Liam's brows lifted in surprise. I guess Eleanor hadn't told him about that, assuming she'd known. The decision could have been made by her friends in Washington.

"There've been a lot of changes while I've been gone."

His words seemed to change the temperature of the room, putting a chill in the air.

"Then maybe you shouldn't have left," Gunnar said. "You ready to talk about that? Because several of us have questions."

"*Many* questions," Tadji said. "And also some declarative sentences."

Liam looked at me, the heat in his eyes sizzling enough to scorch. "I did what I had to do."

"Which was?" Tadji prompted.

There was silence for a long time. And then he looked at me. "What was necessary."

The pain in his eyes was clear enough, and the room went quiet. And so the mystery of Liam's missing weeks still hung in the air.

"Have you been eating?"

I looked at Gunnar, and it took a moment for my brain to catch up with the abrupt shift. "What?"

His gaze narrowed. "You've lost weight you didn't need to lose. I'm making you a grilled cheese sandwich."

"I don't need a grilled cheese sandwich." Never mind that my weight was none of Gunnar's business. But that didn't stop him from playing big brother.

"Tough. I don't need you out there on your own, forgetting to eat."

"I don't forget to eat." I just didn't care that much about it these days. Which, when you put it that way, made it sound like he was right. My jeans had felt a little looser.

Not taking my word for it, Gunnar rose to go into the kitchen.

"I guess we're having grilled cheese," Tadji said, then stood and took my hand. "Come on, Claire. Let's get you fed."

I could feed myself. And did, when I needed food. But the grilled cheese still hit the spot. So did the second one that I accepted after everyone else was satisfied. Gunnar felt better for having done it, and the bread and cheese laid a nice foundation for the alcohol.

We were having an impromptu reunion, after all. And now that the business was done, we decided to make the most of it.

Gunnar played tender at the built-in bar on the other side of the room. "What's everyone drinking?"

He was answered by a chorus of requests.

"Excellent," he said. "You get Sazeracs or you get nothing."

"Claire makes a fantastic Sazerac," Tadji said.

"Oh, I know," Gunnar said with a grin as he added bitters to highball glasses. "Who do you think taught her how to do it?"

"I assumed she taught you," Tadji said with a wink.

"The memory is somewhat hazy," Gunnar said.

She grabbed the first two glasses he'd filled, then gestured toward the door.

"Claire and I are going to take a walk. You gentlemen do what you will."

"Poker?" Gavin asked.

"You cheat," Liam said.

"You just don't like losing." He glanced at Malachi speculatively. "You ever played poker?"

"I have not."

Gavin's grin said all we needed to know about how that was going to go.

Tadji said to me, "Let's go into the orangery."

"You just like saying 'orangery.'"

"True. But mostly I like being in houses that have them."

In that case she'd come to the right place.

The Landreau house was enormous—a late 1920s mansion with a lot of style.

The orangery was pretty much as described: an octagonal peninsula off the back of the house. Five orange trees in terra-cotta pots were blossoming in front of the windows, perfuming the air with floral and citrus scents.

The floor was covered in marble tile, and the ceiling was a cage of glass and steel. If you needed a break from sniffing orange blossoms, there were wicker couches and chairs with deep cushions, and small stone-and-metal tables with matching chairs.

We took seats on the couches. Tadji was already barefoot, and she tucked her feet beneath her as she sat.

"Now that we can talk," she said, turning to face me, "what the hell is the story with Liam?"

"I don't exactly know," I finally said, and told her about our conversation in the garage.

"What do you think happened?"

"No idea. I assume it has something to do with his magic, and that it's not good. But that's based on the look in his eyes. He won't talk about it, and I'm not going to fall at his feet just because he's here."

"Nor should you." She thought for a minute, swirling the liquid in her glass, and nodded. "Ball's in his court until he fesses up."

"Agreed." I took a drink.

It was potent, but layered with flavors. Complex, just like New Orleans. Gunnar did make a pretty good Sazerac.

"I heard about Burke," I said. "Have you heard from him?"

Tadji and Burke, a former Delta member, had been progressing their relationship very slowly—at her request. But he'd been reassigned after the battle, shipped back to DC and PCC headquarters.

"He's doing all right, as far as I can tell."

"And how are you?"

She was quiet for a moment. "Do you believe that absence makes the heart grow fonder?"

"Evidence says yes."

"Well," she said, "then let's just leave it at that."

She was clearly eager to change the subject, so I shifted it back to my first love. "The store looks good."

She looked at me, eyes wide with surprise. And then they narrowed with obvious anger. "What do you mean, 'The store looks good'?"

"Which part are you unhappy about?"

"First of all, the store looks phenomenal," she said, counting off on her fingers. "Second of all, you shouldn't know that. You shouldn't know anything about the store, because you're supposed to be staying away from it."

Perversely, the irritation in her voice made me feel better. If she was angry that I *had* seen her at the store, that meant she wasn't angry that I *hadn't*. She didn't feel burdened by taking it over, or at least not enough to be angry at me over it. That lifted some of the psychic weight I'd been carrying around.

"I just wanted to check on things. How's the dissertation?" I asked, trying to change the subject for my own benefit this time.

"Two more chapters done."

I stared at her. "While running the store on your own? How are you doing that?"

Tadji grinned, pushed hair behind her ear. "Honey, I'm not doing it on my own. I've hired people. There's money in the budget to do that now."

Touché, I thought, with only a little shame that I hadn't been able to get the store to that kind of profitability.

"And, it turns out, I really like being busy. It makes me more productive to have a tight schedule. It's harder to make excuses when you know you have less time. So I made myself a schedule, and I work in the back office while Ezell—he's one of my probationary hires—watches the store."

"There isn't a back office."

She just looked at me, the same way Liam had looked at Gunnar when Gunnar told him about the delivery entry to Devil's Isle.

"Damn, you're good."

"I know," she said with a cheeky grin.

"How do things feel in the Quarter?" I'd missed seeing my regular customers, getting a feel for Containment by watching soldiers moving in and out of the neighborhood. Being in isolation was, well, isolating.

"There's a weird mood," she said, setting her drink on the coffee table.

"How so?"

She frowned, crossed her arms. "Before the battle, we'd gotten comfortable. Maybe not entirely comfortable with Devil's Isle, but we'd gotten used to the way things were."

I nodded. We'd learned to survive during the war. When it was over, it had taken time for us to accept that we were safe, that a battalion of Valkyries wasn't heading for the city, golden weapons at the ready. But we'd made new lives, begun to accept our new world.

"Since the battle," she continued, "it's like we're waiting for the other shoe to drop. For another battle to begin. People look over their shoulders a lot more, wondering if there are more Reveillon members out there.

"But at the same time," she said, "there's a new kind of camaraderie because we fought together. Citizens and soldiers and Paras. We hold coffee klatch on Thursday nights. Someone brings coffee, someone brings a snack, I bring the room and the electricity. And we talk. We're honest. That's a pretty big change."

"It's good," I agreed. "It's very good." I thought of Broussard and the apparent frame job. If anyone knew the word on the streets of New Orleans, it was the woman who ran Royal Mercantile.

And I felt a little pang that I wasn't that woman right now.

"What are you hearing about Containment?"

She glanced back at the doorway, checking that we had privacy. "Nothing about Icarus. If that's part of this. I haven't heard the word since my last myth and mythology class."

"If you hear anything specific, let me know."

"I will." She crossed her legs. "What have you been doing since the battle? Other than delivering goods to the clinic and occasionally spying on my store?"

That was pretty much it. Like everyone else in the Zone, I'd been surviving. There wasn't much to say beyond that. But I told her what there was to tell.

"And how is Moses?" she asked with a grin.

"Grouchy."

"So about the same."

"Pretty much."

She paused. "What are you going to do about Liam?"

"I don't know. I guess just see where it goes."

She patted my leg. "You look exhausted, and you've had a helluva day. You'll get some sleep, let it simmer, and have a clearer outlook."

I hoped she was right. Because right now things were pretty damn murky.

CHAPTER ELEVEN

I was hoping for a ride back to the gas station. It was more than four miles from Gunnar's house, and I'd done plenty of miles today. Besides, the Sazerac was doing its job. My legs felt all warm and soft. By the time we got back to the living room—a good two-minute walk from the orangery—I was ready for bed.

But we found the living room empty.

"Maybe the poker went bad, so they decided to go with a duel?"

"Possible," I said, "but I don't think Gunnar would allow that."

Voices lifted from the doorway on the other side of the room, so we walked that way. And stared.

At the very formal dining table, in a room with walls papered in large flowers, sat four attractive men, shirts discarded, locked in combat. They faced each other in pairs, right hands locked together.

They were arm wrestling.

"Did I drink straight absinthe?" Tadji asked, cocking her head at the scene.

"If so, we both did."

"Not that I'm complaining," Tadji said, her gaze full of appreciation.

Gunnar glanced up at us, sweat popping out on his brow, biceps bulging as he and Gavin struggled for control. "Gun. Show," he muttered through teeth clenched in concentration.

"And are we fighting for money," Tadji asked, "or just to caress our egos?"

"For glory," Gavin said, but didn't take his gaze off his opponent.

Malachi and Liam didn't talk at all. They just stared at each other, knuckles white with effort as they battled.

"Go blow in his ear," Tadji whispered. "Distract him."

"Which one of them?"

"That's my girl," she said with a grin. "Gentlemen, it's getting late. So if you'll wrap up . . . whatever this is, someone needs to give my girl here a ride back to her sanctuary."

There were manly grunts, guttural screams, and finally fists pounded the table.

Gunnar beat Gavin.

Liam beat Malachi.

More power to them.

Gavin rubbed his wrist. "Haven't had a workout like that in a while."

"Y'all have the brains of a fourteen-year-old boy," Tadji said. "Collectively."

"Probably." He glanced at Liam. "Big brother managed a good win."

Without comment, Liam stood and put his T-shirt back on. And didn't bother to avert his gaze. He watched me as I watched him, and there shouldn't have been so much power in a look, in the simple act of a beautiful man pulling a shirt on.

"Oh, you are hosed," Gunnar muttered, sliding behind me to grab his own shirt. "Not that I can fault your taste."

"Physically, no," I said. "But emotionally?"

"Maybe he'll have convincing things to say."

Maybe. But he had to be willing to talk. And he wasn't there yet. I didn't know what could happen between us—but I knew it could only start with honesty.

"You can sleep here," Gunnar said to me. "Plenty of bedrooms."

The idea was inviting—spending the night in a cozy bed in this castle of a house, knowing that I wouldn't be alone. But my being here would put him in danger, and that wasn't worth the risk.

"Thanks, but no, thanks. I'll head home."

"When will I see you again?" Tadji asked, concern pinching her features.

"I don't know." I'd tried to reassure myself that solitude wouldn't last forever. But so far, Containment was still Containment. "Hopefully sooner rather than later."

"If I find out anything on my end," Gunnar said, "I'll let you know. I'm going to have to look into it very discreetly. So it may not be tomorrow. But I'll let you know as soon as I have information."

"We can meet at Moses's house in the morning," I suggested. "Maybe he's found something else about the stub."

Gunnar nodded. "Fine by me."

"While we're making arrangements," Liam said, "I want to see Broussard's place."

Gunnar was quiet for a moment. "That will take time to arrange. The building's sealed, and I don't have authority to let you in."

"How long?"

"A few days, maybe. I'll have to call in a favor."

That didn't calm Liam's obvious impatience. "I'm accused of killing him. I have the right to see the scene, to see what I'm accused of."

"You don't, actually," Gunnar said. He was as calm as Liam was agitated. "You're a suspect in a particularly gruesome murder, and you are absolutely not allowed to contaminate the scene."

"Or risk adding your DNA to the evidentiary mix," I said. "You'd implicate yourself."

"Claire has a point." Gunnar held up his hands. "I'll work as quickly as I can. But you'll only make things worse for yourself if you go without my okay."

"I'm not making any promises."

"Stubborn ass," Gunnar muttered.

"It's genetic," Gavin said, then looked at me. "Since we're wrapping up here, you want a ride back?"

Thank God. "You can take me to the alley. That's as far as you can go."

"If I had a nickel . . . ," Gavin said.

"I'll go, walk you the rest of the way," Malachi said.

"You know where she lives?"

Gavin's question was pouty; Liam's gaze was downright hostile.

"He's already public enemy number one," I said. "Not much harm in his knowing. And there's no need to add anyone else to the list."

After the dark ride back to Mid-City, Gavin turned into the alley.

"Thank you for the ride," I said as Malachi and I climbed out.

"Sure thing," Gavin said. "I'll see you tomorrow?"

"Yep."

Liam looked at me through his open window, a challenge in his eyes. "Be careful," he quietly said.

The tone of his voice, the possessiveness in it, lifted goose bumps on my arms even while it irritated me. "I'm always careful."

"Claire."

I looked back at him, watched gold flare in his eyes. "I told you what I need, Liam."

His jaw clenched, but after a moment the stubbornness in his expression faded, shifted into clear regret. *"Claire,"* he said again, this time an entreaty.

I shook my head. "I get all of you. Or you get none."

He looked away. That I knew we were both hurting was the only reason I wasn't more angry with him.

"Humans, sometimes, are just the worst," I said, when the Range Rover's lights disappeared around the corner. It didn't help that I was tired and feeling helpless. And already missing Tadji, and feeling a little hopeless about that.

"No argument there," Malachi said.

We walked quietly to the gas station. We stopped across the street, where Malachi would wait and watch for me to get safely inside.

Maybe it was time to make a gesture. To take a chance on doing something big. Something right.

"Come on," I said, motioning toward the building. "I want to show you something."

He looked surprised but intrigued. "All right," he said.

We waited to ensure that the coast was clear, and then I headed for the door. "With me," I said.

"You want me to come in?"

"It's only fair," I said, and unlocked it.

We walked inside. I closed and locked the door behind us, then flipped on the overhead lights.

Malachi stared at the room, walked slowly to the first table, looked down at the objects there. *"Claire,"* he said.

"My father saved them from Containment fires," I said.

He walked to the middle table, long and narrow and hewn of thick, dark planks, and picked up a golden bow, ran the tip of his finger down the sinewy string.

"You've kept this secret." He put it down again, then looked back at me, considered. "To ensure that Containment doesn't find out about it."

I nodded. "And that no one gets hurt because they try to find out."

Malachi nodded, looked back at the table. "I don't know how I feel about that."

"Welcome to my world. They'd destroy the weapons if they could. Containment, I mean."

"Or use them for their own purposes." He walked around the table, surveyed the objects on the next one. "I can hardly take it all in."

"I said the same thing the first time."

Malachi frowned at some objects, smiled at others. "There are Consularis and Court objects here."

"Are there? I'd wondered. I don't know anything about how my father gathered these things, but I figured he'd take whatever he could get. I started to catalog it, but I don't know the proper names of everything, and I felt a little stupid writing down human ones."

Malachi was looking at what appeared to be a square tambourine—a rigid form hung with tiny cymbals and bells. "Do you know what this is?"

"Tambourine?"

He smiled. "Something like that. It's called an *Ilgitska*. It's used in a sexual ceremony."

"A sexual ceremony?" I asked, giving it a second look.

"We liked our ceremonies," he said with a smile, probably because of the flush in my cheeks. He picked it up, slapped it against the palm of his hand.

The sound was complex, from the delicate and pretty *ping* of bells to the deep, hollow tones of small brass spheres. I could admit there was something sensual about it, as if each tone had been carefully modulated to stoke desire.

What a weird day this had been. And what a weird night it had become.

"Sound has power," he said with a smile, setting the instrument on the table again. "Your father has done a great service, saving these things."

I nodded. "Thank you. I'd like to think so. I only learned about this a little before the battle. He didn't tell me when he was building the collection, and I didn't know until after he was gone. That hurts. But I know why he kept me from it."

"To keep you safe," Malachi said.

"Yeah. One of the many things he kept from me." I took a deep breath, readied myself, and turned to him. "I need to ask you about Erida."

"You can ask, although I may not be able to answer. What do you want to know?"

I still paused before saying it. "Erida and my father."

He didn't answer immediately. "Was that the question?"

"It was an opener," I said lamely. "They were friends?"

He looked at me for what felt like a really long time. "They were friends," he said finally. "And more."

That confirmed it. "They were lovers," I said. "I thought that might have been the case, after what she told me last night. But I didn't know he was seeing anyone. I never saw her, and he never said anything."

Malachi nodded. "They were very discreet, I understand. By necessity. If they had been found out, she would have been incarcerated, and he would have been punished for harboring a Paranormal."

"Did you know my mother?"

"I did not know her. I've apparently seen her."

"What do you mean?"

"I did not know she was your mother at the time I saw her. Erida told me later."

I told him what I'd believed to be true.

"I'm sorry your father didn't tell you the truth."

"So am I." Because that's what we'd come to. That my father had been lying to me. "Erida said she knew her, but I didn't know her—or anything about her."

"She was a lovely woman, although I understand she was cold."

I nodded. "Come with me." We walked through the kitchenette, then through the narrow door that led to the basement.

The room had probably once been storage for the gas station, and a way to access cars on the first floor via hatches that opened beneath them. It now held rows of metal shelves with water and canned goods, as well as the small cot where I slept.

It also held the trunk that contained only one item—the photograph of the woman with red hair.

Liam and I had taken the photograph away the night we'd discovered this place; I'd taken it back after the battle, put it back in the place where I'd found it.

I lifted the trunk lid and pulled out the picture. I offered it to Malachi, without looking at the image. I'd looked at it too many times already.

"I found the photograph here," I said. "There's no writing on it. I assumed my father had left it, but I didn't know why. She looks like me. And after talking to Erida . . ."

Malachi nodded. "I understand this is your mother. She does look like you." His voice was gentle now.

I looked up at him. "You could both be wrong. This could be a misunderstanding or a coincidence." But that sounded stupid and naive even to me. And I was the one who'd believed a lie for more than twenty years. Who'd been lied to for more than twenty years.

"I understand your father told everyone she was gone. He told Erida the truth only after she found a photograph of her."

My stomach clenched again. "This photograph?" Is that why it had been in the trunk? Had he locked it away so she wouldn't have to see it?

"I don't know. I'm sorry."

I nodded. "Has Erida been here?"

"I knew nothing about this place. If Erida had known, I believe she'd have told me." He looked around. "Or perhaps it would be more accurate to say that I believe she would have told me if she'd known what it held. I don't know how much your father told her."

I nodded, made myself look down at the picture. "This woman was at Talisheek."

His brows lifted. "Was she?"

"Not on our side. She was with the group that had tried to reopen the Veil. Does she work for Containment?"

"I don't know. I don't know anything about her. I don't believe your father spoke about her, and I don't believe Erida asked many questions. But Erida may know more than I do, more that she hasn't told me. You should talk to her."

When I didn't speak, he looked back at me. "It's not her fault your father lied to you."

I knew that, too. But that didn't make it easier.

"You're right." I put the photograph away and closed the lid of the trunk, wishing I could compartmentalize my feelings as easily.

I didn't sleep. Not really.

My brain was spinning with new truths and old lies. Liam and his unknown demons. My mother, my father and his lies.

I tried to flip back through the catalog of memories, of every time I'd asked about my mother, and everything he'd told me in response. I tried to remember his expressions. Had he looked like he was lying?

And that wasn't even the biggest question. The hardest question.

If she was alive, where had she been for the last twenty-two years? Why had she left my father, and why had she left me? Why had she willingly let me go? Did she wonder what I looked like, if I'd survived the war, who I'd grown up to be?

Given the life I'd seen my father lead, I still believed he was a good man, a decent man. Nothing Erida or Malachi had told me changed that. But he hadn't been an honest man. Not about this place, not about magic, not about who he'd been, not about Erida, not about my mother.

Layers of lies, stacked one atop the other. And I was left to unravel them all.

CHAPTER TWELVE

It was already scorching by the time I got to Moses's place. It didn't help my mood when I learned it was missing one magically enhanced human.

"Liam was supposed to stay here," I said to Moses. "He shouldn't be wandering around New Orleans alone."

"He left a note," Moses said, offering up the small sheet of paper pulled from a notebook, the edges still frayed.

"'Went to take a look,'" I read aloud, then looked at Moses. "A look at what?"

"He's here because Broussard's dead. My guess? Broussard's house."

My eyes narrowed. "He should have stayed in the damn bayou. Should have stayed there where Eleanor could keep an eye on him. And he certainly should have stayed here with you until someone could watch his back. Gunnar told him not to go over there."

"If you were in his position, would you do anything different?"

I growled, then glanced around. "Malachi?"

"Sent a pigeon." In the Zone, they were one of the most reliable ways to pass messages. "Said he was going back to Vacherie to check in on the Paras."

I nodded. That meant I was closer to Broussard's place than Malachi was, so it was up to me to find Liam. At least I'd get a look at the scene of the crime.

"You better get moving," Moses said. "I'll stay here in case he comes back."

"You get anything else out of that Icarus file?"

"I'm still looking. Quit rushing my genius."

Everyone was grouchy today. "Stay here, lay low, and keep geniusing."

He grinned toothily. "I got canned foods and a working comp. I don't need to go anywhere else."

Whatever kept him safe.

Broussard made a good living, if his place was any indication. There wasn't a lot of money in the Zone, but he'd managed to get into a gorgeous house in the Garden District just a stone's throw from St. Charles and not far from Gunnar's.

Broussard's house sat behind a fenced front yard full of palm trees and hedges, and a long driveway that would have made plenty of New Orleanians jealous, before or after the war.

The house was an ivory box with symmetrical windows and blue shutters. Double stairs curved up to a red front door. And yellow police tape marked it as a crime scene.

I stood beneath an oak tree on the neighboring property, watching for any sign of Liam. If he was in there, he was being quiet about it.

"At least he hasn't lost his damn mind completely," I murmured. I crept along the hedge that divided the properties, looking for a way in. I found a floor-to-ceiling window already pushed open. Probably how he'd have gotten inside.

I darted across the yard and slipped through the window, which opened into a dining room. Pine floors, plastered walls with crown molding, an enormous inlaid table with curving chairs, an antique rug. The ceilings were high, as were the doorways.

I moved into the hallway, the walls lined with paintings in gilded frames. This was the kind of house my father would have loved to live in, if he'd been able to keep an antique for more than a few days, instead of putting it in the store for sale.

Across from the dining room was a formal living room with the same windows and molding, a brick fireplace that stretched to the ceiling, and a hearth of shiny tiles in shades of green.

The floor above me creaked. I took the double staircase to the second floor.

Liam stood on the landing, staring at the wall.

I was prepared to lay into him—for leaving Moses's house alone, for walking into a crime scene—and then I saw what he was staring at.

FOR GRACIE was painted on the wall in what looked like blood, and there was a stain the same color on the floor in front of it.

Liam's body was rigid, his eyes blazing with anger, as if he might be able to burn the letters off the wall by strength of will alone.

"Liam."

His body jerked, but he didn't turn around. He hadn't heard me come in, which proved he shouldn't have been here alone. He might not have heard hunters, either.

"Are you all right?"

"Would you be?"

"No," I said. "No, if I saw the name of someone I loved spread across the wall, an excuse for someone else's murder, I'd be absolutely furious. But still. You shouldn't have come without Gunnar's okay. Without him clearing a path."

He turned, looked at me for the first time, and I gasped before I could help myself. His eyes glowed golden, fury and grief battling on his face.

"I couldn't wait anymore. They're using me, my family, to hurt people. I want to know why."

I nodded. I couldn't argue with that. And since we were already here, we'd might as well investigate.

"All right," I said. "What do we know?"

He looked back at me, the question clear in his eyes.

"I came here to find you, and I did," I said. "I'm not going to leave you here alone with Containment roaming around."

I didn't mean that as an insult, as a snipe because he'd done exactly that to me after the battle—he'd left me in New Orleans, with Containment roaming around. But it sounded that way, and silence fell again, thick and uncomfortable.

Big-girl panties, I told myself, and walked closer to the wall. "Is it blood?"

I could feel his gaze on mine for a minute, evaluating. And then he shifted his attention back to the wall. "Yes. Don't know if it's Broussard's, but you can smell that it's blood."

I could, now that I'd gotten closer. I looked over at him. "The name and the knife are the only facts that tie the murder to you. You ready to talk about the knife?"

"No."

I sighed. "Then let's bypass the evidence against you for the moment. Let's see if there's something here that tells us about the actual killer. Maybe we'll find something out of place, something that suggests why Broussard was targeted."

His expression didn't change much, but he nodded.

"All right, then. The writing." The letters were written in big, wide streaks, not unlike the way business names and slogans might have been painted onto store windows once upon a time.

"The letters weren't written with just a fingertip."

Liam looked at me. "What?"

I held a finger in front of the wall. "The line's too wide." I fisted my hand, held it against the wall. "And that movement's just awkward."

"Maybe they used something they found here."

We looked around. There was nothing on the landing, no pots of faux flowers or knickknacks that could have been adapted to the task.

"Maybe they came prepared," I said. "To kill Broussard, and to blame someone else for his murder. To blame you for it. So they brought a paintbrush or something. And maybe they were sloppy about it. See any fingerprints?"

Liam stepped closer, peered at the wall. I did the same thing. But if there were fingerprints, I couldn't tell from a look at a dark second-floor landing.

"Can't tell," he said.

"Me, either."

I stepped back, looked at the stain on the floor.

"His throat was slit. Effective, and I guess kind of intimate, because you have to be up close. But it's also not very heat of the moment. You don't accidentally slit someone's throat. That's not something you build up to in a fight. That's something you come here to do."

"And why?" Liam asked. "Money? Love? Punishment?"

"Not money," I said. "There are plenty of nice antiques down there, and none of them were taken."

"You do know antiques."

"I do. Granted, it's hard to get rid of antiques in New Orleans right now. But if the perp's willing to kill for money, why not grab a couple of things on the way out?"

"You're right. I don't see anything obviously missing."

"As for love, you know anything about him being in a relationship?"

Liam shook his head. "No, but I don't think I would have."

"And we don't know anything about punishment. Maybe Icarus matters, maybe it doesn't. We don't know yet."

"That's pretty much it." His gaze locked onto his sister's name again, and I decided it was time to get him away from this spot.

"Let's look around," I said.

The hallway split left and right. "I'll go right."

"Then I'll go left."

We parted in the middle of the landing. The hallway on the left had several open doors. Bathroom, which looked pretty standard. What I supposed was a guest room, since it held a perfectly made bed, a nightstand, and a bureau. I checked a couple of drawers, found nothing. And nothing in the closet, either.

A long linen closet filled the other side of the hallway. I pushed open one sliding door. Most of the cubbies and hanging bars were empty, except for one tower of shelves that held folded sheets and pillowcases. I gave them a quick pat-down, but didn't find anything interesting.

The hallway ended in a doorway, the door half-closed. I listened, ensured that nothing was moving on the other side, then pushed it open.

And found Broussard's office.

"Here we go," I murmured, stepping inside.

The room was big, an enormous curving desk nestled in an oc tagonal bay window. Hardwood floors, a heavy credenza with bookshelves on the other side of the room. A couple of potted plants, a nice rug in the middle of the room.

The books were old, with leather spines, and they weren't about any particular subject. Probably ordered them by the yard to fill up the space.

I moved around the desk. Old-fashioned leather blotter. Pen cup. Memo pad. All of it monogrammed with an equally old-fashioned "B." But there was no pad of paper, and there was no computer. I pulled out my penlight, shone it on the desktop, and found a perfectly clean square where a computer had once been.

"Crafty," I murmured, then sat down in the desk chair—also large and leather. Being careful not to leave fingerprints, I used the hem of my shirt to pull open the left and right drawers, found the usual desk-drawer stuff. Paper clips. Scissors. Stapler. The middle drawer was a keyboard tray. The keyboard was still there, the cord dangling loose at the back.

I looked through the rest of the room, didn't find anything interesting. If Broussard kept secret or controversial information here, it wasn't in his office. Or at least not anymore.

"His computer's gone," I told Liam when we met on the landing again. "You can actually see the edges where the dust had gathered."

"So they took his comp and didn't bother to clean up after themselves."

"That would be my guess. You notice anything else missing?"

"No—although I've never been in here before, so it's hard to say. But there's nothing obvious. No blank space on the wall where a picture was removed, no wall safe with the door hanging open."

"Would have been super handy to find one of those, maybe with a little scrap of paper with the bad guy's name on it."

Liam grinned. "Handy, but unlikely." His expression darkened when his gaze fell on the wall again. "Nothing of value taken, and nothing obvious missing but his computer. He was killed expediently and the perp seemed to be prepared. That confirms our theory—that Broussard found something he wasn't supposed to, and someone didn't want him looking at it."

"Icarus, maybe."

"Maybe. The computer would be a help. Maybe we'll get lucky and find that they've hooked it up to Containment-Net and Moses can somehow backtrack into it."

That would be lucky, and stupid of the perp. But if this was a Containment matter, it was certainly possible.

"You clean up after yourself?" Liam asked. "No fingerprints?"

I shook my head. "I'm good."

"Then we should get out of here," he said. "Containment could come back anytime."

Unfortunately, we'd already overstayed our welcome.

They roared through the front door. Three of them—two men and a woman, all three dressed in black fatigues and combat boots, hair clipped short in military fashion, Containment patches on their arms.

All three pointed guns at us.

"Hands in the air," said the man in front.

"No problem," Liam said, lifting his hands as we walked down the final flight of stairs into the wide hallway. "I'm glad you're here. We've got some information for you."

I managed not to blink, figured he had a plan, and tried to look relieved.

The agents looked momentarily confused, but they were well enough trained that they stayed in position, weapons still pointed. "What information?"

"We saw someone running out of here with a box. Not sure what was in it." Hands still in the air, he pointed at me with a finger. "We saw the tape around the house, figured we better see what was happening. They ran out past us, knocked her down." He bobbed his head toward the open window. "Headed downriver, I think."

The Quinn boys were definitely crafty. And disturbingly good liars.

"You're Liam Quinn," said the female agent. She glanced at me, my hair. "And you're Claire Connolly. We've seen your pictures."

Liam frowned. "I'm not sure what you—did you see the man running? With the box? He looked like a looter, honestly. Ran back down St. Charles?"

The agents had their doubts, but the earnestness in his voice was convincing, even to me. Like synchronized birds in flight, they simultaneously looked out the window.

Liam took the opportunity. He ran forward, taking down the agent in front, then sending the other two off balance. They hit the floor like bowling pins.

"Go!" Liam shouted to me, and began to grapple with the man on the ground.

I didn't have a weapon, not that getting into a gunfight with Containment was a good idea. But I also wasn't about to run and leave him alone with three agents and the same number of weapons. I wasn't that much of a hypocrite.

The two of us would still be outnumbered. But at least the odds would be better.

The female agent was closest, so I went to her first, used the same trick Liam had, and tried to haul her to the floor.

Already off balance, we landed in the dining room doorway together. I smashed my elbow, felt the vibration in the nerve in my teeth. The fingers on my right hand went numb, so I grabbed at the gun with my left, tried to wrangle it out of her grasp.

"Stop!" she yelled, and tried to kick me, but I kept my grip, and my focus, on her hand. I slammed it against the floor, once, twice, a third time.

The gun bounced loose.

I was up in a moment, grabbed it, was about to aim it in Liam's general direction, when a bus hit me from behind.

I'd forgotten about the third agent. And that wasn't smart.

He was at least two hundred pounds of bulk and muscle. I hit the floor on my stomach, his weight added to that, with enough force to push the air out of my lungs and send the gun skittering across the room. He moved to his knees and pulled my wrists behind me.

"I told you to put your goddamn hands in the goddamn air!" he said, nearly yanking my shoulder out of joint.

I didn't want to use magic. Not like this, not in front of Containment agents who already believed we were monsters.

But the woman was on her feet, going for her gun. Liam was still tangled up with the second agent, fists and sweat flying as they grappled. If they took us in after this, we'd be in trouble. Not only a Sensitive and a murder suspect, but fugitives who'd resisted arrest and injured officers in the process.

I didn't have a choice, and that just made me angrier.

I tried to gauge my best options, then gathered up filaments of magic that waited at the ready to be twined and used. To be manipulated against humans.

Alone in the air, the evanescent strands weren't powerful enough to trigger a magic monitor. But gathered together, as I was doing now, they were. An alarm began to wail outside, and the monitor issued an audio warning. *"Containment has been alerted. Containment has been alerted. Containment has been alerted."*

No shit, I thought, and reached out mentally toward the room across the hall, threw the magic at the ornate poker beside the brick-and-tile fireplace in the living room, and zipped it toward me so fast the air sang from the movement.

"Watch out!" The agent scrambled off me. "She's using magic!"

I reached out with the poker and knocked the gun from his hand. It skittered across the hardwood and beneath a sofa. Out of easy reach.

"Good enough," I murmured, and gripped the poker like a baseball bat. "Who's next?"

The air exploded, pain searing across my biceps like God's own fire. I looked back and saw the female agent literally holding the smoking gun.

"You *shot* me."

She'd calmed down, concentration and heat back in her eyes. "You're Claire Connolly, a Sensitive. You're outside Devil's Isle in direct violation of the Magic Act. You will put the weapon down and surrender yourself into the custody of Containment."

"Containment has been alerted. Containment has been alerted."

I ignored the irritating drone of the alarm, the violent throb of pain in my arm, and stared back at her. The flame of my anger was hot enough to scorch anything in its path.

"I'm Claire Connolly, a Sensitive. I helped warn you about Reveillon, and I fought in the Battle of Devil's Isle." I pointed a finger at my chest. "*I* took him down. And you want to arrest me."

She wet her lips nervously. "I'm ordered to take you in. You have magic."

"Not by choice."

"I'm ordered—"

"I don't give a crap about your orders. One of us is going back to the Cabildo today, but it won't be me."

When I felt the other agent moving behind me, I decided we'd had enough talk.

There was more magic in the air, and it waited to be used. Yearned to be used. I knitted it together, wrapped the tendrils around her gun, and yanked it out of her hand. Whatever I felt about Containment, given how much trouble we were already in, I wasn't going to pull a gun on her, so I stuffed it into my jeans.

I saw the shifting of her eyes, but didn't realize until it was too late that she was passing a message to her partner.

He hit me first, grabbing my legs and sending me to the floor. She piled on top, ripping her gun out of my jeans with a scrape against my skin. And then her weight was gone, and he grabbed my arms again and put a knee in my back, mashing my face and chest into the hard floor. I couldn't see, could hardly breathe, couldn't even think about magic.

That's when the world went hot.

It was a kiss by lightning, an embrace by pure electricity. Power subsumed me, coated me, and very nearly drowned me. Had I been stunned? Shot not by a gun but by one of the electric stunners some Containment agents carried?

It took a moment to realize this wasn't human power.

It was magic. Pure and barely controlled.

It was Liam.

I shifted my gaze to look, could just barely see him across the room, standing over the unconscious body of the other agent. The agent on my back couldn't see him; he was too focused on wrangling the handcuffs I could hear jangling behind me. It was better that he hadn't looked, that he was completely oblivious to the golden gleam in Liam's eyes, the fury on his face.

His magic burned like fire, with a rawness that I hadn't felt from Malachi's magic. But I still wasn't sure what it could do. What he could do with it.

He taught me quickly enough.

He condensed his power, his magic, and wrapped it around mine. The same way I braided filaments of magic to manipulate them, he braided the forks of our magic together, and then he used it. He lassoed the agent on my back with the magic and lifted him into the air.

Gasping, I turned over and watched the agent floating upward, his eyes wide with shock.

Liam was controlling my magic. Directing it and making it stronger by adding his own to the mix, like he'd turned up the volume on my own telekinesis.

And then Liam, or I, or the two of us together, tossed the agent across the room like a discarded toy. He flew into the opposite wall, knocking down a gilt-framed portrait on the way, then hitting the floor, eyes closed.

But the envelope taped to the wall—an envelope that had been hidden behind the painting—remained.

It would have to wait.

The female agent aimed the gun again, fired twice in quick succession.

My arm was up and moving before I could register the sound, and certainly before I could grab magic out of the air. I held out a hand, slowed the bullets to a crawl, and then a stop. And then I brushed them away. They clinked to the ground.

"I didn't ask for this," I told her. "Go back to the Cabildo and tell them that."

Tears wobbling in her eyes, she climbed to her feet and ran for the door.

Liam released his magic.

As if that had been holding me aloft, too, I fell to my knees, breathed heavily as silence fell over the room, sunlight glittering through the dust we'd raised during the fight.

I looked down at my fingers, half expecting to see power pouring out like white-blue plasma and my skin charred from the heat. But they were fine. I'd been filled with magic, but my body seemed to be holding. At least for now.

"You're all right?"

I nodded, didn't look at him. "I'm fine."

"Your arm?"

Right. Adrenaline had muted the pain, but it came back now with a vengeance. I winced, rotated my arm and took a look. There was blood, but not a lot.

"Just skimmed me." I looked up. He was sweating from the effort, his knuckles bruised, the hem on his T-shirt nearly ripped off, and there was a cut across his cheekbone. "Are you okay?"

He nodded. He still hadn't come closer, so I figured I needed to be the one who said it.

"You can manipulate the magic of others."

He winced at "manipulate," but there was no helping it, since that was exactly what he'd done. "Yeah."

"Handy." And potentially dangerous, especially in the wrong hands. I didn't think his were the wrong hands, though.

"I didn't hurt you?"

I shook my head, which made it throb with pain. "Just a little worn-out. I'll be fine. Packs a powerful punch."

"Yeah." He ran a hand through his hair. "I've been working on that. Not perfected yet."

He looked at the empty bit of wall space—and the manila envelope taped there.

Then he walked to me, offered a hand. He seemed surprised when I didn't hesitate, when I put my hand in his, let him pull me to my feet.

We approached the wall and Liam pulled the envelope away, was about to run a finger under the sealed tab when a new siren cut through the quiet. Containment had arrived. Again.

"That's our cue to exit," Liam said. He slid the envelope into his shirt, then tucked in the hem to keep it safe. He quickly rehung the painting, then looked at me. "You ready?"

I nodded.

This time, we ran together.

CHAPTER THIRTEEN

We aimed for Moses's house, but stopped about halfway there, just in case we'd been followed or Containment was watching. We didn't want to lead them right to him.

We found a courtyard garden nearly overgrown by mandevilla and jasmine, and all the more hidden because of it. It was cool here, the air perfumed with flowers and brick laid in intricate patterns underfoot. I sat on the ground, my back against the only wall not yet covered with a tangle of green.

He stood near the far wall, looking out at the street through a window made of carefully arranged bricks. He was smart enough to give me room, to give me space. Just like I'd given him once upon a time.

"Welcome to the outcast club," I quietly said, breaking the ice that had gathered between us despite the heat.

"So far, it's a shitty club."

"It doesn't get better." I thought of the Paranormals at Vacherie, the suspicion in their eyes. "Humans are suspicious of you; Paras are suspicious of you. But you do have that cool eye thing going."

He glanced at me, gold still shining in his eyes.

"But harder to hide your magic," I said.

He looked back at me. "Do you see now?"

There was something grave in his voice. Something sad, and something angry.

"Do I see what?"

"Your magic is neutral. Mine is furious."

His hands were fisted on his hips, his lean body still stiff.

"During the battle, he hit me with a blast of magic." He turned back, fingers against his chest like a cage. "I could feel it, sinking in. Affecting me. Changing me. It wasn't just magic, Claire. It was Ezekiel's magic."

Ezekiel had been the leader of Reveillon, a Sensitive who'd suppressed his own magic and been destroyed by it.

I just looked at him, confused. "I don't know what you mean."

"When she was hit, Eleanor lost her vision, but gained her sight. The Para that hit her was a seer, and the weapon carried residual power."

I hadn't known that—hadn't even known it was possible that humans who gained power directly from Paras were affected by it that way.

Did the magic make the Paranormal, or did the Paranormal color the magic?

"And you think Ezekiel's magic had some of him in it?"

He turned back to me, gold churning in his eyes like a tempest. "I know that it did. It took a few seconds before I could move again, before I could do anything other than lie there, the magic like needles in my skin."

"I remember. I went to get Lizzie. You were gone when I got back."

He nodded. "I got to my feet, and it ravaged me, Claire. I had no power over it." His gaze softened, like he was staring at a memory. "A Reveillon member was beside me, on his knees. He'd been hit by something—there was a knot on his head, and he was staring at the ground, totally dazed. And none of that mattered. Because I wanted to kill him. Before I knew it, my hands were wrapped around his neck, and I could feel Ezekiel's fire in my skin, beneath my hands."

Liam stared down at his hands. He extended his fingers, then clenched them into fists, as if he could feel those flames and that power again.

"It was a battle," I said. My voice sounded quiet, far away. "He was trying to kill you. All of us. There's no shame in wanting him dead, or in killing him. That's just war."

"Not sitting there on the ground, only half aware of what was happening. But to the magic that didn't matter." He looked back at me.

Something clenched in my stomach at the look in his eyes. It was feral.

No, I realized. It was *Paranormal*. I knew only some of the basics of Paranormal biology, but I'd seen that primal hunger before—in the eyes of Paras who'd wanted to kill me and everyone else during the war.

"I was so angry. So full of hate I could hardly see through it. It was a haze across my vision." His eyes focused again, and he looked at me. "I held his life, quite literally, in my hands."

"You could use Ezekiel's magic." And it had been a sight—the hot fire that had burst from Ezekiel's mouth. He could literally scream fire.

Liam nodded.

"And still, even though the Reveillon member tried to kill you, you didn't kill him."

"I could have. I could have so easily done it. I could feel his pulse beneath my hands, and see that look of disgust in his eyes. Even dazed, he could see what I was. What I'd become. And when he realized what I could do, that disgust turned to fear. He pissed himself, sitting there, waiting to die."

He went quiet, the memory all but poisoning the air around us.

"You *chose* not to kill him," I insisted.

"No, I *managed* not to kill him." Liam walked toward me, held his thumb and forefinger a millimeter apart. "That's the difference between life and death, Claire."

He paused, seemed to collect himself. "You're worth too much to risk. So I removed myself from the situation. And I removed myself from New Orleans."

I stared at him. "You could have told me."

"How could I tell you that? That I could have taken that man's life as easily as snapping my fingers? That I could have that kind of anger—and that kind of power—inside me? When I'm channeling Ezekiel?"

"Ezekiel was a sociopath."

"And I'm not?"

"No. He'd have done what he wanted and damn the consequences. You just tried to save my life, and yours. You could have killed those agents, but you didn't."

"You could feel the anger?"

I paused, decided there was no point in lying to him, and nodded.

We didn't know if someone had created the Veil or if it had grown organically between our world and the Beyond. If someone created it, maybe this was why. Maybe magic was too much for us—too much temptation, too much power, too much risk. Maybe we couldn't be trusted with it any more than Paranormals could. If magic wasn't the problem, who was good enough, strong enough, to wield it?

Liam looked away, his features fierce, waging his own battle. "I couldn't bring that to your door."

"You think I wouldn't understand?" I stood up, faced him. "That magic is wonderful and terrible? That it makes you feel invincible—and totally vulnerable? Because I do." I put a hand on my chest. "I do,

Liam. I know it better than anyone else. Because, like you, I wasn't born with it. I wasn't used to it. It just *was* one day. And everything changed.

"But even if you had to leave to deal with it to ensure you had control, that was weeks ago, Liam. You couldn't send a message? You couldn't take five minutes to let us know where you were, how you were?"

He turned away, walked back to the gap in the bricks. "It took a long time to get myself ready," he said. "To understand who I was. I had to know who I was before I put you at risk again. Erida helped me—helped me figure out what I could and couldn't do. Helped me try to become myself again." He took a step closer, and I didn't move back. "You think I walked away from you, but I didn't. I took myself away so I could keep you safe, so I could learn control."

I looked up into his eyes, saw the doubts that still flickered there. "And can you learn to live with what you are?"

His jaw worked, chewing over words he couldn't bring himself to say. "I don't know. I care more about whether you can."

"I have magic. I'm an enemy of the state. I've killed. And a bounty hunter once dragged me into Devil's Isle because he figured there was more to life than my becoming a prisoner to my magic."

Liam considered that for a moment. "I don't recall dragging you."

He said it lightly, almost sarcastically. And it loosened some tight knot of tension between us.

"It was mostly emotional," I said, and watched him for a moment. Watched the battle rage in his eyes. And figured that taking this danger away from me was exactly the kind of thing Liam Quinn would do.

"All right," I said.

His brows lifted. "All right what?"

"All right, I accept your story."

"That's good, because it's true." He swallowed, looked to be gathering up his own courage. "And the rest of it?"

Us, he meant.

"I guess I want you to tell me when you're ready."

I walked toward him. Saw the heat flare in his eyes, hotter with each step I took. Then I held out a hand. "Envelope."

His eyes narrowed. "You're cruel, Connolly."

I arched an eyebrow.

"Fine." He took the envelope from his shirt, offered it.

"Thank you."

I removed the sheet of paper, found an invoice addressed to Javier Caval from a place called Henderson Scientific, which was based in Seattle.

"An order for pipettes, a refractometer, polymerase, and other things I don't understand." I passed it to Liam. "This make any sense to you?"

"It doesn't," he said, looking it over. "I mean, not beyond the fact that it's scientific equipment. Lab stuff."

The invoice's memo line said the goods should be routed to Laura Blackwell, president of ADZ Logistics, and listed another address.

"Javier Caval," Liam said. "That name sounds familiar."

"From New Orleans? Containment?"

"I'm not sure. But add him to the list of people we know are involved."

"What about Laura Blackwell?" I asked, and Liam shook his head.

"Don't know her," Liam said.

"So we think Broussard found this invoice. Saved it and hid it, because he thought it was a link in whatever chain he was trying to build. The person who killed him didn't find it."

"They didn't find the paper," Liam agreed. "But that doesn't mean

Broussard didn't go off half-cocked about whatever he'd found. That was his style."

"So what do we do?"

He pointed to Caval's address. "This place is closer. So we check it out."

I stared at him. "We just left two Containment agents unconscious. We need to get out of here."

"One person is already dead in my name," he said quietly. "Did you want to stop looking when you found the gas station?"

I'd been ready to aim a snarky retort in his direction. But I couldn't argue with that. He was right. I'd pushed ahead, and he'd been there with me.

"If they catch you, they won't bother asking questions. Someone wants you to be the fall guy. I know you want to stop this. To fix it. But you can't take chances like that."

"Everyone with magic takes chances. Just by existing here."

I looked at him for a long moment. "All right," I said, rising. "We follow this through. But maybe work on controlling your magic."

A corner of his mouth lifted. "I'll do my best."

All a girl could ask for.

We stood on the neutral ground across the street, looking at the house. It was a newer house by New Orleans standards, probably built after World War II, with white clapboard, a single dormer window beneath a high pitched roof. The deep porch was held up by square columns that narrowed as they rose to the roof. The steps in front were concrete, and no wood or paint had been wasted on decoration—or cleaning up the char marks that still stained the front and sides of the house. The front yard was dirt except for a few scraggly patches of grass.

"I've been here before," Liam said. "This is a Containment safe house."

"A safe house? For who?"

"Humans who talk when they shouldn't, Paras who help when they shouldn't, the occasional controversial visitor. Because despite all the talk, Containment is politically pragmatic."

"But they'll still bitch about Paranormals, paint them with the same brush?"

"That just makes them human," Liam said, the grimness in his voice matching the anger in mine.

"This is another connection to Containment. To whatever's happening here."

"Yeah," Liam said, "I noticed that, too."

"How did you know it was a safe house?"

"Had to park a bounty here three or four years ago. Yale graduate who decided he was going to tell the truth about Devil's Isle conditions."

"You picked him up."

"And parked him here until the PCC could get him out of the Zone again. I think he was a well-meaning kid, but he figured throwing some money around New Orleans would get him special access, special treatment." Liam smiled, crossed his arms. "He was incorrect."

That stirred a memory. "Was this in the summer? And the guy wore this dark Capitol Hill Windbreaker every day?"

Liam looked surprised. "That was him. He come into the store?"

"He did, actually. Came in to get MREs, tried to talk up some of the customers and agents about the prison." I frowned, remembering. "How'd you know what he meant to do?"

Liam's smile went sly. "Because I'm good at my job."

"And as humble as your brother."

We were getting into a rhythm, having the kind of conversation we'd have had before he left. I'd missed that in the same way I'd missed talking with Gunnar and Tadji—I could be myself around all three of them, with no pretensions. Just comfortable in my own skin.

Before we got too far afield, I looked back at the house. "Not much to look at."

"That's the point of a safe house," Liam said with a smile. "Nothing to look at means the house doesn't raise anyone's suspicions. If you were driving past, you wouldn't bother to look twice at this place. That's good op sec."

"Op sec?"

"Operational security," he said.

"What are we likely to find in there?"

"I'm not sure." He cast a gimlet eye on the porch. "But the front door's ajar. That doesn't bode well for anyone using this place as a refuge."

He looked around and, gauging that the coast was clear, climbed the concrete steps.

We stood quietly for a moment, waiting for movement or sound. And then Liam pushed the door open.

The odor that emerged didn't leave many questions about the fate of whoever was inside.

I put my arm over my face, but there was no masking the scent—sweet and rotten and so horrifically strong. And I was suddenly seventeen again, standing in the house across the street from ours. There'd been a barrage of fighting the night before, and I'd wanted to check on the woman who lived there.

Mrs. McClarty was a widow. Her husband died in the first attack on the city; her son had enlisted and had been killed in the Battle of Baton Rouge. She had two daughters, who she'd sent from the Zone to live with relatives before the border had been closed. Because she was alone, we kept an eye on her.

"Mrs. McClarty?" I'd called, and when she didn't answer after a couple of knocks—and when I couldn't see anything through the lace curtain on the front window—I turned the knob and pushed open the door.

It moved with a squeak and let out the thick scent of death. I should have walked away, but I couldn't. I was too young, too curious.

She sat at the kitchen table, her head on the linen tablecloth, arms at her sides. Her eyes were open and blankly staring. A half-drunk mug of coffee, coral lipstick staining the rim, sat in front of her.

She hadn't been killed in the battle the night before; her house hadn't been shelled. She'd been killed by life even while war raged around her.

To my mind back then, that was inspiring and sad. She'd survived the worst of the war, which was a kind of miracle. But she wouldn't have known at that time, and her survival hadn't been worth much in the end, because she still wound up like the rest of us would.

When I'd walked back into our house, my father had stood in the living room with a peanut butter sandwich and an apple on a plate. "Lunch?" he'd asked.

He must have seen the look on my face, because he'd dropped them both and run toward me. When I told him what I'd seen, he wrapped his arms around me.

They'd carried her out a few hours later. Her daughters didn't come back, and no one else took care of the house, so it began to die just like she had. The roof caved in, and the house fell in on itself. And as far as I was aware, that was the end of the McClartys' presence in New Orleans.

I couldn't look at the house then, or think of it now, without experiencing that horribly ripe smell all over again.

"Claire."

I blinked. Liam's hand was on my arm, steadying me. "I'm all right. I'm okay."

"Flashback?"

I nodded. "The smell."

He nodded. "Yeah. I think we're probably too late to question anyone, but I want to take a look. You can stay here if you need to."

I shook my head. "I'll go."

I just wouldn't breathe in while I did.

It was a simple house with slightly shabby furnishings. A worn couch, comfy recliner, scratched dining room table. It was comfortable, and looked lived in and loved. Very different from the showiness of Broussard's house.

A man lay on his back on the floor of the rear bedroom. His body was swollen with death and heat, and the fluids he'd lost in death stained the floor beneath him. Blood and worse, from the gunshot wound in the middle of his forehead. And he wore Containment fatigues.

"Murdered," Liam said.

He moved closer, crouched nearby.

"His hands," he said, and I glanced down. His palms, fingers bore streaky remnants of what I guessed was blood, but it hadn't come from his body. There was no blood anywhere else on him, and the blood on the floor hadn't been disturbed.

Where else might a man have gotten blood under his fingernails?

"He killed Broussard," I said quietly. "Or put Gracie's name on the wall."

"Seems to be a distinct possibility," Liam said.

I held my breath as I walked closer, careful not to step in anything and disturb evidence, or leave a mark that anyone could trace back to me. J. CAVAL was embroidered in gold thread on his pocket flap.

"We found Caval," I said, through the sleeve I was holding over my mouth.

Another wave of odor hit me, and I could feel my gorge rising. "Outside," I said, and didn't wait for him to follow. I dashed to the door, made it to the front porch, and lost what little I'd eaten that morning.

He gave me a moment, then came out, offered his handkerchief in silence.

"Sorry," I said, wiping my mouth and wishing for a tankard of ice water. "Got to me."

"Take your time." He put a hand at my back. We stood there for a few minutes, and I rested my forehead on the porch banister while he rubbed my back in slow, soothing circles.

"It's not the smell per se. Not exactly. It just . . . reminds me."

Liam nodded. "The war?"

I nodded. "Neighbor. I found her."

He gave me another moment to settle.

"Broussard found the invoice," I theorized when I was in control again. "He approached Caval about it. Caval killed Broussard. And someone killed Caval."

"That's what it looks like to me."

"Someone is keeping this from Gunnar, maybe from the Commandant." I wanted to talk to him again. To tell him what we'd seen. But we'd taken a big enough risk going to his house last night. We couldn't go back today.

"Let's get back to Moses's," Liam said. "We'll think it through, regroup, and come up with a plan."

We needed one.

Given the battle we'd already fought, we were extra cautious on the way to Moses's house. We backtracked twice, stopped two additional times to make sure we weren't leading anyone to him. When the coast seemed clear enough, we walked inside.

We walked in together, and we weren't sniping at each other. But there was probably no mistaking the grim expressions on our faces.

"What now?" Moses asked. He was across the room, standing on a chair stacked on a table and picking through a box of parts I was pretty sure hadn't been there this morning.

"Did you bring more stuff in here?"

His gaze narrowed. "My damn house, my damn rules." He pulled out a half-naked Barbie doll. "Could be something for you in here?"

The question was asked with such naked affection I couldn't help but smile. "I am full up on half-naked dolls, but thank you for the very kind offer."

There was a flush across his cheeks when he threw her back in the box. "Suit yourself."

"I don't know what I'd do without you, Mos."

"You'd hear a lot less swearing," Liam said.

"There is that."

"There is what?" Gavin asked, walking into the room with a glass of iced tea in one hand and what I thought was a fried chicken leg in the other.

"Where you'd get that?" Liam asked with narrowed eyes.

"Your scientist lady brought it."

"Darby," she corrected, following Gavin into the room, with her own drumstick and what looked like disappearing patience. "Friend at the lab made it, and we had extra. I wasn't sure if Moses was eating." Hand on her hip, she glared at him.

She was curvy, with pale skin and dark hair in a sleek bob around her face. She favored retro clothes that my dad would have loved, and that made her curves look that much more lush. Today, she'd paired pink ankle-length pants with a pale green short-sleeved shirt that had a Peter Pan collar and tiny pearl buttons on the placket. She wore dark glasses with cat-eye frames and a rolled red bandanna held her hair back.

"I eat!" Moses protested. "Had two cans of potted meat today!"

"More like *rotted* meat," Gavin muttered. "Am I right?"

Moses pointed at him. "That's your word. Your *human* word. It was fine." He sniffed the air. "That stuff, that chicken, smells too fresh."

Darby rolled her eyes, smiled at me. "Hey, Claire. How was the bayou?"

"Wet."

She grinned, looked at Liam. "And welcome back to you. How's Eleanor?"

"Good, thanks. Erida's with her."

"She's still fierce, I assume."

"You asking about Erida or Eleanor?"

Darby smiled. "Either or both."

"Malachi not here?" I asked, glancing around. "We have information."

"Not back yet," Gavin said, pulling off breading and meat with his teeth.

My stomach grumbled, and I obeyed the demand. "Hold that

thought," I said, and headed toward the food. The morning hadn't been appetizing, but the hunger and travel had left me ravenous.

Moses's little kitchen was surprisingly tidy for a man who liked spoiled food. True to Darby's retro style, the chicken was tucked into a red-and-white-checked towel inside a small basket, and the tea was in a Tupperware pitcher the color of avocados.

I poured myself a glass and went back into the living room the same way Gavin and Darby had, with chicken and sweet tea.

Moses had found what he was looking for—a black box with wires that dangled like tentacles—and made his way toward his stool.

"So what's the story?" he asked, short fingers linked together like creatively arranged sausages.

"Well," I said, jumping in before Liam could talk, "I find this one at Broussard's house, standing in front of the murder scene. Long story short, he didn't do it."

"Well, no shit on that one," Moses said.

"No shit on that one," I agreed. "Among other reasons, we may have found the guy who did do it, after we fought with some Containment agents. He's dead."

"The agents?" Darby asked, eyes wide.

"The man we think was Broussard's killer," Liam said. "Small-caliber GSW to the head, and what we're guessing is Broussard's blood still on his hands."

"Busy morning," Gavin said, glancing between us, probably trying to guess if we were still fighting.

When I gave him a look, he just smiled sheepishly. He was a Quinn, just as nosy and stubborn as his brother, and he wasn't about to apologize for it.

"How does it go together?" Moses asked. "Lay out the story for me."

Liam walked to one of the tall windows, leaned against the wall so he could look outside and stay alert, and crossed his arms. "Broussard finds something he isn't supposed to. Something related to this Icarus project."

"The file," Darby said, and Liam nodded.

"He's killed in his home, and not much time elapses between his looking at the file and his TOD," he said. "His computer's missing, and we find an envelope taped behind a picture." Liam nodded at me, and I pulled out the invoice I'd folded and put in my pocket, offered it to Gavin.

Gavin put down his tea, looked over the document. "Invoice for scientific equipment." He passed it to Darby. "Thoughts?"

"Basic lab equipment," she said. "ADZ Logistics. I don't know that company, but I know that name. Laura Blackwell. I'm pretty sure she worked at PCC Research when I did."

"We haven't looked for ADZ yet," Liam said. "The name at the bottom, Caval, is the man we found dead. Broussard had hidden the envelope. Hard to say how long he'd known about Icarus, but he'd apparently managed to put some of its pieces together."

"He thought he'd found a smoking gun," Gavin said. "Something he wanted to keep safe."

"And nearby," I said. "But either word got out that he'd put two and two together, or he confronted the wrong people. Caval decides, or he's instructed, to take Broussard out. He does, leaves a note blaming Broussard's death on Liam. Caval goes to the safe house, is killed before he can even wash his hands."

"He was in a hurry," Gavin said.

Liam nodded. "And he was killed in a different style. Knife for Broussard, gunshot for Caval."

"It's cleaner," I said. "Faster, more expedient."

"Professional," Liam agreed with a nod.

"This is top-of-the-line stuff," Gavin said. "Big enough to merit a Containment safe house and two hits."

"More evidence this is connected to Containment," Liam said. "It's getting uglier."

"Oh, yeah," Darby said. "It is. But very interesting scientifically."

"Discuss," Liam said, when we all looked at her.

"You've got the floor," Gavin said.

"So I've been looking at your file. It's not a molecule. It's actually much more complicated than that." She paused for dramatic effect. "It's a complete biological synthesis."

We were apparently too ignorant to understand the import of that assessment, because you could have heard crickets in the following silence.

"Okay," Liam said. "I'll be the first one to admit I have no idea what she's talking about. What does that mean?"

"It means the file wasn't just illustrating the structure of a molecule," Darby said. "They were *building* something."

"Elaborate," Gavin said.

"Well, without getting into the hairy details, some labs focus on creating new structures—new proteins, new bacteria, new viruses. I can't give you much detail from the stub. There's just not much there, but it looks like a protocol for synthesizing something."

"You can't tell what?" Gavin asked.

She shook her head. "There's not enough left of the file, and what's there is pretty garbled."

"What would you use it for?" I asked with a frown. "The thing you've biologically synthesized."

"Anything. Replacement tissue, research, curiosity, to test drugs. Whatever."

"So the last thing Broussard looks at before he dies is some kind of biological research file."

"Does the invoice look like the kind of stuff they'd need for that?"

Darby nodded. "Creating new tissue is an incredibly complicated process. It needs lots of time, lots of money, lots of very smart people. And plenty of equipment."

"So . . . what?" Gavin asked, swallowing chicken. "Maybe they're trying to figure out how to give humans Paranormal skills? Grow wings or something?"

"Eh, we're several years past the war. I can't imagine they're like, 'Oh, let's suddenly start testing Paranormal tissue to see what makes it tick.' That's not a new research question."

"If someone didn't want Broussard knowing about this, maybe it's too expensive?" I suggested. "Or it's not going well?"

"Or it's generally top secret," Liam said. "But this is merely speculation until we get more information."

Information came in the form of an opening door. Malachi walked in, wearing jeans and a T-shirt that belied his true nature.

That something had happened was clear on his face. He looked absolutely grim, like a man worn thin by exhaustion and grief.

"What's wrong?" Darby asked, moving toward him.

He looked at me. "Cinda's dead."

CHAPTER FOURTEEN

"Cinda's dead," Malachi said again. "Along with another. Two more are sick."

"'I'm sorry' seems like a totally insufficient thing to say," Darby said. "But that's all I've got."

"The words are insufficient," Malachi agreed. "I gave mine to Anh and the others, and they felt insufficient, too."

"The same illness?" I asked.

He nodded. "The illness seems the same—starts as fatigue. Then chills, fever. Rapid heartbeat, rapid breathing. Confusion. Red dots across the skin."

"Hmm," Darby said. "I'm not a diagnostician, but that doesn't sound like your run-of-the-mill infection."

Malachi nodded. "We presume it's contagious, since they live, work, and eat together. And we aren't aware of any other vector."

Darby frowned. "Strangers on the property? New food or water source? Environmental changes?"

"Other than leaving Devil's Isle, no. Anh has lived on the property for five years. She hasn't been ill with anything like this, and she wasn't aware of anything on the property that would cause an exposure problem."

"Did Gunnar get a Containment unit out there?"

Malachi nodded. "Volunteer. The Zone equivalent of Doctors Without Borders. But without hospitalization, there are limits to what they can do in the field." He pulled from his pocket two small vials of crimson liquid, offered them to Darby.

"Blood test?" she asked. She swirled one of the vials, held it up to the light.

"Please."

"Your wish is my command," she said, giving a jaunty head bob. At our blank stares, she asked, *"I Dream of Jeannie*?" Then she waved her hand. "Never mind."

It seemed science wasn't the only thing we didn't know much about.

"How else can I help you?" Darby asked, frowning as she looked up at Malachi. "I'm a lab person, not the doctor you need, but maybe I can find someone to help with diagnosis?"

Malachi shook his head. "I need to talk to Lizzie, but I can't get close to Devil's Isle." He looked at me.

"Yes," I said. "Of course. I'll go tonight, after dark."

"Today of all days," Liam said in a tight voice. "After what happened earlier today, you're going to try to sneak into Devil's Isle? You were in a shoot-out with Containment."

Put like that, it didn't sound very smart. But what choice did we have?

"Delta is as Delta does," I said. "And we've got our delivery procedure, remember? I can handle myself."

That was a lesson I'd been learning. That I could handle myself. I liked learning that.

"I'll go with you."

The concern that furrowed his brow was clear.

"No, you won't. I'll be quieter, faster, less noticeable on my own. This isn't my first rodeo."

"Liam," Gavin said quietly, "this is the package Gunnar talked about. She's been doing this for five weeks."

She's been doing this since you've been gone, he meant. Which was the absolute truth. But it wasn't a truth that Liam wanted to face, given the pained look on his face.

"I hate to bring this up during this non-tender moment," Gavin said, "but there's an illness spreading among Paranormals at the same time Containment's running some kind of secret project involving a biological thingamajig."

"Synthesis," Darby offered.

"That," Gavin said. "Coincidence?"

"There's a biological synthesis?" Malachi asked, and we gave him the brief rundown about our visit to Broussard and Caval, and Darby's preliminary findings.

"I don't think 'science' is a strong enough link between the illness and Icarus," Liam concluded. "There's no evidence the Paras are sick because of anything Containment's done, and we don't know Containment is working on anything that could make anyone ill. They could be trying to create a new product for skin grafts or something." He glanced at Darby. "Right?"

"You got it."

Liam looked at Moses. "You get anything from that file?"

"Oh, are we remembering I'm in the room now?" His voice was the perfect mix of egotistical and long-suffering. That was pretty much Moses to a T.

"Please proceed," Liam said.

He turned to his computer, began typing. "Did more digging on the Icarus file. As we know, Broussard accessed it not long before he died. But that wasn't the first time he'd looked at it. He'd opened it fourteen times over the last two weeks."

"Fourteen times for the same file?" Liam asked with a frown. "That's a lot of views for a file he didn't create."

"Obsessed," Gavin said. "Which squares with what we know about him. He was obsessed with Liam, too."

"He fixated," Liam agreed.

"And there's this." Moses punched a key, had paper spitting out from an old-fashioned dot matrix printer on a shelf beneath his keyboard. He reached down, ripped off the paper, handed it to Liam. "Once again, the idiots who tried to delete the file didn't think about the metadata. Can't get everything out of the file, but I can tell you the address where it was created."

"I want to tear off the perforations," Gavin said, but Liam swatted his hand away.

"Well, what do you know?" He passed the paper to Gavin, glanced at me. "Same address as ADZ Logistics on the Henderson invoice."

"And there's a link in the chain," Gavin said, ripping off the paper's edges with a satisfying *zip*. "Somewhere in Gentilly, looks like."

Gentilly was a neighborhood on the lake side of Devil's Isle.

"We need to surveil the building," Liam said.

Gavin nodded. "Tomorrow morning. It will be getting dark soon, and the building's going to empty out. They won't work at night; the power goes out too often."

"And after what happened today," I said, "if this building matters to Containment, they're going to put extra staff outside it."

Gavin nodded at me. "She's right. We can get out at dawn, get spots, and be in position when the doors open. We'll see who comes and goes, and that will tell us what's happening in there."

"All right," Liam said. "We'll meet in the morning, go take a look."

"Someone needs to get a message to Gunnar tonight," I said. "Tell him about Caval. Killer or not, he needs to be found. His body dealt with."

"And the DNA tested," Darby said. "If that's Broussard's blood on his hands, it will pretty much exonerate Liam from the murder. And then we can just deal with Icarus, and whatever Containment's trying to hide."

"I'll do that," Gavin said, and gave his brother a look. "If only we knew how the goddamn knife got there."

"I'm working on it," Liam said.

"Work harder, please, so we can exonerate your ass."

"You know what we need?" Darby asked. "We need a break." She walked to Moses, looked over the piles. "You got a DVD player in this mess? Or a VCR?"

"Yeah. Why? You gonna put one back together?"

"No, I want to watch it. I've got a stack of movies in the UV."

"You've got a utility vehicle?" Gavin hoofed it to the window, glanced outside. "Darby, that's a golf cart. With an old Coke cooler welded onto the back." He mostly sounded confused.

"Friend of mine at the lab did that," she said with a grin. "We're calling it Rogue Lab."

"Good name," Liam said with a smile. "And very creative welding job."

The cooler was red, probably from the fifties, and had rounded corners and pretty white script. It also had a lot of rust, which made me feel better about the fact that someone had bolted it to a golf cart.

"Keeps the rain off," she said. "And Containment doesn't even look twice. Chick in glasses on a golf cart apparently doesn't inspire a lot of concern. Anyway, there's movies in the box." She looked around at the group. "See if Moses can get a player up and running. It'll be getting dark soon, anyway."

The chatting and plotting began. What would they watch, what would they eat, who got the limited couch real estate in Moses's living room.

They were all eager for company, for normalcy. I understood the urge, and usually I would have been up for it. But not tonight. It was still early, but I was wiped out, emotionally and physically. Murders, battles, and confessions from Liam had left me completely drained—not to mention the hangover from Liam's unexpected magic. That was going to need some time of its own.

I had a lot to think about, and I needed time and space and quiet to do it.

I could feel his gaze on me, the hope in it. But he was going to have to let that simmer a bit. God knew he'd made me do some simmering.

"Rain check," I said. "I'm going to see Lizzie, remember?"

Moses looked back at me, his brow furrowed with disappointment. "Damn it. It's family movie night."

I smiled, but shook my head. "Things to do, people to see."

Moses wrinkled his nose, like I'd mentioned taking out the garbage. "Spoilsport."

"I am," I agreed. I looked at Gavin, Liam. "We surveil at dawn?"

"Fine by me," Gavin said.

"Same," Liam said.

"Why don't I drive you back?" Darby said to me, gesturing toward the window and the UV that sat at the curb. "I could zip you wherever you need to be."

"Actually," Liam said, glancing at me, "I've got some business to attend to, and I think you might be interested in it. You game?"

The spark in his eyes piqued my interest. "Depends. What's the business?"

"We need to see a girl about a knife."

We escaped from the house after Moses gave Liam his own portion of crap about skipping family movie night, then stood on the curb, looking at Darby's UV.

We'd carried the VCR tapes inside; in exchange she'd given us the key. But we hadn't yet climbed in.

"It would be a walk."

"How long?"

He considered. "About a mile."

I did the math, thinking about the three miles I'd need to walk round-trip tonight to get to Devil's Isle, the walking I'd already done today. "I can't ride in this thing. Let's walk."

"Agreed." Liam got the key back to Darby, and then we started walking.

"Where are we going, exactly?"

"To see Blythe."

Blythe was a bounty hunter, a striking woman with dark, choppy hair and sharp cheekbones, generous lips, and plenty of silver tattoos. Very gorgeous and, if I had to take a guess, very impulsive.

She was also Liam's ex-girlfriend.

"You gave her the knife."

"Yeah." Liam ran a hand through his hair, looked a little sheepish. I figured that was the correct response. "All due respect to my brother, I hated that knife. Handle was awkward, blade wasn't balanced, and you couldn't hide it worth a damn."

"So you gave it to your then-girlfriend?"

"Technically, I think she stole it."

"Of course she did." I didn't know much about Blythe, but that seemed to fit. "And why am I along for this particular ride?"

He kept his eyes on the road ahead of us. "You wanted me to trust you, to trust myself. This seems as good a first step as any."

In a city of gorgeous, empty houses, from the historic to the glamorous, Blythe lived in a third-floor apartment in the middle of an otherwise abandoned complex. There was no architecture to speak of, the swimming pool was empty but for a rusting Chevy Suburban, and the courtyard was overrun with weeds.

"Why here?" I asked.

"Anonymity," Liam said. "She's in the middle of the complex, on the top floor. Gives her visibility, but keeps her from standing out."

In any other place and time, I might have said she was paranoid. But not in the Zone. Not in New Orleans.

We took the stairs to the third floor and the outdoor hallway populated with front doors. Liam stopped in front of one—number 313—that didn't look any different from the others. Double anonymity.

He knocked on the door. There was a thump, then shuffling, the jangling of a lock.

The woman who opened the door had tousled hair and wore a tank top over a hot pink bra and mid-calf silver leggings. Her feet were bare, her eyes lined with kohl. A silver snake covered her right biceps, and a silver dragon wound around her left.

"Well, I declare," she said, in an exaggerated accent that was more 'Bama than bayou. "Look who's here. Liam Quinn, the prodigal son returned." She slid her gaze to me. "And little Saint Claire, who I understand isn't so saintly anymore."

I smiled. "Would you like to see an example of my work?"

She smiled back. "Not unless you want to see how my cuffs work. I'm still on the job."

Liam ignored the bait. "Can we come in, Blythe?"

"Why?"

"Broussard. We need information."

She looked at him for a moment. "Were you followed?"

"Are you under the impression I forgot how to do my job?"

"Just checking," she said. "A girl's gotta be careful these days." She waved us in and gave the hallway a second look before closing and relocking the door.

The entry opened into a narrow hallway that led to a small living room. There was a small kitchen on the other side of the entry, and a hallway that ran to the left, which I assumed led to a bed and bath.

The architecture was Generic Apartment. On the basis of what I knew about her so far, the décor seemed to be completely Blythe: Southern, rock 'n' roll, postwar, and a little bit trashy.

There was a motorcycle in the living room, squeezed in beside a worn love seat and a bergère chair covered in rose velvet. The walls bore enormous paintings of fancy men and women at a garden party, all completely naked from the waist down. Ironically, Blythe's clothes—shirts, undergarments, dresses, and pants—were scattered across everything in the room.

"Sorry about the mess," she said, and walked around the bike to perch on the love seat's rolled arm. "Until very recently, I was entertaining company." She winked bawdily, and I wasn't sure how much of the persona was an act and how much was just her vibrant personality. "You want a drink?"

"We're good," Liam said.

"You kill Broussard?"

"I did not."

"I didn't figure you for that. Wasn't really your style. What information you want?"

"I need to know what happened to my knife."

Her face went completely blank. "What knife?"

"Antler handle. The one my brother gave me. Curiously, it was missing one morning after you visited."

"That must mean it was a good visit." She pushed off the love seat, walked into the kitchen. She emptied out a glass, poured a finger of rye whiskey into it, and gulped it.

"Damn," she said with a wince. "Not nearly late enough for rye."

"The knife," Liam prompted.

She held up her hands. "I'm not saying I took it. But if I did, I don't have it anymore. Had a sweetheart, gave it away." She put the glass down, looked at Liam. "It wasn't a very good blade."

"I'm aware."

"Who were you dating?" I asked.

"A very delicious agent named Lorenzo." She patted the kitchen countertop. "We had some very good times."

"Don't need the play-by-play," Liam said. "Last name?"

"Caval. Lorenzo Caval."

Bingo.

"I don't suppose he has a brother named Javier?" I asked.

"Matter of fact, that's Lorenzo's younger brother." She frowned. "Why do you ask?"

"Javier's dead."

Liam's voice was plenty serious, but Blythe didn't get it. "Quit fucking around."

When Liam stayed quiet, her smile fell away, and so did some of the cockiness, the faux accent. "You're serious."

"We are," Liam said. "Found him dead in a Containment safe house. By the look of things, he took out Broussard, and someone took him out."

"Jesus," Blythe said, and turned around, leaned back against the cabinet, crossed her arms. "I knew they were involved in something, but not something that would get them killed."

"What kind of something?" Liam asked.

"No idea," she said, and shook her head when Liam gave her a dangerous stare.

Blythe groaned, turned back to the counter, and poured another finger of whiskey into the glass. "I don't know. My job is to stay on Containment's good side. Not the other way around. I take legit bounties, and I don't get in anyone's way."

"They had something going with Containment," I said.

"They're agents. Of course they had something going with Containment." Blythe knocked back the whiskey like it was bad medicine, slammed the glass down hard enough to make it ring. Then she sighed. "Like I said, I don't have details. They were both impulsive. Lorenzo more so than Javier. Lorenzo figured he was some kind of Special Ops badass." She looked back at us, eyes narrowed. "Was he?"

"It's possible they were involved in a Containment research project. We don't have all the details, either."

"I know Lorenzo doesn't like Paras," she said. "Their mom was a single parent, and she was killed in the war. Lorenzo idolized her, from what I could tell. Took her death hard."

"You know how or when he got involved with the project?"

Blythe shook her head. "That was before my time. But I had the sense it had been a while, that he was pretty enmeshed in whatever it was. He was what I'd call a 'soldier's soldier.' Liked fighting, liked battle, liked having enemies. And then there was the money."

"Money?" Liam asked. "From Containment?"

"Don't know where it came from. Just that he had plenty of it. I do remember him and Javier fighting about it one night. We were hanging, having some drinks, and Javier said something about the money, how good it was." She frowned, crossed her arms, concentrated on the floor as she replayed the memory. "Lorenzo freaked out, started saying how it wasn't about the money but the principle. Started throwing shit around. Not my kind of scene."

"Violent?"

"I'd say Lorenzo liked violence, if that's a different thing."

Liam nodded, considered.

"Did you talk about Broussard to Lorenzo?" I asked, and her gaze shot to mine. There was an expression of amused puzzlement on her face, like she was trying to figure out the joke.

She shrugged. "Probably. We're colleagues, after all."

She didn't get the meaning behind my question. But Liam did. "Someone wrote 'For Gracie' on the wall above Broussard's body and planted the knife to make me look guilty. Which means he understood I had a beef with Broussard and what I cared about."

Blythe's gaze dropped, moved nervously around the room. "Damn it," she murmured. "I don't know. Probably?" She looked up at Liam pleadingly. "Maybe I blew off steam. I don't know. People talk."

I took that as a yes, and watched Liam's face harden into stern lines.

"Have you seen him lately?"

She shook her head. "It's been five or six months." She shrugged. "I lost interest, ghosted him. He was a very serious guy, and I am not a very serious girl."

"Address?"

Blythe rolled her eyes toward the ceiling, then relented. "He's in the barracks in the Quarter."

"The former Marriott?" Liam asked.

She nodded.

"All right," Liam said. "Thank you for the information, Blythe. We appreciate it."

"I don't want it coming back on me."

"It won't," Liam said. "We're breaking it all down."

"She's got issues," I said. Thunder rumbled ominously above us as we headed back toward Moses's house. "Partying hard-ass layered over someone who's more broken than she wants to admit."

Liam glanced down at me. "How'd you get that in a twenty-minute conversation?"

I shrugged. "A lot of agents came into Royal Mercantile. They all dealt with the pressure, with the stress, differently. Some were quiet. Some, like her, were loud. But most had the same gooey centers."

"The Caval brothers do not have gooey centers."

I held up a hand for a high five. "That's an award-winning segue."

Liam slapped my palm. "It was good. But serious. Both Caval brothers were involved in this. And getting paid for it."

"Javier Caval is dead. Lorenzo Caval had your knife." I grimaced. "Javier Caval kills Broussard, Lorenzo Caval kills Javier? That's pretty dark."

"Yeah, if that's how it went down, it is dark. But Lorenzo apparently wasn't above knocking his brother around because of his imagined moral high ground."

"The war created lots of monsters."

"Yeah," Liam said. "And sometimes it just gave monsters an excuse."

"We can't go to the barracks."

"Finally, a place in New Orleans you won't go."

"There are lots of places in New Orleans I won't go. But, yeah, I'm not stupid. We pass this information along to Gunnar, and we let him handle it."

"That's very wise, Saint Claire."

"Don't push it, Quinn."

CHAPTER FIFTEEN

It was pouring by the time I got back to the gas station. I grabbed something to eat and balanced out my magic, getting myself ready for my trip to Devil's Isle.

Since I was already going, I searched through my cabinets, looking for something I could take to Lizzie. My father had stocked the gas station pretty well. But I'd been here for several weeks, and the stuff Moses and I found usually went right to the clinic, so I'd been working through my own stash. And I couldn't rely on my garden plot; a tended garden was another sign of activity. I couldn't risk putting a garden close enough to the gas station to actually make it feasible.

I still had plenty of MREs and the stuff I couldn't stand eating any more often than I had to—including the potted meat Moses loved, even though mine wasn't spoiled. But I figured I could spare another can of crushed tomatoes; it was too hot in New Orleans to make red gravy or soup. I didn't plan to make pumpkin pie, so the canned pumpkin could go, too. A couple of rolls of gauze, a bottle of alcohol, and one of peroxide.

It wasn't a lot, but it was something.

When the moon rose over a sodden New Orleans, I pulled a

jacket over a tank and jeans, stuffed the goods into my messenger bag, and locked up the gas station.

It was a solid three miles downtown, but I loved walking in the dark, even if I was a little more tired today than I might have been. The darkness made me feel invisible, which made me feel powerful. I could slip around houses, through alleys. As long as I was careful, I could see without being seen.

I varied my routes toward Devil's Isle—Bienville, Lafitte, Esplanade, Orleans. Names that were part of the history of the city, even if their streets were mostly empty now. Always a few houses with lights on or candles burning. But most were dark, standing silent and still, as if waiting for the moment when their families would come home again. NOLA was a city that preferred the dark. Shadows softened the rough edges, and moonlight made her sing.

Tonight, I'd taken Canal, planning to hop over to St. Louis Avenue. If I followed that straight down toward the river, I'd pass St. Louis Cemetery No. 2. Like most native New Orleanians, I had a love for the city's older cemeteries, for the tall, narrow tombs, the history, the strange dance of voodoo and Catholicism.

I nearly screamed when a cat jumped in front of me, sleek and black, with eyes that shifted between green and gold in the moonlight.

He sat down on the sidewalk, stared up at me inquisitively.

Maybe I should get a cat. Maybe having someone to come home to at the end of the day would do me good. My father had actually stored tins of cat food in the gas station, maybe expecting he'd eventually take a cat there.

I'd have said having a cat would be a lot less emotionally risky than having a boy, except that I'd had a cat before. Her name was Majestic, and she'd deigned to let me own her until the war began. She ran off after the first Valkyrie attack on New Orleans and never came home again.

The cat that stared up at me now didn't have a collar or tags, so I ventured the question.

"You want to come home with me, live in a gas station?"

Those clearly hadn't been the magic words. With what looked like an imperious sniff, the cat lifted its tail and jogged into the silent street, then disappeared into the dark.

I guess he preferred freedom, hard as it was, to being a captive.

I adjusted my bag, started walking again. And made it nearly a block before I heard the footsteps behind me.

My heart began to race. But this wasn't my first night in the city. If it was Containment, it wasn't even my first Containment fight of the *day*.

But I needed to know either way. I stopped, pretended to tie my shoe, and the footsteps fell silent, too. I stared walking again, and the footsteps picked up again. One block, then another, then another.

He or she was about forty feet behind me. And either the person wasn't very good at tailing people or wasn't worried about being caught.

Unfortunately, the magic monitors in this part of town were armed and ready; the closer you got to Devil's Isle, the better they were maintained. That meant it was tree-branch time again. Or the New Orleans equivalent.

I reached a four-way stop marked by palm trees and Creole cottages. I turned the corner, which put me out of my tracker's direct line of sight, then darted around the next cottage into the narrow space between the houses.

I searched the ground, looking for something I could use, grabbed a wrought-iron bar that had probably been part of a window guard, given the turned metal near the top and bottom.

The footsteps drew closer. I judged my timing, and then jumped out, leading with the bar.

And stared up into Liam's eyes.

"Do you have a death wish?" My voice was as fierce as I could make a whisper. The houses around us were dark, but that didn't mean no one was listening.

"Not especially," he said, his gaze on the iron bar. He used a fingertip to push it away. "Nice weapon."

"It's what I could find. What the hell are you doing out here? We decided I was going alone."

"You decided. I made no commitment either way. You shouldn't be roaming around by yourself."

"I can take care of myself."

"I know," he said. "You absolutely can. But maybe you've got someone who'd like to help you take care."

I stared at him, at a loss for words. "How am I supposed to respond to that?"

"Positively."

If I ignored the insinuation, I could admit it would be good to have another set of hands in case of trouble, and I had a pretty good sense that the trip to Devil's Isle would do him good.

I sighed and tossed the bar away. "I assume if I tell you to go home, you're going to skulk around behind me anyway?"

"Pretty much."

"You've got to go where I tell you. No sneaking inside to get to your town house."

Something hard passed across his eyes. "I know I can't go back there."

"Fine," I said, and started walking. "Do you have any idea how loud you are? I'm half surprised Containment didn't hear you coming, send out a patrol."

"I think you've been around Moses too long."

I lifted my brows and he just smiled. "You introduced us."

"Yeah, so part of that blame falls on me."

"Part of it?"

"No more than ninety, ninety-five percent."

It had been designed to keep Paranormals in, to segregate them from the humans in and outside the Zone, to keep us safe from their magical machinations. But it had also been designed to intimidate, and the concrete wall that surrounded the former Marigny, the current Devil's Isle, was plenty imposing for that.

It was more than grim. Concrete and steel and barbed wire, with an electrified grid on top to keep fliers inside and at bay. The sections of the wall repaired after the battle were a little lighter than the old ones, but the grid still glowed eerily green, reflecting the color back on the wet asphalt. If you listened closely enough, you could hear the buzz of electricity and sizzling dust motes.

"We're going to the Quarter side," I told Liam, and steered him to the upriver side of the triangle, instead of the newly rebuilt front gate that rested in its river-facing point.

We walked toward the river, waited across the street beneath the shade of an oak tree, its branches arcing over us like guarding fingers.

Reveillon's explosives had taken out large segments of the wall. Containment had taken the opportunity to finagle the architecture, building a concrete divot into the wall big enough to accommodate a loading dock.

A bright yellow truck was currently pulled up to the dock, its nose facing the street as agents moved boxes out of the back and piled them along the concrete platform. Floodlights illuminated the dock, showing the streak of red paint across the truck's front panel, and CONTAINMENT written in block letters in reverse across the windshield so the car in front of the truck could read the text in the rearview.

"Well," Liam said when we reached the dock, "that's imposing." He let his gaze rise to the enormous steel gate that kept the loading dock secure when it wasn't in use.

"Welcome to the shiny new delivery entrance," I said. "Crazy it took domestic terrorism to get them to add one."

"Before, they were focused on literal containment," Liam said. "They wanted Paras behind a wall, away from everyone else. That was the primary concern. Probably wouldn't have imagined the prison would still be here seven years later."

"Poor planning on their part," I said.

"Intentionally poor planning," he said, and we watched agents begin to load items into the back of the truck they'd just emptied.

"Taking things out of Devil's Isle?" he wondered, as a man loaded a neon orange box into the truck, the paint so bright it nearly glowed in the dark.

"Apparently so," I said. "Let's get moving."

Liam followed me fifty feet farther down the wall. Then I drew to a stop and pointed at the small metal door in the wall, set atop three concrete steps.

"The door opens into a corridor, and that corridor leads to a small room in one of the clinic's back annexes," I explained. "The door's opened, and Lizzie gets notified. She's the only one with access to it."

"So she could walk out of Devil's Isle if she wanted."

"She could. Could have done it during the battle, too. But she won't. That's not who she is."

"She stays inside, agrees to continue caring for the patients, and they don't put cameras on the door so you can make deliveries," Liam said. "That's a good system."

"It's a compromise system, but it's better than nothing." It reminded me why Moses and I skulked around in dusty, moldy houses full of sadness and unfulfilled hopes. Because at the other end of this corridor were Paras with wounds that still hadn't healed, Sensitives who'd become wraiths. People we'd never be able to save.

"Let's give it a minute," I said. Just because there weren't cameras near the door didn't mean there weren't human patrols keeping an eye on us.

"Lower-level agents aren't supposed to know about this," I murmured, stepping back into the shadows as a couple of agents zoomed by in a jeep. "Just Gunnar and a few of the higher-ups, and even then it's 'don't ask, don't tell.' I don't get caught, and they don't come looking."

"I don't like it," Liam whispered. "I understand it, but I don't like it."

"There's a lot not to like in the Zone," I said, pulling the chain from under my shirt. "But we stay here anyway." I waited until the jeep rounded the sharp edge of the prison, then touched his arm.

"Let's go," I said, and we bolted across the street and up the stairs. It didn't escape my notice that he put his back to me, guarding me with his body while I futzed with the lock. But I wasn't going to argue about it.

I unlocked the door and pushed it open.

As always, I half expected to see a Containment agent waiting, and I could feel Liam tense behind me, probably from the same thought. But the corridor, while dimly lit and not really welcoming, was empty.

"It could take her a few minutes," I said quietly, stepping inside.

"Should I close the door?"

"You want to be inside Devil's Isle behind a locked door?"

"No," he said. And that from a man who'd lived in Devil's Isle. He pushed it closed just enough to keep agents outside from getting suspicious, but not enough to engage the lock.

"What now?" he asked.

I leaned back against the bare concrete wall. "Now we wait."

The minutes ticked by. Five, then ten, then fifteen. The longest I'd ever waited to make a drop was seven minutes. We could have left—dropped off the package and left Lizzie to find it—but we needed to talk to her.

Still. Fifteen minutes felt like a long time. I was nearly convinced some rogue agent had intercepted Lizzie when the door opened at the other end of the hall. Liam and I jumped to careful attention.

Lizzie stepped inside, closed it behind her. She wore pale blue scrubs, the visible skin showing forks of fire that danced like moving tattoos. But that was no ink; it was actual fire, an impressive and dangerous part of who she was.

She nodded at me, cast a suspicious look at Liam. I'd proven myself to her, at least as far as she was willing to trust me. But Liam had been AWOL for a long time, and if her expression was any indication, she wasn't thrilled about the fact that he had been gone.

She walked forward, her feet silent in thick rubber clogs. "Sorry for the delay. Minor crisis, but it's fixed now." She glanced at Liam. "I heard you were back."

"I am."

"Containment's all abuzz about you." She glanced at me. "And you, too. Hear you put on a pretty impressive show earlier today."

"We were checking out Broussard's house. They found us."

"And you made your escape." She cocked her head at the bruise on Liam's cheekbone. "That hurt?"

"Doesn't feel great."

"I bet not."

"You heard anything new inside about Broussard?" I asked. "About why he was killed, or who killed him?"

She shook her head. "Plenty of speculation about whether it was or wasn't Liam. Plenty of complaints about Broussard. But it's all been talk. Some have said it was a Reveillon member who didn't get snatched, maybe someone in Containment jealous of Broussard's position, but nothing specific. No names."

I nodded. "You've heard about the Paras at Vacherie?"

Lizzie nodded. "Word got to me. Haven't seen anything like that here. Just the usual complaints."

"Any idea what's happening?"

"Based on what little I know, sounds like an infection of some kind. A serious one, maybe something that affects blood or bone. A systemic infection they're having trouble beating."

"Would that normally be fatal?" I asked.

"It certainly could be without the right care. Among other things, fevers are dangerous, and they can cause big problems. But the red flag for me was the petechiae."

"Say that again," Liam said.

"Petechiae," Lizzie repeated. "The red marks. They're caused by internal bleeding that seeps through the skin. Can indicate sepsis—when an infection has spread through the body, and the immune response makes the situation worse."

"So you think it's an infection?"

"From here," Lizzie said. "But I'm miles away, haven't seen a patient, and I'm working based on communications from laypeople and the one nomedic who's been to Vacherie."

"Nomedic?" I asked.

"Nomad medic," Lizzie said with a smile. "The volunteer docs who travel through the Zone. Lifesavers, but very unique individuals."

Learned something new every day.

"My staff's on alert about the symptoms. If we see anything like that, we'll let you know." Her features softened. "Tell Malachi I'm sorry."

"I will."

Lizzie's gaze shifted to Liam, and she looked at him for a long, quiet time. "You leave because of the magic?"

"Yeah," he said after a moment. "Yeah, I did."

She nodded, watched him again. "I can see it."

That made me jerk. I'd thought she'd been staring him down because she was angry and hurt, and trying to figure out exactly how much anger and hurt were there.

"Like Eleanor?" I asked.

"Not quite. I can't usually do it," she said, frowning at me. "I can't see any of yours. But there's an aura around Liam. A haze."

"It was Ezekiel's magic."

"And he was a Sensitive."

Liam nodded.

Lizzie moved forward, eyes narrowed as she looked him over. "Sensitive plus human shouldn't equal Sensitive, should it? Unless there's something in that DNA of yours. Eleanor was hit by a weapon, after all. Not the usual way of obtaining power."

"I'd give it back if I could."

"I can see that. I can see that you're fighting it."

He looked surprised by that. "I'm not fighting it. I think it's fighting me."

This time she grinned. "Magic in a human body. Of course it's fighting."

"Because Ezekiel was evil."

"He wasn't evil." She pulled a stethoscope from the pocket of her shirt, wrapped it around her neck. "He was dying. Death by magic."

The fate of all Sensitives who didn't learn to control the magic. And an important distinction that Liam needed to hear.

"That wasn't the magic's fault," she said. "Or his. I'm not condoning what he did. He was a sad and narrow-minded fool. But if he'd been given the right tools?" She lifted a shoulder. "Might have been a different story."

She took another step closer to Liam. "You have the tools. You have knowledge and people. As long as you stay out of here, you'll be fine."

I think she'd given me the same speech.

"I'm trying my best," Liam said.

"Good. That's all any of us can do." Lizzie looked at me speculatively. "And speaking of trying our best, what did you bring me?"

I opened my bag, offered up the goodies. She packed them into the wrinkled plastic grocery bag she pulled from a pocket.

"This will be great," she said, holding up the square bottle of peroxide. "Surprisingly effective on cold-iron wounds." Paranormals didn't heal well from attacks by cold-iron weapons; that's why they'd been so effective and changed the tide during the war. "Stupid I didn't try it earlier, but it's a human treatment, not a Para one. Doesn't even exist in the Beyond."

There was a scratch at the clinic door that had Liam and me whipping around, readying ourselves for a fight. A Containment agent, or a wraith that had escaped his room?

"Don't fret over that," Lizzie said. "Just a visitor." She put the bottle in the bag with the other gear, then walked back to the door. "Someone wants to see you."

Lizzie opened the door, then stepped out of the way. "Come on in," she said.

There, sitting expectantly at the door, was Foster Arsenault, Eleanor's golden Lab and a very good friend of Liam's.

Liam murmured something low, something in Cajun, and went to one knee. Foster bolted toward him, tail wagging like a tornado.

"Oh, buddy," Liam said, burying his face in the dog's neck. "I'm so sorry."

I had to look up at the fluorescent lights in the ceiling, breathing through pursed lips, trying to force the tears back. When Foster made a whooping whine that sounded like a complaint, I laughed, let the tears fall anyway, and wiped them away.

"I think he's mad at you," Lizzie said with a grin.

"He should be," Liam said, scratching Foster's chin so his back leg thwacked rhythmically against the floor. "I left him, too."

"You did," she agreed. "Gavin took him to Pike, and Pike brought him to me right after the battle. He wanted a chance on the outside, was worried how Foster would handle it. I told him I'd find a family for him while you were gone, let him hang out in the clinic for a couple of days. I hoped it might do the patients good."

"Did it?"

"It did," she said, stroking Foster's head. Tongue lolling, he sprawled on the floor and basked in the attention. "And now I can't seem to get rid of him. The Paras enjoy him. And he seems to calm the wraiths."

That snapped my head up. "He does?"

She nodded. "Animal therapy isn't a cure, but it helps. I'm not sure why, but I don't really care. Anything that makes their lives easier and doesn't hurt anyone else is fine by me." She looked up at me. "Better a dog than permanent sedation."

I nodded. That was an easy choice to make.

"How's Pike doing?" Liam asked, stroking Foster's flank. "Claire told me he got snatched."

She grinned. "Pike? He's great. Living in your house."

Liam opened his mouth, wisely closed it again. "I probably owe him that."

"Damn right you do." Lizzie sighed, then looked down at Foster. "You ready to get back to work?"

He made a rolling bark that sounded like a song, got to his feet, and headed for the door.

"If only all our staff was so efficient," she said with a smile. Then she looked at Liam. "It's good to see you. But you made a hell of a mistake, leaving."

She let her gaze flick to me, then back to him. "Maybe you've got a chance to fix that. If I were you, I'd be groveling."

That was a note I was happy to leave on.

It had been a market, a meeting spot, a place to discuss and protest. And it had been a place for the rebellion of joy, where dance and music and camaraderie battled back, at least for a little while, against the difficulties of life.

Congo Square was a park on the lake side of the Quarter, just off Rampart and St. Peter. It had once been a field at the edge of the city, then a park lined with bricks and trees, and then, for a little while during the war, the place where doctors set up tents to help those injured in battle. The tents were gone, and rain had washed away the blood that had stained the brick during the war. Even now, the bricks still had scars from the fighting, great gouges where Paranormals' weapons had pierced and shattered them.

That didn't stop the hardy people who'd stayed from taking back the park. Because Congo Square was for New Orleans, for the survivors.

Even though the world was dark, there were three dozen people in the park. A woman sold yaka mein from a pot in the back of her truck, and a man fried beignets in an enormous kettle nearby. In one corner, a beautiful woman with dark skin, a tignon wrapped around her head, listened while the woman in front of her, her tiny frame and wrinkled skin putting her easily in her eighties or nineties, blotted her eyes with a tissue. The woman, a priestess or conjurer, pulled something from a hidden pocket in her skirt, pressed it into the older woman's hand, and sent her on her way. A gris-gris maybe, a powerful voodoo charm that was banned, like every other form of magic.

But these were all sideshows for the main attraction—the music and dance. In the middle of the park, a circle of men and women stood with drums of every shape and size. Some were handheld, not much bigger than tambourines. Others were more than a foot long and hung from wide straps around the neck or shoulders. Some were too big to hold, their glossy vessels in chrome stands that seemed too beautiful to have survived the war.

But they had survived and now built—one drum at a time—a song that was just as layered and complex as the city itself.

Rat tat. Rat tat tat. Rat tat. Rat tat tat.

Foom. Bum bum. Foom. Bum bum.

Chik chik chik. Chik chik chik. Chik chik chik. Chik chik chik.

In front of the drummers, women danced. They wore white blouses and circle skirts in a patchwork of colors, bells on their ankles adding another layer to the song as they spun, stamped their feet, swung their arms.

The drums beat through me, like my heart had adopted their rhythm. For a little while, it was like the war hadn't come to New Orleans at all. Like tourists might be lined up at Café Du Monde and outside the voodoo shops, like Bourbon Street would be a giant boozy party.

"It's why we stay," Liam quietly said. "And it's why we fight."

I couldn't argue with that.

It was nearly midnight by the time we reached the gas station. We stopped across the street, taking precautions.

"Thanks for letting me tag along. It was good to see Foster."

"It was good for you to see him."

He nodded, and we stood in silence that was almost companionable but for the tension in the air.

Neither of us was ready to walk away. Neither of us was ready to move closer.

"I should get inside, try to get some sleep."

He nodded, and his body tensed. He'd wanted to reach out, I realized. Wanted to touch me, but was working to hold himself back. We were holding ourselves back from each other, still looking for that place of comfort and trust. But I didn't think we'd find it tonight. Not out here in the darkness.

"Good night, Liam."

"Good night, Claire."

And we went our separate ways.

CHAPTER SIXTEEN

I got up before dawn, snuck out of the station before the sun was up, and hopped on the scraggly bike I'd found in an alley behind the station and fixed up. The bike had been my consolation prize; I'd found a motorized Simplex in a warehouse off Canal Street, but didn't have the parts to get it running again.

We had picked a house as a neutral meeting spot for our Icarus building surveillance. It was halfway between mine and Moses's, although only Malachi and Liam knew enough about the gas station to understand that geometry.

Since Malachi had stayed behind today—figuring someone needed to stay with Moses, just in case—I met Liam and Gavin there, at the low cottage overgrown with palm trees, a years-old For Sale sign still hanging by one corner in the front yard.

"No one's going to buy this place now," Gavin said quietly as I climbed into the Range Rover he'd parked at the curb.

"No," I agreed.

Even in the milky predawn light, it was obvious the house was in bad shape. The roof had caved into the middle of what had probably been the living room, and plants had grown in the void, a few stalks and branches already reaching up and out toward the sky, searching for sunlight.

If that wasn't a metaphor for those of us who'd stayed, I don't know what was.

The humidity was oppressive even though the sun hadn't yet risen. Since we were possibly heading to a Containment building, I tucked my hair under a cap, the damp tendrils that escaped blowing in the breeze from the SUV's rolled-down windows.

Liam seemed more relaxed as we drove toward ADZ, but his eyes still held that spark of intensity, of interest, of possessiveness.

"How's your arm?" he asked.

"Sore and bruised, but okay. Thanks." I'd have a scar, but I figured that just added to the mystique.

Gavin glanced at me in the rearview. "What's wrong with your arm?"

"She got shot yesterday."

Gavin's eyes went wide, and the vehicle wobbled as he jerked the wheel. "You got shot? By Containment?"

"It just grazed me. I mean, it didn't feel good, but I've done worse to myself in the store." My dad had done a pretty good job of teaching me how to repair things instead of throwing them out and buying something new. Learning to use saws and hammers brought plenty of cuts and bruises with it.

Since I wasn't ready to walk down memory lane with my dad, I put the thoughts aside.

Gavin whistled. "Figures you didn't tell your guardians. They wouldn't have let you out of the house."

I snorted. "They'd have tried not to." I thought I could probably get around Malachi and Moses, although Malachi would have a pretty easy time finding me. He could surveil from the sky.

"You talk to Gunnar?" Liam asked.

"Not directly," Gavin said. "Passed along a message about Caval, signed it with an alias he'll recognize."

"Beau Q. Lafitte?" I guessed.

"*Mais*, you aren't still using that name?" Liam asked.

"Damn right I am. It's got years of life left in it. Unlike this eyesore of a building," he said, driving slowly past the address on the invoice.

He was right; it wasn't much to look at. Low and squat, made of white-painted brick with long horizontal windows. Probably built in the 1970s, with lots of orange and avocado on the inside. There was no landscaping to speak of, just a long strip of low grass behind a strip of parking spaces. The sign in front, equally squat and unimaginative, read ADZ LOGISTICS in plain black letters. If this was some kind of Containment outfit, maybe they wanted to be unassuming.

"Doesn't exactly look like a hub for innovation or research," Gavin murmured.

"No, it doesn't," I said. "But if you're involved in the murder of a Containment agent, you probably try to keep your work on the down low."

"Probably so," Gavin agreed.

"We've got more information about Caval," Liam said, and told him what we'd learned from Blythe.

"Blythe gave your knife away?" Gavin whistled. "That's cold-blooded."

He drove to the next stop sign, then headed across the neutral ground to the southbound lanes of Elysian. He pulled into the parking lot of an abandoned insurance agency and positioned the car so we could see the building.

ADZ's parking lot was empty, and the building was dark. Hard to tell if anyone actually used the place now. We'd have to wait to learn that truth.

And wait we did.

Dawn began to color the sky after twenty minutes of sitting in the car, twenty minutes of listening to Gavin eat a granola bar louder than I'd have thought possible of a human.

"Like a damn chipmunk," Liam said.

"Boy's gotta have energy. Never know what you're going to get into."

"The bottom of that wrapper, it appears."

"You're hilarious, brother. I missed your wry sense of humor and wit."

Liam punched Gavin, and it jostled him and sent granola crumbs into the air like flakes of delicious snow.

Gavin muttered something in Cajun French that didn't sound flattering. But I just sat in the backseat and smiled, my gaze on the road. For the little while that we'd been a group of friends—that short period between my being attacked by a wraith and the battle—I'd gotten used to their sniping. It was good to hear them irritate each other again.

But when a car turned onto the road—the first we'd seen since parking—we went quiet. We all hunched down a little and watched a white Mercedes pull into the lot.

"Damn," Gavin said. "Nice wheels."

"No kidding," Liam muttered.

A woman in a suit stepped out of the car, closed the door behind her.

A woman with long red hair. The woman from the photograph.

"Merde," Liam murmured. But I didn't even think to respond. Before I knew what was happening, I was out of the vehicle.

"Claire!" Liam's whisper through the open window was fierce and demanding, but I didn't process it. The sound was only a buzz in my ears. I was striding across the street, the neutral ground, the other lanes.

This was my mother. And she'd parked at the Icarus building.

I started running, and the cap flew off my head. I hadn't bothered to consider what I might say when I caught up to her. It didn't seem to matter. I just wanted answers. Or acknowledgment. Or both.

She was a beautiful woman. Tall and slender, with red hair, green eyes, and pale skin. She wore a suit of burnt orange, a cream-colored camisole beneath the jacket, heels in the same shade.

She was nearly to the front door when I stepped in front of her. She didn't flinch, just studied me until awareness dawned in her eyes.

"You're my mother."

She looked at me with clinical detail. "You're Claire Connolly?"

My throat suddenly tight with emotion, I could manage only a nod.

"Then yes. My name is Laura Blackwell. I'm your biological mother." She said it matter-of-factly, like she was confirming the humidity level.

My thoughts spun so quickly it literally made me dizzy. Laura Blackwell, the president of ADZ Logistics, the woman identified on the lab invoice, was my *mother.*

When I continued to stare at her, she rolled her eyes and motioned to the building. "I'm a busy woman, Claire, so while I assume you have questions, I need to get back to work." She looked at me expectantly.

"You left us."

"If by 'us' you mean yourself and your father, yes. I did."

A full five seconds of silence followed that with no elaboration. "Why?" I asked.

"I wasn't cut out to be a spouse or mother. Your father's interests diverged from mine, and I realized I didn't have the instinct for motherhood. You were a well-behaved child, but I simply wasn't interested in you, intellectually or emotionally. Your father wanted a child, and I could admit to some curiosity about the biological processes. I considered it a kind of experiment. I hypothesized that the maternal feeling would grow, but it didn't."

She looked at me expectantly, as if she'd provided an entirely reasonable explanation and was confident that I would buy it immediately.

She sounded like a scientist, a woman who—not unlike Broussard—saw the world in very clear terms. In black and white with no shades of gray, even while she was talking about emotions and abandonment.

"So that was it? You decided being a mother wasn't for you, so you walked away?"

"You're being emotional."

"I'm human."

"Then try harder. As my child, you should have ample intelligence at your disposal." She sighed. "As you didn't appear to know my name, I assume your father upheld his end of the bargain."

My blood ran cold. "What bargain?"

"He wouldn't discuss me, and I wouldn't interfere with his raising you, ask for alimony, complicate the divorce, or cause any of those other irritations. Not that I would have interfered—I had no interest in it. But giving you a 'normal childhood' seemed his only concern."

Because he'd had integrity, and knew how to love, I thought. And had somehow managed to negotiate a life for me even while his heart was probably breaking.

"Did you love him?"

"I was fond of him, of course, but that's hardly the point. There's no logic in tying yourself to someone else if you aren't happy. I wasn't happy, so I moved on."

With a slender manicured finger, she pushed back her sleeve, checked the time on a delicate gold watch, then looked at me again.

"I've given you all the time I have. It will have to be enough. I hope you know that I don't regret having had a child."

She said it like she was making an offering, like her lack of regret was a gift. As consolation prizes go, it wasn't much.

The anger rose so quickly I had to clench my fingers to keep from striking her, from slapping that smile off her face. How dared she talk about regret? She'd broken my father's heart, walked out on him, walked out on me without another look. She might not have felt regret, but she also apparently hadn't felt any sense of honor, any sense of obligation to follow through on the commitment she'd made by having a child in the first place. She'd just, apparently, moved on to better things.

It wasn't the first or last time a parent had walked out on a child. But it had never occurred to me that someone could be so cold about it. She was a blank canvas, and seemed baffled, or maybe exasperated, that I didn't see it her way.

For a moment, I felt like I was floating outside my body, watching myself try to sort through my roiling emotions. I knew, as I seemed to watch myself watching her, as I stared down at mother and daughter, that it would take time to process the emotions. To accept who she was, and be grateful that my father had shielded me.

That unleashed another torrent of emotions—but this time on his behalf. She had no idea what he'd gone through as a single parent, to keep me safe and alive and fed, especially after the war started, when the money dried up and he had to get what he could from selling MREs and bottled water.

"How could you just walk away, like you had no responsibilities?"

"I did have responsibilities. Important ones. I made good on those."

"Like Icarus? Is that one of your responsibilities?"

Her body went rigid, her face very controlled. And there was something else in her eyes—something I didn't know her well enough to assess. But it was a lot darker than the bafflement it had replaced.

"I have nothing more to say to you. And since you seem like a relatively intelligent person, perhaps you've gotten lucky and have more of my brain than your father's." She plastered a smile on her face, a bitterly cold smile. "Icarus is none of your business. It is mine, and I protect what's mine very, very carefully. You can walk away right now, or I can call a Containment agent and have you taken out."

She looked at me expectantly.

"I'll just be going," I said, and it took every ounce of control I had to say that civilly.

She nodded. "I assume I won't be seeing any more of you. I don't need the distraction."

Five-to-one odds said she'd be calling Containment whether I walked away or not. So I planned to head in the opposite direction of Gavin and Liam, to keep attention away from them.

But the plan didn't matter.

They came around the corner, three Containment agents with comm devices in hand, stunners on their belts. They'd gotten ahead of me. She'd signaled them somehow while we were still in the parking lot. While we were talking, while she was meeting her grown daughter for the first time, she'd called them.

Betrayal was a knife in my heart, but she was unapologetic. If anything, she looked irritated by my response. She held up her palm, showed me the small device she held. A panic button of some sort.

"You're disrupting my work," she said flatly. "I don't have time for this. And if you've run afoul of Containment, that's not my problem. You're your own responsibility.

"George!" she called out to one of them without taking her eyes off me. "We have an intruder."

"You called Containment on me?" I could barely force the words out.

"You're interrupting my work." Again, that irritation.

"Hands in the air," one of the agents said, and for the second time in as many days, I lifted my hands. But this time, I kept my gaze on my mother.

"I'm glad you left us."

Her jerk was so small, so minor, that most people probably wouldn't have noticed it. But I did.

"I don't have time for this. I have work to do." She looked at one of the agents, tall and slender with dark skin and deeply brown eyes. "You've got it, Chenille?"

"Ma'am," Chenille responded. Her gaze kept flicking back and forth between us, obviously noticing the resemblance. But it didn't change the grim determination in her expression.

"We aren't done," I called out as she opened the door.

She glanced back at me, one perfect red eyebrow lifted dubiously. "Aren't we? It certainly appears to me that you're done, Ms. Connolly." With that, she slipped inside, leaving me alone with the agents.

My mother turned me in to Containment.

I closed my eyes, thinking this was it—my last moment of freedom. I'd be taken into Devil's Isle to waste away until the magic took me. Destroyed me.

I willed Gavin and Liam to leave, to stay in the vehicle and drive away. To get themselves to safety. Maybe they'd be able to come up with a plan to get me, too, or maybe not. At least I wouldn't have to worry about them.

But then things got more complicated.

A truck zoomed down the street and pulled up to the curb. Big and green and jacked up on enormous tires, with angry guitars blasting through the windows. There were two men in the cab, two men in the back. And two of them looked very familiar—Crowley and

Jimmy, the hunters who'd attacked us outside Vacherie. They'd come back to New Orleans. Had they guessed we'd show up here? Did they know about her, or about ADZ?

They jumped out, the man from the front passenger seat holding up a piece of paper and pointing at me.

"I've got a duly authorized bounty on that woman," Crowley said, in that unusual gravelly voice of his. "On Claire Connolly!"

Every system in my body seemed to freeze at the word "bounty."

Before, I'd been just a person of interest, a human with an outstanding warrant. Creating a reward for my capture would bump me right up on the hunters' priority lists. It wasn't much of a surprise that they'd done it, not after what had happened at Broussard's house. But it still sent a wave of sickness through my stomach. It was one thing to live quietly, to stay out of Containment's sight. It was entirely another to know that hunters had been actively searching me out.

Apparently refusing to abandon me, Liam and Gavin ran across the street. Gavin waved a piece of paper in the air like a competing bounty. Probably registration on the vehicle. But I doubted that would stop the Quinn boys. And neither would the fact that there was definitely a bounty on Liam, and probably one on Gavin now, too.

"Hey!" Gavin called out. "Hey! Over here! She's ours!"

Everyone looked back, their expressions surprised or confused or concerned as they moved forward. Gavin held up the paper one last time, then shoved it into his pocket. "We've got dibs on Claire Connolly. Agent Jackson offered us the bounty personally."

Crowley stepped forward. "You know that's not how it works," he said, then slid a look to Liam. "We got here first, so we get the bounty."

"How the hell'd you get off Montagne Désespérée?" Gavin asked.

"Shrimper," Jimmy said, just as Gavin had predicted.

Crowley's and Liam's eyes narrowed as they looked each other over. "You attacked them?" Liam asked.

"I tried to bring your friends here in for questioning." Crowley's jaw was tight with anger. "I'm guessing this is your brother."

"You'd be right," Gavin said. "Bummer you didn't figure that out when you had your chance."

Crowley's gaze didn't leave Liam. "Seems like I've got a pretty good chance now. If you aren't careful, the both of you, we'll take the couple other bounties available to us for the Quinn brothers. I'm not going to do that now due to professional courtesy. Unless you get in my way."

Liam's features were hard, his eyes shifting blue and golden. And that hadn't escaped the other bounty hunter's notice. "You're going to want to back off and walk away."

Crowley's stare stayed steady. This was just business for him—a lot of money and probably a little pride. "Why should I?"

"Because she's mine."

Crowley's brows lifted. "So that's how it goes, is it? And what if I don't walk away? You going to kill me, too?" Several heads in the group turned to stare at Liam. "Or maybe we should just cut to the chase and execute all our bounties right now."

"Everyone step back," Chenille said. "We've got the prisoner, and we're taking her in."

"Can't step back," Crowley said. "You don't even have a wagon here. Rules are, we locate a target at the same time as Containment, the one with wheels wins the prize. We got transpo, we get the bounty."

"We've got a superior claim," Gavin said again, shaking his head.

"Bullshit," Crowley said, slid his glance to Chenille. "How about a trade? I'll take Connolly, and you can take the brothers Quinn."

Chenille's lips curled in the way of villains everywhere. "They're wanted, too?"

"They are," Crowley said. "Might even go without argument, if they think they'll make it to the prison same time as Ms. Connolly here."

"You'll take us in over your dead body." Liam's voice was fierce.

"Or yours," Crowley said. He pulled a toothpick from his pocket, slipped it between his teeth, chewed. "Makes the transport easier."

For a moment, there was nothing but tense silence, everyone gauging the others, watching to see who'd strike first. With the sun beating down, I wouldn't have been surprised to see tumbleweeds drifting by.

We played chicken . . . until Crowley made the first move.

He jumped forward, grabbed my arm, dragged me across the parking lot, and shoved me behind him, his meaty hand still around my arm. He was bigger than me, stronger than me, and I wasn't going to dislodge his fingers by sheer force. I'd have to get creative.

His other men took that as their signal to move. They jumped out of the truck, and two of them began engaging the Containment officers. The third, either brave or stupid, headed for Liam and Gavin.

"I like these odds," Gavin said, swinging when the man lunged for him. The man was big, but spry enough to dodge the shot. He ducked, then grabbed Gavin by the waist and tried to throw him down.

He was bigger than Gavin, heavy and bulky compared to Gavin's lean ranginess, but Gavin managed to stay on his feet as they moved backward, hit a light pole.

Liam strode forward, chin down and a bullish expression on his face. He grabbed the man by his shoulders, ripped him away from Gavin, and tossed him bodily a few feet away.

"That's my baby brother, asshole."

"Oh, now you come to my rescue?" Gavin asked, using one hand to push himself up, the other to support the spot on his back where he'd been mashed into the steel post.

"Better late than never," Liam said, adjusting his stance while the man rose again and made another lunge.

"You need better moves," Liam said, neatly dodging to the side and avoiding the blitz. But the man skidded to a stop on the concrete, came back again, tried to jump on Liam's back.

"Son of a—," Liam yelled, his body bowed under the weight of the man.

Instinctively, I yanked my arm away from Crowley, but barely made a dent. "Not yet, little lady," he said, and began dragging me toward the truck.

No way was I going in the back of that truck.

What the hell? I figured. They already knew I was a Sensitive. Seeing me do magic now was just icing on the cake.

I reached out for power, felt a few delicate tendrils in the air. By some freak of geography, there weren't many out there, so I was going to need to make this count. Best way to threaten a bully? With his own weapon.

I wrapped magic around the butt of his gun, yanked it out of his holster, then popped it into my hand.

"You're going to want to get your hand off me."

He instinctively felt for his holster, and I saw the jolt when he realized it was empty. Slowly, he looked at me.

"Well," he said with a leering grin, "looks like the bounty was telling the truth." He raked his gaze over me, making me feel grimy. "But maybe I'll have some use for you."

I whipped the knife from his other holster, and when it was

seated in my hand, I pointed it toward his balls. "Say that to me again, Crowley. I dare you."

"Put the gun down!"

We looked back. Two of the agents and two of Crowley's men were rolling on the ground. Liam was helping Gavin stand. Chenille had a gun and swung it from person to person, unsure which of us was the best target.

It was time for us to take our leave. I had a pretty good idea how to make that happen.

I put the knife in my pocket, raised the gun at Crowley. "Turn around and face her."

Crowley muttered under his breath, but turned around.

I glanced at Liam, gave him a nod, then used the rest of the magic I'd gathered to push Crowley toward Chenille. He hit her like a bull, sending both of them to the ground.

We took our chance, running back across the street toward the SUV. Along the way, I snatched up my ball cap, rolled and stuffed it into my back pocket.

Liam was in the lead. "Keys!" he shouted at Gavin, who threw the keys over Liam's head and into his waiting hands. Liam yanked open the door and we jumped inside. Then his keys were in the ignition and we were zooming down the street.

We were a quarter mile down the road when their engine roared behind us. The bounty hunters were giving chase. Booms echoed through the air, and we ducked as metal pinged against the vehicle's exterior.

"Son of a bitch! This is my brand-new car!"

"It's neither new nor your car," Liam pointed out, speeding up along the straightaway.

"Plan?" I asked.

"Not getting taken to Devil's Isle"—Liam winced as the car caught a pothole—"and not leading them to Moses."

"I like both of those plans," Gavin said, grabbing the chicken stick as the vehicle bounced.

"Need enough of a lead," Liam murmured, his eyes shifting between the road and the rearview, "and then we're golden."

He gunned it, putting a half mile between us and the truck.

"Now we need a switch," Liam said, and jerked the car into a hard right turn onto a side street that slung us all against the left side of the car.

"Damn it," Gavin muttered. "I liked this car."

"They've seen it."

"I get that, but it doesn't mean I have to like it. Alley coming up on your left, two hundred feet."

Another tight turn, and Liam slid the Range Rover into the alley with scant inches on each side, then floored it over pockmarked asphalt and gravel.

"There!" Gavin yelled. "There's a truck in the garage twenty feet back. On your right."

Liam threw the car into a stomach-hurling reverse, and we lurched forward as he drilled backward through the narrow lane, then screeched to a stop.

He parked the Range Rover kitty-corner so it blocked the alley behind us. We climbed out of the SUV and walked past a dilapidated house and into the garage Gavin had spotted.

Weeds grew through the garage's dirt floor. But the truck was . . . interesting. It was a Ford, probably from the forties, relatively small and plenty curvy, the original paint long ago rusted into mottled red.

Liam's gaze narrowed. "This isn't a truck. It's a paperweight."

"Probably runs better than yours," Gavin said. "Just need to find out if it moves."

I walked toward the cab, running my fingers over the bed. The body felt solid, and the tires were new. And there was something I liked about the narrow bed, huge curving wheel wells, and chrome details.

There was a thin layer of dust on the door handle. The truck hadn't been driven in a while, so at least we weren't poking around in someone's everyday car. That didn't give me much comfort about the mechanics, but I liked the look of it. It was love at rusty first sight.

"I want it."

They both looked back at me.

"This thing?" Gavin asked.

"This thing. I like it, and I want it. Keep an eye out," I said, then opened the driver's-side door. I checked beneath the floor mats, behind the visors, but didn't find a set of keys. Fortunately, the car was old enough to work a trick I'd learned from my father, who'd been afraid I'd find myself stuck in New Orleans without a way home.

I grabbed my hat, pulled it on and stuffed my hair beneath it. "Pocketknife?" I asked, holding out a hand to Liam. He watched me curiously while Gavin stood at the edge of the garage, keeping an eye on the street.

Liam pulled a multi-tool from his pocket, handed it over.

"Thanks," I said, and slid onto the front seat.

Either the leather was in really good shape, or it had been part of the apparent restoration. Half the work was done for me on the hotwiring, too. The panel that covered the wires beneath the steering wheel was gone, the wires new and labeled with tape. That was a very good sign. Even if the body was rough, someone had taken the time to replace the wires. That meant there was a pretty good chance the mechanics were good, too.

"Thank you," I murmured, carefully stripped a bit of insulation from the ignition wires, twisted them together, and connected the bundle to the battery.

The engine roared to life, echoing like thunder in the narrow garage.

I stuffed the bundle back into the cavity, then sat up and revved the engine. "Squeeze in, and let's get the hell out of here."

Gavin climbed in, slid over on the leather bench seat. "Damn, Claire. You are a badass."

"I can fix things," I said simply, but I noted the pride and interest in Liam's eyes.

I patted the dashboard. "I'm going to call her Scarlet."

"She's not exactly subtle," Liam said, but there was no disapproval in his voice. Just caution. "You'll have to be careful."

"Oh, I will." Because she was mine now.

I put Scarlet in reverse, stretched an arm on the back of the bench seat, and brought her into the light again.

CHAPTER SEVENTEEN

I learned, when we were bumping back toward Mid-City, that while I liked Scarlet's curves, I did not like her suspension.

"Well," Gavin said, "that was an interesting trip."

"What was that paper you were waving around?"

"Vehicle registration," Gavin said with a grin.

Nailed it.

"You want to tell us what happened out there?" Gavin asked the question, but I could feel Liam's gaze on me.

I forced words out, even though my chest had gone tight with emotion. "That's Laura Blackwell. The woman whose name was on the ADZ Logistics invoice. The president of the company."

The car was silent for a moment, and I assumed they were debating whether to ask me to elaborate. I saved them the trouble.

"She's my mother," I said, looking out the window to watch the buildings pass.

"Your mother?" Liam said quietly. "She wasn't dead."

"No. My father lied to me." And I was still working my brain around that one. "She apparently left my father, and didn't want to revisit that part of her life. I guess he wanted to close that chapter."

"I'm sorry, Claire."

I nodded. "She didn't tell me anything about Icarus. She said she'd 'protect what was hers.'"

"And yet she called Containment on her own daughter," Gavin said, then whistled low. "What a stone-cold bitch."

"Can't argue with that. And I guess Containment has issued a bounty on me now."

"And me," Gavin said happily, adjusting in his seat and squeezing his shoulders between me and Liam on the bench. Maybe people had been smaller when this car was built. Or it hadn't been meant for the tall, broad-shouldered Quinn boys. "About damn time. I was beginning to feel left out. Now we're the Three Wanted Amigos."

"Oh, good," Liam murmured.

"Here's my question," Gavin said. "How'd Crowley manage to get there at just the right time? That's a pretty damn big coincidence."

"No way that was coincidence," I said. "Either they'd been watching the building, thinking we might show up if we connected it to Icarus, which seems really unlikely, or someone inside called Crowley when they saw me."

"Containment guards were patrolling," Gavin said. "More evidence this is a Containment problem."

I didn't like the implications. But the connections to Containment were undeniable.

"The more we learn about this," Liam said, "the deeper into Containment it goes."

Gavin nodded. "And the more they try to rein us in."

"We're running out of time."

Liam meant me and him and Gavin—and everyone else on the run. And he meant New Orleans. And he meant Paranormals. Everyone still touched by a war that had never really ended. Only the tactics had changed.

"Yeah," I said. "Something is brewing again. And someone doesn't want us to know what it is."

Without a better option, we went back to Moses's place. Our being there was enough to put him at risk, but there wasn't any help for it.

We walked inside, found Moses at the computer table with an open can of beans, the lid ragged-edged and sticking up from the can.

"Lunch?" he asked with a smile, but it faded when he looked at us. "What the shit happened? You get into a scuffle again?"

"Containment showed up at the building, as did Crowley's bastards." Liam pulled a handkerchief from his pocket, then came over and pressed it to my temple.

"Glass, I think," he said quietly, his brow pinched in concentration as he dabbed carefully at my forehead. I hadn't felt a cut there—at least not separate from the million other little injuries—but the pressure stung a little.

I winced, hissed air through my teeth.

Liam went still. "You all right?"

I nodded. "I'm fine. Thanks."

He lifted my hand, held it to the handkerchief. "Keep pressure on it."

"Sure."

Moses was looking at me when Liam walked away, and he raised his brows comically a few times. The narrow-eyed stare I gave him put a little pink in his cheeks.

Malachi walked into the room, looked us over, then frowned at the sight. "What happened?"

"Long story short," Gavin said, "Claire just outed herself to her mother, who works at ADZ, there's a bounty on all of us now, and

Crowley and Containment got into a gunfight over the bounties." He held up a finger. "And I had to get rid of the Rover, and Claire knows how to hot-wire a car."

Malachi looked at me, a mix of pity and anger in his eyes. "That was a dangerous thing to do, to confront her. But necessary, I suppose."

I just nodded, feeling miserable by the reminder.

"No point beating her up for trying to talk to family," Moses said. He cocked his head to the side. "She was at ADZ, eh?"

I nodded. "Going into the building. She called Containment on us."

"No wonder your father got rid of her. Good riddance, I say."

But my father hadn't gotten rid of her. She'd gotten rid of him, and me, soon enough that I didn't have a single clear memory of her face.

Tears—of sadness, of frustration, of pent-up emotion—stung my eyes, and I looked away, blinked them back.

"I need to get some air," I said, and headed outside before anyone could stop me.

I walked down the street in broad daylight, angry and hurt enough in that moment that I'd have dared Containment to take me. And I'd have thrown everything I had at them. Every last ounce of magic.

I was so tired of pretending.

A few doors down, past Moses's butter house, was a cottage with a swing bolted to the roof of the front porch. Plastic beads, which would probably never degrade, still hung from the gingerbread at the house's corners.

I tested the steel chain, the slats of wood. And when it held, I sat down, pushed off with my feet. The swing rocked back and forth, then back again. I closed my eyes and let myself grieve, let sadness cover me like the dark water near Montagne Désespérée.

I heard him walking toward me, his footsteps on the sidewalk.

Liam walked purposefully. Not slowly, but intentionally. He took his time.

The porch creaked when he stepped onto it. I kept my eyes closed, let him look me over.

"I'd ask if you were all right, but that seems like a stupid question."

"I don't know what I am." I rubbed my hands against my eyes, my damp cheeks.

Silence, then: "Can I sit?"

I opened my eyes, scooted over to one side of the swing, wrapped a hand around one of the chains. The swing shivered when he sat, but it held.

"I'm disappointed," I said. "Does that make sense?"

He pushed the swing back. "It does."

"I feel stupid saying that. Disappointed about my mother. I thought she was gone, that I'd never have a chance to so much as see her. And now I've had that chance, and she's not what I wanted. Not even close."

"She never was," Liam quietly said.

"I know. That's what hurts the most."

"It's okay to grieve."

"I guess." I rested my head on the back of the swing, looked up at the porch's ceiling. Someone had painted a mural there—a second line marching down the street behind a bride and groom, all bold colors and slashes of paint. There was water damage in some spots, flaking paint in others. But it was still a beautiful representation of what had been.

"Before the war," I heard myself saying, "when other kids went shopping with their mothers, or their moms dropped them off at school, or whatever, I wondered what that was like. My dad tried hard to keep me from feeling different. But I did. I did feel different, but I didn't grieve, because I hadn't exactly lost anything."

"It was already gone," Liam said.

I nodded. "Yeah. And now, I got it back, but that's almost worse. I've learned that my father lied to me—probably to protect me. That my mother was cold and didn't care anything about me. That she was still in town and apparently working for Containment, although I'm not certain if he knew that. And that's on top of learning he was a Sensitive, collected magical objects, and was dating Erida. And he didn't tell me about any of it."

"You've had a hard few weeks."

My sigh was half exhaustion, half laugh. "Yeah. Something like that."

Silence fell again, the only sound the creak of the swing as Liam pushed it back and forth, back and forth.

"Magic killed Gracie," Liam said. "Now I'm magic. I've had to deal with that, to accept it."

"You're just wrong."

He shook his head. "You don't get it, Claire. Your magic is different."

"Magic is magic. It isn't good or bad any more than that tree"—I pointed to a magnolia overtaking the postage stamp of a front yard—"is good or bad. It's entirely what we make of it."

The swing was perpendicular to the run of the porch, so we faced the side of the house next door, a cottage not unlike this one. He kept his gaze on that house, with its blue paint and rotting wood.

"You didn't inherit evil from Ezekiel," I quietly said. "That's not the way it works. And magic didn't kill Gracie. *Ignorance* did. Ignorance and fear that kept the wraiths who killed her from getting help when they'd needed it. Wraiths didn't cast a spell on her, and no spell was cast on them. They were victims of human ignorance just like she was, because we refused to let them control their magic. They were victims of the war, just like Gracie."

I nudged him with a shoulder. "Once upon a time, you introduced me to Moses so I'd understand that not all Paras were bad. I'd say that operates for humans, too."

"It's impolite to throw my words back at me."

"Yeah, it is."

We rocked in silence for a few more minutes. And when Liam put his hand over mine, I didn't pull away.

By the time we made it back to Moses's house, Darby had joined them, her utility vehicle parked in the narrow space between his house and the one next door.

Her ensemble—a red top and circle skirt with white polka dots—was a big contrast to her grim expression.

"We were waiting for you to get back," Malachi said kindly, then nodded at Darby.

She didn't waste any time. "They were definitely synthesizing something."

"Who was?" Gavin asked, obviously confused. I couldn't blame him.

"Whoever created the Icarus file. I was right about it being the plan, for lack of a better word, for the synthesis—the creation—of something biological."

Malachi's brows lifted. "What kind of something?"

"A virus."

"Oh, shit," Gavin said.

No details necessary to think a government department creating a virus was a bad thing. A very, very bad thing.

"What kind of virus?" Liam asked.

"Call it what you will," she said. "It's a completely *new* virus. A virus that was created in the lab from scratch. Thus, the term 'synthesized.' It's got elements of other viruses. Protein structures borrowed here, phage structures borrowed there, but the makeup, the totality, is completely new." She lifted her gaze to Malachi, and she looked absolutely bleak. "And the research isn't just theoretical."

The air seemed to leave the room completely.

"Vacherie," Malachi said.

She nodded. "I tested the vials." She pulled a folder from a vintage leather satchel on top of one of Moses's stacks, then took out a sheet of paper that showed two graphs.

She came toward us, pointed to the graph. "That's from the stub file—the bit we found on Containment-Net." Then she pointed to the graph on the right. "That's the test of the Vacherie Paranormals' blood."

The lines on the graphs were almost exactly the same.

"Merde," Liam said as Gavin crossed himself.

"Icarus involves a virus," Malachi said. "A virus that sickens and kills Paranormals."

But not just Icarus, I thought as sickness overwhelmed me and the edges of my vision went dark. I reached out for the wall with a hand, let myself slide to the floor so I wouldn't keel over.

"Claire!" Darby said, and I heard her voice move closer. "What's wrong? Are you all right? Are you sick?"

"Tell her," I said, staring at the floor. "I can't— Just tell her."

"Claire's father told her that her mother was dead," Liam quietly said. "Turns out, she's not. She's the president of ADZ Logistics. She's part of Icarus."

Even Darby went pale. "Oh my God." She held up a hand. "Wait, just wait. Let's not panic. Just because she runs ADZ doesn't mean she was involved in this."

"She's involved. She's Laura Blackwell."

"What does she look like?"

I gave her the description.

"PCC Research," Darby said. "I remember seeing a woman like that at PCC Research, or before I left, anyway. She was very beautiful. A striking woman. She wasn't in my division, and we were very segmented, so I didn't know her. I just saw her around."

"What division?" Liam asked.

Darby's milk-white skin went somehow more pale. "Biologics."

My mother was alive.

My mother was a scientist.

My mother was a *murderer.*

"I need a really good Cajun swear," I said miserably.

"Start with '*fils de putain,*'" Gavin said. "Means 'son of a bitch.'"

I repeated it back to him, and only slightly mangled it.

"Not bad," he said. "We need to work on the accent, but that's not bad."

Liam slid to the floor beside me. He didn't touch me, probably could sense I wasn't ready for that. But the fact that he'd literally moved down to my level just to be supportive nearly wrecked me.

"How does the virus work?" Malachi asked. "How did it kill them?"

Darby stood up, looked at Malachi. "Given the symptoms you've described, I'm thinking it acts like a bacterial infection, triggers the crazy immune response—the septicemia or septic shock."

"How could Containment have infected them?" I asked, looking at Malachi. "You said they got boosters before they left Devil's Isle, right? Shouldn't that have protected them from illnesses, even this one?"

"Wait," Darby said, throwing out a hand. "What do you mean, 'boosters'?"

"Immunity-boosting injections," Malachi said, "given to the few Paranormals who got passes just before they left Devil's Isle."

"Maybe they weren't immunity boosters," Liam said darkly, then looked at Malachi. "Did all the Paras at Vacherie receive the injections?"

Malachi was quiet for a moment, but his expression seemed frozen with rage. "All but one. He was late to the clinic check-in and missed it."

"Is he sick?" Darby asked.

Malachi shook his head. "Not him. But all the others received the injections. And they're either sick or dead."

"It's a small sample," Darby said. "Too small to be certain, but awfully coincidental if the one guy who didn't get the injection also didn't get sick. Is anyone in Devil's Isle sick?"

"Not according to Lizzie," Liam said.

"If you want to hurt Paras, why inject only the ones who are leaving Devil's Isle?" Gavin asked. "You could do more damage administering injections to those staying behind."

"Because Devil's Isle is in the middle of New Orleans," Liam said. "It's surrounded by humans. And Containment doesn't want them sick."

"Where the Paras are in isolated areas," Malachi said, "there are only a few humans around."

"So maybe they're still testing it," Gavin said, "or very carefully deploying it."

Liam nodded. "You deploy first to Paras heading outside New Orleans until you confirm it's not contagious, that it won't spread to humans."

"Gunnar wouldn't have let this happen." They were the first words I'd said in a while, and they were twisting my stomach into knots. I looked pleadingly at Malachi. "He wouldn't have."

"She's right," Liam said. "Gunnar's a stand-up guy. He's part of Containment, but chain of command isn't as important to him as integrity. He wouldn't have authorized the intentional infection of

Paras, and certainly not their murder. And if he hadn't authorized it, but someone wanted to do it anyway, he'd have spread the word."

"Which means he probably didn't know about it," Gavin said. "So either Containment's not in it, or they're in it up to their eyeballs, but only a very few people have access."

"Containment's in it," Liam said. "The file was on their network. Containment guards were outside the building where Blackwell was working. The Caval brothers are involved, as is a Containment safe house."

"I'm stuck on the efficiency thing," Gavin said. "Why would anyone in Containment, or affiliated with Containment, do this? You want to take out Paranormals, take them out in Devil's Isle. Hell, they could have let Reveillon have the run of the place. Why even bother fighting back?"

"Because Reveillon killed Containment agents," Malachi said. "They wouldn't have just destroyed Devil's Isle and the Paras in it. They'd have completely seized power. That's different."

"Maybe," I said, "but if you destroy Paranormals, you destroy the reason for Containment's existence. No Paranormals, no federal money, no Devil's Isle."

Liam looked at Malachi. "Do you know how many received the injections?"

Malachi shook his head. "Not precisely. We understand there are approximately forty Paras with passes right now."

"Forty counts of murder," Moses said, his voice low and stained dark with anger.

"Forty-two if you count Broussard and Caval," Liam said. "Broussard found out about Icarus, about Caval."

"They killed Broussard because he found out too much," I said to Liam. "And they pinned his death on you because it made sense and bought them some time. Steered the investigation away from what Broussard had been looking into."

"Yeah," Liam said, "that sounds about right."

"We need to talk to Containment," Darby said. "Stop the vaccinations immediately."

"And how do we help those who have already been infected?" I asked.

"What about an antiviral?" Gavin asked, looking to Darby. "They've been developed for some viruses, haven't they?"

"Antivirals take luck and money—and, most important, time," Darby said. "We don't have any of those resources right now. And that plan assumes this particular virus would be susceptible to an antiviral. Not all viruses are."

"Maybe we'll get lucky," Gavin said. "You've got brains and a lab. It's worth looking into."

"I won't refuse to help," Darby said, "but you can't rely on that. You're going to have to do this the old-fashioned way—you're going to have to go to the source."

"We have to tell Gunnar the whole story," I said. "We have to warn him."

"Forty targets," Liam quietly said. "God willing we can save some of them."

Darby would pass the message to Gunnar, this time on the way back to her lab. We decided to meet in our old haunt, an old church in the Freret neighborhood. Gunnar hadn't been there before, but it was time to bring him into that particular circle, and we hadn't met at the church in weeks anyway. Gavin stayed with Moses. Malachi could come separately, as he always did.

I asked Moses for a small favor before we left, and he provided it without comment. Then we drove Scarlet to the church, simple and beautiful and largely abandoned.

Two short steps led to double doors in front. The walls were planks of white wood, the paint peeling, the words on the sign out front long since worn away, except for APOSTLES. Maybe that was the only word that mattered.

We parked around the corner and took the standard wait-and-watch approach before climbing out and walking to the front steps. The doors were unlocked but heavy. Liam pushed one open, and we slipped inside.

The church had a small foyer and a larger sanctuary, wooden from floor to vaulted ceiling. The quiet, the dark, the sameness of it made me feel a little better about everything. When it felt like everything was changing, the few places that had stayed the same were comforts.

I walked to the lectern at the front and put my palms flat on its surface, the wood smooth where other people had done the same thing throughout the church's history. I slid my hands to each side the way a preacher might have while looking over his congregation, pondering their burdens and sins, trying to figure out how best to reach them. A hundred years of wisdom and power worn like a stain into the wood. Maybe some of it would seep into my fingers; we needed all the help we could get.

"What an absolute horror show."

"It's not your fault," Liam said.

"She's my mother. My blood."

"And instead of making the kinds of decisions she makes, you're doing what you can to fix the world, not tear it down."

We heard a flutter of wings overhead, a soft *coo.* A mourning dove, its feathers a pale and shimmering gray, landed on one of the exposed wooden beams that held up the church's roof.

"I've always thought the sound of doves was creepy," Liam said as he looked up and studied the bird.

"Agreed. And very sad."

Without warning, the heavy oak doors began to rattle and shake, like they were being assaulted from the outside.

"Shit," Liam said, and pulled a gun from his pocket. It was smaller than the .44 he kept in his truck. Black and sleek, it looked like a Containment service weapon, for those who preferred guns over stunners.

I came around the lectern, stood beside him, body braced for a fight. "Containment shouldn't know where we are. Gunnar wouldn't tell."

The doors flew open, bodies silhouetted against the brilliant sunlight outside.

"*Whoa,*" Gunnar said, his features clearing as he stepped into the room, keeping his body in front of the doorway to protect the rest of them from any violence we might accidentally do. "It's just us."

"Sorry," Liam said, putting the gun away. Malachi and Erida stepped inside behind Gunnar.

"Door got stuck," Gunnar said. "We figured we'd beaten you here, or we would have just knocked."

"They're coming for you," Malachi said.

"What do you mean?" Liam asked.

"Containment," Gunnar said. "They've increased the bounties on all of you."

"Because of what happened earlier?"

"Which was what?" Gunnar asked. "We were told to meet here, but didn't get details."

"What are you doing here?" Liam asked Erida, ignoring Gunnar's question. His tone was as sharp as his gaze. "You're supposed to be with Eleanor."

"I don't take orders from you," she said, tossing her dark hair over her shoulder. She wore leggings, knee-high boots, and a short-sleeved top, and looked ready for either military action or a polo competition. "And I wouldn't have come if Eleanor was not safe. She's with Roy, and she's safe. I'd stake my life on it."

"You have," Liam growled.

"Why do we need help?" Gunnar asked. "What's going on?"

"You found Caval?" Liam asked.

Gunnar's eyes went hard. "I did. Received a message from what was possibly the worst alias I've ever come across that Broussard's killer was an agent named Caval and telling me where to find him. Forensics found him, is testing the DNA." He looked at Liam. "I assume you found him like that?"

"We did. How we got there is involved, and we'll get to that. How long will the testing take?"

"Should have the results later today, tomorrow at the latest. If it's Broussard's blood, that will help put you in the clear. Would help more if we could explain the murder weapon."

"Let me lay it out for you," Liam said. "We believe the Paras who've been dying have been infected with a virus—the same virus found in the Icarus file Broussard located on Containment-Net. We think Containment, or an outfit connected to Containment and run by a scientist named Laura Blackwell, synthesized the virus. We think Containment administered it to Paras with passes via an 'immunity booster.' It's the reason the Paras at Vacherie got ill and the reason they're dead now. It's the reason Broussard is dead."

Gunnar just stared at him, and I saw the instant rejection in his eyes. The dismissal of the possibility that his organization was responsible for something like that. "You've got it wrong. There is no way in hell Containment would administer a virus to Paras or anyone else."

"We've got it right," Malachi said. "Blood samples verify." He offered Gunnar the papers Darby had printed.

"Three dead?" Gunnar frowned, ran a hand through his wavy hair as he looked down at the papers.

"So far," Liam said, "of the forty who received injections. They're all potential victims."

"There's no illness inside Devil's Isle," Gunnar said. "I'd know."

"The only Paras who received the injections, as far as we're aware, have passes," Liam said. "None have returned yet."

"I don't know anyone named Laura Blackwell," Gunnar said. "If she's part of this, whoever she is, she's not on our payroll."

"If she's not being paid by Containment, she's being paid by the PCC," Liam said. "Containment's in this, neck-deep." He glanced at me, hesitant to take that next step.

I might as well pony up. "And she's my mother."

Gunnar blinked, then stared. "She's your— But your mother is dead."

"No, she's very much alive and working at a place on Elysian called ADZ Logistics. She's my mother, was married to my father, left shortly after I was born because she wasn't interested in being a parent."

"Oh, Claire," Gunnar said. "I'm sorry. And what a dick move."

"No argument," I managed.

"The Icarus file that Broussard found was created at ADZ," Liam explained. "We went to surveil, and she was the first one to drive into the lot. Claire confronted her, and she called Containment on us."

"Darby discovered the file was a plan for the synthesis of a biologic," Malachi said. "Paras with passes have been getting ill, and she matched the virus that sickened them to that synthesis and the so-called immunity boosters."

"You have hard evidence the injections contain the virus?"

Malachi's gaze was hot. "We have her test results. Would you like to sample the injection and see?"

"I'm not doubting you. I wish I could doubt you. I want you to be wrong."

"But?" Liam asked.

"But I couldn't find anything about Icarus, so I asked an ally in the department. He laughed it off, said I had too much going on to worry about a pet project from someone in DC."

"Interesting," Liam said.

"Isn't it?" Gunnar looked at me, sympathy in his eyes. "I'd tell you that you shouldn't have confronted your mother. Except I'd have done exactly the same thing in your situation. Not that that does a lot of good."

I nodded. "Yeah. Not my wisest move. But it had to be done."

"I'm really sorry."

"So am I."

Gunnar looked at Liam. "And Broussard? Caval?"

Liam nodded. "Broussard was killed by Javier Caval. He and his brother, Lorenzo, were involved in a Containment project—some sort of black ops program that paid very, very well. And because fate is a twisted bitch, a mutual friend gave Lorenzo my knife—the one used to kill Broussard."

I took up the story. "We think it's possible he might have killed Javier; apparently they had a falling-out over the project. Lorenzo lives in the barracks on Canal, and that's all we've got on him."

"I knew the Caval brothers," Gunnar said. "Not well, but I knew of them. Some minor demerits for causing trouble, starting fights."

"Impulsive?" I asked, and Gunnar nodded.

"I'm not aware they're involved in anything unusual. But then again, I probably wouldn't be. That's for their division commanders. I need to get someone to the barracks," he said, almost to himself. "Pick Lorenzo up, see what he knows."

He considered that for a moment, then looked at Malachi. "I presume you're in communication with the Paras at Vacherie?"

He nodded. "The nomedic, as he's referred to, is still there, treating as he can."

"Good," Gunnar said, then ran a hand through his hair. "As soon as I leave here, I'll make arrangements for medics at the other facilities." He looked at Malachi. "And I'll make sure this isn't held against them for leave purposes. They worked too fucking hard for what little freedom they were granted."

"I agree, and I appreciate it."

Gunnar paced to one end of the church and back, his brows furrowed as he looked at the floor, worked through his mental steps. "I have to talk to the Commandant," he said when he reached us again. "About stopping the injections, about stopping the project, which is against so many laws and international treaties it would take me an hour to explain it."

"Not to mention fundamentally wrong." Malachi's voice was a low rumble of anger.

Malachi wasn't the only one pissed. "I'm not saying it's not wrong," Gunnar said. "I'm saying it's illegal. Inside my organization, that matters."

"When it suits you."

Gunnar took a step toward him. "We stood between the armies that came from your world to destroy ours. Are we perfect? No. Have we been doing the best we can to keep peace in this world? To salvage what we could? Yes."

"I will not stand over more dead bodies."

"Hey," I said, and stepped between them. "Both of you, back off. This situation royally sucks, and it can suck for multiple reasons at the same time. It's not a damn competition."

They stared at each other for another long minute before moving apart again.

"If strings are being pulled in DC, it's going to be tricky."

"He can't just sit on this," I said. "He can't not do anything."

"I didn't say he wouldn't act," Gunnar said. "But there's a chain of command. It's the military, and it's part of the game. If we want him to bypass that system, we're going to have to make a pretty damn convincing case. Well, *I* will. Because that's my job."

"Mentioning Eleanor's name might help get things moving in DC," Liam said, glancing at Gunnar. "She's connected enough, and she'd be on board. Use that however you need to."

"Appreciate it," Gunnar said, with an expression that backed up the words. "We're going to need all the help we can get."

CHAPTER EIGHTEEN

We waited at the church, biding our time, to learn what, if anything, the Commandant would or could do to stop the nightmare.

We sat on the floor where pews had once been. Malachi, Erida, Liam, me. Liam had pulled bottles of water from the priest hole under the floor, passed them around. We waited quietly, talking through what we knew of the project and what we didn't yet know.

I heard the rumbling first, the sound of a thundering engine a few blocks away. Then garbled words filled the air.

"What is that?" Erida asked. We rose and moved into the foyer, peered through the stained glass to look outside.

It was a Containment vehicle, a heavy-duty truck with its bed covered by canvas. A troop carrier, probably. A man stood in the back of the truck, megaphone in hand.

"Attention! Containment has issued bounties for Liam Quinn, Claire Connolly, Gavin Quinn. If you have information regarding these individuals, please communicate with a Containment agent or your block captain. Attention, Containment has issued . . ."

The truck rumbled on, its passengers oblivious to the fact that it had just driven past two of the three fugitives they wanted most of all.

"Someone is running scared," Malachi said, glancing back at us. "They aren't insulated enough—or the project isn't far enough along—that they believe they're immune from setbacks. They're afraid you'll stop them."

"Good," I said. "Because we will."

We just had to stay free long enough to do it.

What he didn't say, of course, was that that concern might also cause Laura Blackwell and Lorenzo Caval to go crazy. To hurt more people.

It took three hours for the door to shake and be pushed open again. Gunnar came in, and once again, he wasn't alone.

A woman stepped in behind him. A beautiful woman. Pale skin and long, dark hair pulled into a high knot. Her eyes were a glassy blue that edged toward green, her nose thin and straight, her lips lush. She was tall and lean, wore jeans and a Tulane T-shirt with the kind of self-assurance that told me she could wear a uniform or a cocktail dress with the same confidence.

"This is Rachel Lewis. She's a colleague, and she's trustworthy," Gunnar said, the word spoken like a kind of promise. Which was good, because everyone looked at her with obvious suspicion.

Probably sensing that, she met each of our eyes in turn, checking, appraising, and promising she wasn't an enemy. And then her gaze—liquid and intense—fell on Malachi, and she went absolutely still.

I glanced at him, found the same intensity on his face, except that it was marked with temper. Usually cool, calm, and collected, Malachi now looked ruffled, on alert, by the slender woman who stood in front of him.

"Captain," he said, biting off the word like it had left a bitter taste in his mouth.

"General," she said. If her emotions were roiling like Malachi's seemed to be, she was doing a much better job of hiding it. And wasn't that interesting? Had we finally met someone who challenged his remarkable control?

"You're acquainted?" Gunnar asked.

"During the war," she said, without taking her eyes off Malachi. I could understand that, too. He was a very intense eyeful. "There was a unit of human and Para soldiers who assisted with the closing of the Veil."

"Black ops," Gunnar put in, and she nodded.

"But we haven't seen each other since." Even with her pretty Southern accent, her words were clipped.

"No," Malachi said, and there was nothing pleasant in his tone now. "We haven't."

"Well," Gunnar muttered, "let's sidestep whatever this is and get down to business. The Commandant is very concerned about what we've found. Rachel is the Commandant's operations director, and she's on loan to us for the time being."

"I take it the Commandant believes us?" Liam asked.

"There's no documentation that confirms Icarus is a project of Containment in New Orleans."

"No *official* documentation," Liam said, and Gunnar nodded.

"Exactly. But Containment resources are clearly being used," Gunnar said. "You've found ample evidence of that."

"How do you reconcile that financially?" I asked.

"The orders came down from on high," Gunnar said. "Long story short, Icarus began as a joint project of the Senate's Armed Services Committee and the FBI. It was initiated after the Veil was identified, before the war. A countermeasure in case something came through."

"Preventive genocide?" Malachi asked.

"I'd definitely call it a biological weapon," Gunnar said. "Beyond that, we're assuming facts they didn't know. There was only the unknown, a lot of fear, and a desire to protect the public, for better or worse.

"The plans didn't get very far," he continued. "There were vague ideas about synthesizing something with biological stopping power, but since they didn't know anything about what was living in the Beyond—or specifically about Paranormal anatomy—they didn't move past the idea stage. When the war started, the project was put on hold, and the materiel, money, and personnel shifted to conventional weapons."

"Like cold iron," I said.

"Like cold iron," Gunnar agreed. "Laura Blackwell was on the synthesis team, but she lost her job when funding was cut off. And that was the end of Icarus. Or it was supposed to be."

"And then what?" Liam asked.

"The war kept going. Tens of thousands dead, property destroyed. The more reasonable politicians realized that developing a virus to infect an entire world was pretty fucking unethical. But not everyone was reasonable."

"Fear makes people . . . well, people," Liam said.

"It does," Gunnar agreed, his face hard.

The plan was obviously unethical, but it was understandable in wartime, when humans had been concerned for their very existence. I'd seen the army that still waited on the other side of the Veil. Those soldiers weren't overly concerned about our genocide; it was their primary motivation.

On the other hand, biological agents weren't choosy. They would kill soldiers and civilians both, the guilty and the innocent. However horrible war was, it wasn't supposed to be that bad.

"The unreasonable politicians?" I prompted.

"They restarted Icarus. Created ADZ Logistics as a shell company and funneled money through the PCC directly to that entity."

"And Laura Blackwell was back in the lab," I said.

Gunnar nodded ruefully. "That's what it looks like."

"What's next?" Malachi asked.

"A lot of work on a lot of levels," Gunnar said. "Big picture—the Commandant is communicating with several members of the Senate's Oversight Committee, requesting a review of Icarus.

"As for Broussard," he continued, looking at Liam, "the blood on Caval's hands was verified as Broussard's, and the writing on the wall at Broussard's house included one of Caval's fingerprints."

"Lorenzo?" I asked.

Gunnar shook his head. "AWOL. Cleaned out his bunk. No obvious link to Icarus left behind. His sheets, pillow were still there, and they will be tested. But it doesn't matter for now. There's ample evidence Liam is innocent, and the Commandant has demanded the charges be dropped immediately. He can't rescind the bounty because of the magic Liam used at Broussard's house, because there were witnesses, and the Magic Act is still in place. But the murder charges are off the table."

I reached out, squeezed Liam's hand. "Good," I said. "That's something, anyway."

Gunnar nodded. "One step at a time." He glanced at Rachel, gave her the go-ahead to continue.

"We're working on warrants right now," she said. "As soon as the lawyers do their jobs, we'll go to ADZ Logistics, where a group of Containment agents and a team from the CDC will inspect the premises and seize any remaining biologicals."

"You need warrants to inspect a Containment site?" Liam asked.

"No," Rachel said. "But it's not technically a Containment site. It's privately owned, as far as all official records show."

"It's off the books," Liam said.

"It is," Rachel acknowledged with a nod.

"As we discussed earlier," Gunnar said, "we've sent additional physicians to work sites. Leave has been temporarily halted until we're sure it's safe."

"So you'll punish Paranormals?" Malachi accused.

"We'll keep them inside Devil's Isle," Rachel said. "For better or worse, it is the most secure and safest facility we can provide for them at this time. There are also no instances of illness inside Devil's Isle, which Lizzie has confirmed. You're welcome to confirm that with her directly, if you can."

There was a challenge in her voice. Captain Lewis was good.

"If this is being directed at the higher levels," Liam said, "the Commandant will take heat."

"He is aware of that," she said. "But as long as Devil's Isle remains under his command, he'll act accordingly."

"We'll help however we can," I said.

Rachel gave Malachi a quick glance before looking at her watch. "I'd like to get back so we can go over the op."

"Sure," Gunnar said. "Sure." He looked around the church. "You all good for tonight?"

"We're fine," Liam said. "We'll meet back here in the morning?"

"Let's make it Moses's house," I said. "He gets testy when he's not included."

"Can't argue with that," Liam said. "Dawn, then."

Arrangements were made, and Gunnar and Rachel left.

"I need to make some contacts," Malachi said. "I'll see you in the morning."

"I've also got something I need to take care of," Liam said, then glanced at me. "You can get back okay?"

I nodded.

"Then I'll see you."

The promise, however vague, was enough to have a blush rising in my cheeks. He'd spoken those words to me, for me, and my body eagerly responded.

Since we were preparing to face the music all the way around, I approached Erida, the only one who hadn't yet arranged her getaway.

"Can I talk to you before you leave?"

If the request made her suspicious, she didn't show it. But then, her poker face was nearly as good as Malachi's. "All right."

"Maybe outside?"

Her brows lifted, but she nodded, followed me through the back of the church and outside again. The sun was setting, the sky streaked with orange and purple.

I walked a few feet away, giving myself time to prepare, then turned back to her. "I know you and my father were lovers. Is that why you hate me?"

Her body jerked at the question. It didn't bother me that I'd shocked her.

"I don't hate you, Claire. I don't even really know you."

Given what I'd seen lately, I didn't think knowing someone was a requirement for hating them. So I stayed quiet.

"If you mean," she went on, her voice softer, "do I hate you because you are your mother's daughter . . ." She paused, seemed to gather her thoughts. "I didn't know your mother well. I only knew what he told me, that she had broken your father's heart."

"He told me she was dead."

"You mentioned that," she said. If she'd judged my father for the lie, it didn't show in her face.

"And now I know she isn't. You'd know that now, too."

She inclined her head. "Malachi told me."

"I thought my father and I had this nice simple life. Antiques and MREs. That my mother had died, but we survived together." I looked at her. "But that's not true. She was still alive. He had magic, and he had you." I paused. "Why didn't he tell me?"

As if to give herself time, Erida went over to the wisteria that climbed over the church's back wall, ran her finger across a cluster of lavender flowers. Then she turned back. "I don't know. I thought he had, and that you simply didn't want to be near a woman you saw as a poor replacement for your mother."

"He told you that?"

"No," she said, with a soft smile. "I thought perhaps he sought to soothe my feelings. I imagine he wanted to keep you safe in the way he knew how—by keeping you away from magic and keeping magic away from you."

The same protective instinct that had driven Liam into the bayou.

"He loved you, Claire, and he wanted to build a wall around you to keep you safe. So he compartmentalized his life."

"You shielded Royal Mercantile from the magic monitors." It was a guess, but I was pretty sure I was right.

She nodded. "He was concerned he might use his magic without thinking, trigger the alarms, and bring Containment. He didn't want you left alone if he got dragged into Devil's Isle."

But I ended up in Devil's Isle anyway. Not dragged, but there because I'd used my magic, triggered Containment, and had to ask Moses to erase the evidence.

"He had such plans for you and the store, for life when things got back to normal. He was working on a second location for the store—an old Apollo gas station in Carrolton."

So he'd told her about the gas station, or at least part of it. "You don't know if he finished it?" I tried to keep my voice neutral, but it was hard.

Grief was clear in her eyes. "I don't know. I shielded it while he was restoring it, but I had to leave New Orleans. Fighting in Shreveport was getting heavier, and I was needed. I was gone for two months . . . and he was gone by the time I got back."

"I'm sorry."

"I know you lost him. But I lost him, too."

I nodded.

"I haven't been to the building since he died. It's been so long, I'm not even sure I could find it again."

We'd both lost my father. Maybe it was time to find something new.

"I know where it is," I said. "He finished it. Maybe I can show it to you sometime."

She looked at me for a long time, a dozen emotions swirling across her face. "I'd like that," she finally said, the deal between us done, and maybe something forged.

I drove Scarlet back to the gas station, parked her in a narrow slot in the alley behind it, covered her with a couple of tarps I found in a nearby garage. They'd keep her safe for now, or at least make her appear uninteresting to casual observers.

It was ironic that I couldn't park my newly adopted car in the gas station I lived in, but none of the garage doors were operable. They'd all been closed and sealed to keep the temperature and humidity consistent. So until I came up with a better plan, it was the alley for her.

I came around the block, waited halfheartedly for a bit to ensure that all was clear, and then stared.

The Snoball sign I'd found in Moses's butter house—and walked away from—was propped beside the gas station door. The grime had been cleared away so the metal gleamed, the letters brilliant and enticing.

I walked toward it, knelt, and ran a finger down the raised ridges of each letter. Memories of another time, as if swollen by the history they contained.

The air changed, shifted, raising the hair at the back of my neck.

Slowly, I rose to my feet and glanced behind me.

Liam stood fifteen feet away, hands at his sides, longing laid bare on his face. His eyes shimmered—blue, then gold, then blue, his brows drawn together with an intensity that reminded me of a warrior, of a wolf. Of a man on a mission.

Lust rose so hot, so bright, it might have been a forming star.

"You looked like you wanted that. Back at the house near Moses's, I mean."

I nodded, and felt like gossamer glass, fragile and ready to break. It took two tries to get out "Thank you. It will look good in there."

Liam nodded.

"I'm sorry," he said, and I could see the truth of it in his eyes. "I'm so sorry I left you alone."

I ran to him, and he welcomed me with strong arms.

"I'm sorry," he said into my hair. "I'm so sorry. I thought I was doing the right thing."

In his arms, I broke, shattered into a million pieces. "You left us."

"I know. And I'm so sorry."

"I didn't know my mother. She left. The war came, and my friends left. My teachers left. My father died. He left." I looked at him, let him see the truth in my eyes. And when he realized it, regret settled into his face. "The battle came, and you left. You left when we needed each other most."

"I thought I was saving us, shielding you. Instead, I put myself far away from the one person who makes me stronger. Because we're stronger together." He tipped my chin up. "I love you, Claire. Maybe it's too soon for that; maybe it's too late. I don't even care if you say it back. I love you. And I will never leave you again."

I lifted my head, searched for his mouth. He met my lips softly, careful but hopeful. His fingers slid into my hair as he moved closer, melding the long line of his body with mine.

I felt my body warming, loosening, relaxing for the first time in weeks, melting in the heat of his arms.

The rain fell suddenly, the sky letting go just as we had, and soaked us to the bone immediately.

He pulled back, pushed wet hair from my face. "We should probably get inside. If you're okay with that."

"I demand it," I said with an answering grin.

Before I could argue, and probably because he knew I would, he picked me up, carried me to the door.

I unlocked it and flipped on the lights, but Liam switched them off again.

"Don't need lights," he murmured, shutting the door and leaving us in darkness. The room was pitch-black, and there was a moment of exquisite anticipation before he found my mouth again and steered me backward until my hips hit the lip of a table.

He hoisted me onto it, pulled me hard against his body while rain pelted the roof like a corps of drummers. His mouth pummeled mine, assaulted and possessed it. He kissed me like a man long denied, like a man returning from war.

And maybe that wasn't far from the truth.

I dug my fingers into his hair and wrapped my legs around his waist, nearly moaned from the feel of him, hard and ready, at my core.

Our kisses became brutal, full of heat and anger and promise. I pulled back, yanked at the hem of his shirt, slid my hands against the bunched muscles of his abdomen. His body was strong, lean muscle honed from hard and honest work.

He pulled the T-shirt over his head and I let my hands roam against skin still damp from the downpour, every inch of skin and muscle taut.

"Your body . . . is a wonderland," I said, when I couldn't think of any other way to finish that sentence.

Liam snorted, pulled my shirt over my head, found my breasts with his hands. I arched forward into his fingers as fire erupted under my skin, fire that only he could control.

Then even that bit of lace was gone, and we were down to rain-sodden jeans. I caught my lip between my teeth, smiled at him as I reached for the snap of his jeans.

"Are you sure—?"

I cut off his question with a kiss. "I need you," I murmured against his lips. "I've needed you for a long time. I just didn't know it until we met. And then I told myself I didn't. And then you came back."

"And I'm not leaving again."

"You may have mentioned that."

Then the rest of his clothes were heaped on the floor, and he was hot and heavy in my hand, his arms braced on the table as he dropped his forehead to mine, struggled to breathe. He reached back, pushed artifacts carefully but decisively away, and pressed me into the table-top. Then his hand was at my core, inciting.

"Now," I said, and his hands were at my jeans, and then I was bared to him, too.

He was already hard, his body primed and ready. "Now," he agreed. He thrust, locked our bodies together. He paused, his body shaking with desire, arms corded as he sought to gain control.

"Claire," he muttered, his breath heavy at my temple.

"Don't stop now," I said, and wrapped my arms around his neck as he climbed onto the table above me, his gorgeous face above mine, one hand behind my head to cushion it, as his hips worked.

"Never," he said, and pressed his mouth to mine, found my center again, and sent us both over the edge.

CHAPTER NINETEEN

I woke with a mission. It was stupid, and it was dangerous, but there was a fire in my belly, enough curiosity to kill a very fat cat, and enough anger to get me up and moving before the sun rose.

And before Liam climbed out of my bed, where he still lay, one hand thrown over his head, the other on his abdomen.

I ate half an energy bar that was somewhere between hardtack and cardboard, chasing it down with a bottle of water.

I hid my hair beneath a cap, pulled on a tank top, capri leggings, and tennis shoes. I'd stay cool in the humidity that already fogged across the city, and in case I was noticed, I'd look like a jogger. At least at first glance. And if nobody questioned whether there were many joggers in postwar New Orleans.

She didn't live far away, according to the information Moses had waiting on a note on his front porch, tucked between the screen door and the main door. That had been the favor I'd asked of him yesterday.

We needed to find out where Laura Blackwell might strike, where she might try to deploy her particular weapon. Maybe, if I watched her, I'd find some clue. I wasn't sure what that might be—a giant photograph of a spot where the Veil crossed, a printed set of Google directions accidentally discarded in her yard? I'd know it when I saw it; the point was the looking.

But that's not why I was doing it. That was just the collateral benefit.

I wanted to know who this woman was. And maybe, in the tiniest hidden recess of my heart, in the Corner of Lost Causes, I wanted to be proven wrong.

She lived near Tulane in the Audubon neighborhood, one of the fancier areas of New Orleans. It was too far to walk, but I didn't want to chance getting caught and having to dump Scarlet. So I left her at home, safe and covered, and rode my bike downtown.

I came within a block of her address, stopped, and stared.

Where there'd once been a grid of streets with small cottages, camelbacks, and shotguns, a tall brick wall towered. The bricks were clean and ran in perfectly aligned rows down the wall, which bowed prettily until it curved around away from me. I got off the bike, locked it to a tree, and walked toward the gate.

There was a pretty cottage-style gatehouse in the middle of the divided avenue that led inside. The cottage house was dark, and the gate was open. I wasn't sure if I'd happened to visit when there wasn't a guard, or if the gatehouse was just for show, because there weren't enough people left in New Orleans to cause concern.

I made my decision and crept closer.

I stayed close to the wall, walked inside.

The houses were brick with tile roofs. All of them new, all of them immaculate. The roads were no longer grids, but sweeping avenues that curved around landscaped lawns and sidewalks marked by trees and wrought-iron benches.

They'd torn down the houses that had been here before and constructed an entirely new neighborhood. One that was gated and walled from the need around it. It was Devil's Isle in reverse—the renovation of a neighborhood with a wall to keep unmentionables out.

The sun was beginning to color the sky as I followed the main road around. The houses weren't just new; they were enormous. Two stories, lots of dormers, two- or three-car garages, huge windows with pretty mullions.

This was a beautiful neighborhood. Before the war, it would have fit well in a suburb for the wealthy who commuted into the city for work every day. But to be here? Now? The only big business in New Orleans was Devil's Isle, and Devil's Isle was run by the PCC—Containment, specifically. Maybe the PCC had set up the neighborhood for the Containment bigwigs. Maybe the Commandant lived here, in one of these set-back houses with the cobblestone sidewalks and hanging ferns.

A street sign atop a fluted black pole—gas lamp mounted on top—told me I'd reached the place I wanted: Hidden Ridge Circle.

I wrapped my fingers around the pole, the painted metal cool beneath my hand, and tried to catch my breath. I hadn't been running, but being close to her again made my lungs feel like they'd been belted, tightly wrapped and very constricted.

I could walk away now. She'd almost certainly call Containment again if she saw me, and it would be hard to hide among these sweeping lawns, especially when my only way out was the narrow gap in the wall.

But I had to look. My feet were already carrying me forward, bearing me to the end of the dead-end circle where my mother lived.

It was a story and a half high, with a small brick porch. The windows were bare, the house lit even in the early hours of the morning.

I adjusted my cap, rolled my shoulders, and began walking like I belonged there.

And then I was there, standing in front of the house.

In front of my mother's house.

There wasn't a single item of decoration outside except for the number on the house. No chairs on the porch, no flowers in urns by the door, no extraneous plants in the landscape. Just the solid brick house in a corner of a gated neighborhood of fraternally similar houses.

I bent down to tie my shoe, glanced to the side to look in the front window. It was probably supposed to be a dining room, but the room was empty except for the wrought-iron chandelier that hung low in the middle of the ceiling, waiting for a table to be slid into place beneath it.

I could see the edges of a kitchen beyond, but nothing else.

I stood up, stretched, took a look at the yard. It sloped gently to the back, a hill created where there hadn't been one before; this part of New Orleans had been as flat as the rest of it. If I wanted another look inside, I'd have to get closer.

I walked around to the back of the house, where a live oak's branches skimmed over the lawn. Since the tree was dozens of years older than the houses, they must have managed to build around it.

There was a wooden deck at the back. Light blazed through windows above it. I crept beneath the wooden slats across a bed of mulch, then around to the stairs—the only way I'd be able to get high enough to see. I took a testing step, putting my weight on one tread to ensure it was quiet, before moving to the next.

The window came into view halfway up the stairs. I peeked inside, was immediately faced by disappointment when I didn't see her in the eat-in kitchen. I took the opportunity to study it.

There were no knickknacks, no art, no kitsch in the kitchen. No canisters or napkin holders or towels or bottles. Just empty granite countertops and tall cherry cabinets. The kitchen table was the same shade, but there were no place mats, no centerpiece. A family room flanked the kitchen on the other side. I could see a couch, a coffee table, and nothing else. No pictures, no television.

The emptiness had to be something she'd chosen; if she could get the house, she could get the stuff to put in it.

She walked in. Tall and slender, long red hair falling over her shoulders. She was a lovely woman; in other circumstances, I might have said that I'd have been happy to look like her when I grew up. Now? Not so much.

She wore a belted robe of pale turquoise that draped silkily to the floor. She opened an enormous glass-doored refrigerator, pulled out a plate of food, and moved it to the table. Leftovers for breakfast, or something she'd already prepared?

She sat down at the kitchen table, where she'd already placed a napkin, fork, and small cup of orange juice. A laptop was closed in front of her, and a manila folder lay to her right. Her feet, which were bare, were flat on the floor as she put the napkin in her lap, opened the folder, and began to eat.

And that was it. She read and ate methodically. She certainly didn't look sad or deprived. She just looked . . . focused.

This wasn't the kind of life I'd said I wanted. And yet it was exactly the kind of life I had. Except that I lived alone by circumstance. Not by design.

My mother. Living alone in her mansion, in a neighborhood of mansions, in a city still broken and stained by war. A woman who'd married and borne a child and then left. A woman who'd created a killer no one could see coming.

Feeling suddenly ill, I crept down the stairs, waited at the bottom with a hand on the railing until my breathing slowed to normal levels.

Whoever she was, I was still me. I was still Claire. And that was fine. That was enough.

I'd just keep saying that until it felt true.

I walked toward the front yard, stopped when I saw a truck newly parked in the driveway.

It was the same yellow truck we'd seen in the loading dock at Devil's Isle, with the same streak of red paint across the front panel. A man climbed out of the back with a clipboard. He strode quickly to the front door, rang the bell, waited for Laura to open it.

She did so without smile or "hello," without even meeting his gaze. She reached for the clipboard, signed, and looked at him expectantly.

The driver opened the back of the truck—and pulled out what looked like the same neon orange box loaded at the Devil's Isle dock. It was no less bright today, and in the morning light I could see dark numbers stenciled along one side.

My mother opened the door for him, let him take the crate into her house. Then she closed the door in his face.

He gave the door a dour look before jogging back to the truck and speeding away.

So what did my mother have from Devil's Isle, and why? What could Devil's Isle have to offer her?

"You looking for something?"

I turned quickly, found the neighbor on his front porch, small dog tucked under his arm like a football. My heart stopped, then thudded hard twice before starting up again.

I didn't know how much he'd seen. So I decided to pretend there'd been nothing to see at all. I offered a nervous laugh, and didn't have to fake the nerves.

"Shin splint," I said, pointing to my lower leg. "Just trying to walk it off. I was hoping the break would help me loosen it up. Running on concrete just *kills* me." I gestured to the truck with a smile.

"And then I got a little nosy. Not often you see a delivery truck like that around here!"

"Sure," he said, and didn't sound at all convinced.

"Anyway, I better get going. Have a good one!"

I jogged out of the neighborhood, found my bike, and raced home.

I walked into the gas station, expecting darkness and silence and safety.

Expecting him to be gone.

I hadn't expected much of Liam Quinn. Wasn't that always my mistake? My prejudice?

He wore jeans and a T-shirt, his feet bare. He stood in front of one of the tables, palms braced on the tabletop as he stared down at an open book.

There was something so right about his standing there, about his bare feet and intense expression. Like he was a warrior poet, a scholarly knight.

He looked up when I walked in, his body instantly on alert. And he didn't relax much when he realized it was me. He didn't ask me where I'd been. Could probably see I was flustered. Might have been able to see the grief in my eyes. But he didn't ask about it. Not yet.

For my part, I had absolutely no idea what to say or do.

He filled in the blank. "It's your place. But I'm staying until you kick me out. And if you try to kick me out, I might not go."

I closed and locked the door. "All right."

"How do you feel about that?"

"I have no idea."

He watched me for a moment. "Fair enough."

Hope was like an ember in my belly. Small and hot and greedy. But that wasn't thinking. It wasn't even feeling. It was anticipation, and anticipation wouldn't get me through this moment. Whatever this moment was. So I ignored it, focused on what was.

I walked toward him, and it took a couple of tries to get words out. "What are you reading?"

"I'm not entirely sure." He showed me the cover. It was a big book with leather binding, the paper inside thin enough to see through. The pages were covered in minuscule calligraphy in a language that didn't look even remotely familiar.

"A spellbook?" I asked.

"Do Paras need spellbooks?"

"I have no idea. That would be a good question for Malachi."

Liam nodded, closed the book. "For all we know, could be recipes. Or a romance novel."

"Love in the Beyond?"

"Something like that. I assume it happens."

"Did you see the tension between Malachi and Rachel? That was pretty interesting."

"I'd rather not think about Malachi at the moment."

His body brushed against mine, and lust bolted through me, leaving me nearly breathless. If this was going to be our relationship, if I was going to get weak in the knees every time our paths crossed, I was in trouble.

His lips were on my ear, growling and nipping, sending shivers down my body. "I can't stop thinking about you."

He was doing a pretty damn good job of making me think about him, too. "We have problems to deal with."

"Like?"

"A biomedical conspiracy?"

"Oh. That." He turned our bodies, pinning me back against the table, his thigh between mine. And then his lips crushed against mine, his body hot and hard and ready, his mouth eager.

"I want you again," he murmured. "I have a lot of making up to do. And if we can't have pleasure, if we can't live, what are we fighting for?"

I couldn't find a single reason to argue with him.

"You want to tell me where you were this morning?" he asked, when we were walking to Moses's house.

"You won't like it."

His jaw tightened. "Try me," he said after a minute, in a tone that confirmed to me he wouldn't like it.

"I went to see my mother."

I'd been right. His jaw twitched, and every other muscle in his body tensed as well.

"At her house," I added.

"How did you—? Moses," he said, answering his own question. "You got her address from Moses."

"He did me a favor."

"That was . . . reckless," he finally said.

"You did know that about me." He'd called me that plenty of times. While he didn't like worrying, I was pretty sure he was turned off by cowardice and turned on by whatever category of bravery "reckless" fell into.

"I'd hoped it had worn off."

"You hoped, in the time I've been living alone in a gas station full of illegal magical objects, while being hunted by Containment and hanging out with illegal magical people, that I'd become less reckless?"

He was silent for a moment. "Good point. And what did you find?" His voice had softened with something that sounded like pity, and made me want to curl up in an uncomfortable ball.

"I found her. Sitting at a table, eating her breakfast. She was alone in an enormous house—not even a picture on the wall—everything just so. Just the way she liked it."

He reached out, took my hand, squeezed it.

"There's no room for me in her life. Maybe never was. Maybe not my father, either."

"That matches what she told you at the building."

"I know. Maybe I thought she was lying. Or maybe I just wanted to see for myself. Who she is, why she's done what she's done. Maybe I thought that if I saw her, I'd understand better. She's my *mother.* If that's the extent of her life, it's sad, at least to me. But I don't know if that's the extent of it. I don't know any more about her than she does about me."

"Do you want to know more?"

"I don't know. I didn't expect to walk into a fairy tale. But I didn't expect to pity her, either. I didn't go just for my own benefit," I said, changing the subject. "I wondered if I'd see anything that was useful. And I might have found something."

"Reckless," he said again as we reached Moses's house. "And what did you find?"

I nearly answered, but caught a whiff of something in the air. Something delicious.

I glanced back at the road. Darby's utility vehicle was parked at the curb. "Breakfast," I said. "I found breakfast."

Technically, it was second breakfast. But I'd earned it with the morning's exercise. And it looked to be worth it.

Darby stood in the middle of the room in a pale green dress with a nipped-in waist, her dark hair gleaming. And she held a silver tray of chocolate chip cookies. Real chocolate chip cookies. Not freeze-dried. Not dairy- and gluten-free. Not rehydrated.

Cookies.

"How do you do this in a war zone?" I asked her, gesturing to the ensemble.

"Practice and denial," she said with a grin. "And we're working on a little something in the lab that keeps the power on."

"If there's going to be food every time I come over here," Gavin said, a cookie in each hand, "I'm coming over here more often." He looked us over. "Coincidence, you two arriving at the same time."

Liam didn't take the bait, but stared his brother down.

"About damn time," Gavin muttered, taking another bite. "But don't mind me."

Liam took two cookies, handed me one. "Thank you, Darby."

"You're welcome."

She offered the tray to Moses, but his lip curled. "Gross."

Malachi took one, tried a careful nibble. His eyes lit up like a kid's on Christmas. No words, just another careful bite. And then another. I wasn't sure he cared much for human food; Darby's cookies might have changed his mind. And for good reason—they were delicious.

"Damn," Liam said, taking a bite. "These are amazing."

"You'd be surprised what lab equipment can do."

Liam swallowed hard.

"I'm kidding. *Kidding.*" She put the tray on a pile of electronics. "What's the latest?"

"Gunnar not here yet?"

"He isn't," Gavin said as he and Malachi both reached for another cookie.

"Don't ruin your dinner," Liam told him, which advice Gavin completely ignored.

"I think I saw something this morning," I said, and told them about my visit to see Laura Blackwell. I'd decided to call her that. It was the best way I could think of to cope with it.

"On my way out, a truck pulled up." I looked at Liam. "Remember that big yellow truck we saw at the loading dock? The one with the paint on the front panel?"

"I don't remember the paint, but yeah."

"Same truck pulled into her driveway. And the driver gave her something he'd loaded out on Devil's Isle."

"What was it?" Gavin asked. He'd stopped eating his cookie.

"I don't know. Didn't see what it was. Only the box. Blinding neon orange." I estimated the dimensions with hand gestures. "Had stenciled numbers on one side."

Darby bobbled on her heels, took a stumbling step backward before "Oh, shit," she said. "Oh, shit."

Gavin caught her by the elbow, steadied her again. "What's wrong?"

"The numbers stenciled on the sides—were they 'three-oh-five'?"

A wave of sickness roiled my stomach. "Yes. Why?"

Gavin led her to the couch. "Sit down. Take a breath." He looked back at Moses. "Bottled water?"

"Kitchen," Moses said. "I'll get it." He hopped down, disappeared into the kitchen, and we all looked back at Darby.

"Darby," Malachi prompted, "what's in the box?"

"I can't be sure, but . . ." She trailed off, rubbing a finger over her lips as she stared into the middle distance, preparing herself for something.

"In the early years, like Gunnar was saying, the PCC was trying to learn about the Veil. Where it came from, what it was made of, what it could do. When I joined PCC Research, we were young and curious and stupidly excited to have discovered this thing. One of our tasks was figuring out a way to look through it. Some kind of device that could let us see what was happening on the other side."

"A periscope," Liam suggested.

"A porthole through the portal," Darby said with a rueful smile. "That's what we called it, and thought we were pretty clever."

Moses came back, offered her the bottle of water. Darby took it with a smile of thanks, but didn't twist the lid.

"We futzed around for a little while, played with optics and lenses, tried to stick them through the Veil. At first, we couldn't manage it because the Veil's not a tangible thing. It's energy—a passageway made of energy. A doorway from our world to theirs. Then we got this idea."

She took a moment to gather herself, while the rest of us waited, completely silent. "We decided we could use harmonics to disrupt the energy in a tiny portion of the Veil and make a little window." She mimed pushing curtains aside. "We created this awkward little machine—the decharger—and got it to work once."

"What did you see?" I asked, thinking of the battalions of warriors I'd seen.

Darby smiled. "Nothing but rolling hills. Which is one of the reasons we were so damn surprised when the war actually started. Hindsight."

Several of us grunted in agreement.

"Anyway, the Veil was breached right after that, so it wasn't necessary anymore. And then I was fired, and that was the end of my work on the decharger."

"The decharger was in the orange box," I said.

She nodded. "Yeah, but I haven't heard anything about it in a really long time."

"Someone heard about it," I said. "Laura, maybe because she was at the PCC before."

"Claire and Liam first saw it being moved out of Devil's Isle," Gavin said. "Why would a PCC Research implement be stored there?"

"There were buildings in the Marigny used for Containment

storage before it became the prison," Darby said. "It was probably in one of those. But what would she want it for?"

"If it was working," Malachi asked, "could it be used to slip something into the Beyond? Through the window?"

"Like what?" Darby asked, but then her expression fell, and the room went absolutely silent.

"Like a virus," Liam said.

"You use the decharger to open the Veil," I said, "and you use the virus you've already created and, what, just toss it in?" I looked at Darby.

"Aerosol," she said, misery clear in every line of her face. "She'd need an aerosolized version of the virus for actual deployment through the Veil."

Gavin reached out to squeeze Darby's shoulder supportively. She put her hand over his, tried for a weak smile.

"How much product would she need to pull this off?" he asked. "Does she have enough to do real damage?"

"The size of a virus is measured in nanometers," Darby said. "Tiny. You can fit a lot of them into a small space. In 1979, a missing filter at an anthrax plant in the Soviet Union killed a hundred people in a few hours. That was an *accidental* release."

"Presumably she wouldn't have wanted the decharger unless she had something to deploy," Gavin said.

"So she's got a virus, and she's got a way to sneak it into the Beyond," I summarized. "But we don't know how much she's got, or how many Paras she could kill."

"Say that Cajun swear again," Moses requested.

"Fils de putain." This time, the Quinn boys said it together.

"No," Darby said, and walked across the room, kicked at the wall with a heel, then looked back at us. "The PCC wouldn't do this. We aren't at war. There'd be no reason for it."

"Maybe they don't know."

She looked back at me. "What do you mean?"

"Gunnar said the PCC is funding the research," I said. "That doesn't mean they want to deploy it this way, for genocide."

"That would mean it's Blackwell's doing." Liam's voice was somber, and he reached out, squeezed my hand, offered the same kind of support Gavin had given Darby a moment ago. A reminder that I wasn't alone. That we were in this together.

"Or hers and Lorenzo Caval's," I said. "I obviously don't know Blackwell very well. But after our conversation yesterday and what I saw this morning, I'd say she's really focused on her science, her work. Single-minded." I rubbed my neck, trying to relieve the tension that had gathered there. "Maybe I'm projecting, but she seems unbalanced. Not because she left us for work, but because she seems to wear blinders about everything else." I told them what I'd seen of the house, of her manner.

"It was just a snapshot, what I saw. But there was something really, I guess, *absent* about it."

"She has a mission."

I looked at Liam and said, "Yeah, but not based on some moral code. I don't think she cares about Paras or humans, for that matter. She has a *task*, and she's not going to stop until she gets it done."

"And you add in Lorenzo Caval," Liam said, "who hates Paras because of his mother's death."

"Yeah. Now add those together—single-minded scientific focus and Paranormal bloodlust."

"And you get murder," Moses said.

"Yeah." I paused. "She was at Talisheek, when Nix tried to open the Veil."

"I thought about that," Liam said.

"Maybe she wanted to sneak in a sample," Darby said. "Was hoping for an early test of the aerosolized virus."

I nodded in agreement.

"If she does this," Darby said—"infects the Beyond, and kills all those people—it's my fault."

"It's not," Malachi said. "Claire's right—the context does matter. This device wasn't created for murder. It was created for curiosity—for the basic human instinct to learn. She's warping that, corrupting it."

"We have to do something," Darby said. "We have to tell someone, or—"

There was a knock at Moses's door.

Gavin checked the peephole. "Gunnar," he said, and opened the door.

This time, Gunnar was alone. He wore fatigues, his service weapon belted at his waist. And he didn't look injured, which meant he hadn't been hurt during the raid on the ADZ building.

That was a little more weight off my chest.

"What did you find?" Darby asked, jumping to her feet.

"Not a damn thing. ADZ was cleared out completely. A couple of desks, a couple of refrigeration units that couldn't be hauled away quickly or easily. That was it."

There was a lot of swearing, including a few more attempts at Cajun.

"How'd they move so fast?" Liam asked.

"Could be your visit yesterday scared them off," Gunnar said. "Could be Lorenzo Caval has contacts in Containment, and we've got a leak. Probably heard about the warrant, or about the op, and made his move."

"Rachel?" Malachi asked.

Gunnar barely managed to hide a smile. "She's fine. I'll tell her you asked."

Malachi didn't look thrilled about that, but he didn't object.

Gunnar's gaze fell on the plate of cookies. "Chocolate chip?"

"Yeah," Darby said. But the excitement had gone out of her voice. "Help yourself."

"Thanks. I'm starving."

"Broussard set all this in motion," Gunnar said. "Found the file, figured out at least some of the rest of it. They probably figured they were nearing the beginning of the end."

"And speaking of endings," Moses said, "we think Blackwell's written a really shitty one."

"Brace yourself," Gavin recommended, and Gunnar stuffed the rest of the cookie into his mouth.

"Go," he murmured over it.

"PCC Research built a window into the Veil once upon a time," I said. "Pretty good chance that's now in Blackwell's hands, and she's going to try to deploy the virus there."

Gunnar choked, coughed, and wasn't helped by Gavin's slap on the back.

"And how do we know that?" Gunnar wheezed, and we walked him through the details.

"The decharger was just delivered today," Darby said. "If it was in a storage facility in the Marigny, it hasn't been maintained. It's going to need work. Maybe substantial work."

If nothing else, Laura Blackwell seemed to be a planner. I glanced at Gunnar. "What did Caval do for Containment?"

"Electrical engineer. Worked on the generators."

Of course he was, and of course he did.

"Damn it," Darby muttered. "Damn it all right to hell."

"If she's going to deploy it through the Veil, she's going to have to get to the Veil."

But the Veil, which ran like a fault line along the ninetieth line of longitude, was thousands of miles long.

"We need to identify her target location," Liam said. "Talisheek?"

That was where the Veil had opened the first time, and where defense contractors had nearly opened it again last year.

"It's guarded now," Gunnar said.

"She's a scientist," I said. "She'll want to put the virus through in the most, I guess, efficacious place. The place with the highest chance of success." I looked at Malachi, my stomach sinking with a horrible realization. "In the Beyond, does the Veil pass through any large cities? Population hubs?"

A shadow passed over his eyes when he figured out what I was suggesting. "You think she'll equate success and Paranormal deaths."

"I think they both might." And I wished I could apologize for her, wished that might have meant something. I wished there was a connection between Laura Blackwell and me other than a slim biological thread—something I could use to keep her from doing this horrible, horrible thing.

"In the Beyond, the Veil runs primarily through rural areas," Malachi said. "We were aware of it before you were, and we avoided it when building our cities."

That was something, but it didn't help us narrow down the strike zone. Even if we divided the Veil into sections and tried to assign people to search them all, there was a good chance we wouldn't find her in time.

Maybe there was a building she'd want to be near, a battlefield that was meaningful to her. Or maybe she'd pick the spot that required the least effort—the one easiest to get to.

"We don't have enough information," I said.

"Puzzle it out the best you can," Gunnar said, grabbing another cookie and heading for the door. "I'm going back to the Cabildo. I'll get back to you—or send Rachel—as soon as I can. I need more warrants."

He looked back and narrowed his gaze at me. "And don't do anything rash while I'm gone."

He closed the door heavily behind him, sending a cloud of dust into the air.

"I think he meant me," I said, and there were general murmurs of agreement.

"Of course he meant you, Red," Moses said with a grin. "You're the only one needs supervising."

"I don't need supervising."

But even Liam's look was doubting.

Since they were so certain I was going to do something reckless, I figured I might as well oblige.

"He's battling bureaucracy and people with power," I said, looking at all of them. "She could be making a move right now."

Moses rolled his eyes. "She's setting you up, in case you can't tell. Preparing to drop the hammer."

"You want to go to her house," Liam said, and I nodded.

"She's probably not there," I said. "But evidence might be. And if I can be the one who stops her, I'm damn well going to try."

CHAPTER TWENTY

"I guess we can be grateful you were reckless the last time," Liam said as we bumped toward my mother's house and her pretty walled neighborhood. Gavin, Liam, and I were squeezed into Scarlet's front seat. "Else we wouldn't know about the box or the decharger."

"You should always be grateful I'm reckless. It's one of my better qualities."

I gunned it, the rebuilt V-8 under the hood roaring like thunder, then patted Scarlet's dash. "That's my girl. My sweet, sweet girl."

"She ever touch you like that?" Gavin asked Liam with a grin.

"No comment."

"You're both hilarious," I said. "Maybe we could talk about what we're going to do when we confront my apparently evil mother."

They both went quiet.

"That wasn't sarcasm," I said. "I'm serious. She's evil, and though I'm still processing the emotions of learning that my mother is the scientist version of Maleficent, I'm very eager to take her down."

"Well," Gavin said when we reached the neighborhood. "She's spared no expense for herself."

"Being morally disgusting evidently pays well," I said, pulling

Scarlet to a stop a couple of streets away in front of a house that was obviously empty—windows open, floors and walls bare.

"I think you're right," Liam said, "and there's a good chance she's not here. But just in case." Liam pulled his .44 from his waistband, then looked at me. "You armed?"

"No. But I'll be fine."

We climbed out of the car, tried to walk as nonchalantly as possible down the quiet suburban street. We strode up to the front door just as casually, found the house dark.

I knocked, waited for a response. And when nothing happened, I tried the door.

"Locked," I said.

"Can you use magic?" Liam asked.

"No. Magic monitors are armed," I said, gesturing over my shoulder at the pole-mounted monitors along the curb.

"Not worth the risk," Gavin said, then pulled the gun from its holster. "Stand back."

"That's not exactly low-key," Liam said.

"Yeah, neither is this bitch, and neither is her plan." Gavin aimed, and we scuttled to the other side of the porch.

Two pops, and the door swung open.

"And I call you reckless," Liam muttered.

"Yeah," I said. "And I'm not the one with a gun."

The house was empty.

I took the second floor, walking slowly through each room, taking in the tall ceilings and attractive paint colors, the crown moldings. And the complete absence of décor. The master bedroom held a bed, dresser, nightstand. The nightstand held a single lamp and an old-fashioned wind-up alarm clock. Prevented her from being late, I guessed, when the power went out.

The nightstand's drawers were empty, the dresser's full of neatly folded clothes in tidy piles. Even the socks were paired and fitted into an organizer that looked a little like an egg crate. I didn't see any evidence that she'd packed a bag, but how would I know?

The bathroom held the usual necessities. The makeup and bath products were high-end brands, must have been shipped into the Zone, but there was nothing extraneous. Nothing that didn't have a specific purpose. And here, like downstairs, we saw no art, no flowers, no cocktail tables or objects. There were four smaller bedrooms on this floor; all were empty except for a yoga mat in the room closest to the master.

I went downstairs again, found Liam in the kitchen.

"Coffeepot's still warm," he said, checking the glass carafe with a fingertip. "She hasn't been gone long."

Gavin came in through another door, the orange box in his arms. "Empty," he said. "But here. Confirms she's in possession of PCC property and her likely intent."

"Getting it through the Veil," Liam said, and Gavin nodded.

"You find anything?" he asked.

"Nothing useful," I replied.

"She gets nervous, decides to abandon this place," Liam said, hands on his hips as he looked around. "Goes into the wind. Or she decides she's ready, and she's off to deploy. Doesn't care if we know where she lives, because she's on task, focused."

"I don't think she'd run," I said. "She doesn't seem to care what people think, and she's got some kind of federal benefactor, maybe thinks she's untouchable."

Liam nodded. "Agreed."

I glanced back, realized the laptop was still sitting on the table.

"Computer," I said. I pulled out the chair, sat down in the same spot where my mother had sat with her coffee and orange juice, and turned the machine on.

It wasn't even password-protected. The computer's desktop blinked on, showing a photograph of Jackson Square after dusk.

"She left her computer behind?" Gavin asked, moving closer. He and Liam stood behind the chair, looked over my shoulder.

"She was in a hurry," I said. And that made me worry even more.

The computer's desktop was immaculate. No random files, no temporarily stored documents or gifs. Just a neat line of links to the hard drive and important folders.

I spent ten minutes opening documents and folders, searching the hard drive for anything that might give us a clue about her location. Plenty of scientific documents that I didn't understand, but I figured Darby would be interested in them.

I skipped those, opened up the Internet browser, then pulled up her search history. And my heart stuttered.

The last phrase she'd searched had been "sola fluids."

"What's a sola?"

"A what?" Liam asked, moving closer.

"Sola. It's what she searched for last. 'Sola fluids.'"

"Not 'sola,'" Gavin said, walking toward us. "So La. As in 'Southern Louisiana.'" He peered over my shoulder. "SoLa Fluids. It's a petroleum processor on the river. One of the few still operating in the Zone."

"Where is it?" I asked.

"Near Belle Chasse."

"The Veil runs through Belle Chasse," Liam said. "There was a skirmish there during the war. A few Court Paras tried to go back through."

"I remember." Their effort hadn't worked, but the fight had been the topic of conversation in the Quarter for weeks.

"Belle Chasse," I murmured, thinking it over. The Veil ran through it, it was close to New Orleans, and it was probably a place she'd heard about before. She wouldn't want to leave this to chance. And there was nothing else on the computer that looked like she was trying to nail down the geographic part of the search.

"I think that's the best we're going to do from here," I said. "Let's find Gunnar."

Gavin was already striding to the door. "Moral of this story?" he said. "Murderers should always clear their browser history."

I grabbed the computer and followed them out.

There were days when it was nice to be free of the burden of cell phones. There were no three a.m. e-mails, no social media stress, no worries about Internet arguments with strangers.

And no way to easily arrange for the arrest and capture of a homicidal maniac.

We dropped Gavin off near Moses's house so he could find a vehicle, then drove directly to the Cabildo, Containment's HQ. We waited outside while Gunnar talked to the Commandant about what we'd found and where we thought she might strike.

The guards outside the building gave us the stink eye. But whatever Gunnar had said to them on his way in had them staying in position, weapons still holstered.

Fifteen minutes later, he came out. And he didn't look happy.

"Senator Jute McLellan," he said, climbing into the truck and slamming the door. The truck vibrated from the ferocity of his anger. "Go back to Moses's."

"Which is who?" Liam asked when I put the truck in gear and drove away from the Cabildo before the agents could change their mind.

"The head of the subcommittee that's been sneaking funds to

ADZ. War disrupts the economy, and Senator McLellan doesn't care for that. So he and his friends decided Icarus was a wise investment."

"No more Paranormals, no more war?" I asked.

"Pretty much." He smiled slyly. "Capital police are now on their way to have a very long talk with Senator McLellan."

"Good," Liam said. "Assuming they can make it stick."

"No evidence to date that he's involved in the research, just the funding, so his lawyers will probably have a field day. But the money was appropriated, and that's got his mark all over it. He'll have plenty to answer for."

"And closer to home?" Liam asked.

"Commandant has scrambled jets out of Pensacola," Gunnar said. "And there are a few troop carriers on the ground with some fancy ordnance that the army's been working on. But we might still beat them to the spot."

"And in the meantime," I guessed, "we do what we can."

"We do what we can," Gunnar said. "So drive fast."

Refusing to give up after the loss of his briefly beloved Range Rover, Gavin pulled up to Moses's house in an enormous red Humvee.

"Only in a war zone, where gas is hard to get, would my brother drive something like that."

"I'm in a war zone," Gavin said through the open window. "I'm driving a vehicle that's ready for war."

Admittedly a better argument.

The rest of us stood outside Moses's house, preparing to stop my mother. Moses watched us from the top step of his front porch.

"She'll be there," he said, pointing generally southeast and toward the ninetieth line of longitude. "Or somewhere along here. We go in teams, secure the virus, take her down. In whatever order necessary."

He glanced at me, concern in his eyes.

"I'm fine," I said. "Really. She's not my mother. Not in any way that counts."

It was the first time I'd said it, and it was absolutely true. We had a biological connection. Shared genetic material. My origin story was connected to her, but that was the only thing between us. She hadn't been my mother in any way that mattered then, and she wasn't now. She wasn't confused, or lost, or whatever fairy tale I might have told myself growing up. She was just a woman.

Saying it aloud lifted the rest of the weight from my chest.

Liam reached out, squeezed my hand, and didn't let go.

"Claire, Liam, Darby, and I approach her directly," Gunnar said. "We aren't entirely sure where she'll be positioned, but I'd like two teams—Rachel and Malachi, and Erida and Gavin—to approach from the other directions. We're at six o'clock, you're at two and ten."

The split made sense—one Paranormal and one human on each of those teams—but no one looked happy about their particular team. Which was probably fine by Gunnar.

"Darby, tell us what we're looking for."

"The decharger's pretty small," she said, and held out her hands to form a small square. "Maybe four by four. It's a black disk, about two and a half or three inches thick. You'd press it flat against the Veil," she said, mimicking the move. "It's powered by the Veil itself."

"And the virus? The aerosolizer?"

"She could be bringing the virus in any kind of container. It depends on how it needs to be stored and how much she was able to process. Probably a canister. Something that would fit into a generator, or gun. And the mechanism has to be small enough to fit into the window created by the decharger."

"Disk, canister, generator, gun," Gunnar said. "Generally, keep an eye out for metal and plastic."

"Pretty much," Darby said with a nod.

"We'll take the virus and the decharger, and give them to Darby. She'll secure and transport."

Darby held up an old, dirty Igloo cooler, patted the side. "High-security transport, right here."

"Claire, Liam, and I will ride in the truck. Gavin will take Darby, Rachel, Erida. Malachi will fly in. Any questions?"

We all shook our heads.

"Then let's hit the road."

Ten minutes later, Gunnar was practically jumping in the front seat of the truck. "Can this thing go any faster?"

"I'm driving eighty on a postwar highway," I said. "Unless you want me to flip the truck"—we all grimaced as I hit a bump and we went momentarily airborne before thudding down again—"then no, we aren't going any faster."

Like the road to Houma, the road to Belle Chasse was mostly empty. Empty businesses and houses, then a stretch of green on both sides of a pitted highway. And somewhere ahead of us, a woman and a weapon of mass destruction.

We slowed as we neared the target area, the white towers and spires of the Apollo refinery looming in the distance like a twisted Oz.

Gunnar and Liam peered through the windows as I drove, looking for a vehicle, a sign, a woman with red hair.

But I saw her first.

"There," I said, and slowed the truck, pointed to the field on the river side of the road.

She stood on the levee half a mile up the road, the wind whipping her hair like Medusa's snakes. Scientist that she was, she'd traded in the sharp suit for cargo pants and a trim tank.

There was something small and black in her hands. There was a plastic box also at her feet, and a canister hanging from a strap around her neck. Aerosolizer and virus, I guessed.

She was staring in front of her, as if trying to locate the Veil, figure out what she was looking at, how exactly to accomplish her work. That meant we weren't too late. There was no sign of Lorenzo Caval, but there wasn't time to wait for him.

We had to move.

The Hummer slowed behind us, then pulled up alongside. A shadow passed over, wings momentarily blocking out the sun, and then Malachi landed on the road in front of us, ivory wings casting sharp shadows on the asphalt.

Hair tousled from the flight, he looked like an avenging angel. And today, that probably wasn't far from the truth.

"He is just . . . gorgeous," Gunnar said, his voice a little gravelly.

That broke the tension in the car by a long shot. "I thought we had to focus on the mission?" I said.

"He's part of the mission," Gunnar said. "A very admirable part."

As Malachi retracted his wings, Rachel and I rolled down our respective windows. But her gaze didn't move from him as he strode toward us.

"You got her?" I asked.

"On the levee," Gavin said, leaning forward.

"Caval?" Malachi asked.

"No sign of him," Liam said. "Could be Blackwell decided he's disposable."

"Or maybe he's completely AWOL," I said. "Got smart, relatively speaking, and decided it was better to bail before she did this thing."

Gunnar didn't look convinced by either option. "A man willing to kill his own brother out of a completely warped sense of priorities isn't worried about being caught. He's worried about the mission. We go as planned," he decided, "but stay alert."

"We'll keep going," Gavin said, "come up from behind."

"I'll circle around, come over from the river side," Malachi said.

Gunnar nodded. "We aren't going to wait for you to get into position. We go now, secure the virus before she attempts to deploy it."

"I'm sorry," I said to no one in particular as we climbed out of the car. "I'm sorry for whatever she's about to do."

"You didn't make her choices for her."

I looked up at Malachi, saw understanding in his eyes, and nodded.

"You're right," I said, looking back at my mother again. "But I'm going to be the one who stops her."

"I want to talk to her first," I said as we walked across the field—which was at least a couple of acres wide. Laura had descended from the levee and was walking in small circles, probably trying to nail down exactly where she needed to aim.

She'd been near the Veil at Talisheek, but didn't have magic, so she wouldn't be able to sense it or see it. She'd have to rely on longitude to find it, and even then it waved back and forth across the line of longitude.

But I could sense it fine. It was difficult to grasp the sheer size of the Veil. It wasn't a curtain drawn between us. It was a split in our world, extending up and side to side infinitely. It shimmered high enough to reach the atmosphere, far enough that it disappeared across the horizon. It was big and it was powerful, and it was holding back the river of magic and Paranormals on the other side.

In preparation for her work, Laura had pulled out the decharger. She held it in one hand while inserting the virus cartridge into a device shaped a little like a fire extinguisher.

"Laura."

She froze, turned back, aiming her biological weapon. I didn't think it would do anything to me—no humans had gotten sick yet—but I still lifted my hands.

I was getting sick of doing that lately. Of feeling like a criminal.

Her lip curled angrily. "I don't have time for you. I have work to do."

I could see them moving in my peripheral vision. "Your work is over. You're surrounded, and we'll be taking the decharger, the virus, and the weapon."

"I'm not turning anything over. I have work to do. A job to finish." She turned around to face the Veil, lifted the decharger.

"And did I mention Containment troops are en route? You turn them over to us now, and this will go a lot easier for you."

"Goddamn it." I heard Gunnar's voice behind me. "Ms. Blackwell, I don't want to shoot you, but I will. If it's between you and the Veil, I'll take you out."

She didn't move for a moment, then glanced back over her shoulder. "Why are you being irrational? This is science. The culmination of years of research."

"And you'd destroy a civilization that was millennia in the making."

She turned back, gasped as Malachi landed in front of her, wings extended and golden fury in his eyes.

She took a stumbling step backward, and Gavin was there to grab her. He pinned her arms while Malachi strode forward, not bothering to hide his wings, and wrenched the decharger away from her.

"You are a disgrace to humans, and to your daughter."

"Darby!" Gunnar called, and she ran forward, holding the cooler open, held it out while Liam removed the canister from the gun, laid it carefully inside the box.

"Got it," Darby said, and slid the cover back into place. "Virus container contained."

"That's my work," my mother said vehemently, struggling in Gavin's grip. "That's a lifetime of work."

"Suffice it to say," Liam said, "you should have focused on something a little less nasty."

"And speaking of focus," Gunnar said as he cuffed her, "where's Caval?"

"I don't know what you're talking about."

"You do," Gunnar said. "And it was pretty stupid of you not to let him help you today. The two of you together could have actually accomplished your genocide. But you didn't. We beat you." He pointed at Malachi. "A Para beat you." Then me. "And the daughter you abandoned beat you. But you'll have plenty of time to think about how they beat you when you're in prison."

The words that spewed from her mouth were overwhelmed by the noise that filled the air: sirens roaring toward us as Containment cruisers and armored vehicles raced toward the levee.

"And here comes the cavalry," Gunnar yelled over the din. He pulled a comm unit from his belt. "Prisoner and package are contained," he said.

All of the vehicles visibly slowed—all but one, which steamed toward us, undeterred by Gunnar's order. And then it lifted its muzzle and pointed the weapon directly at us.

"Caval," I murmured, and watched, hypnotized, as a streaking star shot from the muzzle and flew toward us.

"Incoming!" Gunnar screamed, pushed me and Liam to the ground, then grabbed Laura Blackwell and pulled her down, too.

They hit the ground together, the shot flying barely inches over their heads. And it didn't stop. The round kept on going, heading for the thing directly behind them, the enormous, invisible target.

While we watched in horror, the round hit it square on, and the usually invisible Veil shimmered and rippled like pebble-strewn water, shuddered like video from a broken camera.

"Holy shit," Gunnar said, while we all held our breath.

The scar was small at first, so little it was nearly invisible, a bit of dust that had ghosted across my vision and would be cleared away when I blinked.

I looked back, watched Containment agents wrench open the vehicle's door and drag a man from it. A man who looked a lot like Javier Caval.

We'd found Lorenzo.

But the hole expanded, and the char around the edge became clearer, like a cigarette burn in fabric. And it was growing larger, the circle expanding exponentially with each millisecond that passed.

"Malachi!" I screamed, and heard the *thwack* of wings on the wind behind me.

"No," he said, and the horror in his voice nearly buckled my knees. "No!"

It took me too long to realize that if I could move objects, maybe I could move the separate sides of the Veil, stitch them back together with magic. After all, the edges of the tear wrought by Paranormals had been locked together by Sensitives. Why wouldn't we be able to lock them together now?

I reached out for the power. The air was swimming with magic, but not the familiar kind. It was magic from the Beyond, from the same place the rest of our world's magic derived. But this magic was real, original. It hadn't been filtered through the Veil, through the atmosphere and objects of this world. It was pure, different from anything I'd felt before. And maybe because it hadn't been filtered through the human world, it hurt.

I began to spin the filaments of magic around me, pain erupting across my arms like pins and needles in a limb that had fallen asleep.

And all the while, the gap in the Veil grew ever larger.

"No," I said through clenched teeth, gathering every shred of strength I had, every ounce of energy in reserve. I looped magic around one side of the Veil's breach and then the other, used magic to try to force them together.

Sweat broke out on my arms, the pain like fire across them as I desperately tried to bring one side toward the other, to stretch what remained.

I wiped sweat from my brow and tried again. But it didn't work. I could move the Veil only when there was Veil to move. It was disintegrating faster than I could hold it together.

"Claire."

"No," I said to Liam, then shook off his hand. "No. I'm going to do this. I'm going to fix this. Help me, Liam. You have to help me."

"Claire, baby, I would. But you can't fix this."

I didn't want him to be right. But he was.

No matter how hard I tried, how hard I pulled, there was nothing left of the Veil to stitch together. Not enough magic to patch the hole that Containment had created.

The gap was big enough now to see through. Instead of seeing more of Louisiana, we could see glimpses of the Beyond—and the crimson uniforms of those who waited for us on the other side.

Laura Blackwell hadn't infected the Beyond.

She'd helped destroy the Veil.

CHAPTER TWENTY-ONE

The charring edges of the Veil disappeared into the distance. If anything remained of the barrier, it was too far away to matter now.

The Beyond now filled our vision, obscuring what we might have seen of Louisiana.

They were mounted on white destriers, a dozen that I could see. Paranormals all of them, and all in battle gear. Golden armor with long crimson robes beneath, golden helmets topped by crimson combs or feathers, and gleaming golden weapons in their hands. The horses were enormous white stallions with thick legs, long curling manes, and wide and flaring nostrils.

I didn't see the female commander who'd waited in the Beyond the last time the Veil had nearly been opened, the woman who'd looked into my eyes with murder in hers. But that didn't ease my fears. They were different shapes, sizes, skin tones. But they all looked ready to fight.

Some of the Paras had wings like Malachi's. Others had streaks of crimson down their foreheads, noses, and chins, and the same crimson along the tips of their fingers. They were called Seelies, members of the Court of Dawn, the faction that had broken through the Veil and led the war against us.

"The Court of Dawn!" Malachi screamed. "Be ready!"

We had a few humans and Paras, a few Containment vehicles, and a couple dozen soldiers—only enough people to threaten a scientist into backing down.

They had two dozen mounted soldiers with armor that resisted human weapons, or had before Containment had tweaked the ordnance. God only knew what would happen now.

"General!" Rachel ran toward Malachi. "Would you like the field?"

He stared at her for a moment. Then his expression shifted, went hard, and he looked back at his meager troops. Paranormals had a long way to go toward parity, but that Containment was giving Malachi control of the human troops was a pretty big deal, or so it seemed to me.

"Create an arc," he said, and began pointing to locations. "Soldiers in front, armored vehicles at each end, pointed into the Beyond. You take that end," he told her, pointing to his right. "I'll take the other. They'll try to flank us; it's what they're trained to do. Don't let them, Captain."

That single word—his saying her title—contained enough heat to scorch. And the look in her eyes said she knew it. I had a sense that a kiss between Malachi and Rachel would have plenty of heat.

The promise of that, the reminder of love and connection, made me feel incrementally better. I looked back at the Beyond. Or as good as one could feel when staring down a group of people who wanted us dead and our world to boot.

"What about us?" Erida asked.

"Take as many as you can, and don't stop short of killing them. They won't stop short of killing you." The loathing in Malachi's eyes looked ancient, built from years of anger and mistrust.

A horn trumpeted from their world, long and low and wavering, and lifted the hair on the back of my neck. A flashback threatened, but I shook it off. Not here, not now.

The woman at the front of the line of horses screamed, and they let loose.

The Battle of Belle Chasse had begun.

"We'll stand together," Liam said, gripping my hand as we took positions in the front line. My hand was damp, my heart beating like a timpani as the soldiers galloped toward us.

Liam's eyes were completely gold now, as dense and shimmering as Malachi's. But there was no mistaking the human fury in his eyes, or the look of hatred he directed at those who would destroy us.

"Stay with me," he said. "We stay together, work together, we'll be fine."

But then the army crossed into our world, and all hell broke loose.

As if guessing our plan, one of the Seelies, her white hair streaming beneath her gilded helmet, charged us.

"Claire!" Liam called out as I moved first, darting to the side when she arrowed her stallion between us with an evil grin.

She was close enough that my hair rustled as she passed, close enough that I could smell the clove scent of her skin, the warm odor of horse, her well-oiled armor.

She circled around and came again, whipped the bow from her back with one hand and the arrow from her horse-mounted quiver with the other, and fired.

I smiled, gathered magic, made my best guess about velocity . . . and grabbed the arrow in midflight.

It shivered in the air two feet from my face. Holding it steady, I turned, pivoted it with a fingertip, and looked up at her. "You want to walk back into the Beyond?"

She screamed and charged.

I propelled the arrow toward her, and she barely dodged it, the metal tip grazing her shoulder. She screamed again, launched another arrow, fired.

Her movements were so fast I didn't have time to prepare, to grab that arrow. I hit the ground on my stomach, heard the arrow whiz over my head, and then her stallion was nearly on me.

I screamed as I was hauled to my feet and looked up into golden eyes.

But this time, it wasn't an enemy.

Liam crushed his mouth to mine. "Together," he said.

My head was spinning, but I nodded. "We'll try it again." I had only a moment before the next round. "Behind you!" I yelled, and pulled him to the side, inches from where a golden lance slid into the ground.

I'd seen one of those before, knew they were heavy. But with the two of us together . . .

"I have an idea. But it's a little dirty."

"They'll kill us if they can," he said. "Dirty's fine."

I glanced back. The soldier who'd thrown the lance—a man this time, a Seelie with dark skin and beard with the same crimson stripe—galloped toward us.

"A Seelie walked into a bar," I said, and Liam nodded.

"Right there with you," he said, and took my hand.

There was plenty of magic in the air, especially now that it was funneling through the open Veil, but it was weird and wild, and that much harder to wield. It took precious seconds to pry the enormous lance from the ground, to get it horizontal. And we had only seconds to move.

"On three," Liam said. "One, two, *three*!"

We raised the lance to the Para's chest height.

The horse galloped toward us, passed cleanly beneath the bar. But the rider hit the bar, then hit the ground, and didn't get up. We let the lance fall; it was heavy enough, dense enough, that it didn't even bounce.

The earth shook, and we looked to see smoke rising from a mortar round fired on the other side of the battlefield where soldiers, horses, and Paranormals had fallen.

Fuck war, I thought, and let myself look away. I had to if I was going to get through this.

Behind us came a banshee scream. A female Seelie, golden sword lifted over her head, ran toward us, her gaze aimed at me, maybe because I was smaller and she believed I was weaker, the easier target.

But Liam had decided no one would get to me. No one would get past him.

His eyes glowing gold, he put a hand on the ground like a sprinter on the block, then pushed off. They ran toward each other. Liam leaped, propelling his body an inhuman ten feet into the air—maybe borrowing her magic for the trip—arms back and ready to strike.

They met with a blaze of fire and power that sent a shock wave of magic through the air; then they hit the ground with enough force to put a dent in the earth and send dirt flying.

The Seelie swung the sword. Liam blocked it.

I watched for a moment to intervene, for a chance to lend him a hand, to grab the sword or the woman, but they were a blur of action as he fed off her magic and matched her strike for strike.

I was so focused I heard it before I realized what it was—the buzz in the air, the sound of speed and danger. And even when I looked up, all I could see was the gleaming edge of the golden arrow headed straight toward me.

"No!"

Erida leapt toward me, pushed me toward the ground.

I heard the arrow land with a horrible punch of flesh, and Erida jerked above my body.

"Oh, no," I murmured, maneuvered out from under her and tried to roll her over—or as much as I could, given the arrow piercing the middle of her chest. "Oh, Jesus, Erida. Why did you do that?"

She smiled a little. "That's not very gracious of you."

"I'm grateful and pissed off . . ." I trailed off, looked her over, tried to figure out some way to help her, to move the arrow.

But there was only acceptance in her eyes. She reached out, squeezed my hand. "I did it for your father. Because I loved him best of all. And you were his child. He was gone before I wanted him to go. But this is a gift I can give him, even now."

Bon dieu, I thought, borrowing one of Liam's favorite phrases as tears streamed down my face.

She shivered, blood at the corner of her mouth.

And I knew what I could give her. "The gas station," I said. "Remember what you told me about it?"

Jaw clenched, she nodded.

"He finished, Erida. But it's not just a gas station. It's a museum. All those magical artifacts Containment tried to burn, tried to get rid of, he saved. Books, weapons, objects. Hundreds of them."

She squeezed my hand, tried to smile against the pain. "He saved them."

"He did." I wasn't exactly sure why, but I could make a good guess. "And there's a bunker in it, too. Food, beds, a kitchen." I swallowed back tears, tried to dig out the strength to do this. "It wasn't just going to be a store. I think he saved the objects for you, and I think he meant for the three of us to live together. To be a family. Me and you and him."

Tears slipped from her eyes, gratitude clear in them. "Thank you, Claire. Thank you for that."

"Thank you for making him happy, Erida. Even if it wasn't for nearly long enough."

She squeezed my hand again, then closed her eyes tightly against an obvious burst of pain. There was a sudden intake of breath, and then her eyes opened and she went still, even as the battle waged behind us.

Liam shielded me, watched me, and waited. I brushed the hair from her face, then linked her hands atop her chest and climbed to my feet. I would grieve for Erida, for what she'd meant to my father. But I couldn't do it now.

There was fighting to be done.

There was more blood. More death. The Paras, for their part, were fierce warriors. But though Containment's new mortar rounds were still being tested, they were ferocious. They cut through armor just as they'd cut through the Veil. Unfortunately, only half a dozen rounds had been manufactured thus far. And they'd all been depleted today.

When smoke spread like fog across the field, the scents of gunpowder and blood in the air, the world fell quiet.

Malachi emerged through the smoke that swirled around his boots. His wings were folded but still visible. The top arc on his left wing was ripped, his blood brilliantly crimson against the ivory feathers.

"Is this it?" Liam asked.

"This was probably a sentinel unit assigned to watch the Veil for breaches," Malachi said.

Liam surveyed the devastation. "They're only the first wave."

"The first part of the first wave," Malachi corrected. "A guard unit. They'd have passed along a signal, a warning, the moment the Veil began to open." He wiped sweat and smoke from his face. "A battalion will be next, whichever is closest. And when they come, they'll come with weapons and death. We need to prepare."

He walked toward Gunnar, who was talking to a few of the troops.

Liam reached out, squeezed my hand. "I'm going to go speak to them."

"Go ahead." I watched him walk away—temporarily, this time—and then turned back to Laura and Caval. They were on their knees twenty feet away.

There was a bruise across Laura's cheekbone, a smear of blood from a cut on her collarbone. But unlike many of the others, they were alive. They were the reason for it all.

I strode toward them, stared down at them. "How could you be so selfish?"

She pushed her hair from her eyes. "I did what I was asked to do."

"You were fired. Icarus was killed. But you decided to keep going. To keep developing a weapon."

Her eyes were clear, and utterly free of guilt. Free of conscience, if that was possible. "I had a job to do, a mission. I wasn't going to just stop because someone got scared. Because someone wanted to ignore reality. You think Paranormals are our friends? Look around you."

She would never change her mind. She was at least forty, and wasn't able to see the world outside her myopic vision. And it didn't matter. I didn't matter to her, and she didn't have to matter to me. I wasn't her responsibility, and she wasn't mine.

I looked at Caval. "You destroyed the Veil."

His smile was wide and totally without doubt. "We beat them before. We'll beat them again."

"You won't be beating anyone," I said. "You'll both be in prison. Locked away for the rest of your lives. Away from your money, away from your lab. You'll have plenty of time to think about all your achievements."

"We have friends."

"Not anymore," I said. "The jig is up, and your friends are as much underwater as you are."

Liam and Gunnar walked back with half a dozen Containment agents.

One of the agents, an MP badge on her fatigues, stepped forward. "Laura Blackwell and Lorenzo Caval. You're under arrest for murder, several counts, terroristic acts, and other charges that will be made known to you."

They were pulled to their feet, and two of the agents took the prisoners toward one of the vehicles for transportation.

But the other agents stayed behind. And they looked at me and Liam with grim expressions. They'd seen us do magic. Big magic. Powerful magic. Liam had been cleared of murder, but we'd still violated the law.

We were still criminals.

One of the agents stepped forward. Gunnar tried to move in front of us, to protect us, but I held out a hand, shook my head.

"Claire Connolly and Liam Quinn, I'm sorry, but you're under arrest for multiple violations of the Magic Act. We're going to need to take you in."

"No," I said. "I don't believe you will." Because I was absolutely done.

The agent's eyebrows lifted.

"We won't be putting our hands in the air. We won't be going with you and we won't be going into Devil's Isle." I took Liam's hand, smiled at him. "Little help?"

"Always."

I reached for the magic, gasped at the sheer volume of it. It was flowing from the Beyond now, filaments filling the air like millions of fireflies. So much magic I could feel it floating between my fingers.

"Damn," Liam said, swallowing hard. "There's a lot of it."

And there'd be more than this eventually. More magic in our world, more humanity—if that was a thing—in theirs. Because the Veil had been ripped open, and there was no turning back.

The agent put a hand on his weapon.

"Nor will you be pointing those at us," I said, and lifted my hand.

Liam's magic joined mine, braided around it, and together we lifted every weapon in the group into the air, let them float twenty feet above their heads.

Some of the agents jumped, scrambling to keep their guns. Others just stared at us, openmouthed and afraid—or openmouthed and completely awed.

"In a few hours," I said, "maybe sooner, battalions of Paranormal troops are going to storm through that gap and into our world. They've been waiting for an opportunity to go to war, and Lorenzo Caval just gave them one."

"Call the Commandant," Liam told them. "Tell him to get ready for war."

I squeezed his hand, my partner and my friend. "And tell him we're ready to fight."

Love Liam and Claire? Then meet Ethan and Merit!
Read on for a look at the first book in
Chloe Neill's *New York Times* bestselling
Chicagoland Vampires series,

SOME GIRLS BITE

✣

Early April
Chicago, Illinois

At first, I wondered if it was karmic punishment. I'd sneered at the fancy vampires, and as some kind of cosmic retribution, I'd been made one. Vampire. Predator. Initiate into one of the oldest of the twelve vampire Houses in the United States.

And I wasn't just *one* of them.

I was one of the best.

But I'm getting ahead of myself. Let me begin by telling you how I became a vampire, a story that starts weeks before my twenty-eighth birthday, the night I completed the transition. The night I awoke in the back of a limousine, three days after I'd been attacked walking across the University of Chicago campus.

I didn't remember all the details of the attack. But I remembered enough to be thrilled to be alive. To be shocked to be alive.

In the back of the limousine, I squeezed my eyes shut and tried to unpack the memory of the attack. I'd heard footsteps, the sound muffled by dewy grass, before he grabbed me. I'd screamed and kicked, tried to fight my way out, but he pushed me down. He was preter-naturally strong—supernaturally strong—and he bit my neck with a predatory ferocity that left little doubt about who he was. What he was.

Vampire.

But while he tore into skin and muscle, he didn't drink; he didn't have time. Without warning, he'd stopped and jumped away, running between buildings at the edge of the main quad.

My attacker temporarily vanquished, I'd raised a hand to the crux of my neck and shoulder, felt the sticky warmth. My vision was dimming, but I could see the wine-colored stain across my fingers clearly enough.

Then there was movement around me. Two men.

The men my attacker had been afraid of.

The first of them had sounded anxious. "He was fast. You'll need to hurry, Liege."

The second had been unerringly confident. "I'll get it done."

He pulled me up to my knees, and knelt behind me, a supportive arm around my waist. He wore cologne—soapy and clean.

I tried to move, to give some struggle, but I was fading.

"Be still."

"She's lovely."

"Yes," he agreed. He suckled the wound at my neck. I twitched again, and he stroked my hair. "Be still."

I recalled very little of the next three days, of the genetic restructuring that transformed me into a vampire. Even now, I only carry a handful of memories. Deep-seated, dull pain—shocks of it that bowed my body. Numbing cold. Darkness. A pair of intensely green eyes.

In the limo, I felt for the scars that should have marred my neck and shoulders. The vampire that attacked me hadn't taken a clean bite—he'd torn at the skin at my neck like a starved animal. But the skin was smooth. No scars. No bumps. No bandages. I pulled my hand away and stared at the clean pale skin—and the short nails, perfectly painted cherry red.

The blood was gone—and I'd been manicured.

Staving off a wash of dizziness, I sat up. I was wearing different clothes. I'd been in jeans and a T-shirt. Now I wore a black cocktail dress, a sheath that fell to just below my knees, and three-inch-high black heels.

That made me a twenty-seven-year-old attack victim, clean and absurdly scar-free, wearing a cocktail dress that wasn't mine. I knew, then and there, that they'd made me one of them.

The Chicagoland Vampires.

It had started eight months ago with a letter, a kind of vampire manifesto first published in the *Sun-Times* and *Trib*, then picked up by papers across the country. It was a coming-out, an announcement to the world of their existence. Some humans believed it a hoax, at least until the press conference that followed, in which three of them displayed their fangs. Human panic led to four days of riots in the Windy City and a run on water and canned goods sparked by public fear of a vampire apocalypse. The feds finally stepped in, ordering Congressional investigations, the hearings obsessively filmed and televised in order to pluck out every detail of the vampires' existence. And even though they'd been the ones to step forward, the vamps were tight-lipped about those details—the fang bearing, blood drinking, and night walking the only facts the public could be sure about.

Eight months later, some humans were still afraid. Others were obsessed. With the lifestyle, with the lure of immortality, with the vampires themselves. In particular, with Celina Desaulniers, the glamorous Windy City she-vamp who'd apparently orchestrated the coming-out, and who'd made her debut during the first day of the Congressional hearings.

Celina was tall and slim and sable-haired, and that day she wore a black suit snug enough to give the illusion that it had been poured onto her body. Looks aside, she was obviously smart and savvy, and she knew how to twist humans around her fingers. To wit: The senior senator from Idaho had asked her what she planned to do now that vampires had come out of the closet.

She'd famously replied in dulcet tones, "I'll be making the most of the dark."

The twenty-year Congressional veteran had smiled with such dopey-eyed lust that a picture of him made the front page of the *New York Times*.

No such reaction from me. I'd rolled my eyes and flipped off the television.

I'd made fun of them, of her, of their pretensions.

And in return, they'd made me like them.

Wasn't karma a bitch?

Now they were sending me back home, but returning me different. Notwithstanding the changes my body had endured, they'd glammed me up, cleaned me of blood, stripped me of clothing, and repackaged me in their image.

They killed me. They healed me. They changed me.

The tiny seed, that kernel of distrust of the ones who'd made me, rooted.

I was still dizzy when the limousine stopped in front of the Wicker Park brownstone I shared with my roommate, Mallory. I wasn't sleepy, but groggy, mired in a haze across my consciousness that felt thick enough to wade through. Drugs, maybe, or a residual effect of the transition from human to vampire.

Mallory stood on the stoop, her shoulder-length ice blue hair shining beneath the bare bulb of the overhead light. She looked anxious, but seemed to be expecting me. She wore flannel pajamas patterned with sock monkeys. I realized it was late.

The limousine door opened, and I looked toward the house and then into the face of a man in a black uniform and cap who'd peeked into the backseat.

"Ma'am?" He held out a hand expectantly.

My fingers in his palm, I stepped onto the asphalt, my ankles wobbly in the stilettos. I rarely wore heels, jeans being my preferred uniform. Grad school didn't require much else.

I heard a door shut. Seconds later, a hand gripped my elbow. My gaze traveled down the pale, slender arm to the bespectacled face it belonged to. She smiled at me, the woman who held my arm, the woman who must have emerged from the limo's front seat.

"Hello, dear. We're home now. I'll help you inside, and we'll get you settled."

Grogginess making me acquiescent, and not really having a good reason to argue anyway, I nodded to the woman, who looked to be in her late fifties. She had a short, sensible bob of steel gray hair and wore a tidy suit on her trim figure, carrying herself with a professional confidence. As we progressed down the sidewalk, Mallory moved cautiously down the first step, then the second, toward us.

"Merit?"

The woman patted my back. "She'll be fine, dear. She's just a little dizzy. I'm Helen. You must be Mallory?"

Mallory nodded, but kept her gaze on me.

"Lovely home. Can we go inside?"

Mallory nodded again and traveled back up the steps. I began to follow, but the woman's grip on my arm stopped me. "You go by Merit, dear? Although that's your last name?"

I nodded at her.

She smiled patiently. "The newly risen utilize only a single name. Merit, if that's what you go by, would be yours. Only the Masters of each House are allowed to retain their last names. That's just one of the rules you'll need to remember." She leaned in conspiratorially. "And it's considered déclassé to break the rules."

Her soft admonition sparked something in my mind, like the beam of a flashlight in the dark. I blinked at her. "Some would consider changing a person without their consent déclassé, Helen."

The smile Helen fixed on her face didn't quite reach her eyes. "You were made a vampire in order to save your life, Merit. Consent is irrelevant." She glanced at Mallory "She could probably use a glass of water. I'll give you two a moment."

Mallory nodded, and Helen, who carried an ancient-looking leather satchel, moved past her into the brownstone. I walked up the remaining stairs on my own, but stopped when I reached Mallory. Her blue eyes swam with tears, a frown curving her cupid's bow mouth. She was extraordinarily, classically pretty, which was the reason she'd given for tinting her hair with packets of blue Kool-Aid. She claimed it was a way for her to distinguish herself. It was unusual, sure, but it wasn't a bad look for an ad executive, for a woman defined by her creativity.

"You're—" She shook her head, then started again. "It's been three days. I didn't know where you were. I called your parents when you didn't come home. Your dad said he'd handle it. He told me not to call the police. He said someone had called him, told him you'd been attacked but were okay. That you were healing. They told your dad they'd bring you home when you were ready. I got a call a few minutes ago. They said you were on your way home." She pulled me into a fierce hug. "I'm gonna beat the shit out of you for not calling."

Mal pulled back, gave me a head-to-toe evaluation. "They said—you'd been changed."

I nodded, tears threatening to spill over.

"So you're a vampire?" she asked.

"I think. I just woke up or . . . I don't know."

"Do you feel any different?"

"I feel . . . slow."

Mallory nodded with confidence. "Effects of the change, probably. They say that happens. Things will settle." Mallory would know; unlike me, she followed all the vamp-related news. She offered a weak smile. "Hey, you're still Merit, right?"

Weirdly, I felt a prickle in the air emanating from my best friend and roommate. A tingle of something electric. But still sleepy, dizzy, I dismissed it.

"I'm still me," I told her.

And I hoped that was true.

The brownstone had been owned by Mallory's great-aunt until her death four years ago. Mallory, who lost her parents in a car accident when she was young, inherited the house and everything in it, from the chintzy rugs that covered the hardwood floors, to the antique furniture, to the oil paintings of flower vases. It wasn't chic, but it was home, and it smelled like it—lemon-scented wood polish, cookies, dusty coziness. It smelled the same as it had three days ago, but I realized that the scent was deeper. Richer.

Improved vampire senses, maybe?

When we entered the living room, Helen was sitting at the edge of our gingham-patterned sofa, her legs crossed at the ankles. A glass of water sat on the coffee table in front of her.

"Come in, ladies. Have a seat." She smiled and patted the couch. Mallory and I exchanged a glance and sat down. I took the seat next to Helen. Mallory sat on the matching love seat that faced the couch. Helen handed me the glass of water.

I brought it to my lips, but paused before sipping. "I can—eat and drink things other than blood?"

Helen's laugh tinkled. "Of course, dear. You can eat whatever you'd like. But you'll need blood for its nutritional value." She leaned toward me, touched my bare knee with the tips of her fingers. "And I daresay you'll enjoy it!" She said the words like she was imparting a delicious secret, sharing scandalous gossip about her next-door neighbor.

I sipped, discovered that water still tasted like water. I put the glass back on the table.

Helen tapped her hands against her knees, then favored us both with a bright smile. "Well, let's get to it, shall we?" She reached into the satchel at her feet and pulled out a dictionary-sized leather-bound book. The deep burgundy cover was inscribed in embossed gold letters—*Canon of the North American Houses, Desk Reference*. "This is everything you need to know about joining Cadogan House. It's not the full *Canon*, obviously, as the series is voluminous, but this will cover the basics."

"Cadogan House?" Mallory asked. "Seriously?"

I blinked at Mallory, then Helen. "What's Cadogan House?"

Helen looked at me over the top of her horn-rimmed glasses. "That's the House that you'll be Commended into. One of Chicago's three vampire Houses—Navarre, Cadogan, Grey. Only the Master of each House has the privilege of turning new vampires. You were turned by Cadogan's Master—"

"Ethan Sullivan," Mallory finished.

Helen nodded approvingly. "That's right."

I lifted brows at Mallory.

"Internet," she said. "You'd be amazed."

Photo by Dana Damewood Photography

Chloe Neill, *New York Times* bestselling author of the Chicagoland Vampires Novels (*Blade Bound*, *Midnight Marked*, *Dark Debt*), the Dark Elite novels (*Charmfall*, *Hexbound*, *Firespell*), and the Devil's Isle Novels (*The Veil*, *The Sight*), was born and raised in the South but now makes her home in the Midwest—just close enough to Cadogan House, St. Sophia's, and Devil's Isle to keep an eye on things. When not transcribing Merit's, Lily's, and Claire's adventures, she bakes, works, and scours the Internet for good recipes and great graphic design. Chloe also maintains her sanity by spending time with her boys—her favorite landscape photographer (her husband), and their dogs, Baxter and Scout. (Both she and the photographer understand the dogs are in charge.)

CONNECT ONLINE

chloeneill.com
facebook.com/authorchloeneill
twitter.com/chloeneill